The Plane That Wasn't There

by John Norlin

Harry —
Whenever two or more old
fighter pilots get together and
talk turns — as it inevitably must
— to combat flying, there's an
unwritten rule that the right
hand always shoots down the
left. May you always be the
right hand!
Hope you enjoy the story.
Jim Norl

Library of Congress Cataloging-in Publication Data
ISBN: 0-87714-308-0

Denlinger's Publishers, Ltd. Edgewater, FL 32132

DEDICATION

In memory of Dick Webb, who said it wasn't there.

The Plane That Wasn't There

ACKNOWLEDGEMENTS

All writers owe huge debts to others, most of which they can never repay. I can only acknowledge owing debts to the following people.

My deep thanks to my old high school pal, Nancy Arneson Prosa. It made no difference what anyone else ever said to me, it wasn't until Nancy suggested I ought to write that I really began to think I should or could.

I really need to mention my appreciation of Marcia Buckingham, the Director of Operations at Denlinger's. Without her direct encouragement, I wouldn't be writing this right now.

Thanks are definitely due to three people who have encouraged me, sometimes with a rap up alongside the head - and I'm talking about the three ladies who read through my manuscript drafts. Start with Lois Griffin, who helped me come up with new ways to say things, and add in Barbara Holmes and my sister-in-law, Pat Dobbin, both of whom made large red marks all over my early work.

Finally, behind every man there stands a woman (usually telling him he's wrong) - in my case, it's the love of my life, my wife of 40-plus years, Marge. She has been my rock and my traffic cop, my cookie-baker and my best pal for all of these years. And she has believed in me when even I wasn't sure.

PROLOGUE

April 4th, 1962.

An airplane taxies along next to the runway at Sungshan International Airport in T'aipei, T'aiwan. International treaty says it's not supposed to be there.

What the hell's going on?

* * *

The young man sitting by the window smiled at the stewardess who offered him the pillow. She was beautiful, he thought, and she damned well should be. Civil Air Transport only hired former Miss China winners as stewardesses for their Mandarin Jet. He turned and grinned at the big man seated next to him.

"CAT really means this Flying Oriental Palace thing, don't they, captain?" the young man asked.

"They sure do, Mike," the big man replied. "And, as long as we're in civilian clothes, don't call me 'captain' or 'sir', OK? I'd just as soon the people we're going to visit weren't reminded of our ranks. While we're on this trip, it's just 'Bill', OK?"

"Yessir, Bill," Mike replied, then realized what he'd said. "Maybe I'd better just look out the window, huh?"

Bill laughed and reached for the drink on the table in front of him.

"Hey, look," Mike pointed out the window at a small, black airplane that taxied past the airliner, its pilots dressed in bright orange flight overalls. "There's a B-26."

"No, it's not," Bill spoke quietly.

"Sure it is," Mike insisted, leaning back so Bill could look out the window. "See it?"

"We can't see it," Bill insisted quietly but firmly. "It's not there."

Mike looked at him with eyes wide. "It's - - 'not there'?"

"That's what I said," Bill replied. "No bombers are allowed on T'aiwan by the United Nations treaty that turned it over to the Chinese after World War Two. A B-26 is a bomber, even if it was an 'A-26' when it started out and they just renamed it during Korea. So it's not there."

"Oh!" Mike responded. "Sort of like you and I are wearing

civilian clothes on this trip because American Air Force people don't go to Hong Kong on official business, right?"

"Something like that," Bill laughed. "At least, they don't go in comfort on the Mandarin Jet!"

"OK," Mike replied. "I think I understand, then."

They both laughed.

ONE

The pilot pulled the plane to a stop in front of the CAT maintenance hangar, as previously arranged. Harry Lindsay grinned without mirth at his co-pilot and former student, "Tiger" Ch'en.

"OK, Tiger," Lindsay scanned the area around them, "let's get her shut down and out of sight as soon as we can. No sense advertising she's here."

"Yes sir, Colonel," Tiger agreed, quickly performing the shutdown checklist.

"Good," Lindsay nodded approval. "We're home. And I'm glad to be here."

"Same here," Tiger's English was slightly accented, but he'd learned it well. "I'll miss Japan, but I'm happy to be home, too."

"We'll go back," Lindsay replied, releasing his belts. "Now let's get out of here and turn her over to ground maintenance. We've still got a briefing to make before the day's over."

The two men made their way to the customized door at the rear of the aircraft, passing through the former bomb bay area turned into a cargo compartment by previous owners. As they stepped out the door to the ground, two men appeared at the open doorway of the hangar.

"Well, Hamilton's here, anyway." Lindsay recognized their Southern Air Transport (SAT) project officer from Japan as one of the men. As he and Tiger made their way toward the hangar doorway, carrying their traveling bags, Hamilton and the other man came forward.

"Good to see you made it OK, Lindsay, Tiger." Hamilton thrust out a hand, then realized that the two men had their hands full of bags. "I'd like you to meet our Chinese project officer, Mister Winston Kung."

"Colonel Lindsay and I have met before," Kung announced, coldly. "We played golf together." He turned to Lindsay. "How are you, Lindsay? Did the training go well?"

"Hi, Winston," Lindsay greeted the man coolly - they hadn't been friends. "The training went fine. We had an excellent instructor. The plane's almost as fast as a fighter, and we're ready to start flying her regularly." He knew Kung was a manager in the

CAT organization, but this was the first time he'd known Kung might have a government function, as well. The plane and its crew were contracted to the Chinese government by SAT. "Listen," he went on, "our arrival here has probably been noticed by at least half the damned population. You know as well as I do what that means!"

"Not a problem. Lindsay," Kung smiled coldly. "Our cover story is we've just received CAT's new corporate airplane. The cargo bay will be fitted with removable seats to carry corporate executives. Of course, we'll move it into the hangar right away to start the modifications."

"OK," Lindsay nodded. "What do we plan to do about the paint? CAT's colors won't provide much cover in the middle of the night."

"We'll leave it black," Kung answered.

"Won't that look odd?" Tiger piped up.

"We won't need to worry about that," Kung replied coldly. "If anyone does look, I'm sure the Special Intelligence Division will remind them not to see it."

Tiger looked at Lindsay, who nodded. The Special Intelligence Division, the ChiNats' version of the CIA and FBI rolled into one, had plenty of power to do just what Kung said. So Kung was SID!

"As I told you, Winston," Hamilton broke in, "their instructor, Calloway, said they're the best pilots he's ever trained in the plane."

"Well," Kung responded, "we need to get several things settled. I'm sure the two of you want to finish up business and get some rest after your trip. And we," he nodded toward Hamilton, "have arrangements to handle, as well. Besides," he added, "your new crew's waiting to meet you."

"We need to drop this stuff off somewhere." Lindsay held the bags out.

"Leave it in the office back there." Hamilton pointed to the rear of the hangar. "Winston's arranged for you to use it, anyway."

The two pilots walked toward the office while Kung and Hamilton stayed near the entrance.

"I wish you could have gotten someone else," Kung finally spoke. "I don't trust Lindsay."

"I don't know, Winston," Hamilton looked after the two pilots thoughtfully. "He'll handle the regular job fine. We'll just have to be careful about our part."

"This could create a problem," Kung warned.

"Well," Hamilton replied, "I didn't get a choice of pilots. We have to use what we can get, and Lindsay's the only retired American fighter pilot we could find who speaks Chinese."

"I know," Kung interjected, "and we've got to have an American pilot because of the contract with SAT. Damn the luck, anyway! I wish our navigator spoke decent English, but we can't have everything. And Li's perfect for the job."

"I'm still not sure why you want a frogman as a navigator." Hamilton was puzzled.

"Simple," Kung replied. "Li's been on the mainland on spy missions several times. He was born in the area we're targeting – that's part of why I selected him. And he studied navigation as a part of his naval officer training, before he became a frogmen."

Hamilton was impressed. "Will he do what we want?" he asked.

"I doubt it," Kung replied. "There's only one frogman I felt would go along with our plans, and he's not trained in navigation. Besides, we need him on the ground, to receive and deliver our special packages."

"That makes it shaky," Hamilton shook his head.

"Be patient," Kung answered. "Here they come," he added, as Lindsay and Tiger approached.

* * *

The two pilots nodded to the other two men already in the room, then sat down as Kung and Hamilton walked to the front of the room. Hamilton stood back as Kung stepped forward to speak.

"Colonel Lindsay, Captain Ch'en," he nodded to Lindsay and Tiger, speaking Chinese, "this is your crew. Commander Li is your navigator and Mister Chou is your kicker - he'll make sure your delivery leaves the plane."

Lindsay and Tiger nodded greetings to the two men, who politely nodded back.

"As all of you know," Kung continued, "your job is to crew the airplane Lindsay and Ch'en have just delivered on night flights over the Chinese mainland, where it will drop supplies to frogmen, who penetrate the mainland on spy missions. The airplane will also drop medical supplies to be distributed to villages as part of our propaganda program."

"In one week's time, gentlemen," Kung smiled coldly, "we should make our first delivery. My superiors are anxious to get started. Are there any questions?"

"None," Lindsay replied.

"Good," Kung continued. "Lindsay," he turned to Lindsay, "you're in charge of everything to do with the crew and plane. We," he nodded toward Hamilton, "will let you know when we need a mission flown, and we'll provide a listing of locations where we want the supplies dropped. You must let us know which location you've selected and the exact time and date you plan to make the drop at least three days in advance so we can get the frogmen into place."

He stopped for a moment. "Charles," he said in English, "I think I've covered everything we discussed. Is there anything you want to add?"

"Nothing now, Winston." Hamilton smiled from where he stood. "Except to let you know, Lindsay, that I'm staying at the Grand Hotel, and Winston has found me an office and phone at the CAT building downtown. I'll get the number to you later."

Lindsay nodded understanding.

"Good," Kung replied, turning to the crew and speaking Chinese again. "Does anyone have any questions?" he asked.

"Only one thing," Tiger spoke up. "How often will we fly?"

"One mission a week," Kung replied, "in addition to two flights a week as the corporate plane."

"That's far too ambitious," Lindsay disagreed. "Low-altitude high-speed night flights take a lot out of the crew and the plane. We may have to adjust to something closer to once every three weeks for the night missions."

"I'd rather not," Kung responded, obviously irritated. "Maybe we can cut back on the corporate missions and maintain the rate of night flights."

"Well," Lindsay continued, "we'll have to see how the plane holds up – and how the crew holds up, as well."

"Oh, come now, Lindsay," Kung showed his impatience, switching to English. "We're paying you damned well to fly these missions."

"You're also paying me not to fly them into the side of a mountain!" Lindsay responded hotly, also in English. "If you want to keep us flying, you'll listen to what I say."

"Hey, guys," Hamilton jumped in, "we're all on the same side here! Let's not lose sight of our objective. Lindsay," he turned toward Lindsay with a tight smile on his face, "Winston needs the best rate you can deliver. Anything less cuts into the effectiveness of his program. Remember, this helps our intelligence people, too."

He turned to Kung. "Winston, I know you need the best rate you can get, and I know Lindsay will give the best he can. Let's not get into a hassle about it, OK? We can talk it over later – we should be able to agree on a rate somewhere in between."

Lindsay nodded. Hamilton was right. There was room for negotiation. And he was tired – the five-hour flight from Tokyo had been long, on top of two months of hard flight training. It was time to break this party up and go get some sleep at his little bungalow. He wished there was someone there to greet him, but she'd gone back to the states months ago to get the divorce and left him not really caring about what happened next.

"OK, Charlie," Lindsay said. "We can talk this over later. Right now, I'm tired. I'd like to sleep for awhile and get back with you guys, maybe tomorrow, to talk about it. OK?"

"OK," Kung agreed, grudgingly.

"Good," Lindsay turned to Tiger and Li. "I want you two here at about oh-nine-hundred in the morning for a crew meeting. Now let's get out of here!"

* * *

"Well, at least Chou will be aboard to drop our packages," Hamilton congratulated Kung in the car. "I sure hope we can trust him."

"We can," Kung smiled mirthlessly. "He'll do anything I want."

"Good!" Hamilton was excited. "It won't be long now before the money starts coming in!"

"Yes," Kung agreed. "I only hope the mission rate's a lot better than once every three weeks."

TWO

Woops! Olson's eyes popped open. Wouldn't do to get caught with the eyes closed. The guys would never let their supervisor live it down, even if it was a terrible first mid shift and he was dog-tired after Hong Kong! There might be some coffee left - almost three hours old. Maybe strong enough to keep him awake the rest of the shift.

Staff Sergeant (SSgt) Mike Olson, U. S. Air Force, focused on the plexiglas panel in front of him. Etched on it was a map of the area of China across from T'aiwan. This was where the guys, working from behind the plexiglas, plotted any action going on in the area. There were teletypes back there, with information coming in from other watch centers and radar sites. There were also headsets that fed information from a restricted-access room in the building.

The guys who worked in that room were Chinese linguists. They never talked much to his guys - except, of course, when they passed information. Olson knew the information was more accurate than anything that came from the ChiNat radar stations and was probably coming from the Communists. Somebody – maybe it was the ChiNats –monitored the ChiCom radio system and passed the information to the watch center.

But that stuff happened on day shifts, not on slow, sleepy mid shifts. Olson poured some of the thick, black coffee into his cup and walked slowly back to the desk. Not in any hurry to sit down again, he was still standing when the lead airman behind the map, Smitty, suddenly jumped to his feet and pulled his headset down over his ears. Olson and the others looked at him suspiciously. People sometimes played jokes on mid watches, but Smitty looked serious about this. In a moment, he called out, "Hey, Sarge! We've got activity!"

Olson was alert immediately. If this was real, it was what they trained for. But the middle of the night? He yelled, "Are you sure, Smitty? Or are they pulling your leg?"

"Hey," Smitty responded, "it's the shift chief! He doesn't joke around!" He made a mark on the map, on the coast across from T'aiwan, then spoke into his microphone. He listened, then wrote some identifying data alongside the mark. In a moment, he made another mark, this time a short way inland from the first, and drew a line between the two, indicating it was the same aircraft. Then he listened to the earphones again and reached up and put two slash-marks by the last plot, indicating the plot had stopped.

"What the hell's going on?" Olson demanded to know.

"Low altitude," Smitty answered. "It's faded out." He listened to the headset for a moment, then made a mark alongside the last plot. "The altitude was only 30 meters - less than 100 feet off the ground! They've lost it, though."

"Shit!" Olson snapped. "Is this a trick or something?"

"I don't think so," Smitty responded.

"How about practice, then?" Olson asked. "Ask about that. There's nothing on the teletypes. We should see something from ChiNat radar!"

"Only if it's ChiComs, Sarge," one of the teletype operators volunteered, "unless it's special interest to the ChiNats."

Smitty looked up from talking into the microphone. "Back room says they're sure it's not practice...hold it!" He held up a hand to show he was listening to the headsets once again, then made a mark further inland on the map. "Got it again! It's going like a bat out of hell! Must be a fighter or something."

"Damn!" Olson shook his head. "Any indications of a 'thunder-kitty' initiation?" Initiations of new members into the ChiNats' elite Thunder Tigers included mainland penetrations.

"Nothing," Smitty answered. "We'd see ChiNat fighters in the strait for cover if they did. And this one's gone way too deep into the mainland."

"Yeah," Olson responded. "It's real, then. OK. Time to call the ops officer! Chuck," he spoke to the lead teletype operator, "better get a fresh pot of coffee started. Captain will want coffee!" He picked up the telephone with a direct line to the house of the operations officer, just across the street.

"Captain Armstrong," the captain's voice responded. "What's up?"

"Sorry to bother you, sir," Olson said. "This is Olson at the watch center. We have a probable penetration going on over the mainland. Think you should come in, sir."

"Huh, Mike?" the captain answered. "A real one, at this time of night?"

"Looks like it, sir," Olson responded.

"OK," the captain hesitated a moment. "Get the coffee ready. I'm on my way."

"Fresh pot's already starting, sir," Olson replied. "See you in a minute or two."

* * *

Hot damn! Lindsay thought, this is what it's all about. Less than 100 feet off the ground, going over 300 knots, both engines screaming, and dark as hell outside! Oh, yeah, there was moonlight, but they couldn't see much at this speed. Just had to fly it by instruments, even if they knew every inch of the route like it was their backyard – Li had seen to that! Li was sitting in the special jump seat behind him right now, calling out checktimes. Lindsay was touching the controls in case he needed to grab them, but Tiger had control. Let's face it, Lindsay thought, Tiger has better eyesight than I've got, and quicker reflexes.

"Three seconds to climb to 200 meters," Li announced, checking his watch carefully. "Two... one... now!"

"Altitude two zero zero, roger," Tiger pulled back on the yoke and the fast-moving plane slid upward to 200 meters on the altimeter, just as the ground lifted under them into a ridge that peaked about 50 feet below the plane's belly.

Li smiled. He and Tiger Ch'en had become friends, but they were also a damned good team.

* * *

"Dammit!" Smitty barked into the microphone, startling Olson and the captain, who had just walked into the center. "Say that again, please!" He listened intently.

"Coffee's ready!" Chuck announced, still waiting for the rattle of the teletype to announce activity.

"Captain, Sarge," Smitty broke in, "back room says the bases at Fuchou, Changchou, and Liench'eng are running around in circles, but they don't have any aircraft ready to fly. Nobody has strip alerts scheduled for nights. Looks like they got caught with their pants down!"

"That will change," the captain observed dryly. "OK, Mike, first things first. Coffee, then the full story." He stepped to the coffeepot and poured a cupful into one of the spare mugs. After the first sip, he took a cigarette from his shirt pocket, lit it, and turned back to Olson. "Now, what's going on?"

"We're not really sure, sir," Olson responded, moving to the map. "We picked up the intruder here, at the coast. Low altitude - thirty meters - and high speed, around three hundred knots. The track was repeated again, here, and then faded out. We thought it might be a Thunder Tiger penetration, but there's no cover flight off the coast. So now we have an intruder somewhere over there, down low, going fast. There's no indication of aircraft type yet, and -"

"Gotcha!" Smitty jumped to the map. "Looks like it jumped the ridge into the valley." He made a mark, then drew a dashed line to it from the last point.

"That's it, sir," Olson concluded. "You're up with us now. Not sure who or what, but there's something out there and the ChiComs are watching it closely, just like we are."

"OK," the captain said, crushing out his cigarette in the nearby ashtray. "Let's tell Colonel Harding what we've got." Colonel Harding was the station commander. "Grab the second phone, Mike, and back me up."

* * *

"Checkpoint!" Tiger called out to Li. "Heading 300, as planned. How are we for time?"

Li was looking carefully at his watch. "We've gained one second on the plan," he answered, "not bad. OK, be ready for the next turn, heading 360, in about thirty seconds. Otherwise, we'll make a mess of several tea fields on the side of a hill."

From the corner of his eye, Lindsay watched what little he could see of the terrain slipping by at breakneck speed. Talk about adrenaline pumping! Aerial combat has nothing on this kind of flying, he thought. Up there, the enemy could make a mistake. Down here, the ground didn't make mistakes - you had to go around it! And this close to it, there wasn't a lot of space to go around!

* * *

"That's right, Colonel," Olson agreed with the captain. "There's not much chance of air combat, sir. They couldn't find anything down that low in the dark, even if they could get off the ground."

The colonel responded thoughtfully. "OK, Sergeant Olson. And you're still not seeing any activity from the ChiNats?"

"No sir," Olson responded.

"Alright. Bill," he spoke to the captain, "keep an eye on it until it's over. So long as it doesn't look like it's going to start a flap, be sure I get briefed on it in the morning at my office. And then I'll take it to the general and his staff."

"OK, Colonel," the captain answered. "If you don't mind, I'd like to come along for the briefing to the general."

"OK, Bill," the colonel chuckled. "Just don't try to use it as an excuse when we whip you on the golf course this afternoon, OK?"

* * *

"Everything OK back there, Chou?" Lindsay asked the kicker, who was watching the sky toward the rear.

"All clear," came the kicker's voice.

"Good, thanks," Lindsay wasn't comfortable with him yet, but Chou had every reason to keep a sharp eye out for enemy fighters - if they got shot down, he went with them!

"Still nothing from Matsu?" Li asked. The radio site at Matsu would relay initial reports of reacting activity to them so they could avoid dangerous areas.

"Nothing!" Lindsay responded. "All quiet."

* * *

"Got it again!" Smitty's yelp got everybody's attention. "It went north, and now it's jumped to another valley." He made another mark on the map, then announced, "Lost it again. It's dropped." He marked data next to the last plot. "Still unidentified, still non-Communist, altitude was 450 meters." he announced.

"I'd hate to be flying at that kind of altitude and speed!" the captain observed, his coffee cup about halfway to his mouth. "Damn', Mike!" He looked over toward Olson. "He probably isn't more than forty or fifty feet off the ground!"

"The Thunder Tigers do that, sir," Olson answered.

"Wonder what kind of plane it is," the captain peered at the map. "Still no report on the aircraft type, Smitty?" he asked the young man with the marker.

"No, sir," Smitty answered. "Funny, too. No information on the size, either. Just nothing, sir."

* * *

"Second checkpoint's coming up in twenty seconds," Li broke the silence. "It's a road intersection. We should pass directly over it at heading 30."

"OK!" Lindsay announced. "See it, Tiger? Just a little left of centerline."

"Roger!" Tiger announced, "about three or four degrees short of heading three zero. Turning to adjust." He swept the airplane to the left, then back to the right, so the compass showed the aircraft again heading 30 degrees, with the nose centered directly over the intersection. "OK, over checkpoint at -," he hesitated. "Now!"

"Right!" Li responded. "Forty-five seconds to our next turn."

"Damn'!" Tiger interjected. "Off by a good fifty feet! What happened?"

"Probably some breeze here in the valley," Lindsay answered. "Not to worry."

"She flies like a dream, Colonel," Tiger spoke up. "Would you like to try it?"

"Not on your life!" Lindsay replied. "You've got it, Tiger. I'm just enjoying the ride!"

* * *

"Captain," Smitty spoke up, standing behind the map, "what is this, anyway? This guy's going straight into the mainland."

"I don't know," the captain answered, pulling out another cigarette and setting his coffee cup down. "I don't think the ChiComs know, either. So it's anybody's guess."

"You think maybe somebody's defecting, sir?" Chuck asked.

"I doubt it," the captain responded. "A defector would head straight into Fuchou and land right away. This guy's staying below radar, and going deep inland."

* * *

"One minute to next turn," Li called out, then sat back and took a deep breath. "It's going great so far," he commented. He turned to look behind him. "*Ah yi!* Fool!" he yelled at Chou, "put the damned cigarette out! Now!"

"What?" Chou answered indignantly. "You turtle's egg! I can smoke if I want to! You're not the captain!"

"Chou!" Lindsay realized he had to take control immediately. "Put the cigarette out! Anyone looking this way can see it, and it spoils your night vision! Out! Now!"

"OK, Captain," Chou answered, now contrite. "It's out." He crushed the cigarette under his foot.

Li simmered. Fool, he thought, you can call me all the names in the world, but we're already in enough danger without your foolishness making it worse!

* * *

"Got it!" Smitty called out, moving quickly to the map. Everyone's head immediately turned.

"Headed northeast," Smitty marked the map. "Faded in and out again. It just barely got up into the radar radiation pattern. They don't even have an altitude reading."

"Looks like it's heading right at Nanp'ing," Olson noted.

The captain blew out a puff of smoke. "They might just be testing their air defenses. But it's sure headed inland, wherever it's going."

* * *

"Chou," Lindsay called out. "Better start getting ready. Only a few more minutes to the first drop point – don't want to miss it, after all this!"

"OK, Captain," Chou responded.

"Don't forget to check in when you get in place," Lindsay cautioned. "And be sure to strap yourself in so you don't fall out."

"I will, Captain," Chou promised.

* * *

"Got it again!" Smitty called out as he stepped to the back of the map.

The captain crushed out his cigarette, then looked up to see Smitty putting the next mark on the board.

"Looks like it's turning toward the north," Olson commented.

"It's faded out again," Smitty announced.

"It's turned," Olson concluded. "That's tight in there, and it would have bought the next ridge already. It's already turned."

"That's damned good flying," the captain observed. "Haven't seen too many pilots who could do that, especially in the dark. I wouldn't even try it, and I'm a damned good pilot, if I say so myself!"

Olson nodded. "He's either scared shitless or he's got brass balls. That's some pretty rugged country!"

"Jesus," the captain gave a short ironic laugh, "the colonel and general aren't going to believe this, are they? They're old pilots, too. Maybe it's a good thing I'm going to show up with the briefing in the morning, huh?"

"Yes sir," Olson agreed. "I don't think they'd believe it, otherwise!"

"Hey, Mike," the captain went on. "How about you and me both going to this briefing? The colonel and general both listen when enlisted people talk, and I think the two of us can convince them we really did see this. You got anywhere you need to be before about eight-thirty or nine?"

"No, sir," Olson replied, "I sure don't. The wife won't mind if I'm a little late getting in. All I do is go to sleep, anyway."

* * *

"Checkpoint dead ahead, heading 65 degrees," Tiger called out. "Crossing checkpoint... now!" he barked out the completion.

"Perfect!" Li exulted. "We're right on track and only two seconds ahead of schedule! Ready to turn right to 90 degrees in fifteen seconds."

"Cargo door opening," Lindsay called. "Chou, do you hear OK?"

"I hear you fine, Captain," the kicker responded. "The packages are ready. The door's open."

"Right turn to 90 degrees," Li announced, "Three... two... one... now!"

"Right to nine zero," Tiger responded, as the plane began the turn. "And 90 degrees!" he announced, the plane leveling off.

"There's the signal!" Tiger called as a pinpoint of light flashed at them. "We're dead on it!"

"Drop now!" Lindsay called out.

"Gone!" Chou called.

"Right on target!" Lindsay called out. "Great! Closing the door!"

"Next turn to 115 degrees in fifteen seconds, drop to altitude 150 now!" Li called. "It's going to get tight."

* * *

"OK, so now where did it go?" the captain puzzled, looking at the map.

"Well, sir," Smitty answered, "I don't think there's any way to tell."

"We'll find out when it pops out of that valley, sir, whichever end it comes from," Olson interjected. "I think the longer it stays down, the bigger the chance it's coming down the valley toward Fuchou!"

* * *

"Chou," Lindsay called to the kicker, "start getting the second drop ready."

"Plenty of time, Colonel," Tiger spoke up.

"We only have about ten minutes, Tiger," Lindsay reminded him.

"Yes, sir," Tiger laughed. "Like I said, plenty of time!"

* * *

"Fuchou still can't get a plane in the air, Captain," Smitty reported. "They won't make it. That plane's going to bust out of the valley right over Fuchou before too long."

"Yeah," Olson agreed, "if it hasn't crashed into a hillside somewhere!"

"Definitely possible," the captain added, "but that pilot's been running up and down those valleys for how long, almost an hour now? And he obviously knows exactly where he's going."

"That's right, sir," Smitty agreed. "He stays below the tops of the ridges when he's not jumping over them. There's not a lot of space in there, and he must know where he is."

"Well," the captain turned back toward the map, "we should know what he's going to do next pretty soon."

* * *

"Checkpoint... now!" Tiger called out.

"Good!" Li responded, "left turn to 80 degrees in three seconds... two... one... now!"

"Left to eight zero, roger!" Tiger repeated the instruction as the plane banked to the left. "And 80!" he announced as the plane leveled out.

"We're past Nanp'ing and the valley's opening out now," Li reminded them. "We're a little faster than planned." He advised, "Drop to 70 meters!"

"Altitude seven zero, roger," Tiger answered.

"OK," Lindsay spoke up. "We're doing great. And there's still nothing from Matsu - guess we caught them with their pants further down than we expected!"

"Yes, Colonel!" Li agreed. "And turn right to 95 degrees in three seconds... two... one... now!"

"Roger, right to nine five," Tiger responded, banking the plane once again. "And 95 degrees," he called as the plane leveled out again.

"We'll break out of the valley and into the plain after the next two turns," Li advised the others. "Remember, the triple-A near the airfield won't hesitate to fire, even if they hit populated areas. Next turn to heading 75, in fifteen seconds," he concluded.

"OK." Lindsay interjected. "Chou," he called out, "be ready for the second drop after two more turns."

"I'm ready now, Captain," came the kicker's voice.

"Good!" Lindsay said, as Li's voice began to call the next turn.

* * *

"This waiting is miserable," Chuck's voice broke the silence. "When's he going to break out of the valley?"

"Chuck," Olson responded, "hang in there, man. He should be coming out onto the plain in a little bit. I expect that's where we're going to see him."

* * *

"Final turn in fifteen seconds, Colonel," Li advised.

"We're ready," Lindsay nodded. This was it, the mad rush down the river, across the plain, then out over the strait. The adrenaline was high - he felt it.

"Turn right to heading 110 degrees in... three seconds," Li called, "two... one... now!"

"Right to one one zero, roger," Tiger repeated, as the airplane jumped to the new heading. "110 degrees."

"Drop to 50 meters!" Li called out.

"Roger," Tiger called back, "five zero meters!"

The plane screamed out of the valley, headed directly at the city of Fuchou at less than 100 feet off the ground.

* * *

"There he is!" Smitty yelled. "Right out of the chute!"

Olson and the captain stared at the mark as Smitty began putting data up alongside it. When he marked the altitude up, the captain grinned.

"I'll be damned!" the captain announced. "He made it down that stretch, and he's coming out at less than 100 feet off the ground! I didn't think it could be done!"

Olson grinned at the captain in relief. "He's going to make it, sir!"

Smitty immediately put another mark up, and started writing additional information alongside it.

"Damn!" the captain barked out. "He's heading straight toward the city! There's triple-A all around the airfield just south of the city. He's going to run right into it!"

"He can't avoid it, sir!" Olson spoke up. "He'll make it cost to shoot at him, though. They're going to have to shoot low and hit the ground. That ammunition will explode when it hits. Maybe he's betting they won't shoot when they could hit populated areas!"

"He's taking a hell of a chance on that!" the captain replied. "The ChiComs don't give a damn' about civilians. Or military people, either, for that matter!"

"Well, if nothing else, sir," Olson continued, "maybe he's headed for the base to make them shoot at their own planes while they're trying to shoot at him! Maybe that'll make them think twice!"

"You could be right!" the captain nodded agreement.

* * *

"Tiger!" Lindsay barked. "Triple-A on the right, firing wild! They can't see us."

"Roger," Tiger called back. "We'll be over the city in a moment. Maybe it'll slow a little then."

"Chou," Lindsay called out, "are you OK back there?"

"Ready, Captain," Chou responded.

"OK, hang on," Lindsay said. "This could get bumpy before we make the drop."

"Yes, Captain," Chou answered. "I'm already buckled in."

"Triple-A, left front," Tiger called out. "Hang on!" The plane fishtailed as it dodged. Suddenly they were over the city and the shooting eased, with only a few tracers now making wild patterns in the sky.

"They can't see us through the buildings!" Tiger shouted.

"Yeah," Lindsay replied, "but we'll clear the buildings in a minute and then there'll be hell to pay!"

"Right, Colonel," Li remarked, "but then we'll be down low and headed right at the airfield."

"Guess we'd better get the cargo door open," Lindsay pulled the lever.

"Cargo door opening," Chou announced.

"Roger, Chou," Lindsay responded. "Not long now!"

The plane continued to weave as Tiger tried to throw off the enemy gunners. Suddenly, the city fell away from beneath the plane.

"Altitude 60 meters," Li instructed, "and heading 110."

"Roger," responded Tiger, pushing the aircraft lower, "six zero meters. Ha!" he laughed wryly, "how am I supposed to hold heading one one zero?" The aircraft was fishtailing as the ChiCom gunners again began firing wildly toward the plane.

"Just put it over the airbase, Tiger," Lindsay urged. "We'll do the rest."

* * *

Olson's eyes were glued to the map. "He's headed straight for the airfield!"

"Not sure I understand why," the captain commented. "They won't like it much." He pulled another cigarette from his shirt pocket and lit it.

"Another plot, sir," Olson called as Smitty began marking again. "This one's between Fuchou and the base."

"He's dropped to 60 meters, Captain," Smitty announced as he put the additional data alongside the plot, "a little higher than before."

"If it was me," the captain shook his head, "I'd be as low on the deck as I could get."

* * *

"I see the airbase, Colonel," Li spoke quickly. He pointed past Lindsay out into the dark. "There's the perimeter lights, see?"

Lindsay finally saw the lights. They weren't what he expected. The ChiCom base commander obviously hadn't cut the lights off, but they weren't that strong anyway.

Within seconds, with the plane still zigging and zagging, they crossed the base perimeter.

"Now, Chou!" Lindsay barked, as they crossed above the runway. He glanced out the side window toward the rear, where he saw the edge of a cloud of paper leaflets scattering in the wake of the airplane. The propaganda on those leaflets would drive the ChiComs nuts!

"Instant clutter," Li chuckled. "Drop to 30 meters. Let's get out of here!"

"Thirty meters, roger," Tiger barked, and the plane dropped, still twisting and turning.

"Cargo door closing!" Lindsay announced. "Clear away, Chou. Good job!"

"Thank you, Captain," Chou responded.

The plane continued to zig and zag through the night as the ChiCom gunners kept firing wildly. A couple of searchlights came on, late, sweeping across the black sky a long way behind them.

Damn, Lindsay thought, we did it!

* * *

"Jesus, Captain," Olson broke in, staring at the map in disbelief, "it went right over the middle of the base!"

"It sure did!" the captain's voice was filled with disbelief. "And there's no telling how much shit's going to hit the fan over this one!"

"Matsu radar just picked it up, Captain!" called Chuck as the teletype rattled.

"OK, keep an eye peeled, guys," Olson turned back to his crew. "I want to know which way it heads out over the strait."

* * *

The plane broke the coastline to the southwest of Matsu as all of them - even Chou - set off a loud cheer. Tracers waved in their direction as the coastal gunners fired a few last futile rounds.

"Good job!" Lindsay called out. "Let's go home!" He grinned. "I think we earned our pay tonight, guys. Except me - hell, you guys did all the work!"

"You also earned your pay, Colonel," Li spoke quietly. "Without you, we wouldn't have been organized at all."

"That's right, Colonel," Tiger agreed. "You're still the boss-man." He glanced back at Li as the aircraft leveled off. "Altitude 1000 meters, heading 80 degrees."

"OK, if you guys say so," Lindsay laughed, "but let's not get too close to Matsu, remember?"

"OK, Colonel," Li agreed. "Maintain heading 80 for about another minute."

* * *

"Captain!" Smitty suddenly yelled. "We've got identification on it! They're calling it a small-type multi-engine aircraft!"

"Is that what I think it is?" the captain turned to Olson.

"Sir," Olson was thoughtful, "It means a light bomber, like the Chinese Il-28 Beagle."

"A light bomber?" the captain asked. "Like the B-26 that wasn't there, remember, Mike? This is going to turn into a world of pure shit!" He turned quickly to look at the telephone. "Mike, get on the other phone!"

"Are we sure it's ChiNats, sir?" Olson pointed toward where Smitty continued to mark plots. "Looks like it's headed off toward Okinawa!"

"Huh?" the captain stopped.

"It turned away from T'aiwan and it looks like it's headed toward Okinawa." Olson pointed toward the plots. "It may not be ChiNat at all. See the way it's skirting around Matsu, like it's trying to avoid fire from the ChiNats?"

* * *

"Hold it on course 85, Tiger," Lindsay grinned. "We'll be out of radar coverage in a little bit. Then we can turn and go home for the night."

"Colonel," Li was serious, "it's been a good mission. But I'm sure the Communists will be ready for us next time."

"I understand," Lindsay answered. "We'll talk about that later, OK?"

"Yes, sir," Li agreed.

* * *

The plane was turned over to the ground crew before Lindsay saw Kung and Hamilton coming toward them from the office area.

Hamilton was smiling. "How did it go?" he asked immediately.

"Fine," Lindsay responded. "We're going to debrief, if you want to sit in."

Kung grabbed Chou by the arm and pulled him to the side. Lindsay could see Chou's attitude turn surly. Maybe Chou didn't like his boss very much, Lindsay thought - too bad. Chou had actually laughed with the rest of the crew as they returned to the island. Oh, well, Lindsay thought, Kung's been pushy as long as I've known him.

They all trooped into the office, where Lindsay opened several bottles of soda and passed them around. As the others sat in the chairs around his desk, Lindsay perched on the corner.

"Good flight," he told Hamilton in English. "Everything went well. We picked up about three seconds on our schedule as we went through the valleys, but the checkpoints showed how we were doing, so it wasn't a problem. We'll insert more checkpoints next time." He nodded toward Li, smiling. "Navigation was great, as expected. We had good visibility, considering the altitude and speed." He nodded toward Chou. "The deliveries went smoothly. Mister Chou did his job well, and both drops were as good as we could have asked." Finally, he nodded toward Tiger. "And I'll let Tiger tell you about the flying part - he took care of that the whole way."

"Well," Tiger started, "there's not much to say. The aircraft handled easily. Fuel consumption wasn't quite as high as we expected. There's not much more to say from my point of view."

Lindsay shrugged his shoulders. "And that's about it. It was exciting, but it went smoothly. Oh, yes," he added, remembering Li's point at the end of the flight, "there's one more thing. Commander Li suggested we won't catch anyone by surprise next time. We need to think about what we'll do if we get a reaction. I know we can probably outfly most of the guns in the area. But I'm worried about an airborne reaction." He turned to Hamilton. "What do you think?"

"Hmm," Hamilton responded, "I'm not really sure what to do. Would a fighter be a threat at that low altitude at night? It really depends on how you feel about it."

"Well," Lindsay answered, "let us think about it and see what we can come up with. We've got to be ready to get ourselves out of trouble if they do get something onto us."

"OK," Hamilton responded, "whatever you think is best. Let me know if there's anything you need. Is there any more major stuff we need to know?"

"Not really," Lindsay shrugged his shoulders. "The rest is just details."

"Can you put it into the report and send it to me?" Hamilton asked. "Or would it be better to talk about it now?"

"There's nothing that important about the rest of it," Lindsay shrugged. "I'll be sure it's in the report. You look like you need to catch up on some lost sleep, so go on ahead, OK?"

"OK," Hamilton nodded, "we'll be on our way, then." He turned back to Lindsay as he started toward the door. "Hope you can get some sleep, too. I'll talk to you tomorrow about the next operation."

"Sure." Lindsay walked to the door with them, noticing that Chou was also coming toward the door. "If you want to stay, Chou, I'll be happy to give you a ride later."

"Thank you, Captain," Chou responded, "but I have to talk to Mister Kung. Thanks for allowing me to work with you," he turned and nodded toward the others, "and the rest of the crew. Mister Li, I apologize for my poor behavior earlier. I realize my smoking was dangerous. I'll behave better in the future."

"Don't apologize, Chou," Li called from his seat. "You did a good job tonight. Thanks."

"And thank you, Li," Chou responded. "Good night to all of you. Captain, I'll see you later. *Tsai chien.*"

The room was quiet as Lindsay picked up the bottles that Hamilton and Kung had left where they sat. He then turned toward Tiger and Li. "What do you two think?" he asked.

Tiger sighed. "A good flight, Colonel. We've got a lot of

information to report." He turned toward Li. "And what do you think, Li?"

"I was surprised," Li responded. "I expected more questions. Especially," he nodded toward Lindsay, "after you said we had good visibility."

"Well," Lindsay commented, "this wasn't an intelligence collection flight. Maybe we should talk to intelligence people, but I guess our contract doesn't say so."

"I overheard Kung asking Chou how the drops went," Li volunteered. "I thought this mission was only supposed to be a test, except for the leaflet drop over Fuchou."

"Well, I'm sure Kung wants to know how well we'll do on the real drops," Lindsay laughed. "And it's the middle of the night – our two project officers weren't awake enough to ask good questions, not to mention the fact that neither of them is apparently an intelligence officer."

Tiger tilted up his bottle to down the last swallow of soda then wiped his mouth as he got up from the chair. "Ah, well," he shrugged, "it's time to get some sleep. Do you want us to meet you here this afternoon to write up a report?"

"Make it about three," Lindsay responded. "Do either of you need a ride? I'm going toward Yang Ming Shan."

"If I could catch a ride with you to the first bus stop, I'd appreciate it," Li answered. He chuckled. "I've got to be quiet when I get home. My parents are asleep, and they won't like it if I wake them up."

"I'd appreciate a ride to the bus stop, too," Tiger responded. "And I've got to be quiet when I get home, too." He grinned at Li. "Maybe we need to find a place away from home, my friend. We could get an apartment near here."

"Hmm," Lindsay added, "a 'swinging bachelor pad', huh? Maybe the company could help out." He grinned at the two as he pulled the office key from his pocket. "Let's go get some sleep."

"And what makes you think we'll be able to sleep," Tiger wanted to know, still grinning at Li, "now that you have us all excited about this 'swinging bachelor pad'?"

Li didn't understand the English words and looked at Tiger with a question on his face.

Tiger laughed. "Come on," he thumped Li on the back, "I can see it's time to teach you some English! Among other things!"

* * *

"Chou says the drop went well," Kung spoke English so Hamilton could understand. "The merchandise should be in our man's hands in good condition. I expect the payment in Tokyo within three or four days. It'll take the buyer that long to actually receive the goods and tell his agent to pay us."

"Excellent!" Hamilton was pleased. "How much opium did we deliver this time?"

"Charles!" Kung admonished. "I strongly suggest we avoid calling our merchandise by its true name. A slip of the tongue in the wrong place and we're in deep trouble!"

"Sorry!" Hamilton blanched. "I'll be careful about it in the future. But how much did we actually send?"

"About two kilograms," Kung replied. "With our mission rate, I don't think we should send more than that with each drop. That's almost four and a half pounds – about half the size of a house brick. If we send any more than that, our customer will soon have more than he needs, and his demand will drop. He doesn't need a lot, he just needs it constantly."

"It's hard to believe this stuff is going to the governor of Fuchien Province," Hamilton shook his head.

"Only indirectly, through his deputy," Kung responded. "Even the old Communists have appetites to be satisfied. And they're the only ones left who can afford to have appetites. Especially at the price we charge."

"Which makes a nice little profit for us!" Hamilton grinned.

* * *

Olson was starting to feel tired. He and the captain had already briefed the colonel. Ending it with a briefing for the general and his staff wasn't always part of the job, but Olson had briefed the general before. Those briefings had been in the center, but this one would be different, at the general's office.

The captain had helped Olson and his crew put the briefing together, until he had to leave to get cleaned up. Even then, he'd come back to sit in on the colonel's briefing. After that, he helped Olson load the material into the colonel's car before they went off to the Headquarters Support Activity compound to brief the general and his staff.

The general seemed surprised they'd brought a sergeant to the briefing. But he recognized Olson after Colonel Harding introduced them. And then the seats were all filled and the briefing began.

The general stood up. "Gentlemen," he spoke, "we had an incident last night involving an aircraft over the mainland. That's all I know about it, so I'll let Colonel Harding introduce our briefers." He turned toward the colonel. "Go ahead, please, John." With that, he sat down.

"Gentlemen," the colonel nodded to the others in the room. "Good morning. While we were sleeping last night, Captain Armstrong and Sergeant Olson had an interesting time in the watch center. I'll let them tell you all about what they were doing." He grinned at the two. "Your floor."

The captain waved toward Olson, who stood up.

"Thank you, sir," Olson had done this before, and the colonel had just made it a lot easier by relaxing the room.

"Gentlemen," he started off, stepping to the easel that held the map, "the briefing I'm about to give you is classified Secret." He took a deep breath. "Last night, an aircraft identified as a light bomber penetrated the Chinese mainland directly across from T'aiwan."

The entire room became totally silent. Several faces turned almost white. These people knew the implications of the words "light bomber".

"As nearly as we can tell, it was not, I repeat, *was not*, a ChiNat aircraft!" Olson halted the reaction and everyone started breathing again.

"We don't know the origin, but it didn't head toward T'aiwan when it exited the mainland. Furthermore, there was no ChiNat support available to assist the aircraft and the ChiNats may have been as surprised at the event as we were. Let me describe what we saw." He turned toward the easel, picking up the pointer. "The aircraft first came to our attention when it appeared here, having already penetrated the coastline."

Everyone in the room stared closely at the map.

THREE

It was time for a break. Lindsay sat back from the desk and spoke to Tiger and Li.

"Hey, guys," he sighed. "Let's break for lunch. We've been at this for four hours already."

"OK," Tiger answered. "There's no sense killing ourselves over it, especially since you talked Kung into a twelve-day mission cycle."

"Yeah," Lindsay chuckled. "But we've still got the corporate flight to Tokyo day after tomorrow."

"Will I need to go along on that, sir?" Li asked.

"No," Lindsay replied. "It should be a nice, normal little trip where we won't actually require any navigating. Do you want to come?"

"I have some personal business to attend to here," Li spoke up. "I need to talk to my parents. I haven't seen them much since I came back from the mainland, and now that Tiger and I live here in the city, I still don't get a chance to see them."

"OK," Lindsay said. "There's really nothing for you to do around here for the two days we'll be gone."

"Well," Li grinned sheepishly, "I also want to ask my mother to help Tiger and me find some things we need for our apartment."

"My mother also volunteered to help, sir," Tiger admitted. "Neither of us has ever had a place of his own."

"Oh, no!" Lindsay tilted his head back with laughter. "I can't believe you two are going to get your *mothers* to help set up your 'bachelor pad'!"

Li and Tiger looked at each other with a blank stare. What was he talking about?

* * *

The plane touched down gently at Tokyo's Haneda Airport and taxied to the SAT hangar. A single SAT car sat in front of the hangar, and, as they got off the plane, Lindsay wondered where the transportation was for him and Tiger. However, the driver, a tall young American with a pleasant smile, came straight to Lindsay.

"Hi, Colonel Lindsay," he greeted Lindsay with an outstretched hand. "I'm Paul Anderson. Mister Calloway asked me to come down and pick up you and Mister Ch'en."

Lindsay was surprised. "Ah, I thought you were here to pick up Mister Kung and Mister Hamilton," he said.

"No sir," Anderson glanced at the other two, who stood nearby with their luggage. "They called yesterday afternoon to set up your visit and said they wouldn't need a car. They have a limo meeting them from CAT, I believe."

Sure enough, a large black limousine came around the side of the hangar and pulled up in front of the two men. The driver jumped out and put the luggage into the trunk after the two men were seated inside.

"Wow!" Tiger was impressed with the limousine. "That's quite a car!"

"I guess we don't rate very highly, Tiger," Lindsay laughed. "At least not enough to get a limo." He looked at Anderson. "Sorry, Paul. No offense intended."

"None taken, sir," Anderson grinned back. "Anyway," he turned toward the bags sitting on the ground, "let's get you guys loaded up and ready to go."

"Don't we need to clear customs?" Lindsay asked.

"Yes, sir," Anderson replied. "But we have our own customs guy right here at the hangar, so we'll take it to him and get cleared."

"Great," Lindsay was ready. "Let's go."

"We're supposed to go by the SAT offices first thing," Anderson said as they put the bags in the trunk. "Mister Calloway wanted me to bring you by so he can take you to lunch, he said."

"That sounds good," Lindsay grinned. "I think I'm hungry enough to take him up on it. And this'll be the first chance we've had to see the office up here. We didn't stop when we were here last time."

"There's not much to it," Anderson closed the filled trunk. "But I'm sure Mister Calloway won't keep you there long!"

"Yep," Lindsay agreed. "He'll want to get a beer right away, I'm sure! That's what he always wanted to do while we were training!"

* * *

At the office building, Anderson led Lindsay and Tiger in to see Calloway. At the entrance to the office area, the receptionist looked up at them - and Tiger Ch'en stopped cold. One thought stuck in his mind - she was the most beautiful girl he'd ever seen! And she was looking at him with a startled look, as though she was as surprised at seeing him as he was at seeing her.

This is ridiculous, thought Tiger, starting to blush. I'm a fully-grown man, not a lovesick child. But she's gorgeous!

Lindsay saw the moment taking place. "Miss," he spoke to the pretty oriental girl, "I'm Harry Lindsay and this is Tiger Ch'en. We're here to see Mister Calloway - and your name is - ?"

The girl blushed. "I'm Yukiko, Yukiko Ishibashi," she stammered, looking helplessly toward Tiger. "I'm the receptionist. I'll announce you immediately." She jumped up, nearly upsetting her chair, and hurried to the door leading to Calloway's outer office. Once there, she quickly pushed open the door and announced, "Mister Lindsay and Mister Ch'en are here to see Mister Calloway." Then she stepped aside, still blushing, and motioned for the two men to enter the door she held open.

With a polite "Thank you, Miss Ishibashi," Lindsay pushed Tiger through the doorway, grinning to himself. Oh, Lord, the Tiger had just been lightning-struck. Lindsay had been there once, himself, back in college - the girl was beautiful and he knew she felt the same way about him, but he was so busy getting an education he pushed all of the feelings aside and he never saw her again.

Inside, a warmly smiling American woman looked up from her desk and greeted them in a low voice that matched her smile. "Good afternoon, gentlemen. I'm Mrs. Oliver, Mister Calloway's secretary. He's on the phone right now, but he should be finished shortly. In the meantime, can I get you coffee, tea, anything?" She stood and beamed a smile at Lindsay, who suddenly realized she was a very attractive woman.

Lindsay asked for coffee, noticing Tiger hadn't reacted at all but was still staring at the closed door.

"I think Mister Ch'en would prefer some tea, if you don't mind," Lindsay smiled at the woman. "He's having a hard time concentrating right now," he added. "I think Miss Ishibashi captured his attention!"

Mrs. Oliver's laugh was deep and relaxed. "Yukiko's very pretty, that's for sure," she commented as she poured the coffee, "and I have this feeling Mister Ch'en made his own impression on her. Cream and sugar?"

As she fixed the coffee, Lindsay collected an impression of her. Medium height, full-figured, light brown hair that probably smelled good – like just-baked bread - if you stood next to her, just a few strands starting to show a little gray. Probably early forties, a little younger than he was. Warm brown eyes that crinkled at the corners when she smiled. A soft kind of prettiness, definitely attractive.

Aw, hell, thought Lindsay, it's "*Mrs.*" and this line of thinking is going nowhere.

"So, Mrs. Oliver," he'd make small talk, "What kind of work does Mister Oliver do?"

Mrs. Oliver turned slowly, the twinkle gone from her smile. "I lost Mister Oliver...that was Major Oliver, Air Force...in a plane crash just after Korea," she said quietly.

Lindsay nearly fell over himself. "Oh, lord, Mrs. Oliver, I'm sorry, I didn't realize...."

"No need to be sorry, Mister Lindsay," she cut him off, smiling again, but with a little pain. "You didn't know. We were living here in Japan. We had no children and not much other family. I wound up finding this job and just staying here. But now," her smile warmed considerably and her voice softened, "you do know. And I think I'd like it if you call me Marion, OK? Everyone around here does."

The warmth of her voice and smile flowed over Lindsay once again. "I certainly will, Marion," he responded, "and I'm Harry, although most folks just call me Lindsay. And," he added with a wishful expression, "I hope you wouldn't mind if I just call you."

"'Harry' it is, Harry," she grinned and the crinkles returned in force. "I'm glad to meet you. And I'd really like to have you call, whenever you can."

"Hey, you two cowboys!" Calloway's voice broke the moment. "Get your asses in here!" His blonde head poked around the corner of the doorway, a grin on his thin face.

Tiger seemed to wake up. "You'd think he'd soften up a little, sometime," Tiger complained, laughing.

"Who, Joe?" Lindsay laughed in return. "Never!"

* * *

Kung had been in the restaurant no more than five minutes. Hamilton didn't even have time to finish his cigarette. And now here he came, a broad smile on his face, very unlike him.

"This is it," Kung said, holding up a stuffed envelope. He slid into the car and opened the envelope, pulling out a thick wad of U. S. currency, mostly hundred dollar bills.

"How much?" Hamilton asked.

"Five thousand for you, just as I said," Kung answered triumphantly. He began counting out bills. As Hamilton watched, he stopped, then lifted the pile he'd counted and held it out. "Here's yours, Charles. Our customer's very pleased with the delivery."

"Five thousand bucks!" Hamilton looked at the money appreciatively as he took it from Kung. "I like this job, Winston. I like it a lot!"

* * *

Lindsay and Tiger finally nodded to each other. They'd covered everything they could think of. Calloway had written it all down.

"OK, then," Calloway put the finishing touches on the last note. "Let me look back over this to see if I can come up with anything more, and then let's break it off. I realize this isn't an intelligence op, but Hamilton could have spent a couple more minutes debriefing you guys. He didn't put anything in the report about half of this stuff."

"Actually, Joe," Lindsay commented, "he didn't write the report either, just paraphrased what I gave him. And my report wasn't really complete. I wrote it awfully fast."

"Hmmm," Calloway frowned. "Well, I hoped Charlie would be better at getting the intelligence information, but I guess that's not why he's there. Anyway, I want you guys to send me a full report after each flight, OK? I want all of the intelligence stuff you can include, too."

Tiger and Lindsay nodded to each other at that.

"OK," Calloway grinned. "Hey, it's past lunch time. Let's go get something to eat." He got up out of his chair. "Where are you guys staying?"

"Your young man, Anderson, has us in a place called the

Katusai Kanko," Lindsay answered as he walked to the door alongside the shorter Calloway, followed by Tiger.

"Oh, shit!" Calloway shook his head. "That's a damned American-style hotel. We'll get you into a good Japanese place, like the one we were in up in Fussa. It'll cost a hell of a lot less, too."

"Sounds good to me," Lindsay nodded.

"Me, too," Tiger agreed from behind them. "I liked the place in Fussa."

They stepped into the outer office, almost running into the receptionist, Yukiko, who was talking to the secretary, Marion.

"Oh!" Yukiko held her hand over her mouth in surprise.

Tiger froze in place. Finally, after what seemed to be a long time, he spoke.

"Miss Ishibashi," he started, then stammered, "I – I'd like to see you sometime, if I could, please?"

The girl bowed nervously. "Of - of course, Mister Ch'en," she stammered back.

"Are you busy tonight?" Tiger asked, hope high in his voice.

"No," Yukiko replied.

"May I see you tonight, then?" Tiger asked cautiously.

"Certainly," Yukiko replied. "I live in an apartment building not far from here. I'll write the address."

Marion handed her a pen and a pad of paper, and she wrote quickly. Tearing the sheet off, she handed it to Tiger.

"Oh, my," Yukiko suddenly stopped. "Can you read the words? I wrote them in *kanji*."

"Of course," Tiger replied. "*Kanji*'s just like Chinese, you know."

"You're Chinese," it wasn't a question. "I forgot. I'm so sorry." The girl blushed.

Both Tiger and Lindsay suddenly realized she'd apologized in Chinese!

"You speak Chinese?" Tiger reacted quickly.

"Of course," the girl blushed even harder. "My mother was Chinese."

"You speak Chinese beautifully," Lindsay decided to break in – if he didn't get things moving, they'd never get to lunch. "Tiger will see you there tonight, then. About six o'clock?"

"Yes," the girl smiled at Lindsay, realizing he'd just spoken Chinese, too.

"Good," Lindsay nodded his head. "Come on, Tiger, we need to get our lunch!"

"Can Marion come with us, too?" Yukiko asked. "It isn't good for a young Japanese girl to go out on a first date without a chaperone."

"I hope she will," Lindsay broke in with the answer, grinning at Marion. "After all, Tiger will have me along as *his* chaperone. I won't let him go out without one, either!" He winked.

"I have a feeling this will be fun," Marion smiled at Lindsay. "I haven't done any chaperoning in a long time!"

"Neither have I," Lindsay grinned back. "You may have to coach me on it."

"I'm looking forward to that," Marion's eyes crinkled with her smile. "See you at six."

Damn', thought Lindsay as they left the office. I almost feel like a schoolboy going to his first dance!

* * *

It had been a really nice evening, Lindsay reflected as he sat in the hot bath the following morning. They'd gone out to dinner and to a floorshow at a large downtown nightclub. Afterward, because it wasn't really all that far, they'd walked back to the apartment building where the two women lived, which was only about a block from the *ryokan* where Calloway had found rooms for them.

Tiger and Yukiko had been very much in their own world together, and Lindsay chuckled at the thought. That left him and Marion to their own devices, and they'd talked quite a bit, finding out they shared a lot of likes and dislikes. The more time Lindsay spent around her, the more he realized that he really liked this woman. That was unusual, especially after his ex-wife had dropped him like a hot potato and gone back to the states after he retired, leaving him pretty bitter about women. On the other hand, they had to head back to T'aiwan this afternoon – takeoff was at noon – and it would be awhile before they'd come back again. But it would be nice to have something to look forward to when they came, he thought. And time with Marion was definitely something to look forward to.

Lindsay shook himself. Between the heat of the hot bath and the warmth of his thoughts about Marion, he was about to go to sleep. That wouldn't work, he thought. He and Tiger didn't have that long until they had to leave for the airport – they still had to get the pre-flight done. And they really needed to get back. It wasn't long until the next night mission, and there was work to be done to get ready. Hamilton had already delivered the next set of possible locations, and they still had some route planning and timing exercises to work out. Twelve-day mission cycles didn't give them any extra time between flights.

* * *

The flight back was uneventful, although Kung and Hamilton were a couple of minutes late and they were forced to hurry to get the plane through its checklist and still make their takeoff time.

Li met the plane at the airport. While Kung's chauffeur loaded Kung's and Hamilton's bags into Kung's car, Li helped Lindsay and Tiger throw their bags into their jeep before they turned the plane over to the maintenance crew.

"You have a good vacation?" Tiger grinned at Li.

"Of course," Li replied. "I even slept in this morning, almost until seven-thirty!"

"Omigosh!" Tiger deadpanned. "You almost missed your morning 'ballet' class, didn't you?" Li was a student of *t'ai-ch'i*, the Chinese self-defense method that looked like ballet, and usually practiced with a group of elders in the park across from the apartment.

"One of these days, I'll teach you *t'ai-ch'i*, Tiger," Li smiled in return. "And then it will be my turn to laugh!"

"Let's go," said Lindsay, returning from surrendering the plane. "I want to change and get to dinner."

"Colonel," Li spoke up as they started off, "I talked to Chou yesterday afternoon. He's not very busy, and I wonder if we can let him help us with our mission planning."

"Sure," Lindsay replied. "I guess I just never thought of it. How do you feel, Tiger?"

"Fine by me, Colonel," Tiger answered. "He might have some things he can add to our planning. At least, he can feel like he's a member of the crew."

"OK, then," Lindsay nodded agreement. "Next time I talk to him, I'll ask him if he'll help us."

"One other thing, Colonel," Li spoke up. "I also visited with one of my old intelligence officers. He says the frogman who's receiving our deliveries is one of the few I don't trust, a lieutenant named Wang. He said he thought Wang was specifically requested by the project officer."

"Is that a problem?" Lindsay asked.

"Not for me, sir," Li replied. "I only hope he does his job right, so we're not wasting our time."

* * *

They were finished for the day and getting ready to leave the office.

"It's been a good day," Lindsay commented, using Chinese as usual. "Tomorrow, we'll go over the route plans with watches and start practicing the route."

"That's called a 'dry run', isn't it, Colonel?" Li responded, using the English term.

Lindsay was caught short by the unexpected reply. "Ah - it sure is, Li!" Lindsay looked at him in amazement. "I see Tiger's started you on English lessons!"

"Yes, sir," Li replied in accented English. "I'm a poor student, though."

"Actually, Colonel," Tiger broke in, "Li knows a lot of English. We all learned it in school. He just hasn't used it in a long time, so it's rusty. But he'll get it back in no time! I'm making him use it at the apartment."

"Tiger's right, Captain," Chou volunteered, also in slow and accented English. "We all learn some English in school. We don't speak it, so it becomes very...what did you say, Tiger?...ah, having rust?"

Lindsay smiled a huge smile. "Hey, I'm really proud of you guys!" He stopped short as he saw looks of consternation appear on both of the men's faces.

"They're not quite *that* good, yet, Colonel! A little slower, please," Tiger cautioned him, then turned and translated to the others.

FOUR

"Hey, Sarge!" Smitty greeted Olson at the door as they arrived for the first mid shift of the cycle. "Will we hear from the phantom bomber tonight?"

"Not this soon," Olson laughed at him. "The ChiComs are too ready for him – they've got fighters on strip alert day and night now. Maybe in another couple of months, when the ChiComs get lax, he'll sneak in and get out fast. But it sure won't happen again this soon."

"So he won't show up, huh?" Smitty asked as they entered the watch center.

"He'd better not," Olson replied, "at least, not until I've had my first cup of coffee and written Chuck's performance report!"

* * *

The words weren't coming easily. Olson put the pencil down, sipped his coffee, and thought more about the words for Chuck's report.

"Shit!" Smitty's voice broke through Olson's thoughts. "Sarge, it's him!"

"Huh?" Olson nearly dropped his coffee cup as his head jerked upward to see Smitty moving into place behind the map. "Who?" The question was rhetorical - Olson already knew what Smitty meant.

"Broke the coast north of Fuchou!" Smitty called out as he marked a plot on the board. "It's our boy!"

"Don't jump so fast," Olson cautioned. "It may just be a practice run." The other shifts had reported the ChiComs were practicing reactions to night penetrations.

"Another plot," Smitty reported.

"OK," Olson responded, checking the latest location on the map. No way yet to tell whether this was real or just practice.

"Faded out," Smitty reported. "Sarge, the other guys said the practices didn't drop tracks."

"Yeah," Olson responded, not happy - he needed to get Chuck's performance report done. "Maybe they're being a little more realistic in their practices, too."

* * *

Here we are again, thought Lindsay as he glanced out the canopy of the plane. Going like a bat out of hell, less than 100 feet off the ground, and Li's the only one who's ever seen the territory we're flying over. This has to be insane. But, then, why am I having so much fun?

*   *   *

"Shit!" Smitty blurted it out. "Sarge, we've got fighters taking off from Fuchou!" Olson's head jerked upward from Chuck's report as Smitty continued. "I don't know what they think they're doing! All they've got is day fighters, MiG-17s! They'll be lucky if they don't run into each other up there!"

"Smitty, you sure?" Olson wanted to know.

"Yeah, Sarge," Smitty confirmed. "Back room says they're scrambling right now!"

A teletype suddenly came to life, and Chuck jumped in front of it immediately. "Sarge!" he called out, "Matsu reports two fighters taking off from Fuchou!"

"Smitty," Olson turned, "switch on the feed from the teletype and plot Matsu's reports on the reacting fighters. I'll call the captain." He grabbed the phone and dialed the ops officer's number. Oh shit, Olson thought, the captain will love this!

*   *   *

Lindsay, with his hands and feet touching the controls, felt their movements and moved with them. Tiger's doing his magic again, he thought, making the plane act like an extension of himself!

"Climb to 250 meters in three seconds, two... one... now!" Li announced.

"Two five zero meters, roger!" Tiger responded, and the plane began climbing, pushing the crew downward into their seats.

This will be a tough stretch, thought Lindsay as the plane reached for altitude. The ChiComs can see us easily. But it's the only way to get over this area where the valley zigzags a lot before it turns gentle and starts meandering along again.

*   *   *

The captain walked in within moments. Olson realized he must have had his clothes right beside his bed, or he wouldn't have been able to get dressed so quickly.

"Our plane again?" the captain grinned at Olson, who nodded. "Hey, Mike, does this thing work for you? It sure seems to be on your shift schedule!"

"Sir," Olson answered, "it has company up there tonight. Fuchou launched a pair of MiGs after it."

"They won't catch it," the captain grinned. "All it needs to do is stay low and the fighters will be blind."

"Won't they be able to see flame from its exhaust, sir?" Chuck asked.

"Probably not," the captain answered. "If there *are* visible flames, they're usually blue, and it's hard to see them at night, even if you're looking straight at them. The only thing they might be able to see is its shadow on the ground, unless it's painted a bright color."

Smitty began marking on the map again. "It's faded in. Looks like it grabbed some altitude!" The captain and Olson turned to look. "And the MiGs have turned toward it!" Smitty continued. "They're closing on it, only about seventy-five kilometers away." He marked the plots on the board as he spoke.

* * *

The radio crackled and Lindsay almost sat bolt upright as the voice came through. "Red flag, red flag," it announced, "we have two tigers at seven five and six." It was the radio from Matsu. Red flag was their callsign, tigers meant reacting fighters, seven five was a distance of 75 kilometers from them, and six meant that the fighters were at a six o'clock, or approximately 180 degrees, azimuth from their last-noted position. Lindsay quickly adjusted the radio to the next frequency in the sequence, then turned toward the rear of the plane.

"Chou!" he spoke quickly into the intercom, "Matsu just reported we've got two fighters coming after us. They're about seventy-five kilometers away, toward the south - behind us and off our left side."

"OK, Captain," Chou answered, "I'm looking that way."

"Good," Lindsay responded, then turned to Li. "How much longer do we stay at this altitude? We're 'sitting ducks' up here. The MiGs are too close for comfort."

"Not long, Colonel," Li responded, grinning at the English term. "Another forty-five seconds."

"They'll be close by then," Lindsay said.

"They won't be close enough to spot us before we drop below radar coverage, Colonel," Tiger spoke up.

"OK, Tiger," Lindsay responded, "but we don't have room for error. And I'd like to have all the room we can get!"

Li laughed. "Colonel, that's why we decided to use this route, if you remember!" he chided.

"I know, Li," Lindsay answered him, "but it doesn't make me any happier, knowing two fighters are back there looking to run right up our tail. We're stuck out here in the middle of the sky, 'fat, dumb, and happy'!"

Li understood the English, and both he and Tiger laughed again.

"Captain!" Chou's voice broke in. "I see them!"

"Where?" Lindsay spun in his seat, looking back over his shoulder, intently scanning the sky behind them.

"A long way back, Captain," Chou reported. "They have their lights on. You can see them flash, at about eight o'clock and not very high."

Lindsay strained to see, then caught sight of the flashing lights. "They're a long way away yet," he noted, "but they'll close quickly."

"Not quickly enough, Colonel," Li spoke up. "Ready to descend to 85 meters in three seconds, two -."

* * *

"There it goes!" Smitty called out, marking another plot. "It's faded out."

"Hmm," the captain commented, lighting another cigarette from the butt of the previous one. "Fighters are still sixty kilometers away from it."

"Yes, sir," Olson responded. "It dropped down into that valley and there's no telling where it'll pop up again. The valley's pretty big. It can wander all around without showing itself, and it can fool around until the MiGs have to go home with low fuel. Unless, of course, they somehow spot it," he added.

"Let's hope they don't," the captain looked around. "Any coffee?"

"Oops, sir," Chuck had a guilty look on his face. "I'm the designated coffee-maker, but I guess I've been kind of busy."

"Stay right there," the captain smiled. "I don't make bad coffee, myself. Where's the grounds and the filters?"

* * *

"Twenty seconds to the first checkpoint, Colonel," Li noted. "Holding heading 250, we should pass exactly over a bridge across the river," he reminded.

"OK," Lindsay responded. "Got the river in sight. Now to find the bridge."

"Is that it?" Tiger nodded ahead of them. "Closing on it pretty fast."

"Checkpoint in three seconds, two... one... now!" Li barked.

"Good!" Lindsay acknowledged.

"Captain!" Chou's voice came over the intercom again. "I see the lights again, sir. They're coming over the hills behind us."

"They're getting close," Lindsay looked back to confirm Chou's sighting.

"They won't see us, Colonel," Tiger chuckled. "They still have their navigation lights on and they can't see much past the inside of their cockpits."

* * *

"Coffee's brewing," the captain announced. "Should be ready in a few minutes."

"Thank you, sir," Olson nodded. "Everything's quiet for the moment."

As if to prove Olson wrong, the teletypes rattled, and Smitty moved to the map again as Chuck read off the coordinates of a new plot.

"ChiComs are over the last plot," he announced as he marked the location of the MiGs.

"I don't imagine our plane's anywhere near there," the captain called back. "The ChiComs won't think it's there, either. They'll head upriver to see if they can spot it."

The teletype rattled again. "ChiComs are climbing, sir," Smitty announced. "Going up to a thousand meters."

"Hmm," Olson added, "they're back in the mountains. Trying to get up high enough to let their own radars see 'em. Those guys are flying with nothing but their controller's voices to keep 'em from panicking."

"Yeah, they don't fly at night," the captain responded. "It's like they figure wars are only fought in daylight!"

"Or maybe they just figure you can't take enough away from them at night that they can't take it all back, and then some, the next day," Olson commented wryly.

* * *

"They're still coming, Captain," Chou announced. "But they're high up."

"They're climbing, Colonel," Tiger added. "We're far enough away that Fuchou can't keep them on radar unless they climb to a higher altitude."

"We have a turn coming up, Colonel," Li spoke up. "Do we want to go ahead with the route? If we turn, they may be able to see us."

"Continue on," Lindsay made the decision quickly. "We can take evasive action if needed. But I don't think they can see us, with the altitude and their navigation lights blinding them. We're just a tiny black shadow on the face of a very shadowy patch of earth down here. Their only chance of seeing us is for us to jump up into their radar pattern, and we won't do that again for awhile."

"About fifteen minutes, in fact," Li added.

"And if my calculations are anywhere near right," Lindsay concluded, "they'll break off and head for home before then. Any longer than that and they risk flying on fumes."

* * *

The captain poured the cups full and passed them out. "Easy, guy," he spoke to Smitty, who was showing nervousness. "The MiGs will make some circles up there before they realize they can't see anything and go home for the night. Hell, it's hard enough to see another plane in the same sky in normal daylight conditions. Make it night, and you're chasing your tail unless radar sees it!"

The teletype rattled again as the captain walked back toward the coffeepot.

"Sir, the ChiComs are turning south," Smitty announced.

"Probably starting to circle," the captain said as he poured coffee for Olson and himself. "If they don't break it off in another ten-fifteen minutes, they won't have enough fuel to do an intercept and still get back to base."

"You're right, sir," Smitty said, listening to his headset. "The guys in back say they're circling."

"They won't find much," the captain sighed, fishing another cigarette from the pack on the desk in front of him. He turned to Olson. "Mike, you and I are going to become regulars on the general's briefing list, you know that, don't you?"

* * *

"Captain," Chou broke the silence. "The MiGs have continued their turn past our course."

"Thanks, Chou," Lindsay responded. "They're circling. But stay alert, please."

"Yes, sir," Chou spoke quietly.

"Forty-five seconds to next checkpoint," Li called out. "After that, we have awhile before the first drop."

* * *

"That's a large valley," Olson explained to the captain. "It could fly around in circles and we wouldn't be able to see anything. There's a navigation radar site at Nanp'ing, but it's no good for anything except stuff up high in the air, and it won't see the plane unless it passes right over top."

The teletype rattled again.

"MiGs are circling," Smitty called out. "And still no word on our boy."

The captain grinned at Olson. "He's 'our boy' now? Looks like we've adopted him, huh?"

"I'd say that's the case, sir," Olson replied. "We could do worse."

"Yeah," the captain nodded, "but now he has to get out of there. They can still make another pass at him when he comes out."

"They only had two pilots on strip alert this evening, sir," Olson advised. "They'd have to get two more ready pretty quickly to be able to take a crack at him on the return run."

"How much activity was there during the day today?" the captain wanted to know.

"Ahh, let me look, sir," Olson was stopped. He picked up the sheaf of reports.

"If there wasn't much activity today," the captain went on, "they might have a couple of aircraft ready."

"Hmmm," Olson looked through the paper. "The activity level

was fairly high today, at least thirty-six sorties out of Fuchou, all in the afternoon, and all extended airfield activity - a lot of touch-and-goes and pattern flying."

"Ah," the captain mused, "that means probably all fourteen planes not on strip alert flew at least two sorties, some of them three. Not a high probability they can launch two of those. Airfield activity takes a lot more out of a plane than most other activity types. The reaction's probably over when these two come home." He stubbed out the cigarette butt in the ashtray.

* * *

"Passing over checkpoint in three seconds," Li called out, "two... one... now!"

"On the money!" Lindsay responded. "Right on schedule and track."

It's going well, Lindsay thought. The ChiCom fighters were still circling a long way behind. Maybe more would come, but the plane would be hard to spot in the dark, especially at low altitude. There were a couple of places where they'd be vulnerable to radar, but Lindsay was sure the ChiComs couldn't take advantage of the momentary vulnerability without monstrously good luck. He didn't think they'd be quite that lucky.

* * *

"It's quiet," the captain commented.

"Yes sir," Olson agreed. "Calm between storms, maybe."

"At least we can get coffee ready," the captain chuckled, "and maybe catch a potty break." He looked toward the other members of Olson's crew. "Any of you need a break?"

Chuck looked a little sheepish. "Think I could use one, sir," he spoke up apologetically.

The captain strode over and took Chuck's headset and microphone. "Go. I'll hold it down for you. Let's hope nothing comes up." He winked at Chuck, who headed for the latrine. "What do I need to do, Smitty?" the captain turned toward the map.

"Just read anything that comes in on the teletypes, sir," Smitty answered.

"OK," the captain looked down as one of the teletypes suddenly began chattering again. "It says raid number one, bearing two six five, distance one two five, altitude a thousand meters."

"Good, sir," Smitty answered on the headset. "Looks like they're breaking off and coming back to Fuchou. They'll be landing in awhile. Matsu will probably only put out a few more plots on them."

* * *

"We'll jump over the ridge in about three minutes," Li noted.

"Chou," Lindsay asked the kicker, "what are the fighters doing?"

"They're leaving, Captain," Chou replied. "They're heading toward the coast."

"Thanks," Lindsay responded. "We'll cross the ridge to the next checkpoint and the first drop soon. Please go to the cargo bay now."

* * *

"Well," the captain returned from the teletype area and fished another cigarette from the crumpled pack, "the MiGs are coming back. And our boy's still up in the valley."

"Yes, sir," Olson agreed thoughtfully. "I wonder what he's doing up there."

"No telling," the captain answered, lighting his cigarette. "Burning fuel, at least," he grinned.

* * *

It was quiet in the airplane, thought Lindsay. They'd hit the next checkpoint soon and then the first drop. After that, it was a long way before they hit the second drop and then headed for home.

"I wish we had more information on the MiGs," Li broke the silence.

"They've gone home by now," Tiger answered Li's doubts. "Just remember, even if they could find us, they'd still have to engage us. It takes a lot of fuel to do that and still get back to base."

"Matsu will let us know anytime aircraft take off that look like they're coming after us," Lindsay added.

"Well," Li stated, "I'd still be happier if we had a better idea where the enemy aircraft are."

"So would the Communists, my friend," laughed Tiger. "And they're not having much more luck than we are right now!"

* * *

"Fighters are almost back to Fuchou now," Smitty advised, adding another plot to the track. "Our boy's still up there, though."

Captain Armstrong stubbed out his cigarette and took a sip of coffee. "If we knew what he's doing, we might have a little better idea where he's going," he commented to Olson.

"Agree, sir," Olson commented, "but I figure there aren't a lot of things he can be doing. I mean, he sure isn't gathering intelligence, with his altitudes and speeds."

* * *

Lindsay looked out the side window as the plane climbed. Li had calculated the climb to a gnat's ass once again. They would clear the ridge by no more than a few dozen feet.

"Be ready to turn left as soon as we drop," Li called out. "It's a tight turn to our next checkpoint."

"Roger," Tiger responded.

* * *

"There he is!" Smitty marked the plot. "Jumping into the valley southwest of Nanp'ing!"

"He ran that valley toward Nanp'ing last time," Olson reminded the captain. "Maybe he'll do it again."

"Whatever, it's awfully narrow," the captain responded.

Suddenly, Smitty stiffened. "Hey!" he called out, "back room says Liench'eng's putting up fighters!"

"They won't do much," Olson shrugged. "Too far away."

"Yeah," the colonel agreed, "unless he turned up the valley and headed toward them!"

A teletype began chattering, and one of the airmen moved to see what it was reporting. "Hey, Smitty," he called, "it's Quemoy radar. They're reporting activity inland, a couple of fighters."

"OK, Stu," Smitty responded, "that's Liench'eng. Pass me the information."

"They've got a long way to go to get to that last plot," the captain noted.

"Yes, sir," Olson agreed. "And they're either awfully brave or stupid if they're going that far out. If he's headed down the valley, he's way out of their range. He'll be out of ChiCom airspace before they can catch him."

"Yeah," the captain agreed, "but they're headed right at him if he's headed up the valley."

* * *

"Checkpoint's a bridge over the river," Li announced, "and it's ten seconds away. Cross it at heading 220."

"Roger," Tiger acknowledged. "Got it, about two-three degrees left of center." He adjusted the angle of the plane's course to head directly for the checkpoint.

"Checkpoint at three seconds," Li announced, "two... one... now!"

"Roger!" Tiger called out, turning the aircraft slightly to resume their course.

The radio squawked. "Red flag, two tigers, at one one zero and eight." Matsu was telling them there were two MiGs 110 kilometers from their last noted point at an eight o'clock position, or bearing of about 240 degrees.

"Shit!" Lindsay called out, "we're heading right at them. They should pass over us right after the drop. And we'll turn and leave the valley right after that, which means they'll have us."

"Don't worry, Colonel," Li noted, "I have an alternate route that will take us well past them before we climb."

"Good, Li," Lindsay breathed his relief. "We'll delay, then, and let them get past us before we jump."

* * *

"Hey!" Smitty called out, "the Liench'eng fighters are going into orbit. They've started circling about seventy kilometers east of the field."

"Hmm," the captain looked carefully at the map, "maybe they're not as stupid as we thought. If our boy headed up the valley, he'll fly right into them. And if he headed down the valley, they can get home pretty quick once they find out."

* * *

"First drop in twenty seconds," Li announced.

"Cargo door open," Lindsay called out. "Chou, be ready!"

"Ready, Captain," Chou answered brusquely.

"Colonel," Tiger interjected, "please watch for those fighters. Chou's in the bomb bay."

"You're right, Tiger!" Lindsay had forgotten about the fighters in the rush to be ready for the drop. "I'll keep my eyes open for them."

"Drop point in three seconds," Li announced over the intercom system, so Chou could hear.

"See the light, dead ahead!" Tiger announced.

"Two... one...," Li continued, "now!"

"Drop away!" Chou announced.

"Good drop!" Tiger called. "Right on target!"

"Cargo door closing. Still don't see fighters," Lindsay called out.

"Good, Colonel," Tiger replied. "We'll extend to be sure. Just keep an eye peeled."

"OK!" Lindsay responded. "Chou, please go to the back and help me watch for the fighters," he added. "I'd really like to have an extra set of eyes."

"Going, Captain," Chou's voice seemed relieved.

* * *

"OK," the captain mumbled, "so now where the hell is he?"

"Hopefully not heading right into that defensive position, sir," Olson answered, his eyes not leaving the map.

"Yeah," the captain agreed. "With the closure rate, he shouldn't be too far away from them right now if he headed that way."

* * *

"Shit!" Lindsay exploded, "there they are! Ahead of us! They're circling! I can see their navigation lights, twenty kilometers or so away."

"If we continue with my alternate plan, we'll cross the ridge just this side of them, Colonel," Li spoke up. "We can try to turn and go back to our original point, but they might spot our wing up during the tight turn and they're close enough to catch up with us if that happens."

"Li," Lindsay's mind was working fast, "you said you were at Liench'eng, once, not long ago. Did they have a radar that nodded up and down?"

"Yes, Colonel," Li replied. "It was a small one, located near the runway with a small rotating radar. That was the only one they had in the area."

"Good," Lindsay's voice signaled finality. "That was the airfield height-finder, then, and they don't have any others, especially any that will see us this far away from the airfield. We're going to cross the ridge directly underneath those fighters."

"I don't understand," Li responded. "They'll see us and will only have to drop down to catch us."

"No," Lindsay insisted, "they'll see the fighters and a shadow on their radar screen almost exactly where the fighters are. They won't know we're below the fighters, causing the shadow! Their radars can't be good enough to see us separately if we're that close."

"Good thinking, Colonel!" Tiger understood. "We'll sneak over the ridge under them and they won't know we're there!"

"Well," Lindsay shrugged, "the only alternative is to turn around and go back down this valley, but I don't like it at all. The valley isn't wide enough to escape their notice, once they have an idea where we are."

"OK," Li agreed. "We cross into the next valley under the fighters. And hope our prayers are heard and they won't see us."

"Prayers? Why, Li," Tiger teased, "I didn't know you were religious."

"I wasn't," Li replied dryly, "until I began flying with you!"

* * *

"He's been down a long time," the captain noted, lighting another cigarette. "He's either coming down the chute, or else he's underneath those fighters by now."

"Let's hope he's coming down the chute, then, sir," Olson responded. "I sure wouldn't want to pop up underneath the MiGs and have them jump on me."

"I wouldn't either," the captain agreed.

* * *

"Good." Li was doing some quick calculations. "We turn left to 150 degrees in twenty seconds. If Tiger judges his speed carefully, we'll be almost directly underneath the fighters when we go over the ridge."

"OK," Lindsay agreed. "Just make sure we go over the ridge at minimum altitude and we don't stay up there long. And," he added, "remember to keep your fingers crossed."

"Sure, Colonel," Li smiled. "But they'll probably see our crossed fingers and come after us!"

"I really wish you wouldn't say that!" Tiger spoke up. "I can't fly the plane while I'm laughing."

* * *

"Sarge," Smitty called out, "Quemoy radar thinks there's more than two fighters in the Liench'eng flight."

"What's that?" Olson wanted to know.

"They just reported they think there's more fighters than they've been tracking," Smitty repeated. "They saw a possible third fighter during the last circle. It separated from the others for just an instant, like it got out of position, fell behind or something."

"That's the best radar the ChiNats can get their hands on," the captain broke in. "Meaning it's the best in the world. It sees the difference in the two fighters out there right now, and they're flying in formation."

"Sir," Smitty went on, "the back room says they're sure there's only two fighters."

"You thinking what I'm thinking?" the captain suddenly looked at Olson, a brightness in his eyes saying he'd just witnessed something impossible. "I think they just saw our boy!"

"You mean you think he went over the ridge with the fighters, sir?" Olson asked, disbelief written on his face.

"He crossed *under* them," the captain answered, shaking his head. "I'll bet on it."

"Holy Toledo!" Olson marveled. "What a night! And we thought his first trip was wild!"

* * *

"Colonel," Li spoke up, "that maneuver lost our exact position. What do you want to do now?"

"How long did we extend to pass under the fighters?" Lindsay asked.

"By my timing, sir," Li looked at his watch, "exactly 23 seconds from the alternate point before we turned and crossed the ridge."

"Good," Lindsay thought for a moment, "then, if we fly a reciprocal route for 23 seconds, we should be near where we'd be if we took the alternate route, right?"

"We'll be close, Colonel," Li agreed, "but not exactly."

"Good," Lindsay nodded his head. "We have a checkpoint down the valley, and we can re-establish our location and timing there so long as we're close. For now, keep us on the course we would have followed from your alternate point, but remember we're about 46 seconds off our timing. And pray we didn't screw up and wind up hitting some hillside on the way!"

"OK, Colonel," Li responded, "then we should turn to heading 95 in three seconds... two... one... now!"

"Nine five, roger," Tiger automatically responded as the plane quickly adjusted its heading.

Chou's voice came over the intercom. "The fighters are still turning, away from us."

* * *

"He can't be in that valley," Olson pointed toward the map, "otherwise he'll fly right into Liench'eng real soon!"

"The MiGs are still circling," Smitty called out as he marked another position on the map. "They have no idea where he is. And the back room says the same two MiGs are getting ready to take off from Fuchou."

"Hmmm," the captain had a thoughtful look on his face, "those old MiGs are right on the ragged edge of trouble, I'll bet. They need lots of maintenance to keep going."

"Why are they putting 'em up, sir?" Smitty asked.

"Looks like they think our boy might be coming down the valley toward Fuchou again," the captain answered.

* * *

"Red flag," the call came in, "two tigers, at one four zero and four."

"Fuchou," Tiger knew the position.

"They don't have anything to chase," Lindsay commented. "They're only getting airborne in case we come back their way. They probably think we're in the valley coming toward them."

"There's about thirty seconds to the checkpoint, Colonel," Li advised. "It's a junction of two streams, and we should pass directly over it on heading 100. Heading 100 in three seconds," he called out, "two... one... now!"

"Left to one zero zero, roger," Tiger responded as the plane adjusted slightly.

"See the checkpoint!" Li called out. "To the right just a bit!"

"Got it!" Tiger twisted the plane to aim toward the checkpoint. "Heading one zero three... four. One zero four," he called as the nose swung past the aiming point.

"Cross it at 100, Tiger," Lindsay reminded him.

"No problem, Colonel," Tiger answered as the nose swung back to point directly at the checkpoint. "One zero zero, right on the button!"

"Crossing checkpoint... now!" Lindsay called to Li, who set the time on his watch and began marking the next call.

"Back on course, Colonel," Tiger chuckled. "Good thinking, again!"

"Now we just have to figure out what the Fuchou fighters are doing!" Lindsay answered.

* * *

"Back room says the Fuchou fighters have been ordered to stay close," Smitty announced. "And the Liench'eng fighters are breaking off and heading back toward the base."

"Guess Liench'eng figures if he hasn't showed up by now," Olson commented, "he's not going to, and they're bringing their folks back."

"Probably," the captain lit another cigarette. "And Fuchou is just hanging around until our guy should pop out of the chute. They want somebody up there just in case. I have a funny feeling the MiGs don't stand a chance of catching him. But we'll let them decide that!"

* * *

"Climb to 580 meters now," Li called out. "And fingers crossed!"

"Climb to five eight zero, roger," Tiger responded and the plane climbed to cross the mountains.

"Why fingers crossed?" Lindsay wanted to know.

"Fingers crossed the Fuchou fighters aren't waiting for us on the other side!" Li answered.

"They shouldn't know we're here - yet," Lindsay chuckled. "They'll find out now, though."

* * *

"There he is!" Smitty called out, marking the plot on the map. "He just jumped over the coastal mountain range!"

"And the fighters are still circling just north of Fuchou," Olson noted.

"He's faded out again," Smitty reported. "Gone down into the valley."

"OK," Olson called back. He and the captain turned to watch the map, while the captain lit another cigarette.

"Fuchou's fighters are still circling," Smitty called out. "They figure he's coming toward them."

"Or they're just not taking chances," the captain chuckled. "Maybe they don't like having him overfly them."

* * *

"Gauges all look good, Colonel," Tiger reported. "We just hit half-way on gas."

"Good," Lindsay replied. "And now we start the last part of this little exercise."

* * *

One of the teletype machines clattered again. "Sarge," Smitty called out, "the back room says the MiGs are being vectored to the southwest!"

"Hmm," the captain stroked his chin. "Looks like they're moving to intercept him between the valley and Fuchou. Probably try to jump in behind him when he comes out into the plain."

"Sarge," Smitty called out again, "Matsu shows the MiGs moving toward the southwest. Wait! - OK, back room says they've been told to circle where they are."

* * *

"OK," Li spoke carefully, "we start the final run in a few more minutes. We have no idea where the Fuchou MiGs are, so we'll have to watch carefully."

"OK," Lindsay spoke up, "Chou, please prepare the second drop."

"Yes, Captain," Chou answered immediately.

* * *

"Matsu reports the fighters circling just south of the river," Smitty called out.

"Right at the mouth of the valley, then," the captain noted.

"Yes, sir," Olson answered. "He'll pop out right under those fighters and they should have at least two passes at him before he can clear the plain and get to the coastline."

"Well," the captain chewed on his lower lip, "at least he seems to have the advantage of maneuverability over the fighters." He lit another cigarette.

* * *

"Colonel," Li spoke up, "with Chou at the cargo door, no one's watching our rear. Can you watch in that direction?"

"Sure," Lindsay nodded.

"And if you have any contacts with the gods, sir," Tiger spoke up, "we could sure use some intervention about now. Clouds would help us get by the fighters."

"Figure the odds," Lindsay quipped. "Not a cloud in the sky, and the moon's almost full! I thought the weather report said we'd have broken cloud tonight."

"Weathermen are notorious for being wrong, aren't they?" Tiger quipped back. "At least half the time."

"Hard to get good help nowadays, isn't it?" Li added, laughing nervously.

* * *

"Holy shit!" Smitty jumped to the map. "He just jumped into the valley, here!" He marked the map to the south of the fighters.

"That valley leads out onto the plain south of Fuchou," Olson reminded the captain. "It's also the last valley before the coastal plain."

"Yeah, I see," the captain responded.

"Back room says the fighters are going east," Smitty announced. "Looks like they're trying to get between him and the airfield."

"Why don't they want him near the airfield?" the captain asked, puzzlement on his face.

"Captain," Olson thought for a moment, "I may know why they're touchy about the field. There was a HUMINT report out of Fuchou after the last flight that said some propaganda leaflets were scattered around the base, leaflets that told the pilots they'd get a lot of money if they defected."

"You think maybe he dropped them when he passed over the base?" the captain asked.

"I didn't put it together then, sir," Olson answered, "and it's not our job, but, yeah, that may be exactly what happened. Maybe they don't want a bunch more of those leaflets dropped."

"Sounds like they don't want their pilots reading the stuff," the captain commented. "Which sounds like they don't trust their people much. Happy people don't pay attention to that kind of bullshit."

* * *

"Where are the fighters, guys?" Lindsay called out. "I don't see them anywhere."

"Colonel!" Li spoke up, "is that them? There, ahead of us, out in the plain?"

"Sure is!" Lindsay breathed a sigh of relief. "Good. Opening cargo door!"

"Right to - 100 degrees in three seconds," Li called, quickly calculating the course to their final objective. "Two... one... now!"

"Right to one zero zero, roger!" Tiger answered with enthusiasm and the plane banked hard to the right.

"Chou!" Lindsay called out, "stand by. We're on the final run."

"Good, Captain," came Chou's reply. "I'm ready."

"Heading one zero zero!" Tiger announced.

* * *

"Got him again!" Smitty called out. "He's heading East, toward Lungt'ien airfield!"

"Lungt'ien?" Olson was puzzled. "It's just an auxiliary field."

"Sarge," Chuck cut in, "yesterday's reports said four of Fuchou's fighters recovered at Lungt'ien, probably spend the night there and return to Fuchou later on."

"Damn!" Olson remembered now. "You're right, Chuck!"

"Then why aren't we seeing activity from Lungt'ien?" one of the younger airmen wanted to know.

"Lungt'ien isn't a regular facility," Olson had the answer, "so they don't maintain a strip alert there. Besides, these guys flew late, so their planes aren't ready for use yet."

"And," the captain added, "they don't have any heavy defensive capabilities there."

"At least none we know of," Olson added. "Lungt'ien's pretty much out by itself. They used it as an auxiliary recovery field back in '58, during the crisis. It's just a bare runway with a couple of maintenance outbuildings and a small overnight quarters for pilots and maintenance people. And it's surrounded by rice paddies, otherwise."

"Sarge," Smitty called out, "back room reports Fuchou controller just ordered the fighters to head toward Lungt'ien."

* * *

There were no lights at the target, but the concrete runway was easy to see in the moonlight.

"Drop point in three seconds," Li called out on the intercom, "two... one... now!"

"Drop away!" Chou reported immediately.

Lindsay turned his head to see the cloud of leaflets spreading rapidly, right over the taxiway area and the buildings alongside it.

"Feet wet!" Li called out, signaling they'd broken out over the coast and were now over water.

"Yes!" Lindsay exulted. "Good mission! Cargo door closing!"

"Heading 80, climb to 1,000 meters," Li called out.

Lindsay glanced out the window alongside him as the aircraft climbed. The MiGs were still coming toward them!

"Jesus!" Lindsay called out. "Fighters at nine o'clock low! About fifteen kilometers away!"

Suddenly the radio broke in. "Red flag, two fire dragons, at one five zero and six," the Matsu controller advised them of two ChiNat fighters – "fire dragons" meant supersonic F104s – coming from Makung airbase, and probably very, very fast.

Lindsay grinned at the announcement. The ChiNats didn't like to have ChiCom fighters wander out over the strait, which the ChiNats considered their own private lake!

* * *

"Woooey!" Smitty nearly screamed with excitement. "The MiGs kept going for the coast, and now Matsu has two F104s out of Makung at Mach plus and fixing to take 'em on!"

"The MiGs don't stand a chance against the F104s," Olson spoke the obvious.

"Back room says the MiGs are recalled," Smitty quickly announced.

"Smart, I'd say," the captain observed wryly. "They're a little outclassed."

"Sir!" Smitty called out, "our guy's dropping altitude, looks like he's headed for the deck!"

"Trying to avoid the F104s?" the captain asked the question. "Or trying to avoid the MiGs, since he may not know the F104s are coming?"

"He's not changing his course, sir," Smitty called out, as if in answer to the question. "Maybe he's just being careful to get out of the way of any shooting."

* * *

Tiger tuned one of the radios to the frequency for the ChiNat F104s, since he remembered it well. "Ha!" he announced as he heard one of the Nationalist pilots talking to his controller, "that's Chung, my old wingman! I flew with him back when he didn't know his stick from his throttle!" he grinned.

"Just get us home, OK?" Lindsay smiled at his young protégé. "I'm ready for a bathroom break!"

"I second that!" Li chimed in, laughing.

"Hey," it was Chou, "did you know there's a relief tube back here behind the cargo area? We don't have to hold our water if we don't want to! We can spread it all over the strait!"

"I'm on my way!" yelled Li, jumping up. "Chou, save me a place in line!"

"OK!" Chou laughed back. "You're next, after me."

* * *

"He's gone," Smitty called out. "He's below radar coverage now. The MiGs are returning to Fuchou, and the F104s are patrolling the coastline."

"OK, Smitty," Olson breathed a sigh of relief. "Keep a watch until everything settles down. Chuck, let the guys handle the teletypes while you fix a fresh pot of coffee."

"Got it," Chuck handed over the headsets to a nearby helper. "It's quiet, anyway, just Matsu reporting the ChiComs and F104s, now."

"Well," Olson turned to the captain, "guess I'd better start getting ready to brief the colonel and the general, huh, sir?"

"Yeah," the captain smiled as he pulled another cigarette from the pack. "Let me get changed and grab another pack of smokes, and then I'll come back to give you a hand. This is getting to be a regular affair!" He hesitated as he reached the door. "Don't forget to call your wife."

FIVE

Kung and Hamilton strode from the CAT hangar as the plane taxied into place. Lindsay climbed out as they approached the plane.

"How'd it go?" Hamilton asked.

"Not as easy as the first one," Lindsay answered casually. "Had some fighter reaction this time."

"Colonel Lindsay used a trick to get us out of a mess," Tiger spoke out as he and Li came up behind them. "He ducked under the fighters and they didn't even know it!"

"Hmm," Hamilton grinned at Lindsay as they continued into the hangar, "that sounds like a pilot magic trick."

"Not magic, Charlie," Lindsay assured him, "just common sense. The controllers didn't see us because we looked like we were part of the flight of fighters while we were visible."

"Oh, *that* sounds good," Hamilton laughed. "By the way, the drops went OK, didn't they?"

"Sure," Lindsay answered. "We were right on target with both of them."

"Good, good," Hamilton nodded as they entered the office. "Keeps the customer happy - I hope!"

"We hope so, too, sir," Li responded. Hamilton looked at him with surprise.

"Your crew speaks English?" Hamilton asked Lindsay.

"Some," Lindsay answered. "Tiger's trying to teach them. OK, everybody," he turned to the others, "let's do a quick outbrief – you want it in-depth in writing, right, Charlie?"

"Well," Hamilton chuckled, "I sure wouldn't mind hearing about how you foxed the fighters. But the details we can do in written form."

"Sounds good," Lindsay responded. "I expect the guys would like to go home and get some sleep."

The outbrief went quickly, with each crewmember giving a quick sketch of his view of the mission. Lindsay gave a detailed description of the escape from the fighters, and Hamilton laughed at it, although Lindsay noted that Kung seemed bored. Ah, well, Lindsay thought, Kung wasn't a flier, and that was already obvious.

When the briefing was over, Hamilton spoke up. "Good job, guys. I think our customer's pleased with your results." He turned toward Kung, who nodded approval. "OK, then," Hamilton resumed, "if there's nothing more, we'll see the detailed report tomorrow, and I'll call you later about any other stuff. Anything else?" The crew all shook their heads. "Good then," he looked toward Kung. "If you're ready, Winston, let's go."

* * *

The rest of the outbrief went quickly, and Lindsay made plenty of notes. When it was finished, he looked at the crew. "Anybody got anything else?" he grinned at them. "If not, that's it. Crew rest until three-thirty this afternoon, so there's nothing more today. See you guys at nine tomorrow morning."

Tiger and Li jumped up and put their soda bottles away, followed by Chou, who seemed to hang back. The other two were out the door by the time Chou had carefully put his bottle away.

"Something wrong, Chou?" Lindsay asked.

"I could use a ride, Captain," Chou answered.

"Sure," Lindsay responded. "Let's take the other guys to their place," Lindsay suggested, "and then I'll take you home."

* * *

"See you tomorrow morning!" Lindsay waved to the two tired young men. He put the jeep in gear and headed back toward the main boulevard, then turned to Chou.

"It looked like Mister Kung was concerned about something tonight," Lindsay said. "He pulled you to the side right after we landed."

"Yes, Captain," Chou answered thoughtfully. "He wants me to do a good job."

"I think he should take my word for it, Chou," Lindsay commented. "You've done everything we've asked you to, and we're happy you're a member of our crew."

"I'm glad to know that, Captain," Chou showed a rare smile. "I haven't been happy since I left the army to join the SID. But I'm afraid I'm doing something that's wrong."

"What's that?" Lindsay asked, curious.

"On both flights, Mister Kung has given me an extra package to drop, Captain," Chou looked worried. "I don't know what's in the package, but he told me it's very important that I drop it. Captain," Chou looked toward Lindsay with troubled eyes, "if it's important, then why isn't it in the regular packages?"

Lindsay wasn't quite sure how to answer the question, but he didn't want to upset Chou. "Maybe it's something that can't be put into the packages because it's got to be handled differently."

"Yes," Chou seemed relieved. "Maybe that's what it is."

"Why don't you ask Mister Kung?" Lindsay suggested. "He'll be happy to tell you."

"Oh, he won't tell me," Chou responded with conviction.

"Why not?" Lindsay asked.

"He doesn't have to tell me anything," Chou replied. "I have to do what he wants."

"What?" Lindsay questioned.

"Mister Kung knows some things which could put me in prison," Chou admitted, hanging his head, "and I have no choice but to do what he says."

"What have you done so awful you could be put in prison?" Lindsay wanted to know.

"Oh, Captain," Chou answered. "I'm ashamed to tell it, but I lost my temper and killed a policeman. I was working undercover in a whorehouse," he went on, "and the policeman demanded the girls pay him a lot of money or he was going to put them all in jail. I lost my temper and killed him. Mister Kung took care of the problem. But he never lets me forget. If they found out it was me, I probably wouldn't live long enough to go to prison. They'd shoot me and say I tried to escape."

"Jesus!" Lindsay lapsed into English.

"I can't see any way out of this," Chou went on.

"I understand," Lindsay responded. "But maybe Mister Hamilton could inform Mister Kung what he's doing is wrong."

"I'd appreciate any help, Captain," Chou answered. "I'm not a very smart man, I know, and I can't see a way. But you're smart, and maybe you can help me."

"I hope so," Lindsay responded. "Let me talk to Mister Hamilton."

"Thank you, Captain," Chou seemed relieved.

"Changing the subject," Lindsay continued, "I've wondered for a long time why you call me 'Captain'."

"That's easy, sir," Chou smiled. "When I was in the army, the highest ranking officer I ever saw was a captain. It's the highest rank I know to call anyone."

"Then I consider it an honor," Lindsay laughed.

* * *

Olson woke to the bed shaking.

"Hey, honey!" his wife shook it again, "time to wake up and get something to eat! Here's your coffee." She put the cup down on the bedside table.

"Oooooh!" Olson moaned. "Marie, my mouth feels like I've been eating cotton and my head feels like it's stuffed full of it!"

"That's what you get for staying up late off a mid shift!" she laughed at him. "You should tell the general to let you come home on time! You hardly even spoke when you came in this morning!"

"I know," Olson answered. "Oh!" the recollection came to him, "then I bet I didn't tell you what happened, did I?"

"What?" her bright blue eyes crackled under the long auburn hair.

"He promoted me," Olson smiled and lay back on the bed. "To Tech Sergeant. Effective the first of the month."

"Mike Olson," she stopped cold, "you know what'll happen to you if you tell lies? Your nose will grow real long and your thingie will shrink to nothing!"

"It's true, baby," Olson smiled. "When I finished the briefing, the general told the colonel to make sure the orders were published, effective the first of the month!"

"Oh, God, Mike," she gasped. "I'm so happy for you! Tech Sergeant!"

Olson grabbed and caught her by the arm. With a yank, he pulled her onto the bed and close enough so he could wrap one of his arms around her. "And now, since my thingie isn't shrunk, I'm going to use it on you!" he laughed, unbuttoning her jeans with his free hand.

* * *

Another trip to Tokyo! Lindsay wasn't sure he'd heard right as he put down the phone. Hamilton and Kung wanted to go to Tokyo again because Kung had some business to take care of. It was a chance for him and Tiger to see Marion and Yukiko. And maybe they could take Li along with them this time. Li could use a couple of days off, Lindsay thought. With the exception of Sundays, when he'd go to visit his parents, Li rarely went anywhere or did anything except work and physical exercises.

Even Chou might like to have a couple of days off, since Kung would be gone. Chou didn't seem to have much of a personal life. The only thing that seemed worthwhile in his life was the respect the other crewmembers accorded him. Maybe, thought Lindsay, they should take Chou to Tokyo with them too, someday, just to see if he was really alive.

In the meantime, the crew was out getting lunch. Lindsay would tell them about the trip when they got back. They'd better be ready to take off early tomorrow morning. Hamilton wanted to leave early. For now, though, Lindsay needed to ask the SAT office to notify Tokyo they were coming.

* * *

The flight to Tokyo went smoothly. Having Li on board made it much better, of course - he and Tiger kept them laughing the whole flight. Kung was late arriving for takeoff, but they pushed the plane a little and made their scheduled arrival time at Haneda. Now they were riding with Paul Anderson into Tokyo, since the CAT limousine had once again met Kung and Hamilton.

The three younger men seemed to be enjoying themselves immensely. And they obviously got along well together, with the other two making sure Li saw everything there was to see on the way. By the time they arrived at the SAT offices, the three younger men had decided Tiger would ask Yukiko out that evening and they'd ask if she had two friends, so the three could go out together.

It was going to be interesting to introduce Li to Joe Calloway, Lindsay thought as the car pulled into the office-parking garage.

In the office, Yukiko wasted no time jumping up and greeting Tiger. She was obviously pleased to see him.

The introduction to Li went well. Yukiko blushed when Li, in his very matter-of-fact way, said Tiger was the luckiest man he'd ever seen, since he'd met Yukiko before Li could fall in love with her.

Next, while Lindsay was still peeling off his flight jacket, the youngsters arranged Li's date with Yukiko's friend Kumiko and started talking about finding a date for Anderson. Finally, Lindsay had to break in, and, leaving Anderson to help Yukiko and Kumiko find a date for him, he led the two young Chinese off toward Calloway's office.

At the door, his knock was answered with a roar, "Lindsay, get your asses in here and get a beer!" Yep, Lindsay thought, Calloway knew they were coming!

"Joe," Lindsay pushed the door open, "I'd like to have you meet our other front-end crewman, Li Yao-shan. Just call him Li, for short."

Calloway appraised the young frogman quickly. "Li, it's a privilege to have you as a part of the team. I've heard and read a lot about your work."

"I hope some of it's been good," Li responded, a little proud of his English.

"Most of it's been outstanding," Calloway replied. "Lindsay," he turned, "you got lucky. I think you've got a real top-quality crew."

At that point, the door to the office opened, and Marion came in with a tray with beer and sodas. She smiled at Lindsay. "Hi, Harry," she spoke quietly as she set the tray down. "They said you were coming in this morning. I'll talk to you later?"

"I'll track you down, wherever you are," Lindsay answered. "By the way, Marion," he added, "meet our other crewman, Li. Li," he continued, "this is my friend, Mrs. Oliver, Marion."

"Mrs. Oliver," Li bowed, "it's a pleasure to meet such a very special friend of my friend, Colonel Lindsay, especially such a beautiful lady."

"Mister Li," Marion smiled at him, "it's a pleasure to meet such a nice young rogue and friend of Colonel Lindsay."

"Mrs. Oliver," he smiled back, "I've been called a rogue many times, but never by anyone so lovely, and no one's ever made it sound so nice. I understand why Colonel Lindsay cares about you very much!"

Marion blushed lightly. "Joe," she said, "I'll be at my desk if you need anything." She smiled back at Li. "I hope you enjoy Tokyo a lot, Li. And Tiger," she scowled at Tiger, "you and Yukiko keep him out of trouble."

"Yes, Mrs. Oliver," Tiger bowed. "If we can."

When the door closed behind Marion, Joe waved toward the others. "Get a drink and sit down," he ordered. "Now, Lindsay," he turned to face Lindsay, "I want to hear all about this thing with the fighters first-hand."

When they finished the briefing, Calloway laughed. "Jesus, Lindsay, I like the way you handled the fighters. You guys did a great job."

"Thanks, Joe," Lindsay responded. "And now that we've got big heads, what's on the agenda for the rest of the day?"

Calloway stood up. "Well," he said, "since you let us know you were coming, I talked to the boss and he said the girls can take the afternoon off and show you around Tokyo. Even Kumiko, so Li can have an escort while Tiger and Yukiko are mooning over each other. Anderson's off, too, since I suspect you'll be asking him to go along, but I'm afraid I can't help find him a date. Anyway," he waved toward the two younger men, "you two get out of here and let me talk to Lindsay."

"Go get checked into the *ryokan*," Lindsay suggested. "Take my bags along, and I'll be there in a bit."

"I could use another beer," Calloway started off. "How about you?"

"Still just a one-beer guy," Lindsay chuckled. "But don't let me stop you!"

"Well, I've done some research on some questions from last time," Calloway reached over and took another beer from the tray. "For one thing, Charlie Hamilton isn't an intelligence guy – he started with SAT operations in Central America and then came here to the Far East office. After he got here, he came up with this project, so they let him take it over and run it."

"Well," Lindsay shrugged, "he's easy to get along with, actually a fairly nice guy. I think he gets a lot of pressure from the customer, Kung. I knew Kung before this project, and the guy has all the makings of a real asshole. In fact, he's got our kicker upset, and I wish you or Charlie would do something about it."

"Hey," Calloway took a drink of the beer, "customer problems are out of my league. Those are Charlie's ballpark. That's why he's the project officer. But I guess I can see if he can't do something with this guy Kung and the problem he's causing for your kicker."

"I don't believe there's anything he can do, Joe," Lindsay shrugged again, "but I figure you ought to know there's a problem."

"OK," Calloway agreed. "Anyway, I'd keep an eye on it. My horse and half my kingdom for a customer who doesn't think he knows it all!"

"I hear that," Lindsay agreed. "By the way, what do you think of Li?"

Calloway's face turned serious, "He's a pro. And I'm damned glad he's on our side!"

"Yeah," Lindsay nodded, "so am I. You got anything else?"

"Guess not," Calloway finished up the beer. "Why don't you get out of here?"

"OK," Lindsay stretched his arms and legs. "I want to get to the *ryokan* and get cleaned up and change clothes." He got up from the chair and started toward the door, then stopped. "Hey, what are you doing for dinner tonight?"

"Nothing," Calloway answered.

"I'm going to see if Marion won't go to dinner with me again. Why don't we meet you, and let's eat some *sushi*?" Lindsay asked.

"OK! See you at the *sushi* place near Marion's at six?" Calloway wanted to know.

"Sounds good!" Lindsay replied. "Six it is!"

"Remember to stop and take Marion with you," Calloway reminded. "Not that I figure you'd forget!"

* * *

The wad of bills felt thick in Hamilton's hand. Another five thousand bucks! This time Kung had taken a little longer in the restaurant. But the money made up for the time spent waiting. Of course, he'd suggested going inside with Kung, but Kung had said he'd just be bored and he'd be just as well off waiting in the limousine. The driver had even brought him a beer from inside the restaurant, and the car certainly had been comfortable enough.

* * *

Lindsay was reviewing the route for the next mission when the phone rang. "That you, Lindsay?" Hamilton asked.

"Sure is, Charlie," Lindsay replied. "What's up?"

"Hey," Hamilton answered, "Calloway wanted me to talk to Kung about a problem with Chou. I'm not sure I understand everything, but I don't think he's being unreasonable. All he's doing is asking Chou to do his job, and do it right."

"I understand," Lindsay responded. "But Kung has him upset, and I wish he'd quit pushing. I want Chou to feel good about his job, and Kung makes him uneasy. That makes *me* uneasy."

"OK," Hamilton agreed, "I'll talk to Kung. But Chou's his direct subordinate, and I don't think he'll do much. And Kung *is* the customer, so I don't feel I can ask a lot of him, either."

"I hear you," Lindsay replied. "I hope Kung realizes my crew doesn't need outside crap. We've got enough to worry about while we're doing our job."

"I know what you mean," Hamilton responded. "By the way, are you ready to pass along the mission information this afternoon?"

"Yep," Lindsay answered. "I'll drop it by your office right after lunch."

"OK," Hamilton said. "See you then."

SIX

The new stripes felt good, Olson thought as he walked in for the first mid shift of the cycle. Marie had sewn them on for him just today. In a month, the first payday at the new rank would be another good day! There was sure a lot right with the world right now!

"Hey, Sarge!" Chuck greeted Olson. "The stripes look really good!" Chuck stuck out his fist, thumb up.

"Yeah, Sarge!" Stu added. "Like to see that!"

"You passing out cigars, Sarge?" Smitty teased from behind the map.

"Nope," Olson replied, "just candy bars. You guys would stink the place up too much with cigars!" He turned to the shift chief he was relieving. "You'd think they'd never seen anyone get promoted."

"Yeah," the other shift chief answered. "Good to see it though, Mike. Congratulations!"

"Thanks," Olson shook the proffered hand. "Anything going on?"

"Nope," came the answer. "Looks like you get a normal mid shift."

"Yeah," Olson laughed, "don't say it that way. We keep getting these screwy nights, every first mid since I got back from Hong Kong!"

"I hear you," the other shift chief chuckled. "Think he's working your shift schedule?"

"Almost looks like it, doesn't it?" Olson replied. "Two sets of mids and two flights!"

Shift change was completed, and Olson called to the others. "OK, Chuck, you help the young guys study for their five-level test for awhile. Smitty, how about working with Stu on plot board skills so he can rotate with you and Chuck? The rest of you get ready - we'll start cleanup in two hours."

* * *

Lindsay was ready to climb into the plane when he saw Hamilton.

"Hey, Charlie," he asked, "did you get a chance to talk to Kung yet?"

"Yeah, I did," Hamilton seemed nervous. "He sort of pooh-poohed the whole thing, said he thought Chou was just trying to fish for sympathy."

"Hmmm," Lindsay was a little perplexed. "He didn't seem that way to me, but I guess I won't get involved in it at this point. It just better not screw up our crew."

"Well," Hamilton commented, "keep an eye on it. If anything further needs to be done, let me know."

"OK," Lindsay responded, "will do. See you when we get back."

"Sure," Hamilton grinned, "have fun."

* * *

The book was dull, the course was dull, and Olson had already put away two cups of coffee trying to stay awake.

"Shit!" Smitty yelled. "Sarge, we got work."

"On the board, Smitty," Olson threw the book into the desk drawer. "Chuck, Stu, everybody, positions. What is it, Smitty?"

"He's going in again!" Smitty replied, marking the map.

"You sure?" Olson moved quickly to the ops officer's phone.

"Got to be!" Smitty called back, "low altitude, broke the coastline northeast of Quemoy, and he's moving fast!" He marked another position. "Headed inland, going northwest."

"Damn!" Olson growled. "Maybe he *is* working our schedule! Just hope I don't have to write his performance report, too!" He picked up the phone and rang the bell at the captain's quarters.

* * *

Lindsay grinned with excitement. Low and fast, in over the coast, just like before. Just a different location.

* * *

"Stripes look good, Mike," the captain pulled off his jacket and glanced toward the map.

"Thanks, sir," Olson answered.

The captain nodded. "OK, where are we now?"

"He broke the coast just above Quemoy, sir," Olson answered. "He stayed at low altitude up this valley here, then jumped west, over to the valley, here, north of Changchou. That's all we have so far, sir."

"Oops!" Chuck broke in as a teletype machine started chattering. "It's Quemoy!" He began reading information to Smitty at the map.

"Fighter reaction from Changchou," Smitty called as he plotted the information. "OK," he announced, "back room says they have two fighters lifting off from Changchou."

"They're awfully close," Olson noted. "No more than 65 kilometers away. And he's staying up high. There's nowhere to duck down there."

"Yeah," the captain agreed, "but they're trailing him, and they're not at full speed yet. He has all the lead he needs."

* * *

"Red flag," the radio squawked. "Two tigers, six five at six." The transmission ended.

"They can't catch up with us before we're gone," Li commented. "The valley splits there, so they won't know which direction we've gone."

"And they don't know that we're going somewhere else altogether," Tiger laughed.

* * *

"Faded off," Smitty called out. "Headed for the valley floor there. And he can go either way."

"Hey," Chuck called out. "Another raid from Quemoy. Looks like Liench'eng, back inland."

"Going to try the old hammer and anvil routine?" the captain smiled. "I doubt it'll succeed. Our boy probably expects it, and he's probably already got something planned."

* * *

"Red flag," the radio squawked again, "two tigers, one zero zero at ten."

"Liench'eng's up," Lindsay called out. "Ready to start the fun!"

"OK, left to 120 in three seconds," Li called, "two... one... now!"

"Left to one two zero, roger," Tiger responded as the right wing rose into the air and the plane made a hard turn, almost reversing direction, and started back down the valley toward the coast.

"Now the fun begins," Lindsay laughed. "Changchou will go berserk!"

* * *

"The Liench'eng flight's circling," Smitty announced, marking another plot. "They haven't moved."

"Probably not sure which way to go," the captain commented. "The river splits there and he can either go west, away from the Changchou MiGs, or go north, putting him east of Liench'eng. They're playing it safe."

"The Changchou MiGs are closing on where our guy went down into the valley," Olson watched Smitty mark another plot.

"Wonder which way he went," the captain mused. "They'll have to make a decision, and there's a fifty-fifty chance they'll pick the right one."

"I hate to disagree, sir," Olson responded, "but they only have a thirty-three percent chance."

"Huh?" the captain turned to stare.

"There's a third way, sir," Olson continued to stare at the map. "Back down the river, toward Changchou."

"Aw, that's crazy!" the captain shook his head. "Why would he do that?"

"He's pulled the fighters off to the north, sir," Olson pointed out. "That puts him over Changchou, with the nearest planes seventy-five kilometers away."

"What if they think the same way?" the captain asked.

"Simple, sir," Olson answered. "He watches the fighters to see what they do. If they start back toward Changchou, he goes the opposite way. Nobody can see him in the valley there, it's too deep. And he has them where he wants them — not sure where he is, but with him knowing where they are!"

"But what will that accomplish, Mike?" the captain asked. "It puts them out of the way if he wants to overfly Changchou, but it doesn't get him back up into the mainland?"

"Who said he needed to get back in over the mainland, sir?" Olson asked the obvious question.

"Changchou fighters are turning west," Smitty called. "Looks like Liench'eng's covering the north route and Changchou's taking the west one."

* * *

"I see the fighters," Chou called. "They're crossing the valley behind us."

"Good," Lindsay answered. "Just what we wanted. How long to the first checkpoint, Li?"

"About half a minute, Colonel," Li answered. "Then we start the sequence."

* * *

"Changchou fighters are still going west," Smitty called out as he marked the map.

"They're trying to follow the west branch of the river," Olson pointed out the valley area to the west of where the river divided.

"Not much chance they'll see him, much less catch him in those valleys," the captain commented. "Those are deep valleys and not very wide. The MiGs can't make the turns and they can't get down there to him."

"*IF* he decided to go that direction, sir," Olson reminded him.

"Yeah," the captain lit another cigarette.

"Liench'eng's still orbiting," Smitty marked another plot.

* * *

"Checkpoint's a bridge over the river," Li reminded them. "We cross it, then jump up and immediately turn back upriver."

"Roger," Tiger answered.

"Ready?" Li started, "time to start. Checkpoint's about 10 seconds out."

"Got it!" Tiger called out, "dead ahead, 180 degrees."

"Call the checkpoint," Li said.

"Roger!" Lindsay replied. "Now!"

"Climb to 80 meters!" Li called. "Now!"

"Eight zero meters, roger," Tiger echoed.

"Drop to 45 meters, now!" Li called out immediately.

"Roger, four five!" Tiger responded and the plane nosed downward.

"Left to 345 degrees, now!" Li called out.

"Left to three four five, roger," Tiger called back and the plane stood on its left wing.

"Holy shit!" Lindsay murmured, watching the ground pass by no more than a few meters below the wingtip.

"Three four five!" Tiger called as the plane leveled off, headed back up the valley.

* * *

"Got him!" Smitty called out, marking another plot. "Heading for Changchou, down the valley!"

Olson glanced at the captain, who shook his head.

"Damn!" the captain chuckled, "right on the money, Mike! How'd you guess it?"

"Didn't, sir," Olson smiled. "It was the only way he could go without having them on him when he came out of the valley."

"So he's headed for Changchou!" the captain shook his head. "But it'll be awfully tight whether or not he can get out over the strait before the fighters can get close enough for a shot."

"He might make it, sir," Olson looked carefully at the map, but shook his head, as if not believing himself.

"Changchou fighters are being recalled and told to go to combat power," Smitty called.

* * *

"Hey," Tiger called as the plane turned, "where are the MiGs?"

"We should see them any time now," Lindsay answered. "Changchou's got to recall them to try to cover against us. Chou, please watch carefully to the left front."

"Yes, Captain," Chou answered.

"There they are," Lindsay spotted the navigation lights, "and they must be on combat power. They're moving fast!"

"I see them, Captain," Chou responded.

"Good," Lindsay nodded. "Now for the Liench'eng fighters."

* * *

"Changchou fighters are heading for home," Smitty called as he marked up a plot.

"Our boy should reach the plain soon," Olson noted.

"Yeah," the captain responded, "and those fighters will be right on his ass as he passes Changchou. I don't like that, not at all!"

"Hmmm," Olson thought for a second, "neither do I, sir. And I'll bet he doesn't either. So I'll bet he's not going where we think he is."

"Huh?" the captain raised an eyebrow.

"He's headed back up the valley," Olson nodded in agreement with himself. "That jump up into the air was meant to pull the Changchou MiGs back to base." He turned toward the captain. "They're on combat power, so they're done for the night when they get back to the plain and don't have a target. In fact, sir, I'm surprised those two fighters have managed to hold together this long."

"Oops!" Smitty's voice broke in. "Got an airplane with problems."

"See what I mean?" Olson grinned.

"One of the Liench'eng fighters has power fluctuations," Smitty called. "Liench'eng's ordered them back to base."

"Ah, well," Olson shrugged. "Sometimes you miss by a bit."

* * *

"OK," Lindsay spoke up. "Now we pull the Liench'eng MiGs to the south, and then we can pass them and go up the valley to our drop."

"Yes, sir," Li answered.

"Good," Lindsay grinned. "Start the sequence, Li."

"Yes, sir!" Li responded.

* * *

"He still hasn't shown up," Smitty called out. "Fighters are almost to the plain."

"He should have come out a couple of minutes ago, sir," Olson told the captain. "He's gone back up the valley."

"Looks like you're right again, Mike," the captain chuckled. "Damn', son, you're getting to be more like a Tech Sergeant every minute! Right all the time!"

"Hopefully not that bad yet, sir," Olson answered.

"Back room says Changchou's telling the fighters to land," Smitty called.

* * *

"Drop to 60 meters and turn left to 35 degrees now!" Li called.

"Drop to six zero and left to three five, roger," Tiger answered as the plane's right wing lifted toward the sky while the left wing pointed straight at the ground and the aircraft dropped. It pushed through the turn, driving the crew down into their seats, then leveled out as the turn completed. "Six zero and three five it is," Tiger called out.

"That should start them this way," Lindsay nodded smugly.

"Hopefully, they've already started," Li nodded agreement. "They have to take our bait. We have to clear the valley and be into the next one before they can get near us."

* * *

"There he is!" Smitty jumped to mark another plot. "He's south of Liench'eng, headed southwest."

"There's lots of territory down there without coverage," Olson noted. "If anybody's going to catch him, it'll have to be Liench'eng. Smitty," he called, "where are the Liench'eng MiGs now?"

Smitty spoke into his microphone, then relayed the answer. "They're still limping home," he answered. "The back room says they're going slow because of the power problems."

"OK," Olson responded, turning back to the captain. "There it is, sir," he said. "Liench'eng probably can't send anybody else, and our boy's loose in the interior for awhile. Looks like time for coffee."

"Sure does, Mike," the captain lit another cigarette.

* * *

"Watch carefully, Chou," Lindsay called. "The fighters should cross behind us, but they'll be to our left side after the next turn."

"I'm watching, Captain," Chou responded. "I haven't seen anything, yet."

"OK," Lindsay answered, "'Into the valley of death rode the six hundred'-."

"Poem?" Li asked.

"Yeah. 'Charge of the Light Brigade'," Lindsay answered.

"None of them came back, did they, Colonel?" Tiger asked.

"Right, Tiger," Lindsay answered. "I hope we have better luck."

* * *

"They're getting ready to land at Liench'eng," Smitty called out. "Back room says they'll bring the lame one down first."

"OK Smitty," Olson replied.

"Hey, Sarge!" Smitty peeled off the headset and microphone and put them on the table. "I need a potty break."

"Sure," Olson called out, "Chuck, take Smitty's place, just in case."

"Aw, shoot, Sarge," Smitty protested, "nothing will happen while I go to the potty."

"Hey," Olson replied, "we've still got a penetrator loose over there. No telling what can happen, and I don't want us uncovered if something pops up, y'know?"

"Yeah," Smitty agreed, "you're right. I'll hustle back."

"Hey," Chuck called, "you don't have to hurry, Smitty. The guys can handle the teletype center. Besides, I want to find out what it's like to write backwards on the map for real! Like does it make you sterile or something?"

"Up yours, too," Smitty laughed as he left the room.

* * *

"Still no fighters to our left," Chou reported.

"They may be too low to see," Lindsay responded. "And they should be fifty kilometers away from us, flying the other way, so we might miss them."

"I'm watching carefully, Captain," Chou didn't sound reassured.

"OK," Li warned. "We're ready to jump over the ridge. Let's hope the Liench'eng fighters aren't waiting for us."

"Li," Tiger responded, "you're a damned pessimist!"

* * *

"Alright," the captain sat back in the chair and put his feet up on the desk, "so what's he going to run into at Swatow?"

"I don't know, sir," Olson responded. "We don't get reports on that area. Nobody's close enough to keep an eye on it."

* * *

"Fingers crossed," Lindsay spoke as the plane climbed to clear the ridge. "Chou," he called out, "please keep a sharp lookout."

"Yes, Captain," Chou responded.

"Here we go, Colonel," Li smiled grimly. "Over the ridge."

"Five three five meters!" Tiger called the altitude as the plane leveled off.

"Descend to 125 meters," Li called out, "now!"

"One two five meters, roger," Tiger echoed and the nose of the plane dropped toward the valley ahead of them.

"Captain!" it was Chou's voice. "I see flashing lights. To our left. Over there, low to the ground."

"Where, Chou?" Lindsay didn't see.

"To the left, there, Captain!" Chou called out. "Near the town lights!"

"Chou, I can't see them," Lindsay called back. "We're too low now. All I could see were the lights of the town. Are you sure you saw flashing lights?"

"I think so, Captain," now Chou didn't sound very sure, either. "Maybe it was only my imagination."

"One two five meters," Tiger announced as the plane leveled out.

"Forty-five seconds to next checkpoint," Li announced.

* * *

"Oh, shit!" Chuck's face went almost white. "It's him!"

"What, Chuck?" Olson wanted to know.

"He just jumped over the ridge east of Liench'eng," Chuck began marking the information. "And the back room says they've still got one fighter up at Liench'eng with plenty of fuel left to chase him!"

"Damn!" the captain interjected. "That fighter will be on him like a duck on a Junebug! It'll catch him before he can find any maneuvering room!"

"The MiG may not be able to see him," Olson started, hopefully.

"Let's hope not, Mike," the captain responded, "but I wouldn't give him a wooden nickel's chance in hellfire. That valley's damned tight, and he can't wriggle around enough to get away from somebody who knows where to look for him unless it's really cloudy and he can slip around in the shadows. The MiG can catch up with him in no more than forty or fifty kilometers because it can go almost twice his speed."

A teletype rattled. "Hey," Stu called out, "Quemoy just reacquired the Liench'eng fighter, the one that didn't land." He quickly read off the data to Chuck at the map.

"They've got a good shot at him," the captain shook his head, lighting another cigarette. "He may not be able to get away. The

MiG pilot doesn't have another aircraft blinding him with nav lights, either."

"The Liench'eng fighter's moving pretty fast," Chuck called out as he marked another plot. "He must be on combat power."

* * *

"Chou," Lindsay called, "do you see anything back there?"

"No, Captain," Chou answered.

"OK," Lindsay made a decision, "start preparing the first drop. Let me know when you're ready."

"Yes, Captain," Chou answered.

* * *

"The MiG's moving pretty fast," Chuck called out as he put up another plot. "Our boy ought to be right about here right now, if he's keeping up the same rate of speed."

"Hey," Smitty was back in the room, "what's this?"

"Liench'eng MiG's after our boy in the valley, Smitty," Olson answered quickly. "Get on the board and help Chuck. This one could get nasty real fast!"

"On it, Sarge!" Smitty picked up an extra pair of headsets and plugged in next to Chuck's. "Where we at, Chuck?"

As Chuck briefed Smitty, Olson turned back toward the desk, where the captain lit another cigarette. "Better cross our fingers, sir," he suggested. "Hopefully, our boy's paying attention! If not, that MiG's shooting fish in a barrel!"

"Another plot on the MiG," Chuck announced. "It's only at seven hundred meters altitude."

"Yeah," the captain nodded. "He doesn't need to get any higher – they're not that far from the base radar. He's low enough to spot our guy. And it won't be long."

* * *

"Two minutes to drop," Li announced. "Dead on at 35 degrees."

"Roger," Lindsay agreed. "Chou, is the drop ready?"

"Yes, Captain," Chou replied.

"Good," Lindsay answered, "I'll open the cargo door in about forty-five seconds. Please be ready."

"Yes, Captain," Chou responded.

* * *

"The MiG's still moving fast, Sarge," Chuck called out again.

"He might only be ten or fifteen kilometers behind our guy. Back room says he hasn't seen our guy yet, but he's getting approximate location reports from his controller."

"OK, Chuck," Olson answered, turning toward the captain. "They're guessing where he is, same as we are, sir."

"Looks like it, Mike," the captain answered. "Figure another two minutes at the most before he catches up."

* * *

"Cargo door open," Lindsay called. "Prepare to drop."

"Yes, Captain," Chou answered.

"One minute to drop," Li chimed in. "Steady on heading 35."

"Hey, sir," it was Tiger's voice. "Anybody check our six?"

"Shit," Lindsay cursed in English. "Looking now." He spun around in his seat and immediately saw the MiG's navigation lights above and behind them. "We've got one right behind us!" he called. "About ten kilometers away, looks like he's catching up, and not very high!"

"Chou saw aircraft lights, Colonel," Li offered.

"Yeah," Lindsay agreed, "now what do we do?"

"Hold on tight, Colonel," Tiger answered. "We make our drop and try to avoid getting shot down, that's what we do."

"OK, Tiger," Lindsay agreed, "do some magic and get us out of here."

"Roger, sir," Tiger grinned. "A little bit of magic coming right up."

"Thirty seconds to drop," Li called out.

"Thirty seconds, Chou," Lindsay passed the information along. "Be ready to hold on tight. We could have a very bumpy ride!"

* * *

"Another plot," Chuck called out. "Now about five kilometers behind."

"Back room says L" Lien[Lienchéng Liench'eng's telling the pilot to look toward the ground," Smitty chimed in. "They must figure he's pretty close."

"All we can do is keep our fingers crossed, huh, sir?" Olson questioned.

"We could try some silent prayer, too," the captain agreed. "Every little bit might help!"

* * *

"See the light!" Tiger called out.

"Three seconds to drop," Li called, "two... one... now!"

"Drop!" Lindsay called.

"Drop away!" Chou responded.

"Cargo door closing!" Lindsay called out. "Chou, hold on tight back there. We're going to take evasive action!"

"Yes, Captain," Chou answered.

* * *

"Back room says the MiG reports seeing something!" Smitty called out. "He's going down to take a look!"

"Quemoy reports the MiG faded off the radar screen," Chuck chimed in.

"He's going too fast," the captain noted. "He's either going to overshoot or bury himself in the paddies."

* * *

"MiG's right behind us!" Lindsay yelled, "but high and coming too fast!"

"Hold on!" Tiger called out, and pulled back the throttle, causing the plane to slow.

Red tracers streamed overhead as the MiG opened fire, still too high to depress fire enough to hit the plane without diving into the ground. In a second, the MiG shot past, then began to climb and turn quickly to try another pass.

* * *

"The MiG's climbing out of the valley!" Chuck called.

"Back room says the MiG reported attacking a 'black hostile airplane'," Smitty called out. "He's going to try again."

"The MiG didn't get him!" Olson said.

"He won't make that mistake again," the captain cautioned, lighting another cigarette. "This time, he'll come in low and slow."

"The MiG's turned!" Chuck announced.

"Back room says the MiG pilot's extending landing gear and dive brakes," Smitty announced.

"Maybe the best way to slow down," the captain spoke up. "If he reduces throttle too much, he could lose thrust. With gear and dive brakes, he slows way down but he's got lots of thrust."

"Quemoy shows the MiG starting to turn," Chuck called out. "He's getting in position to start another attack."

* * *

"OK," Lindsay called, twisting in the seat, "I see him. His gear's down. Probably has his dive brakes out, too, trying to slow down enough to shoot at us."

"Let me know when he's in position to start shooting again," Tiger spoke calmly.

"How about if I let you know a little before then?" Lindsay asked.

"If you insist," Tiger answered.

* * *

"Quemoy shows the MiG faded out," Chuck called. "He's got to be in attack position."

"Back room says the MiG pilot sees the target and he's in position for another pass," Smitty called.

* * *

"Colonel," it was Li, "there's a grove of trees not far ahead. The MiG pilot may not realize it. We should turn toward the trees."

"OK, Li," Lindsay agreed. "Do it now. Carefully."

"Tiger," Li started. "Left to 30 degrees heading, now!"

"Roger, three zero," Tiger responded.

"Be ready to climb quickly," Li warned. "I'll try to make sure we can clear the trees and the MiG can't."

"Just remember I'm not really magic," Tiger replied. "Almost, but not quite!"

* * *

"The MiG pilot says he's closing to firing distance," Smitty warned. "The target's directly ahead of him."

"I sure hope our guy knows what he's doing," the captain said.

"I'm with you, sir," Olson noticed the captain was sweating. Then he noticed he was sweating, too.

* * *

"I see the trees," Tiger spoke.

"He's lining up now," Lindsay was watching. "He's in position, in my blind spot – I don't see him."

"Climb now!" Li barked, and the plane hesitated, then jumped as Tiger responded to his own timing. Red tracers shot under the plane as it lifted and barely cleared the treetops. And then the tracers stopped.

"Right to 40 degrees now!" Li called.

"Right, four zero, roger," Tiger called as the plane was already into the turn.

"Where's the MiG?" Lindsay wanted to know.

"Captain," Chou called, "the other plane didn't come over the trees."

Suddenly, there was a ball of flame behind them. The flame reached outward, then fell in on itself.

* * *

The crew in the alert center sat quietly, waiting.

"Sarge," Smitty sounded off, "the Liench'eng controller's calling the MiG. There's no answer."

"Quemoy has lost tracking on the MiG," Chuck chimed in.

"Yeah," the captain added. "He's been down in that valley way too long. He should have come out of there right after the attack."

"You figure he pranged it in, sir?" Olson asked.

"Maybe so, Mike," the captain's answer was somber. He crushed out his cigarette, staring at the butt as though it offended him. Damn, he thought, hate having a pilot crash, even if it was the other side. Hell, we all fly planes. It could be any one of us!

"You think our guy survived?" Olson asked the obvious question.

"I don't know," the captain responded.

"Liencheng's still calling the MiG, Sarge," Smitty added lamely.

* * *

The cockpit was quiet.

"We've passed Shahsien," Li spoke up finally. He looked back toward the lights of the village.

"Looking back won't bring the pilot back to life," Lindsay commented.

"I'm not looking for the pilot, Colonel," Li responded quietly. "My friend's in Shahsien, the one who was my assistant surveyor while I was on the mainland."

"Your friend?" Tiger perked up. "What's he doing in Shahsien?"

"She," Li corrected. "She's teaching there, waiting for my return."

"She?" Tiger glanced over his shoulder. "You didn't tell me about a woman! You had a woman here, and you didn't even tell me!"

"Not a woman as you think, Tiger," Li answered. "This was like a little sister. Her mother was once my mother's servant, although she doesn't know it."

"So she's in Shahsien?" Lindsay asked. "Waiting for you to return?"

"Yes, Colonel," Li answered. "We were lucky and got her moved there from Fuchou, where she was treated badly by the governor and some other important people. The people of Shahsien learned to respect me, so they'll treat her well until I go back for her. When this business is over, I'll take her to my family to be cared for."

"Respect you?" Tiger spoke up. "What did you do, break somebody's head?"

"No," Li remembered, "but I yelled at them a little!"

"Well, I wouldn't want you to yell at me, either," Tiger replied.

"I will if we miss our turn," Li quickly got back to business. "Right to heading 130 in three seconds, two...."

* * *

"Got him!" it was Smitty. "He jumped the ridge here." He marked the location as he spoke. "He made it!"

"Jesus!" the captain almost shouted.

"He's OK!" Olson spit it out, then realized that he almost hadn't been breathing. He inhaled deeply, then exhaled, very conscious of the acts.

"And now what?" the captain asked. "Where the hell's he going now?"

* * *

"We're behind the coastal mountain range," Li spoke quietly. "It'll mask us from the radars until we begin our approach to the second drop."

"Chou," Lindsay called out, "are you OK back there?"

"I'm fine, Captain," Chou's answered. "I've been listening and enjoying being alive."

* * *

"Where's he going now?" the captain repeated the question.

"Changchou, sir," Olson guessed. "He's already pulled their alert fighters out, and they don't have anything left to put up against him."

"Back room says two fighters coming up out of Fuchou," Smitty called.

A teletype began rattling. "Matsu has two MiGs taking off at Fuchou, Sarge," Chuck called out as he plotted it. "Hey, Smitty," he spoke aside, "you want to take this back over and let me go back to teletypes?"

"Why, Chuckie," Smitty smiled sweetly, "you're doing a great job, so I'll let you keep it so you can get sterile, too. I'll go help on teletypes." Smitty handed Chuck his headsets and walked over to the teletypes.

* * *

It was quiet inside the airplane now, with nothing but the sound of the engines running strongly. A little different luck, thought Lindsay, and this is the MiG flying home and we're back there in a heap of ashes on the valley floor, instead. What am I thinking, here? he stopped himself, I've never been concerned about it before! What is this? Have my feelings about Marion got me worrying about staying alive?

"Yes, Colonel," Tiger, still looking straight ahead, broke the silence. "And I feel the same way about Yukiko. You shouldn't think out loud, sir."

"Let's finish our business for the night then," Lindsay replied. "That way, we'll be ready to go back to Tokyo whenever our project officers are ready."

"Let's do it," Li replied. "I'd like to see Kumiko once again, as well!"

"Ha!" Tiger barked. "Li, you have far too many women already!"

* * *

"He hasn't passed over an airfield yet, sir," Olson pointed out.

"There aren't any between him and the strait," the captain had a puzzled look on his face, "unless...."

"If you're thinking what I'm thinking, sir," Olson chuckled, "yep, bet he goes on down for a drop over Changchou itself!"

"You know another thing I'm thinking, Mike?" the captain lit another cigarette. "The general isn't going to like this one bit. I'm not sure I want to tell him the ChiComs lost a plane this morning, but I don't think we've got a choice!"

* * *

"Why are we changing altitude?" Lindsay spoke up.

"With the moonlight, there's enough visibility for Tiger to fly without altitude or heading calls," Li answered, "but he needs to be as close to the deck as possible before then. 100 meters puts him about ten meters above the surface of the stream."

"That makes it close," Lindsay noted.

"Yes, sir," Li responded. "But we can use all the surprise we can get."

* * *

"There he is!" Chuck called out, putting up a new mark. "He went south!"

"He's jumping over to the western fork of the Gold River," Olson told the captain as Chuck put a second plot up on the board right after the first one. "One of its branches leads up to the northeast of Changchou."

* * *

The plane was very low, Lindsay realized. Although the moonlight was adequate to see most of the terrain, Tiger was concentrating his attention on following the river and staying low. Lindsay turned his attention to the route ahead. God forbid they should run up on a grove of trees that was more than 30 feet high!

"Tiger," Li spoke quietly, "take the right fork up there." He pointed toward where the watercourse forked from a stream into two creeks. "It'll lead us to the saddle where we'll jump over into the valley. Then, just head for the city as fast as you can."

"Roger," Tiger turned the plane to follow the right-hand creek.

"Chou," Lindsay called out, "get ready for the second drop."

"I'm already in position, Captain," Chou responded.

* * *

"Picked him up again, I believe, Sarge!" Chuck called out.

"Back room says they have a tentative plot on him here, between the Gold River area and Changchou. It's not firm – not even an altitude."

"Chuck," Olson called back, "ask the back room if there's any further activity at Changchou."

Chuck spoke into the microphone, then looked up. "They don't have anything at Changchou, Sarge," he called back. "They say Changchou can't put up another reaction."

"Good!" Olson smiled. "All he's got to sweat is triple-A."

"That may be plenty, Mike," the captain responded, lighting another cigarette. "But it sure isn't fighters!"

* * *

"There's the saddle," Tiger noted as they climbed. "They should be able to see us on radar now. We still haven't heard of any fighters at Changchou?"

"Nothing," Lindsay answered tersely.

"Heading to the airfield is 190," Li reminded Tiger, and the plane turned to the new heading, picking up speed as Tiger advanced the throttles all the way from cruise speed to wide open, then set the propellers at optimum pitch for speed.

Now all we have to do is avoid the ground fire, Lindsay thought. Unless, somehow, they missed getting news of fighters to us!

The plane sped toward the city as Tiger held the altitude high so he could descend and pick up even more speed.

"Chou," Lindsay called out, "be ready for the doors to open."

"Ready, Captain," Chou's responded.

* * *

"OK," Chuck spoke up. "Got him! He's cleared the saddle and heading for Changchou. He's not trying to hide anything now, either. Back room says he's maintaining altitude!"

"He'll probably drop down to pick up speed when he gets closer in," the captain spoke up.

A teletype rattled. Everyone in the room looked at it in horror as Smitty jumped to see what it said.

"Matsu's reporting the Fuchou fighters are still circling!" Smitty called out, and everyone began breathing again.

* * *

The engines emitted a high-pitched scream as the plane knifed through the air toward Changchou.

"Airspeed 360 knots!" Tiger called out. "Everything normal for full power."

"Do you see the base, yet?" Li asked.

"Got it," Lindsay responded. "The faint lights, there."

"Ready to descend to fifty meters," Li called out.

"Remember that the open door will slow us," Lindsay called out. "Opening cargo door!" he flipped the switch.

"Good, Captain," Chou replied. "I'm ready."

"Starting descent," Tiger aimed the nose of the plane toward the center of the airfield lights. The added speed caused by descent of the plane compensated for some of the reduction caused by the drag of the cargo door, but the airspeed indicator still slipped backward to 350 knots, then to 340.

"There should be ground fire shortly," Lindsay spoke up. "Li, I hope you were right when you said there was limited anti-aircraft artillery on this side of the river except out at the coast."

"Yes, sir," Li answered quietly. "Changchou doesn't expect to be attacked from their north, and they've put their scarce guns facing their enemy rather than their neighbors."

"Approaching the river, Colonel," Tiger noted.

"Be ready, Chou," Lindsay called out. "Drop to run level, 50 meters, Tiger," he added.

"Roger, Colonel," Tiger replied.

* * *

"He's crossing the river now," Chuck called out, marking another plot. "Be over the airfield in a moment."

"He's got brass balls," the captain lit another cigarette, shaking his head.

"Yes, sir," Olson responded. "And he's done it again. Another few minutes, and he's out over the strait."

* * *

The plane was fishtailing as Tiger worked to stay away from the streams of tracers. There were few guns firing in their direction and the ChiComs didn't seem to have an idea where they were located.

"See the runway," Lindsay called out. "Chou, be ready."

"Ready, Captain," Chou replied.

The plane cleared the perimeter fence and shot toward the runway.

Lindsay shouted, "Now, Chou! Drop now!"

"Drop now, Captain," Chou's steady voice replied. "Drop is away!"

Lindsay looked back to see a cloud of leaflets spreading behind the plane as it raced across the runway. In a moment, the plane was clear of the base perimeter and roaring toward the city, tracers scattering through the air like furious blind red bees behind it.

"Cargo door closed," Lindsay called out. "Chou, hang on tight!"

"Yes, Captain!" Chou's voice was less steady than usual.

"Climb to 60 meters," Li called to Tiger, who was busy making the plane zigzag through the sky.

"Roger, six zero meters," Tiger answered, although it was difficult to tell the plane had changed altitude. More wildly fired tracer rounds came their direction and fell into the city.

"Now turn to heading 135," Li called out.

"Roger," Tiger answered, grinning wildly, "heading one three five – more or less!"

* * *

"He's past the base and over the city now," Chuck called out.

"Right over the middle of the damned base," the captain grinned wryly, shaking his head. "Again."

"He's turning!" Chuck called, as he started to mark another plot. "He's headed for the coast now."

"He's out of there," Olson nodded. "He's just got to clear the coast."

* * *

The plane bumped and bounced as it drove toward the coastline, flailing wildly as Tiger turned it randomly to avoid being hit. Tracers flew past them frequently, as ground fire chased them along.

"Coastline!" Lindsay called. "Feet wet!

Just as he called, there was a thump and the plane skidded oddly.

"Hit!" Tiger called. "Near the rear!" He quickly tried the controls. "It's flying OK!"

"Chou!" Lindsay called out. "Are you OK?"

"I'm OK, Captain," Chou answered, "but there's a hole in the side of the airplane. It's not big."

"You've got control, Tiger," Lindsay, speaking English, was out of his belts quickly and headed toward the rear of the plane. "I'll check damage. You know what to do." Li quickly moved to allow Lindsay by.

At the rear of the aircraft, Chou pointed to the fist-sized hole in the fuselage as Lindsay arrived. Lindsay quickly checked the hole and the damaged area around it, and saw that the round had exited through the upper part of the fuselage. There was no damage to the controls or to the structure, only to the aircraft skin. With a sigh of relief, he patted Chou reassuringly on the shoulder and headed back for the front of the plane.

* * *

"They've cleared the coast," Chuck called out. "They'll probably drop off radar pretty soon."

"Another one," the captain noted, as he lit another cigarette. "OK." He blew out a puff of the smoke. "Good job, as usual. Now we wrap it up and get ready for the briefings in the morning." He turned to Olson. "What a way to get to spend your first day in the stripes, huh, Mike?"

"Another day, sir," Olson sighed. "This is getting to be routine. Before long, the general will be tired of seeing us around."

"This one won't be routine," the captain shook his head. "They'll forget about the golf game when they hear about the MiG being lost. ChiComs won't like that much."

"That's true, sir," Olson spoke understandingly.

"He's faded off radar," Chuck called out.

"OK, guys," Olson called to his crew, "let's get this one wrapped and ready to go for the briefing!"

* * *

Kung and Hamilton were waiting in front of the hangar as the plane pulled into parking position.

"How'd it go?" was Hamilton's greeting. "Any problems?"

"Yeah, Charlie," Lindsay answered. "We ran into some, alright!"

"What kind?" Kung was behind Hamilton and looked uneasy.

"A MiG caught up with us," Lindsay answered. "We managed to get out of it."

"Oh," Kung responded, and turned toward Chou, pulling him aside.

"What happened?" Hamilton wanted to know, and Lindsay told him the story of the intercept as they walked toward the office.

"Jesus," Hamilton sounded relieved. "That was close!"

"Yeah," Lindsay answered. "The MiG couldn't get enough additional lift to jump over the trees. And then it blew up."

"Ugly," Hamilton grimaced.

"Yep," Lindsay responded. "Worst part was thinking it could have been us if Li hadn't known about the trees."

"Don't talk like that!" Hamilton exclaimed with a shudder.

"Well," Lindsay opened the refrigerator to get sodas for the outbriefing, "that wasn't the worst moment of the night. The worst moment was when we got hit."

"What?" was Hamilton's response.

"We got nicked as we cleared out over the strait," Lindsay tried to calm the situation. "Just a couple of holes in the skin. It was almost panic for a moment. The MiG was a dogfight, and both Tiger and I have been there and know what to do. But getting hit and not knowing what kind of damage you've got is something else!"

"Can we fix it?" Hamilton was concerned.

"Just a couple of small holes in the skin, Charlie," Lindsay repeated. "Some sheet metal and paint, and nobody will ever know it happened – except us, of course."

"OK," Hamilton's relief was obvious. "Well, you guys have already had a pretty tough night of it. Let's get the briefing over so you can get out of here."

In the office, it was clear Kung was upset about something.

"Something the matter?" Lindsay asked.

"Nothing you need to know about!" Kung's answer was clipped. "But I think we need to leave now! I have to talk to Chou."

"Sure," Lindsay shrugged. "Whatever."

"Sorry, Lindsay," Hamilton also shrugged his shoulders. "I'll talk to you tomorrow."

"OK, Charlie," Lindsay replied as Kung and Chou started toward the door, with Hamilton following.

* * *

In the car, after dropping Chou at his room, Kung turned to Hamilton. "Charles, Chou broke into the opium package before he dropped it. It was probably splattered everywhere when it hit the ground. That idiot destroyed ten thousand dollars' worth of opium! Ten thousand dollars!"

"Damn, Winston!" Hamilton replied. "Ok, it costs us ten grand – five grand each - for this screw-up. So we go to the customer and tell him we'll get together another delivery, and then we'll deliver it after things quiet down, and we'll have our money back again."

"Charles," Kung's voice was coldly furious, "you don't understand the situation. It's not our money that's lost, it's our customer's. When I took you to receive the money that first time, it wasn't the first payment for a delivery, it was payment for the *next* delivery! Our customer pays in advance for the goods, and now we owe him a package."

"What?" Hamilton was stunned. "You mean you already got money from the customer, before we started?"

"Of course," Kung answered. "You didn't think *I* had the money to buy the opium and have it brought here for the first flight, did you?"

"Then what the hell happened to the money you got the first time?" Hamilton began to realize that he knew very little of what was going on. "Where's my share of that?"

"There was nothing left after I set up the apparatus to handle this," Kung answered. "It wasn't easy, nor was it cheap."

"It cost the whole ten thousand?" Hamilton was incredulous.

"That, plus more!" Kung answered. "Don't forget, I had to set it all up. And I'm still paying the customs people and the aircrew people to get the opium brought in so we can send it on the airplane, as well as paying for delivery on the other end. It costs a lot of money to do that, five thousand dollars for each shipment. That much is added to the initial ten thousand to set us up."

"Five thousand dollars each delivery!" Hamilton was shocked. "That's a huge amount of money!"

"It's the cost of doing business!" Kung explained flatly. "If we don't pay the price, we don't make a profit. Charles, listen! Our customer paid us a lot of money, and we failed to deliver his goods. I put the goods aboard the airplane and your crew was to deliver them. That didn't happen, and now we're not only out the ten thousand dollars to purchase the opium, but we also have to pay to get it brought here again so we can deliver it."

"But where are we supposed to get that kind of money?" Hamilton shook his head. "We haven't made that much that we can afford another shipment! I mean, we've only made two shipments – that's only ten thousand altogether! You're saying we have to come up with fifteen thousand dollars – seventy-five hundred each - to make this next delivery? I barely have that much of my money left!"

"The alternative is not making the delivery," Kung announced coldly. "Do you think our customer won't tell our employers that we've sent opium to the mainland for him, for money he's paid us? And what will our employers say about that?"

"Shit, Winston!" Hamilton shook his head dejectedly. "They'll put us both in jail and throw away the key. So what the hell can we do?"

"I've got to get the money from you soon," Kung answered. "I can arrange for another shipment when I have the money to pay for it. But you've got to get me your part of the money right away, do you understand?"

"Sure," Hamilton agreed. "It's here, in the bank. I'll get it for you."

"Good," Kung followed up. "Now, we have to make sure the other crewmembers don't learn about this and give us away. I'll talk to Chou this morning and make sure he doesn't screw up again."

"OK," Hamilton agreed.

"Here we are," Kung announced their arrival at the Grand Hotel. "I need the money no later than tomorrow afternoon, Charles, when I start making the arrangements. Don't fail me!"

"I won't," Hamilton got out of the car.

"You'd better not," Kung responded under his breath.

* * *

Stupid foreigner, thought Kung as the car started back down the hill from the hotel entrance, you know so little about this. Your money covers the cost of replacing the lost material. And now I've got to come up with a plan to overcome this setback and somehow make the delivery! And all I have to work with are one stupid foreigner and my own idiot underling!

Somehow, I've got to get us through the next twelve days, until the plane flies again. And then I've got to make sure the opium's delivered!

* * *

Olson's face was almost ash-white when he walked in the door. Marie had never seen him look so upset!

"Mike," she wanted to know, "what's the matter?"

"This morning's briefing with the general didn't go well, honey," he replied. "He blew up and yelled a lot. We didn't have any answers for the questions he asked and he got really upset about it."

"That's not fair!" Marie's anger lit up her blue eyes. "Why did he yell at you? Did you do something to make him mad?"

"Marie," Olson's face was saddened, "you know I can't tell you anything about it!"

"Damn it, Mike Olson," she was getting angry now, "people don't have any right to treat you that way, just because you have to stand there!"

"It's OK, honey," Olson was almost pleading. "It's OK."

"Well, come on and get some sleep," she answered. Maybe I can't know about the work you do, she thought, but I know you care about it and do your best at it. And I know how much it hurts when you do the best you can and some asshole like this general takes his anger out on you!

SEVEN

Lindsay was barely into the office when the phone rang.

"Lindsay, this is Charlie," Hamilton said. "Are you going to be in for awhile? I need to talk to you."

"Yeah," Lindsay replied, "I'll be here. I have to put together the report – you took off before we could tell you everything, but it was pretty wild. And I have to get those holes in the plane fixed – the maintenance crew said they can get some sheet metal guys on it tonight."

"OK," Hamilton responded. "I won't take up much of your time. See you in about fifteen minutes."

"Sure," Lindsay responded. "See you then."

* * *

Hamilton sat down in the chair.

"What's up?" Lindsay started off.

"How's the report going?" Hamilton asked.

"Not bad," Lindsay answered. "Got the first part drafted."

"Look," Hamilton went on. "I'm sorry I ran off with Kung this morning and didn't stay for the outbrief. I was upset because Kung was upset. I apologize for reacting badly."

"No apology needed, Charlie," Lindsay replied.

"Well, I was reacting to Kung, too," Hamilton continued. "He's the customer and he expects us to deliver whatever he wants, no questions asked. At least that's what he told me. He was upset because some stuff we were supposed to deliver might have been destroyed because Chou opened the package. And that upset me, too."

"OK," Lindsay nodded, "I understand."

"Well," Hamilton went on, "like Kung said, his office goes to considerable trouble to get the stuff ready to deliver. You know, he's got people looking over his shoulder and he's under pressure, even more so now that we've screwed up."

"Charlie," Lindsay held up a hand, "I hope Kung remembers the guy who opened the package is his own guy."

"Oh, he does," Hamilton responded. "He's furious with Chou. And he's upset because Chou tries to hide behind you."

"Well," Lindsay conceded, "maybe I need to talk to Chou about his responsibility to all of us."

"There's no need to do that," Hamilton replied. "I think Kung's taking care of that."

"I still don't want him upsetting Chou," Lindsay warned. "I've still got crew integrity to be concerned about, you know."

"Sure," Hamilton replied.

"By the way," Lindsay asked, "what was in the package that Chou screwed up, just out of curiosity?"

"Oh, just some medical supplies," Hamilton answered. He suddenly realized perhaps he could get Lindsay to stop defending Chou, which would please Kung. "There was morphine. Chou thought he could steal it."

"Morphine?" Lindsay asked. "That's not the kind of medical supplies I'm contracted to deliver, Charlie. That's an illegal drug unless it's administered through a real doctor!"

"Hey," Hamilton hadn't expected the response. "It's medical supplies. These folks over here don't look at it the same way we do, Lindsay!"

"I don't care how they look at it, Charlie," Lindsay replied. "I'm not delivering it. You tell Kung none of it goes on my missions, OK? As far as I'm concerned, it's illegal. I'm not taking it!"

"OK," Hamilton's face showed his concern, "I understand your point. Maybe I can convince Kung we're not going to deliver the stuff and he and his people might as well forget it."

"That sounds like a good place to start," Lindsay agreed. "Be sure to let me know how it goes, OK? Maybe I can help."

"OK," Hamilton nodded. "Guess I'd better go on and let you finish your report. It'll be on my desk tomorrow afternoon?"

"It'll be there," Lindsay agreed.

"Then I'm gone." Hamilton got up to leave. "See you later."

Hmm, Lindsay thought, so Kung's sending morphine in the medical supplies. Maybe I ought to let Joe know about this. He picked up the phone and dialed the international operator.

The phone only rang twice before an operator answered. Amazing, Lindsay thought, that's the first time I ever got the international operator to answer right away! He asked for a line to Japan, and the operator asked him to hold for a moment. The Japanese operator was on the line in a moment, asking him for the number. Hastily flipping through his rolodex, Lindsay found Calloway's number and the operator dialed it.

In a moment, a familiar voice answered the phone. "Southern Air Transport, Special Operations Office!" Yukiko's voice was unmistakable.

"Yukiko, hi!" Lindsay started. "This is Lindsay!"

"Oh, Mister Lindsay!" Yukiko's voice became excited. "How are you, sir? Are you and Tiger coming to Tokyo to visit? We're doing well, sir. Do you want to speak to Marion?"

"We're fine, Yukiko!" Lindsay had to laugh at her excitement. "I'm sorry, Tiger's gone right now and isn't here to talk to you. I need to speak to Mister Calloway, please."

"Oh!" Yukiko's voice registered disappointment. "Mister Calloway isn't here today. He's gone flying, sir. His friend came from Washington, and they went to the base. But he'll be back tomorrow."

"I'm sorry he's not there, Yukiko," the call had gone through too well for everything to work out right. "As long as I'm calling, let me talk to Marion for a minute, though, please."

"Oh, yes, sir!" Yukiko bubbled, "let me get her!"

Well, thought Lindsay, maybe the day will turn out OK yet!

* * *

Kung was furious! Hamilton had met with Lindsay yesterday, trying to calm things down, and all he'd succeeded in doing was getting Lindsay irritated about some non-existent morphine. Hamilton didn't know how to handle such matters. And now Lindsay was upset.

The customer wouldn't be patient for long. He had his own schedule to meet. And he certainly could embarrass them if he told anyone they were involved with him.

This was becoming difficult. Now he had to make another trip to Tokyo, not to collect the next payment, but to calm the customer and assure him of the next delivery. It wouldn't be a problem, but Lindsay and his crew could be difficult if they ever learned anything. Maybe he should get rid of them all. Then he and Hamilton could find a more cooperative crew and the situation would settle down.

In the meantime, he had to calm his customer. He'd already

spoken to Chou, warning him to do as he was told. Now they had to find a suitable place to hide the opium in the plane, so Chou could deliver it. And he had to talk to Hamilton about getting a new aircrew ready to replace this one. What else did he need to do? He didn't know, but the money would be worth it, eventually.

Kung picked up the telephone and told his secretary to place a call to the CAT office in Tokyo for him. First things first. The customer was probably wondering what they'd do about the failed delivery. He needed to set up a meeting.

* * *

Another trip to Tokyo. Lindsay was pleased. He'd get to see Marion again!

Despite the excitement, though, Lindsay had reservations about this trip. It was too soon after the mission, and he hadn't been able to call Calloway yet. In fact, he hadn't even been able to call off the island this morning, although he'd tried three times already.

And now Hamilton wanted to go to Tokyo tomorrow morning, first thing. Usually, they waited five or six days after the mission before going to Tokyo. This time, there wouldn't be nearly as much time to get the plane ready. And he'd have to spend his time preparing for the trip to Tokyo and not on preparing for the next mission.

The entire crew sat around Lindsay's desk.

"Guys," Lindsay started, "we've got another trip to Tokyo, tomorrow. We'll do the standard trip, since the bosses want to leave early. Departure at oh-seven-hundred local, with arrival there at about twelve. Li and Chou," he added, "there's no reason for you two to have to stay here – we haven't started planning the next trip yet – so you can come along, if you want."

"Colonel," Li started, "I'd like to go along. I had a good time last trip."

"OK," Lindsay chuckled. Kumiko had told Marion and Yukiko that she was available whenever Li came back to Tokyo again. "How about you, Chou?"

"I'd rather not, Captain," Chou spoke evenly. "I'll stay here and enjoy the time off. It'll be a good time for quiet and peace."

"We understand," Lindsay knew Chou didn't want to spend any more time around Kung than necessary and had no desire to see any other part of the world. He turned to the other two. "OK, we'll break off now, so you can take care of personal business. We'll meet here at oh-six-fifteen to file our flight plan and pre-flight the plane. Don't forget your passports! And be ready to stay two nights, like I told you last time – if we have a problem with Kung being late, Haneda might make us forfeit our departure time and have to stay longer."

"Well, Colonel," Tiger grinned, "I wouldn't mind an extra day – and night, of course! - in Tokyo!" He turned to Li. "Are you in any hurry to get back, Li?" he laughed.

"Why Tiger," Li smiled back, "it would be a disservice to Kumiko to say yes!"

"The words of a gentleman, Li," Lindsay laughed. "Now, get out of here, and let me try to get a phone call through to let them know we're coming!"

The three crewmembers got up and left the office.

* * *

At six fifteen in the morning it was just turning light outside.

When Lindsay arrived at the hangar, both Tiger and Li were already there, full coffee cups in hand. Lindsay laughed – his crew had started drinking coffee before the night flights, and now they drank coffee about as much as the ever-present tea! What's more, they even knew how to make a pretty good pot of coffee. Lindsay hadn't been able to get a telephone call through yesterday, but had used the direct-line teletype at SAT's office to advise Tokyo of their plans. He just hoped the message had been passed along.

Li was out in the hangar, loading the plane, as Lindsay, fresh cup of coffee in hand, looked over Tiger's shoulder at the paperwork on the table. "Hey, Tiger," he asked, curious, "what's that?"

"Flight plan forms," Tiger answered, his face screwed up as he tried to fill in blanks.

"Why?" Lindsay wanted to know. "You know I keep a copy of filled-in flight plans in the top drawer of my desk, so we can make a new one just by copying the old one!"

"I know, Colonel," Tiger responded, "but I want to learn more about how to fill these out."

"Wait a minute!" Lindsay looked closely at the form in front of his co-pilot. "What's this? Purpose of flight is 'get horny navigator laid'?" He started laughing.

"Aw, Colonel!" Tiger complained. "I was going to show it to Li! Now you've spoiled my joke!"

"No, I haven't," Lindsay held up his hands in protest. "I won't say anything about this. I haven't seen a thing!"

Lindsay filled out a copy of the real flight plan and was heading out the door to file it when Li came toward the office.

"Everything's stowed, Colonel," Li reported. "Now, if our passengers will get here, we'll have an uneventful start to this trip."

Oh yeah? Lindsay thought, working to keep a straight face. Good luck!

* * *

OK, so Kung was five minutes late. The preflight checklist took longer than usual because the crew kept breaking out laughing every few moments. The plane barely started warming up when the car pulled up and let Kung out. Li and the driver stowed the luggage quickly, Kung got in and settled down, and it was time to taxi out and take off.

The flight was uneventful, too. As usual, they were met by Anderson and, as usual, the limousine met Kung and Hamilton. This time, both Marion and Yukiko were waiting at the receptionist desk when they got out of the elevator, and the girls greeted them warmly! Even Kumiko was there, and caught Li's arm immediately. They barely had time to greet the girls when Calloway stuck his head out the door of his office. The question on Calloway's face stopped any further celebration.

"OK, guys," Calloway's greeting was almost growled. "Let's get this part over with."

Once they were in the office and seated, Lindsay led out. "OK, Joe. What do you want to know?"

"First of all," Calloway started, "Why are you so damned early coming up, anyway?"

"I don't know," Lindsay started off. "I couldn't get a call through and talk to you about it, and Hamilton probably hasn't sent his report up yet. My report just got in the mail yesterday, so it won't be here for another few days. But the mission didn't go well, Joe."

"What went wrong?" Calloway asked. He glanced at Tiger and Li, as though expecting to find them wearing bandages.

"We got jumped," Lindsay admitted. "Something went wrong, and our plans to clear our route didn't work. One of the MiGs caught us, and, if Li hadn't remembered a grove of trees near our route, he would've had our asses. But he was pushing it, with dive brakes out and gear down and pretty close to full throttle, and he couldn't make the jump to clear the trees. He hit and blew up."

"Shit!" Calloway winced.

"And then we got hit coming off the mainland," Lindsay continued. "Nothing serious, just punctured the skin of the plane, but it caused the tail to sideslip, and we got a lump in the throat."

"OK," Calloway nodded. "I presume the plane's already fixed."

"That's right," Lindsay replied. "And then," he continued, "there was one more thing. Chou opened a package he was given to drop, and probably caused it to break apart when it hit. The Chinese project officer, Kung, exploded, and Charlie said he thought it contained morphine in the medical supplies."

"Morphine?" Calloway questioned. "Who the hell authorized the delivery of morphine?"

"Kung gave the package to Chou," Lindsay continued, "and this wasn't the first time. They apparently sent packages on the first and second missions as well. I told Charlie I wouldn't put up with it. He finally said he'd try to talk Kung out of doing it again. That was day before yesterday, and I haven't heard anything since then."

"Dropping morphine's asking for trouble," Calloway shook his head. "Not only is it against international law, but you can bet our government would grab anybody who was pushing delivery of the stuff and lock them up forever, I don't care who the hell it got dropped to!"

"At any rate," Lindsay went on, "Charlie may want to deliver his report in person this time. And he said Kung wanted to come early on CAT business. The two of them took off in the CAT limo."

"Well," Calloway shook his head, "I hope you and Charlie can keep this under control. SAT won't support something like this, and it's probably not official on Kung's side, either. Somebody not too far up the line from him is doing this."

"I agree," Lindsay said. "Right now, though, we have no evidence and nobody to blame it on, really. So I guess we'll just try to make sure it doesn't happen again."

"OK," Calloway agreed. "Anyway, let's talk about the mission. I'm worried about the MiG crashing – the ChiComs will be upset about that, and you guys will be prime targets for them."

* * *

The limousine stopped in front of the usual restaurant. This time, both Kung and Hamilton went in. The man they needed to see was waiting for them at a table in a private room. He was smiling, but not very brightly. Hamilton wasn't sure how to read the look. He'd just have to trust Kung, who'd done all of the dealing with the man up until now.

"Good day," the man greeted them in English. "I hope your trip was pleasant." He seemed pleasant enough, thought Hamilton, but he was waiting to hear something.

"Good day," Kung bowed deeply. Hamilton wouldn't bow, of course – it wasn't the way Americans did things. The man motioned them to sit at the low table.

"You asked me to meet you," the man began. "I'm here."

"We had trouble making the delivery," Kung began.

"I'm aware the delivery didn't happen," the man spoke evenly. "I trust there's been no major problem."

"Nothing major," Kung answered. "There was a small accident."

"OK," the man nodded agreeably. "Let's eat, then." He clapped his hands and a young woman came to take their order.

With the order taken, Kung spoke up. "Because of the accident, we may have some difficulty with the airplane crew." He looked at Hamilton. "When they learned of it, they said they prefer not to deliver your property. We're not sure we can convince them to do it, and we may have to find another crew to continue deliveries."

"I see," the man answered. "I'm not sure my 'client' will appreciate further delays. Fortunately, your earlier deliveries have been more than enough to meet his needs and he has enough stockpiled for nearly a month, if he's patient. However, his patience isn't his greatest asset. We must resume the deliveries soon."

"We're trying to do exactly that," Kung spoke up. "We should be able to make another delivery with the next flight."

"I really hope so," the man smiled as the young woman brought their food. When she'd departed, he continued. "I'll be upset if my 'client' has to wait too long for the next delivery. He'll be upset, too." With that, he began eating.

There was no more talk until they finished their meal. With a sip of tea from his cup, the man sat back. "I trust you understand what I need. Now, if I can help you, please let me know. I have to please my client, too."

Kung looked carefully at the man, considering how much help he could ask. "We might need your help," he responded.

"I'll be happy to cooperate," the man reiterated. "I can do things you may not be able to do or arrange on your own. Please feel free to ask, and I'll do what I can."

Kung looked questioningly at the man. "Would it be possible to, ah, eliminate some problems?"

"Yes," the man nodded knowingly. "But we've got to be careful we don't overextend ourselves."

"Yes, that's true," Kung considered the possibilities. This was an unexpected ally! Obviously, the man wanted them to succeed as much as they wanted to.

"Please understand," the man continued, "I don't have a lot of resources. I have contacts and can make things happen. But I don't have any money."

"We understand, and we appreciate your offer," Kung replied quickly. "We might call on you soon, in fact. Let us think about it."

"Well, you know how to contact me," the man smiled. "I'll see you later." With a nod, he left.

"Did I understand that right?" Hamilton asked. "Will he help us?"

"Yes," Kung answered. "He may be a lot of help. But first, we've got to learn how close Calloway is to finding replacements for this crew."

"I'll go by the office and ask," Hamilton said. "I've got to go in and deliver my mission report, anyway."

"Finish your tea," Kung agreed, "and we'll see about it after we check into our hotel."

* * *

Calloway's brow was furrowed as they finished discussing the mission. "I guess that wraps it, then," he commented. "Anything to add?"

"Nothing, Joe," Lindsay replied. "That's all I can think of. How about you guys?" Tiger and Li both shook their heads.

"OK," Calloway grinned. "The girls have the afternoon off again. So you guys get out of here." He herded the group toward the doorway.

Yukiko and Kumiko met them at the door. Marion stood in the background, but she could see Lindsay seemed to want to continue talking.

"Joe," Lindsay remained by the door as the younger men departed, "let's talk for a minute, OK?"

Calloway looked at Lindsay with concern. "Sure," he agreed. "You want another beer?"

"Just coffee," Lindsay stayed with his limits.

Calloway waved to Marion. "Marion, could I have another beer and coffee for Lindsay, please?" he asked her.

"Sure, Joe," she smiled back, "and Harry wants cream and two sugars, right? Or will one sugar and a stir with my finger be sweet enough, Harry?" she teased.

"Just one little kiss and I don't need any sugar," Lindsay whispered back to her and grinned as she left.

"What's up, Lindsay?" Calloway asked.

"Joe," Lindsay started out, "I think we're stirring up a hornet's nest over there with these flights. We've had phenomenal luck so far. In fact, I'm almost inclined to think they're not shooting straight at us. And I'm afraid they might get better fast, now that they've lost an airplane. We weren't a big deal when we were just dropping stuff. But now we've got blood on our hands."

"Hmm," Calloway stroked his chin, "I see." There was a knock on the door, and Marion brought in the beer and coffee. When she left with a wink at Lindsay, Calloway continued. "If somebody's holding back, this could force them to have to go full up, right?"

"Yeah," Lindsay responded, "that's it. There'll be lots of pressure to get us now. And I won't bet on our ability to survive."

"I agree," Calloway nodded. "But we don't have much choice. We've got a contract to deliver, at least for now. I realize we can't expect you to put yourself on the line, but you're the only one we've got who can handle it. I'm the alternative, and I can't speak Chinese or physically handle the flying. And I don't have any real prospects to take your place, yet."

"You know I won't back out, Joe," Lindsay grinned ironically. "But I wanted you to know how I feel. And let you know that we'll think a lot about the routes we fly."

The phone rang. "Joe, I'm gone," Lindsay said as he got up and left. "See you in the morning?"

"Sure," Calloway reached for the phone, "you can meet my buddy, Tom. You'll like him!" Lindsay closed the door behind himself as Marion stepped forward.

"Calloway," Calloway answered the phone.

"Joe, it's Charlie Hamilton," said the voice on the other end of the line. "I'm over in my office right now and was wondering if I can talk to you for a minute."

"Sure," Calloway answered. "You want me to meet you there?"

"Let me come over there," Hamilton answered. "Maybe I can grab some coffee on the way."

In a minute, Hamilton walked in. "Hey, Joe," he put an envelope on Calloway's desk. "Here's the report on the last mission."

Calloway laughed. "Good, Charlie. The guys told me all about it, pretty rough. This business about the morphine has them upset, not to mention me."

"Oh, yeah," Hamilton looked uneasy. "It bothers me too. Not too cool of the customer to pull it, but it puts me in a bad position to tell him we won't handle the job."

"Well," Calloway nodded, "I understand how you feel, but your customer knows we can't do anything like that. I'm sure the people who negotiated the contract didn't have anything like it in mind."

"Well, let me try to keep things together," Hamilton said. "On the other hand, got a question for you."

"Shoot," Calloway answered.

"How are we doing on a replacement for Lindsay?" Hamilton asked. "We talked about being sure we got him replaced as soon as possible so he could get back to work."

"Well," Calloway replied, "I've looked at a couple of guys, but I'm not impressed. The ones I've seen so far can't fly that plane."

"Hmm," Hamilton was concerned. "There's got to be somebody. How about some of the Flying Tigers? Or maybe somebody else who worked with the ChiNats?"

"None available," Calloway shrugged his shoulders. "The few guys who are still around are all flying for airlines. I haven't even found anyone for the backup slot yet."

"I hope you can soon," Hamilton sounded urgent. "What happens if we need some help? You know, they got hit this last mission. Didn't do much damage, but we could wind up with somebody hurt and no way to continue because we don't have anybody to fill in."

"Yeah, I understand," Calloway nodded. "But there just isn't anyone qualified. Even Lindsay wasn't ideal, although he was close enough so we could get him up to speed in a short time. Nobody else fits in without lots of training."

"Look, Joe," Hamilton leaned forward. "I'm afraid if either of our pilots go down, the ChiNats will figure they can do this themselves, probably for less money than they're paying us. And then we're out of a job. More than that, we lose control of it."

"Ah, Charlie, you know the ChiNats can't do that," Calloway chuckled. "They wouldn't last five minutes before the United Nations would yank that island right out from under them!"

"Hey, the UN might never hear about it," Hamilton responded. "All they have to do is cover the plane up while it's not flying. They can hangar it at CAT, just like we do."

"No they can't," Calloway laughed. "Neither CAT nor Air Asia will help them without our OK – they both belong to Air America, and that's who *we* work for! The only other place to put it would be with the ChiNat air force, and they're probably infiltrated with Commies! They'd know all about it immediately! The ChiNats have only one way to go – it's got to be our plane, with our pilots, and them paying us to do the job. That's the only way they can avoid having a bomber on the island – it's a 'private' aircraft that belongs to us."

"Yeah, you're right" Hamilton sighed. "Guess our jobs are secure. But we still need to have backups, and I'd really feel a lot better if we did, Joe."

"I understand," Calloway nodded. "I'll try to expedite things. Just don't get your hopes too high, OK?"

"Well, do what you can, please," Hamilton requested. He picked up his cup and left the office.

Shit! Hamilton thought as he set the dirty coffee cup on his desk. So Calloway didn't have replacements or a backup! Damn'! It would take at least two months to get a pilot trained. And Calloway wasn't in any hurry. Well, maybe they'd have to give him a reason to move! What would he do if the crew was out of action? He wouldn't have a choice. The contract would have to be met, and he'd have to get new people and train them!

He hurried off to meet Kung at the hotel.

* * *

Kung was upset.

"Charles," Kung complained, "can't your people do *any*thing right? Lindsay questions our shipments and Calloway doesn't have the replacements ready. I'm really upset!"

"Easy, Winston!" Hamilton tried to calm him. "There's nothing we can do about it! I'm afraid Calloway won't even try unless something happens to the crew! I think that's what we have to do."

"You want to eliminate them?" Kung questioned. "Or just make it impossible for them to fly for awhile?"

"Whatever, I don't care," Hamilton answered. "I don't think they'll scare easily. And we've got to ensure if they're not dead, at least they won't recover quickly."

"I understand," Kung thought for a moment. "Our new-found friend may be able to help us, but I'm afraid it's going to cost."

"I gave you everything I had," Hamilton stated. "I don't have anything more. I don't even get paid by SAT until the end of the month."

"I'll see what we can do," Kung answered. "We may be able to borrow some. I'll ask."

"I don't want to go into debt, Winston," Hamilton started. "It's not a good idea."

"Nonsense!" Kung countered. "Charles, we've got too much invested to quit now! And there's far too much money to be made from this! Just remember how much we'll have when this gets rolling!"

"I know," Hamilton shook his head. "It's just that -."

"Remember what I said about putting something in to get something back?" Kung prodded. "That's a fact of business."

"Yeah," Hamilton agreed. "If we need to do it, -."

"That's better," Kung was relieved. "You're important to our deliveries, Charles. Being able to deliver by air is much better than anything else."

"Then we'll have to find a way to replace the crew," Hamilton said. "Otherwise, you may have to find another way to deliver the stuff."

"You're probably right," Kung answered. "I don't like violence, but it may be necessary. If nothing else, it may cause Calloway to hurry to find backups for his crew. I'll contact our new friend. We'll find out what he can do to help us before we commit to any action. Is that fair?"

"Yeah," Hamilton nodded, "I guess so."

* * *

The call to the Chinese guy made Kung happier, Hamilton reflected. Although they spoke mostly Chinese, Kung told him most of what they said. The only thing Hamilton insisted on was not paying for a bungled job, just like the Chinese guy expected to get his goods after he'd already paid. Kung argued the guy down to only two hundred fifty dollars for the job.

Finally, Kung turned to him. "Where are they staying?" he asked.

"Huh?" Hamilton responded. "Why?"

"He may be able to send some people tonight," Kung explained patiently. "Where do they stay while they're in Tokyo?"

"I guess they stay at the Katusai Kanko," Hamilton was at a loss. "It's the only American-style hotel in the area."

"OK," Kung spoke into the telephone again. Finally, he hung the phone up. "He'll send one of his people to watch for our 'friends' and call in the others if they arrive," he explained. "They'd be better off not asking questions. Someone might mention it to the police, during the investigation. The *Kempetai* would follow up that kind of lead."

"OK," Hamilton agreed. "What if they miss them?"

"They know the way to Haneda airport," Kung replied. "And I told them when our 'friends' will make the trip, in case they don't go to the hotel tonight."

"What do they plan to do?" Hamilton asked.

"I didn't ask," Kung answered simply.

"Well it's settled, anyway," Hamilton sighed. "And we can sit back and let things happen, right?"

"We still have to make our departure time tomorrow," Kung reminded him. "We can't look like we know the crew will even be delayed."

"Well, then," Hamilton grinned, "would you care to join me in a drink before we get ready for dinner, Mister Kung?"

"I'd be delighted," Kung smiled. It wasn't a nice smile.

* * *

Lindsay and Tiger rode in the back seat, with Li joining Anderson in the front. Li laughed; Lindsay and Tiger were tired. The two of them had stayed up with the girls. Li, as before, let Kumiko know he was very old-fashioned in the way he treated women he respected and had gone to bed alone and early! Perhaps they'd go to bed together sometime, but there was no hurry.

In the meantime, Li thought, his two friends were sleeping while they could. Anderson was driving and talking with Li about the night before. Li looked back at his two friends in the rear seat.

Suddenly, Li realized a car was dodging through traffic behind them. And he had a sickening feeling it was coming after THEM!

"Paul," he spoke quietly, "I think we have trouble behind us."

Anderson looked in his rear view mirror. "Yep," he answered, "looks like they're after us. Four of them." He pushed on the gas pedal and the car jumped forward. "Here." He pulled a snub-nosed revolver from under his jacket, handing it to Li. "And there's a sawed-off shotgun under the seat and shells in the glove compartment."

Li felt under the seat and found the shotgun, then opened the glove compartment and took out a handful of shells. He quickly loaded the shotgun and snapped it shut. "If they're after us," he spoke plainly, "they might wish they weren't!"

"What's going on?" Lindsay's sleepy voice asked.

"Keep your head down, Colonel," Li spoke as the car veered to miss slower traffic. "And keep Tiger's down, too. We've got unfriendly company."

"What?" Lindsay started to sit up.

"Down!" Li barked, and Lindsay instinctively ducked. "Colonel, if you pop up, you'll get in my way, and you could get hurt!" He showed Lindsay the handgun. "Stay down, please!"

"OK!" Lindsay agreed.

Anderson kept the SAT car ahead of the other one but it was right behind them.

Suddenly, Li called out. "Look out, Paul, he's shooting!" and a shot rang out. The bullet hit their car with a ding as Anderson swung wildly.

"Shit!" Anderson shouted as flame spat from another gun.

"What's happening?" Tiger was awake, and Lindsay held him down.

"Somebody's shooting at us," Lindsay answered. "It's under control!" At least I hope so, he thought.

The car swerved again as another shot smashed the glass in the back window. Lindsay suddenly realized this was a Japanese car and the glass was regular glass, not safety glass like on American cars.

"Hey, Li," he called out. "You want to see to shoot back?"

"Sure," Li replied.

"OK," Lindsay turned his body and, with a lunge, kicked out what was left of the rear window. It went crashing across the back of the car and into the road.

"Great!" Li called out. His body turned, he aimed the shotgun at the driver's side tire and pulled the trigger. The roar of the shotgun inside the car was almost deafening and everyone, even Anderson, winced. When Li opened his eyes, he saw the oncoming car suddenly flip over and bounce off the roadway and down an embankment that hid it from sight.

"Got his tire!" Li called out. "Don't slow down, Paul," he cautioned. "There might be others."

Lindsay and Tiger both finally sat up, brushing off glass.

"What was that all about?" Lindsay asked.

"I think we were targets, Colonel," Li responded. "Fortunately, Paul was ready, and the guys doing the shooting weren't!" He handed the pistol back to Anderson.

"Not bad, Li," Anderson put the pistol away. "If anybody got out of there alive, they'll take some patching up!"

"Good driving, Paul," Li responded, nodding.

"Is this some kind of bandit thing, Paul?" Lindsay was angry.

"No bandits here in Japan, sir," Anderson answered, "although we've had some problems with the *yakuza* – local version of the Mafia - when we've been caught in their turf wars. That's why we keep the shotguns, just in case. But I think those guys were after us."

"That's right, Colonel," Li added. "They were looking right at this vehicle and trying to catch it. They didn't look like Japanese, though. They weren't Chinese, either, although they were sure Oriental."

"Did they have round faces, Li?" Lindsay asked.

"Ah - yes, sir," Li answered.

"Sounds like Koreans," Lindsay said.

"Why would Koreans chase us?" Tiger asked.

"That's a good question," Lindsay answered. "And I don't see anyone else chasing us, so let's get off the road and call the cops, OK, Paul?"

"Right, sir," Anderson agreed, slowing the car. "We also need to call my office, to let them know what's going on. They'll send an interpreter to help us deal with the cops."

"Is there any problem with the guns, Paul?" Li asked.

"No," Anderson answered. "They're both registered. I've got the permit for mine, and the one for the shotgun's in the glove compartment."

"OK," Lindsay thought for a second. "Somebody needs to let Hamilton and Kung know we won't be there for a bit. Can the office take care of that?"

"Sure, sir," Anderson nodded. "They're supposed to meet you at the SAT hangar area. But we won't get there for quite a while. They'll be lots better off taking a commercial flight back to T'aiwan. We could finish sometime late tonight or in the morning!"

"Well," Lindsay sighed, "at least this time I won't get mad at Kung for being late!"

"Turn about's fair play, Colonel," Tiger reminded him.

* * *

The young *Kempetai* officer who met them was polite, but his English was limited. Anderson surrendered the guns, along with the permits, which surprised the officer. However, he looked over both permits and then put them and the guns in the trunk of his car. He then began looking over the damages to the car. In a while, another car arrived, this one with three officers in it. One of these obviously was a senior officer.

The young officer stepped forward and bowed deeply, speaking in Japanese, while the senior officer grimaced. Finally, the senior officer turned to Lindsay, the oldest of the group, and bowed.

"Sir," he spoke correct but accented English, "I'm Major Hayashi of the *Kempetai*. I'm the senior investigating officer. I'm sorry to be late getting here, but I went to the crash site to see the other car first. May I please see your identification and that of each of your friends."

"Certainly, Major," Lindsay returned the bow. "I'm Colonel Harold Lindsay, recently retired from the US Air Force and now flying for Southern Air Transport. These two young men are officers of my flight crew, Major Li and Captain Ch'en, and our driver is Mister Paul Anderson of Southern Air Transport." Each of the others handed over his identification in its SAT cover, along with his passport.

"Ah, yes," Major Hayashi's relief was obvious in his smile. "I know Southern Air Transport, of course, sir. We hope it won't inconvenience you to help us in our investigation." He bowed again, more deeply than before.

"I'm sorry for the suspicion, sir," he continued. "Guns aren't often used by honest people in our country. However, I know the reasons why SAT maintains the weapons, and I'm relieved that you and your people work for SAT. It will make our investigation much easier."

"Thank you, Major," Lindsay tried to match the man's politeness. "We'll help you as much as we can. Please let us know how."

"Thank you, sir," the major bowed again. "First of all, I'm sure it's uncomfortable for you out here in the cold. There's a restaurant just over there. Perhaps we can find a cup of tea there and a little warmth." He smiled broadly as he waved for the crew to precede him to the restaurant.

Before long, a car pulled up outside and another officer got out and came in, motioning to the major. The major excused himself, and went to talk to the man, returning in a moment.

"We have news from the crash scene," he said. "Three of the men in the car were killed in the crash. Although people said there was a fourth man, he left before we arrived, but he's hurt. They're Koreans, and we think they're gang members. At the crash scene, we found several guns, two of which had been fired. Your shotgun damaged the front of the vehicle near the driver's side front tire." He looked carefully at Li. "You've been trained in the use of weapons, Major Li."

"I'm a member of my country's military, Major," Li responded. "I'm on loan to SAT for special reasons."

"I see, Major," Major Hayashi smiled warmly. "Military men and policemen are brothers in arms, regardless of their country!"

"That's right, sir," Li answered.

"Colonel Lindsay," the major became solemn again. "Is someone coming from SAT's office, sir?"

"They should be sending an interpreter, Colonel," Anderson responded, advising Lindsay.

"Ah, Mister Anderson," the major smiled toward Paul. "I see someone's just arrived, which is why I asked. In fact, your office has sent three ladies! It looks like they're carrying some sort of thermal bottle. Colonel, I presume you prefer coffee?" He smiled gently.

* * *

Kung and Hamilton arrived at the airport on time, for once. Their smiles didn't last long, and both had to play-act to express concern for their crewmembers, who were being detained and questioned by the *Kempetai*. The SAT maintenance manager suggested they go ahead on a commercial flight - there was one leaving in about an hour, and he'd checked to make sure there were seats available. They thanked him, and hurried to get tickets on the departing plane.

Once the tickets were in hand, Kung called the number he'd been given. The man answered the phone, and Kung asked if he knew what happened. The man answered yes, one of the men had returned and told him. He'd reminded the man there was no payment for failure. The speaker wasn't pleased that the job wasn't done properly, but nothing could be done now. Perhaps later he'd be able to help his new comrades. With that, Kung hung up the phone.

To Hamilton's question, "What'd he have to say?", Kung quickly described the conversation.

"Is that it?" Hamilton asked. "They screwed it up, and they're just sorry?"

"Yes," Kung answered. "Don't forget three of their men are dead. And they weren't paid."

"Damn it, Winston," Hamilton was feeling frustrated again. "There's got to be a way to dump that crew and make Calloway get a new one!"

"I hope so, Charles," Kung responded. "I'm not happy about finding another way to deliver our goods. It's best to send them on your airplane!"

"I agree!" Hamilton replied.

"Well, I want to make another delivery soon," Kung smiled. And I need to be sure to remind Chou of his obligation, he thought. I won't do that, though, until we're ready to send the shipment. That way, Chou won't have time to think about it and foul up! But we also need to keep the crew off-balance, so they won't think about our delivery. And there are ways to do just that.

* * *

The *Kempetai* major finished talking to his investigators and returned to the group.

"Colonel Lindsay," he smiled. "Our investigation's nearly finished and I believe we have all the information we'll need from you." He bowed deeply. "Thanks for your cooperation. I hope we haven't inconvenienced you too much, although I'm afraid it's much too late for you to fly back to T'aiwan today. Besides, we might need to ask you more questions, later. I'd appreciate knowing where you'll stay tonight."

Lindsay reached into his pocket and found one of the cards from the *ryokan*, giving it to the major. "That's where we stayed last night, Major," he responded. "We'll try to stay there again tonight."

"Thank you. You're free to leave now, if you want," the major smiled. "I see the ladies brought a van to take you back."

"If we can take the car back," Anderson offered, "I'll drive, and you guys can ride with the girls. Oh, Major," Anderson looked toward the police officer, "I need a receipt for the guns."

"Of course, Mister Anderson," the major nodded. "I believe we already have a receipt ready. And we'll return the guns to you when the incident is cleared through our system."

"I understand, sir," Anderson smiled and bowed. The major returned the bow with a smile of his own.

* * *

After they told him what happened, Calloway was concerned, but he wasn't sure what about. The situation about the morphine was upsetting, but Hamilton would work on that. This thing about the Koreans, though – that was something else! Maybe the Koreans had made a mistake and chased the wrong car, but maybe they hadn't made a mistake. And Calloway didn't like that idea at all!

The primary argument against it, of course, was why would anyone want to shoot at the crew - and who? Based on the morphine situation, Calloway thought it might be somebody in the ChiNat government, whoever ran the medical supplies. But then there wouldn't be anybody to fly the plane for at least a couple of months, so that was a poor answer!

The Korean involvement could mean the ChiComs were involved – the ChiComs sometimes worked with them - but how would they know about Lindsay and the crew? Unfortunately, the Korean who wasn't killed in the crash had gotten away. Calloway wished he could get his hands on him. Maybe the *Kempetai* would have him in custody soon. At that point, a call to the right people would get him an interview. He'd have to contact the *Kempetai* and see what they could do together.

In the meantime, though, Lindsay and his crew probably needed some protection. He'd send Paul Anderson, with instructions to keep his eyes open and be ready for trouble.

* * *

Morning's light awakened Lindsay, as it usually did, and he felt Marion at his side. He lay still, thoughts running through his mind.

The situation yesterday scared him. Oh, he wasn't afraid of being hurt or killed. What scared him was the thought that maybe he would never see Marion again. This was the second time he'd felt that way, and it wasn't a pleasant feeling. He longed for the old days, when he didn't sweat this stuff. But then he realized that, in the old days, he didn't have Marion, either.

Last night, he asked her to marry him. They loved each other, he knew that, but she said no, at least until he was finished with this dangerous stuff – she didn't ever want to lose the man she loved again. Hell, it didn't make any difference whether she married him or not – they were in love, dangerous stuff or not! But he wouldn't argue with her.

Damn! All he was doing was getting confused. Somehow, he had to get his mind cleared. Being so hung up on his feelings for Marion clouded his thinking so badly that he didn't even feel like trying to think!

Maybe he'd feel better about it if he dozed a little longer. Marion snuggled against him as he closed his eyes again.

* * *

Having Anderson return with them made the crew more aware of the threat to their safety. Li was more sober than usual, and even Tiger had a serious look on his face. Tiger and Li decided Anderson could use the spare room in their apartment as a bedroom. Lindsay got him furniture from the operation's "slush fund". In fact, Lindsay was happy the three younger men decided to stay together. That way, Anderson would be able to keep a closer watch on at least those two crewmembers who actually did all the work!

In his first few days on T'aiwan, Anderson got in touch with local authorities. They were obviously important enough to grant Anderson and Li permits to carry sidearms. And Anderson acquired a couple of handguns for himself and Li, plus ammunition.

In the meantime, Lindsay returned to his own place. They'd been back for a couple of days. One evening, he was reading a book before bedtime when, suddenly, the buzzer at his front gate rang. After checking to see who it was, he went out and opened the gate.

"Hello, Lindsay." It was the owner of the Black Cat Bar, a place he'd frequented before he accepted the flying job. They'd been on friendly terms, but he hadn't seen her since before the whole thing with the plane started.

"Hi, Meiling," Lindsay greeted her. "Won't you please come in?"

"Thank you," the woman stepped through the gate into the small yard. "I won't stay long." She looked around. "It's a very nice house."

"Thanks," Lindsay responded. "How did you find me?"

"It was easy, Lindsay," she answered. "You once said you lived around here. I just asked the people where the American lived. They showed me."

"Ah - and why did you come?" Lindsay was curious. Meiling, like most Chinese, didn't do things without a reason.

"I've heard disturbing news," she answered. "I felt I needed to let you know about it, since we were friends."

"Yes," Lindsay agreed. "I've fallen in love, Meiling, and so I haven't come back to the bar. But you're right, we were friends. We certainly laughed a lot together."

"Yes, we did," Meiling smiled happily. "And I hope your lady's good to you, Lindsay. Is she Chinese?"

"No," Lindsay admitted, "she's an American and she lives in Japan. That's where I've been most of the time since I last saw you."

"Good!" Meiling's smile was genuine. "I've heard American women are different from Chinese women, but, if she makes you happy, then it's good!"

"Thanks," Lindsay replied. "But you say you've heard disturbing news. What is it?"

"Lindsay, do you remember the girl who always teased you about buying drinks for her?" Meiling asked.

"Sure," Lindsay replied.

"She came to me this morning," Meiling continued. "She told me she heard some Chinese men talking at a party she went to last night. She said some of the men talked about a contract offered to a local *t'ang*, you know, a Chinese gang."

"And -?" Lindsay questioned.

"The name on the contract was yours," Meiling answered. "There were some Chinese names, too, but she recognized yours and thought she should tell me about it. I thought it was something you should know."

Jesus, Lindsay thought immediately, maybe the attack by the Koreans wasn't a coincidence! He and his crew were targets! But who set it up? "Yes, it is," Lindsay nodded, "and thank you very much for coming to tell me."

"You're welcome, Lindsay," the woman smiled again. "She also said the men said the *t'ang* hadn't agreed to the contract. The *t'ang*s don't like to disturb Americans. The Foreign Affairs Police don't like it."

"Maybe so," Lindsay knew of the Foreign Affairs Police, a special branch of the civil police that dealt with foreigners.

"I don't know what they'll do," Meiling concluded, "but I felt I had to let you know someone wants you dead."

"Did your girl hear who put out the contract?" Lindsay asked.

"No, the men didn't say," she answered. "Now I've told you all I know. So good luck, and I'll say goodbye." She turned and walked to the gate. "Be careful, please, Lindsay. You were a good customer. Come back to see us again." She turned and left, the gate clicking shut behind her.

Lindsay walked back into the house and closed the door. He suddenly felt alone and threatened.

* * *

The phone at the apartment rang twice before Tiger finally grabbed it. "*Wei!*" he shouted the Chinese greeting.

"Tiger," it was Lindsay. "We've got a problem and I need to talk to all of you, Paul too. I'll be there as soon as I can. You guys wait for me, OK?"

"Sure, Colonel," Tiger agreed readily. "What kind of problem?" Li and Anderson came into the living room when they heard the word "colonel".

"Sounds like a spin-off of the one we had in Japan," Lindsay answered. "We need to figure out how to deal with it here."

"OK, sir," Tiger was quick to catch on. "Should Li or Paul come for you?"

"No," Lindsay answered. "From what I understand, the problem's just developing, it hasn't gotten to that level yet."

"OK, sir," Tiger said. "We'll see you soon, then. Please be careful. We don't want to lose you!"

"Yeah, Tiger," Lindsay replied. "I don't want to lose me, either!"

When the jeep arrived in front of the building, Li and Anderson were already standing out front. Their guns were hidden, but ready, when Lindsay got out.

"Hey, guys," Lindsay protested as they closed around him and ushered him into the building, "it's not *that* bad, yet!"

"We don't want to take any chances, sir," Anderson spoke calmly, as both he and Li kept their heads turning.

They were inside the apartment, the door locked behind them, and Lindsay laughed out loud. "You guys make this seem like a combat operation," he choked out, "and I haven't even had a chance to tell you what it's all about!"

"Just being cautious, Colonel," Li answered. "We're not interested in having a bunch of Koreans jump out of the woodwork and try to run us down in a car!"

After they all laughed, Lindsay finally got their attention.

"Look, guys," he started, "I've heard one of the *t'ang*s here – Paul, that's a Chinese gang – has been offered a contract on us. My source says the contract hasn't been taken, probably because the *t'ang* doesn't want trouble with the Foreign Affairs Police."

"That's serious, Colonel," Tiger said. "The Chinese people fear the *t'ang*s a lot."

"True, Tiger," Li spoke up, "but it's also true the *t'ang*s fear the Foreign Affairs Police more." He turned to Anderson. "Paul, the Foreign Affairs Police don't always go to court to deal out justice, and nobody questions them. And they don't like to have the *t'ang*s become involved with the Americans." He turned back to the others. "Any action against us would probably bring the Foreign Affairs Police down on the *t'ang*s." Tiger nodded his agreement.

"What should we do, then, Li?" Lindsay asked. "I realize the *t'ang*s probably aren't interested in a contract on us, but I'd like to make sure. Do you think the Foreign Affairs Police would remind the *t'ang*s they'll be in trouble if anything happens?"

"I'll bet on it, Colonel," it was Tiger who answered. "My younger brother deals with the Foreign Affairs Police a lot, since Americans come to his restaurant. One of his school classmates is a policeman, in fact. I'm sure my brother would talk to his classmate and ask him to tell the *t'ang*s the police know we're being targeted. That would probably take care of the problem."

"And I think, if the *t'ang*s get a warning," Li added, "they'll be sure no one else bothers us, either. Isn't that right, Tiger?"

"I think so," Tiger agreed. "Let's call my brother and see if he'll help us."

* * *

Kung was pleased. Proposing a contract with the *t'ang*s was a stroke of genius. Obviously, the *t'ang*s wouldn't accept the contract – it didn't offer enough money for the risk involved. But Lindsay and his crew would hear about the contract, and they'd be more concerned about their own safety than about what they delivered. Now he'd have to find a place in the plane to hide the package and then talk to Chou just before the mission, telling him where the package was and reminding him of his obligation. That should take care of the immediate problem. Then there was the long-term problem, replacing Lindsay and his crew.

Suddenly, Kung realized that the man in Tokyo could be the key to the problem. He and Hamilton would know the drop point and time of delivery, since they coordinated the location of the agent receiving the supply drop. Once the package was safely on the ground, the ChiComs could do whatever they wanted about the plane and its crew. They'd just have to coordinate all of this properly with the man in Tokyo. He should be able to have his 'client', the deputy governor, let the Communist air force know when and where the plane would be - after it had dropped its cargo, of course. He'd ask the man in Tokyo to handle this. It should only require a telephone call.

Kung reached for the telephone on his desk, making sure one of the office lines was open. This would have to be a direct call. It was one thing to make arrangements for a meeting in Tokyo through the CAT office there, but he couldn't take a chance on the Chinese receptionist at CAT in Tokyo listening in on this discussion.

* * *

The planning for the mission looked good, Lindsay thought. There were only three days left now before the mission went. He'd selected the route into the drop point they picked from the list. Now he'd let Hamilton know which point they'd use and when they'd be there.

Lindsay picked up his telephone and dialed the number for the receptionist at Hamilton's office at CAT.

* * *

Kung was feeling even better. His conversation yesterday with the man in Tokyo had gone exactly as he'd hoped. The man would deliver the information to the Communists when he was told to. All he needed was the information, and a phone call would provide that.

On top of that, Kung had just hit a beautiful drive off the fifth tee and the other three players weren't happy because each of them already owed him money. He walked down the fairway with the director of the SID's anti-espionage unit.

"Ah, P'eng," he smiled, "it's been a long time since the last time we talked. How's work going?"

"Pretty good, Winston," his friend replied. "I stay busy. I'm surprised how many spies the enemy can put into our government offices and where."

"Oh," Kung responded, "that doesn't sound good!"

"Well," his friend went on, "we manage to find them all. For instance, we found one in the Ministry of Defense last week, reporting the condition of our airfields to a Communist agent. She was taken care of."

"That sounds serious," Kung wasn't really interested, but it was too boring not to talk at all. They came to his friend's ball in the fairway, and P'eng selected his club, took a practice swing and finally stroked the ball toward the hole, landing about forty yards short of the green. "Ah," Kung nodded, "good shot."

"Thanks, Winston," his friend acknowledged as he handed the club back to the caddy. "At any rate," he continued as the two resumed walking toward Kung's ball, "we find them everywhere." He smiled at Kung. "We might even have one in your office!"

"Oh?" Kung responded as they arrived at his ball. He reached for the club the caddy had selected, took a practice swing, and stroked the ball very nicely toward the hole, running it up over the fringe of the green and to within about six feet of the hole.

"Oh!" P'eng was pleased with Kung's shot. "Very good!"

"Thank you," Kung nodded his pleasure, then handed the club back to his caddy.

They started forward. "Yes," P'eng continued as they walked, "several weeks ago, Japanese authorities told us a possible mainlander was residing in Tokyo. His paperwork said he was from Hong Kong, but he didn't respond when one of their officers spoke Cantonese to him, so they felt the papers could be forgeries. We asked them to keep an eye on him, and they've reported that he's contacted the Communist embassy several times. This morning, we received a report that someone in your office called him yesterday."

"Hmmm," Kung hid his surprise. "Do you know who it was?"

"No," P'eng replied. "But we'll keep an eye on him. The person who called him will call again and then we'll be able to catch them easily." He reached for the club his caddy offered and took a practice swing.

Kung smiled as he watched his friend hit the ball, placing it nicely on the green but about 20 feet from the pin. He'd win another hole from P'eng, at least, and probably from the other two, who'd hit poorly from the tee and even more poorly from the rough. And he'd be careful how he passed information to the man in Tokyo from now on. Maybe there was a different way to call the information to the man. He'd have to think about it for awhile. Not too long, though – the delivery information should be available today or tomorrow.

EIGHT

Second mid shift this cycle, Olson thought as he showed his identification badge to the gate guard. Maybe the penetrator wouldn't go on his watch this cycle. Only tonight and tomorrow night left. Ah, well, it kept things exciting for one of the three mids, at least. Of course, it made for an exciting briefing the following morning, too.

Olson remembered the last briefing well – the general yelled at him, as if Olson had anything to do with what happened except to report it. Everyone else at the briefing ducked their heads or turned their faces, even Captain Armstrong and Colonel Harding. Nobody wanted to contradict the general. It hadn't been a very good day. And the general hadn't said anything more since then. Neither had the colonel or the captain, who hadn't even come into the watch center during Olson's team's watches.

Nothing else was changed, of course. Everything else in the watch center was the same as before. But maybe it was best nothing happened on this set of mids, Olson thought. If anything did, he might tell the captain how he felt about the way he'd been treated, whether it got him in trouble or not.

The crew was busy at routine tasks when he finished relieving the previous shift chief. The promotion board was due to meet soon, and Olson needed to finish writing recommendations for his eligible guys. Hopefully, it would be a quiet night.

* * *

Kung watched the plane take off. The package was safely on board; only he and Chou knew where. It was bigger than any of the previous packages. This one might have to supply the customer's 'client' for as much as three months, as they'd already agreed. Kung had been lucky, and the cost of the contents wasn't much more than the price for the smaller packages. He'd visited Chou during crew rest the previous evening and forcefully told him the package had better be delivered properly. If not, he'd turn Chou over to the police, along with all the information about the death of the police officer. Chou was frightened enough that Kung was sure the package would be protected until it was dropped.

The call to Tokyo was no trouble. Hamilton simply made the call from his phone at CAT to the SAT office in Tokyo, and then had it forwarded from the SAT receptionist's switchboard to the boarding house where the man stayed, on the pretense Hamilton was making arrangements to live there when he returned to Japan. A local call from the SAT office wouldn't be remarkable to an anti-espionage officer looking for inter-island spy communications. Kung had advised the man, using Chinese so the SAT receptionist couldn't understand if she listened, of the delivery location and the approximate time, warning him he had to ensure the drop was completed before the attack took place or he'd get no package. After all, as Kung pointed out, it was as much to the man's advantage to ensure the delivery was completed as it was to theirs.

Ah, yes, Kung thought. It was going very well.

* * *

On board the plane, Lindsay activated their flight plan to Okinawa. Then he sat back and watched as Tiger controlled the climb to altitude and heading to start the flight.

The weather would be clear tonight, Lindsay thought. The forecast for the mainland was light scattered clouds. There probably wouldn't be enough cloud to hide them, but enough to let them see the area. That ought to make it a little easier to fly at low altitude.

* * *

It was quiet, and Smitty's promotion recommendation was finally done. Now Olson was getting ready to start Chuck's. Smitty and Chuck were both studying on correspondence courses at the moment, Smitty with the headsets on. It was quiet.

The quiet was shattered by Smitty's voice. "It's our guy!" He jumped up and ran to the map. "Here we go again!"

"Yeah!" Chuck ran to the teletypes, joined by the rest of his crew.

Olson put aside the folder with the promotion write-ups. Here we go again, he thought. I sure hope it's not as bad as last time. "Stu!" he called out, "how about getting the coffee ready? Captain will want a cup."

"Got it, Sarge!" Stu shouted back.

"He's way north of Fuchou," Smitty called out, marking plots. "What the hell's he doing so far north?"

"Maybe he figures he can get into the interior before they can get a reaction anywhere near him," Olson answered. "Any reaction from Fuchou will have to go fast to catch him."

"He's headed inland," Smitty spoke up as he marked another plot. "And Fuchou's reacting!" he announced.

A teletype started chattering as Olson picked up the telephone and dialed the captain's number. This should be interesting, he thought. I wonder what the captain will say about coming over here again after that round with the general. The phone rang on the other end.

"Armstrong," the voice on the other end mumbled.

"Sir, this is Sergeant Olson in the watch center," Olson announced. "We have a situation."

"On my way, Mike," the captain's voice was crisper. "Coffee on, yet?"

"Going on now, sir," Olson answered.

"Good," the Captain said. "Be there in a couple of minutes."

* * *

At seven hundred meters' altitude, the countryside passed below slowly in the moonlight. Lindsay knew better, though. This altitude would take them past the first mountain range near the coast. Then they'd drop down into the valleys to confuse the radars and avoid the fighters. For the moment, though, the going was clear.

After the row he'd raised, there shouldn't be a problem with the medical supplies on this trip, Lindsay thought.

Li carefully watched his timing, while Tiger almost gleefully flew the airplane. It was going smoothly.

The radio squawked. "Red flag," Matsu radio called, "two tigers, one four zero at six." Two MiGs at a distance of 140 kilometers at 180 degrees.

"Two MiGs up from Fuchou," Lindsay said. "We're too far away and going further. They might come part way, just to make sure we don't turn back."

"We'll drop down soon, anyway," Li responded. "Only two minutes before we're past the coast mountain range and drop down. Then we zigzag through the valleys until we reach our delivery point."

It's going just fine, thought Lindsay.

* * *

The captain walked in as Smitty put the first fighter plot on the map.

"Evening, sir," Olson's greeting was reserved. "He's north of Fuchou, headed northwest at 700 meters. The fighters just took off, and don't have much of a chance of catching up. He'll be over the mountain range soon, and the coast radars will lose him."

"Good, Mike," the captain responded, looking toward the coffeepot. "Coffee ready yet?"

"It will be in a minute, sir," Olson answered. "Other than that, it's quiet right now."

The captain took a cigarette from the pack he pulled from his pocket, then offered the pack to Olson. "Care for one?" he asked, then stopped. "Sorry. I forgot you don't smoke. You didn't start after last time, did you?"

"No, sir, I didn't," Olson answered. "I don't know what I did wrong at the briefing, but I have no reason to want to smoke. So I won't."

"Mike," the captain breathed a sigh, "that was a bad show by the rest of us, wasn't it? We just sat there and let the general tee off, and nobody was willing to tell him he was out of line."

"It's OK, sir," Olson tried to defuse the situation, "I don't blame you."

"Well I do," the captain continued. "He blew up about that pilot pranging it in. We all felt bad about it, but there's not one of us who wouldn't be bragging proud if we shot him down in a dogfight! So what's the difference? He was trying to shoot down our guy and he didn't make it. Probably not a really good pilot, I'd say."

"I understand that, sir," Olson nodded.

"Aw, shit, Mike," the captain kept on. "I've been avoiding talking to you, mostly because I didn't really know how to say I screwed up in not backing you. I'm sorry, OK? It looks like we'll get another chance this morning, and I hope I've got the guts to stand with you if he starts again."

"Sir, I appreciate that," Olson started, "but you've got a career - don't just throw it away."

"You've got a career, too," the captain countered. "And mine's not worth a damn if I can't feel good about it. I guess it was just reflexes that made me duck. But I don't think it'll happen again."

"Sir," Olson almost felt embarrassed, "you don't need to feel that way. I hope the general won't have a chance to get so upset this time."

"Well," the captain grinned crookedly, "if he does, we'll see what happens. Now let's check our boy out, OK? Looks like a quiet run for him tonight. He's way out past the range of the fighters, that's for sure."

"Yes, sir," Olson noted, "and it looks like Fuchou is just doing their defensive patrol thing near the airfield, again."

* * *

Lindsay smiled. They were past the mountain range. Now it was time to drop down into the valley and turn to follow the river. The fighters wouldn't come this far – at 150 kilometers, it was beyond the range of their radar coverage. The Fuchou pilots weren't experienced enough to do night flights without solid control.

This mission's going fine, Lindsay thought.

* * *

Time passed slowly after the plane dropped off radar. Smitty sat back and waited, getting up now and then to mark another plot on the fighters. But there wasn't anything on the plane after it dropped behind the mountain range. No telling where it was now. The captain sat quietly, sipping his coffee and smoking and things were, well, just *quiet!* It was like something was waiting to happen, suddenly, but nobody knew what.

Olson got a cup of coffee and sat back down, staring at the plotting map, then looking at the topographical map on the wall. If the plane hadn't turned north, then it should have broken off before it reached Nanp'ing and gone further northwest, up toward the mountain range between the coast and the Yangtze River valley. That mountain range was around two hundred miles inland. Hell, even the ChiNat radars couldn't go that deep with any hope of accuracy. That was probably just about as far as any aircraft could ever hope to penetrate the mainland and have a chance to get back out.

* * *

The flight was going smoothly, Lindsay thought. With the moonlight, it wasn't necessary to call out altitudes. Li still called out the course adjustments, though.

They'd dropped down and come down the river to its big junction, then turned back up the other branch of the river, toward the northwest. Ahead lay the mountains and the province border, Lindsay knew, but their target tonight wasn't that far. And, unlike their previous missions, they weren't going to drop leaflets on this mission. In fact, this time they were going to go out the same way they'd come in.

The plane was responding to Tiger's control like it was a part of him, Lindsay noted. Maybe his nagging premonition of something not right was wrong, too. They'd have to see.

* * *

Smitty announced it. "Sarge," he spoke up, "the back room guys say they've got something odd."

"What's that?" Olson asked.

"A radio beacon came up a little bit ago," Smitty pointed to a place on the map. "It's in the high frequency range, which means it can be heard a long way off. Direction finding took shots on it, and they figure it's located somewhere out near the Yangtze River, but it's not stationary. It's moving, and at a pretty fair speed, like an aircraft."

"It's not showing on radar?" the captain asked.

"Sir, that's too deep for ChiNat radar," Olson noted, "and the ChiComs don't routinely track their own aircraft. It's not far away from that bomber base up there, though. I've never heard of them using beacons on bombers, although they could."

"Sarge," Smitty cut in, "it's faster than a bomber. The speeds they're talking about, it's probably a fighter."

"Another fighter," the captain shook his head. "But it's on the wrong side of the mountains. They won't be able to watch it on radar, even if they've got a decent radar up there."

"Sir," Olson cut in, "I hate to say this, but that beacon lets them watch it, the same way we can, with direction finding. And they can still put HF radios in most of their planes, so they can also talk to it over the mountains. It may just be a fluke, because nobody knows where he is. But if our guy jumps up at the wrong time, that fighter could catch up with him."

The captain suddenly looked at the teletypes. "They're silent, except for Fuchou," he noted. "The ChiNats don't know that other plane's there?"

"Remember, they can't see it on radar, Captain," Chuck started. "The teletypes only report what the ChiNat radars can see."

"OK, so we can't tell if the ChiNats know what's going on?" the captain asked.

"That's right, sir," Olson answered. "We can't, unless they're the ones reporting to the back room. The guys there can't tell us where the information's coming from. You know the rules, too, sir – you've got the clearance."

"Nuts," the captain was irritated. "For all we know, our guy is flying blind, although somebody must be telling him about reacting fighters. So there's a probable ChiCom fighter not too far from where he ought to be, but the ChiNats probably can't tell him because they might not know about it."

"Sir, we don't have any way of knowing," Olson shook his head. "We don't even know for sure it's a fighter. All we can say is that it's a radio beacon and we think it's moving as fast as a fighter would fly. And we have no way of contacting the plane."

"Damn, I hope somebody's telling him he's got company out there," the captain grumbled. "He's gonna pop up and have something on his ass!"

"Well," Olson was quiet, "he hasn't shown up in awhile, sir. Maybe he won't be where they can see him!"

"Shit, Mike," the captain apologized, "I'm just worried he's gonna get creamed and never know what hit 'im."

"They've got to find him first, sir," Olson replied carefully. "That's not easy to do. He's staying low, and they don't have radar coverage that deep in the mainland."

"They may not know where he is," the captain looked at where Smitty marked another plot on the beacon, "but it looks like that beacon knows where it's going! Smitty," he spoke to the man at the map, "is the beacon crossing over the mountains there? Right there, at the province border?"

"Looks like it, sir!" Smitty answered as he marked another plot. "It's moving into Fuchien Province!"

* * *

A smooth flight so far, Lindsay marveled, with clear skies and moonlight. They'd turned to start the delivery run.

"Drop point in two minutes thirty seconds," Li called.

"Chou, are you in place?" Lindsay asked.

"I'm ready, Captain," Chou's voice was steady.

"OK," Lindsay replied, "opening the cargo door." With that, he pulled the lever. "Drop point in two minutes fifteen seconds," he added.

"Colonel," it was Li, "it's time to change frequency on the HF radio so we can continue to monitor Matsu."

"You're right, Li," Lindsay began turning the radio dial to the next frequency. Suddenly, there was a squawk in everyone's headsets, and Lindsay turned down the volume and then tuned the radio to the squawk. With the volume reduced, the sound was loud and clear, a radio signal.

Li spoke up. "Colonel," he said, "there's no radio signal like that in this area. The people here complained because the radio stations were all too far away to hear clearly. I tried to help them tune in radio signals and swept the frequency bands pretty thoroughly. That signal wasn't here then."

"Colonel," it was Tiger, "there's a sound inside it, like Morse code. Do you hear it?"

"Yeah, I do," Lindsay listened intently. "It's repeated. Tiger, it's a radio beacon!"

"Colonel," Li was concerned, "it wasn't here before."

"Everyone stay alert!" Lindsay warned. "I don't know what this means, but I don't like it!" He moved the tuning control to the new Matsu frequency.

"One minute thirty seconds to drop point," Li called.

The plane hurtled on through the night. Lindsay turned to look outside as Tiger and Li concentrated their attention on flying.

"One minute to drop point," Li's voice startled Lindsay, who was intently scanning the sky.

* * *

"That beacon's moved inside the province border," Smitty noted. "It's about 40 kilometers past the border now."

"It looks like it's headed toward a place, just like it expects to find something there," Olson noted.

"Yeah," the captain agreed, lighting another cigarette. "And the chances our guy is somewhere around there are pretty high. Don't ask me how, but I'll bet that beacon knows exactly where to go to find what it's looking for. And I'll bet our guy has no idea he's got company."

* * *

"Thirty seconds," Li announced. Lindsay continued to scan the sky.

"See anything?" Tiger asked.

"Nothing," Lindsay answered.

"No, Colonel, I mean ahead of us!" Tiger chuckled. "The drop point!"

"Ah... sorry, Tiger," Lindsay shook his head. "I'm still worried about that beacon. It might be a reference point for an airplane to home on out here. Although," he added, "I don't know what an airplane would be doing out here."

"Three seconds," Li called.

"See the light, dead ahead!" Tiger interrupted quickly.

"...two... one... now!" Li continued the countdown.

"Drop now!" Lindsay chimed in.

"Drop away!" Chou responded.

"Good drop!" Li called out.

"Cargo door closing," Lindsay called. "Chou, please watch behind us." Lindsay reached forward and turned the control knob on the HF radio. The sound of the beacon blasted, louder than before, into the ears of the crewmembers. "Damn'!" Lindsay blurted, "it sounds like it's closer than it was before!"

Li was listening to the sound. "Colonel!" he spoke up, "that's a five-digit number it's transmitting! That's the radio signal for an airplane, not a fixed site! That's an airplane, and it's close to us!"

"Oh, shit!" Lindsay turned and scanned the sky again. Suddenly, he stopped and pointed. "Something's up there, but it's not showing any lights. It could be a fighter!"

"Is it close enough to see us, Colonel?" Tiger asked.

"I don't think so," Lindsay answered. "It's not very close, but it seems to be coming right at us."

"Colonel," Li remarked, "I saw airplanes in Nanch'ang that had strange bulges in front. The intelligence officer said they were MiG-19s, and they have radar to attack other airplanes."

"Damn!" Lindsay exploded, "that's probably one of them! It's got us on radar, and the beacon's how the controllers know where it is! But how can it talk to the controllers unless -?" Lindsay stopped. "It's got to have HF radio! And we have HF radio, too. Maybe we can find out what's going on!" With that, he began turning the dial on the radio, moving it through the frequency band.

"The shadow's getting larger, Colonel," Li called out. "I believe it's getting closer, and it seems to be dropping toward our altitude!"

"Steady, Tiger," Lindsay called, noting that Tiger was turning his head.

"Just checking the terrain, Colonel," Tiger answered. "We may have to do some tight flying."

"What's that flash?" Li suddenly called.

"Christ!" Lindsay looked backward to see a streak of light coming toward them. "Missile! Hold it straight. Steady - ready to break – steady - break now!"

The plane stood on its left wing and turned. The missile flashed through the space where the plane had been. It exploded in a ball of flame far in front of them.

"Hold on," Lindsay called. "Those things come in twos. He's got another one."

"Should I climb out of this valley?" Tiger asked.

"No," Lindsay answered. "Stay in the valley for now. He might not be able to get close enough to use his cannon. That's a big plane, and it's not as agile as we are, especially at these speeds."

"Captain," Chou called from the rear of the plane, "I see the airplane itself now. It's above and behind us."

"Thanks, Chou," Lindsay replied. "That was a heat-seeker, like our Sidewinders, Tiger. It couldn't have been radar-guided if he's still above us."

"I agree, Colonel," it was Li. "I saw some of those missiles. My intelligence officer said the Communists retrieved some of our unexploded Sidewinders during the battle in the strait, and copied them."

"If it's a heat-seeker," Lindsay went on, "then he can shoot any time he wants to. The Sidewinder can't turn worth a damn, though. As quick as this plane is, we can out-turn nearly anything he can send at us."

"Except for cannon shells, Colonel," Li reminded him. "He's trying to get closer, perhaps to shoot at us."

"Captain," Chou called out, "the enemy airplane is dropping lower."

"Thanks, Chou," Lindsay responded.

Suddenly, there was a squawk from the radio that Lindsay hadn't stopped tuning. "- getting closer to try cannon," came a muffled Chinese-speaking voice from the radio.

"Good," came a response from farther away. "Be careful."

"Roger," responded the first voice. "Descending. Landing gear and dive brakes extended, airspeed slowing to 700 ... 650."

"Roger," came the second voice.

"Power three-quarters," the first voice reported. "Airspeed now steady at 550 kilometers. Adding power."

"Roger," acknowledged the second voice.

"Power is almost maximum and airspeed now increased to 600," came the first voice. "I have the enemy aircraft in my sights, but it's too far to shoot."

"Roger," the second voice acknowledged.

"We're very low," the first voice sounded nervous. "I'm closing to cannon distance now."

"Be ready to break, Tiger," Lindsay said.

"Tiger," it was Li, "there's a small ridge to our left front. Behind it's a valley that leads toward the coast. Go there when you break."

"Understand," Tiger didn't turn his head.

"I'm within cannon distance," the first voice reported.

"The plane's close!" Chou called.

"Roger," came the second voice. "OK to fire."

"Break now!" Lindsay called to Tiger, who jerked the plane toward the left. A stream of red tracers flew through the air behind them.

"Good!" shouted Lindsay as the MiG tried to turn to bring its cannons to bear again. Just as it came around to attempt a shot, Lindsay called, "Break back!" and Tiger flipped the plane the other direction, zooming across in front of the MiG. The MiG pilot was too surprised to shoot and began a hard turn to follow the plane.

"Report," the second voice demanded.

"I'm too low!" called the first voice. "It's too hard to keep up with the enemy, he's too maneuverable!"

"Shoot him!" ordered the second voice. "Do it the way we practiced!"

"I'm trying!" the first voice responded.

The MiG was coming around behind the plane, which was now flying straight and level, at a right angle to the nearby valley.

"Sorry, Colonel," Tiger called out, "but I've got to turn now if we're going to get to the valley." With that, he started the tight turn to the left to head for the valley.

This time, the MiG pilot was ready, and a spray of cannon shell tracers flashed past the plane as it headed for the entrance to the valley.

"Damn!" Tiger realized that, in the moonlight, he'd misjudged the distance. If they flew directly at the valley, the MiG would be straightened out and in firing position before they could reach it. With that, Tiger motioned to Lindsay, who understood he was going to go straight until the MiG was almost in firing position, then make a tight 360-degree turn to get behind the MiG and slip into the valley when the MiG had to turn away to keep from crashing.

Lindsay turned in his seat to watch the MiG come around behind them. Just before he turned, he noticed that Tiger had cheated just a bit and had already started edging the plane into its turn enough so they were headed almost right at the ridge that stuck out into the valley. "Careful, Tiger," he cautioned. "Don't give us away yet."

Lindsay turned his head and saw that the MiG was nearly all the way around.

"What's happening?" the second voice asked.

"He's turning away," answered the first voice, "but I'm catching him now."

Lindsay saw that the MiG was leveling off and setting up to fire. "Now, Tiger," he called.

"Just a second, Colonel," Tiger was concentrating. He seemed to count in his head, then flipped the plane into a hard left turn, in time to avoid the stream of tracers that again flashed by.

Lindsay realized they were very near the ridge, so close he could see individual bushes standing out from the ground. "Shit!" he breathed, as the wingtip seemed to dodge between bushes as the plane turned. Suddenly, the ground dropped away as the ridge fell behind them.

Lindsay turned his head to see where the MiG had gone, in time to see it was trying to follow them across the face of the ridge. With a sick feeling in the pit of his stomach, Lindsay realized the MiG was going to hit the ridge. At the last second, the MiG pilot seemed to realize it also, and the MiG started to pull right and upward, but it was too late. There was a loud scream on the radio, and the MiG hit the ridge, then exploded in a huge fireball.

The radio came alive. "Are you there?" It was the controller. "Do you read me?" There was a moment of silence, then the voice returned, this time with concern. "We don't see the beacon. Are you OK?" There was another pause, and the controller began calling the MiG, over and over.

Lindsay tuned the radio back to the frequency for Matsu. Another plane down. He felt sorry for the pilot, but the controller had pushed the pilot too hard, even when the pilot wasn't happy about pursuing the attack. And the pilot obeyed, instead of telling the controller to cram it!

Well, maybe he couldn't tell him to cram it, Lindsay thought. That's one difference between the way they do things and the way we do things! And it looks like it just cost them another plane and another pilot.

"Chou," Lindsay called back to the kicker. "Are you OK?"

"Yes, Captain," came Chou's steady voice.

* * *

"The beacon just quit," Smitty announced, marking a point on the map.

"That's out in the middle of nowhere," Olson noted. "Did our boy take out another one?"

"No way of knowing," Smitty smiled, "but I won't bet against him!"

"We'll just have to wait, huh?" Olson grinned. "It won't be long before we find out. He'll be coming out soon enough. He shouldn't have enough fuel left to fly around in there much longer."

The captain had remained silent through the banter. Now he spoke up. "If another fighter's down, the ChiComs will be frantic," he commented.

"Hey, Sarge," it was Smitty. "Back room says there's a transmitter calling an aircraft callsign and not getting any response."

"ChiComs use the same frequency range we do," the captain commented, doubtfully. "Signals in that range are line-of-sight; there's no way anyone could hear anything in that frequency range from this far away."

"Captain," Olson reminded him, "some of their aircraft are still equipped with HF radios. HF transmissions follow the curve of the earth a lot better than the VHF and UHF range stuff we use on fighters. If they put HF in a fighter, it could be picked up from this far away."

"Yes, sir," Smitty agreed. "That's how we were getting the beacon."

The captain stared at the map. "Sure is a long way back in there," he finally commented. "I'd like to know what the hell our boy's doing now."

* * *

The plane was traveling back across the ridge. In the bright moonlight, Tiger was almost skimming the tops of trees as they raced to return to the same course they'd flown coming to the drop point.

"There's the river, Colonel," Li pointed to the large stream. "We follow it until we get to the river junction, and then return the way we came."

"And hope Fuchou doesn't have anybody up!" Lindsay responded.

"Yes sir," Li answered.

* * *

The silence in the watch center was thick enough to cut with a knife, Olson thought. Everyone was watching the map. The ChiCom fighters from Fuchou had been recalled and were getting ready to land. But there was no sign of the plane.

The captain suddenly stood up and started toward the coffeepot, breaking the tension. "I don't know about you guys," he said, "but I need to go get rid of some used coffee. I'll be back in a minute." He set his coffee cup down and walked through the door into the hallway.

"Little bit edgy tonight, huh?" Smitty nodded after the captain.

"Yep, Smitty," Olson nodded in agreement. "He's not happy about that last briefing with the general."

"Understand, Sarge," Smitty replied, "But will it be any different this time?"

"I don't know," Olson answered. "I know the general was upset, but I think he was wrong to jump on me in front of everybody."

"Well, I hope it won't happen again, Sarge!" Smitty responded. "I sure wouldn't want to be in your shoes, though," he added.

"Yeah," Olson agreed, "I'm not sure I want to be in them, either!"

* * *

It was almost time to jump up and run for the coast, Lindsay thought. Li would call the climb soon. He hoped there wouldn't be any further reaction from Fuchou. They'd had a busy enough night of it, already.

* * *

"Damn, yes!" Smitty yelled it as he jumped toward the map. "Got him! He's coming out!"

The captain sat down on the desk next to Olson. "Looks like he's way up north," the captain commented. "That's where he went in, right?"

"Yes, sir," Olson agreed.

"He's headed due east, Sarge," Smitty called as he marked up the next plot.

"Avoiding any reaction from Fuchou," Olson remarked calmly.

* * *

"Still no report of activity from Fuchou," Lindsay remarked, breaking the silence. "I guess they won't put anything up."

"That's good, sir," Li responded.

* * *

"No activity from Fuchou," Smitty called. "Looks like our guy's clear to the coast."

Olson looked toward the captain. "Guess we need to think about briefing the general, huh, sir?" he asked. "I don't know what to tell him about the beacon."

"I think," the captain answered slowly, "we need to tell him all we know is it was a beacon, it was active during the time the plane was in the area, it moved, and then it quit."

"Will he accept that, sir?" Olson wanted to know. "Or will he get upset again, like he did last time?"

"I don't know, Mike," the captain answered. "If he does, I hope I'll have the good sense to deal with it like a man! In the meantime," he grinned at Olson, "I think I need another cup of coffee. How about you?"

* * *

The plane broke the coast and Li called for the descent so they could escape radar coverage quickly. The plane dropped to a low altitude.

"Great flight!" Lindsay said to the crew. "Tiger, take a break. I've got it for now."

"Thanks, Colonel," Tiger grinned. "I need to hit the relief tube!"

"Don't use it all up," Li put in jokingly. "The rest of us have to go, too."

"I'll be right back, then," Tiger assured Li. "I wouldn't want you to have to cross your legs any longer than necessary."

OK, thought Lindsay. We're out of there, and the crew can relax and laugh a little to let off the pressure. But it was another close one, and it took all of Tiger's flying abilities to get us out of it. I think Calloway will be interested to know the MiG was outfitted with HF radio.

* * *

The plane rolled to a stop in front of the CAT hangar. There was Kung's car again, Lindsay thought, with Kung and Hamilton getting out and standing beside it, both in overcoats because of the cold. They didn't look particularly happy to be there. Lindsay laughed.

Lindsay undid his seat belt and followed Tiger down the length of the plane and out the rear hatchway. Hamilton met him as his feet hit the ground.

"How'd it go, Lindsay?" Hamilton seemed more concerned than usual. Must be just his nerves, Lindsay thought. They started toward the office.

"Not bad, Charlie," Lindsay replied, "but we had another close call."

"What was that?" Hamilton asked.

"A MiG jumped us right after we made our drop," Lindsay answered. "Just one, an all-weather job. It got in a few shots at us."

"What happened?" Hamilton asked. "How'd you get away?"

"We were making a turn to throw it off," Lindsay responded,

"and it plowed into a hillside because it couldn't turn as tightly as we could."

"Jesus!" Hamilton shook his head. "You guys live right! But it was an all-weather job?"

"Yep," Lindsay answered. "Moonlight was bright enough we could see it pretty well. Besides, it closed on us very directly, like the pilot didn't need a visual sighting."

"Hmm," Hamilton seemed thoughtful. "Sounds like they're getting serious about trying to catch you guys! You think maybe we ought to postpone further missions for awhile? If I were you guys, I don't think I'd be ready to go back in there again soon. In fact, I don't think I'd want to ever go again!"

"You weren't a combat pilot, were you, Charlie?" Lindsay asked.

"No, I wasn't," Hamilton admitted. "I never flew in combat."

"Let's go do an outbrief, then," Lindsay responded, leading the way. "I'm tired, and I'd like to head for bed."

* * *

After the colonel's introduction, Olson walked to the easel that held the map they'd prepared. The group he was briefing was the same as the last time, and they were obviously uneasy over what might happen.

"General, gentlemen," he acknowledged the audience. "This morning, we had another penetration of the mainland by an aircraft identified as a light bomber. The penetrator entered mainland airspace well north of Fuchou and flew toward the northwest. Fighters were sent up from Fuchou, but made no attempt to pursue the penetrator, which dropped out of radar coverage far north of Fuchou and west of the mountain range. We didn't see the penetrator again until it returned to this same location, over forty minutes later, when it climbed up and flew out directly to the east, exiting the mainland."

The entire group breathed much easier. No controversial action, no aircraft losses, no reaction from the general.

"We had one unusual activity during the penetration," Olson continued. "A beacon, origin unknown but mobile, was seen moving from here -" he indicated the spot where the beacon was first plotted, "- to here." He pointed to the location where the beacon was last seen. "This point could've been reached by the penetrator during the time it was active but out of radar coverage. We also received belated reports that a radio transmitter was monitored calling an aircraft repeatedly after the beacon disappeared. We believe -."

The general came up out of his chair with a curse. "Dammit, Sarge! You 'believe' - you don't know shit, do you? What the hell was it? You can't answer that, can you? What the hell good are you people if you can't give me solid answers? -."

"Sir!" Olson's barked response stopped the general cold. "I don't know what you expect me to be, sir, a liar or a fool, but I'm giving you the best answers I can. I wasn't out there to see what happened, sir!"

"Sergeant, don't be a damned fool!" the general's aide, a captain, growled at Olson.

"Jeff, shut up!" It was Captain Armstrong, standing up and walking to Olson's side, his size commanding attention. "General, I think you might want to listen to Sergeant Olson, sir. I sat there and watched what he was seeing this morning, and I'll be damned if I could come up with any better way to say what we saw. We've all been around enough to know the sarge is giving you the best he can, sir. If it's not enough, then nothing's ever going to be. But it's the best we can come up with. If you want to yell at anybody, sir, maybe you ought to yell at *me*. Sarge here can only stand and take this, but at least I can get back at you out on the golf course this afternoon!"

The general stopped cold, then started laughing. "Damn it, Bill," he looked at the captain, "you're right! I'm too damned worried about whether or not the ChiComs are going to holler about having a bomber over here during my watch!" He turned to Olson. "Sarge, the captain's right, and I guess it's time I admitted it. I owe you a couple of apologies, one for now and one for last time. I think the captain just put this into perspective, as he often does. I don't like seeing aircraft losses, but I also need to remember that they're not *our* losses, and I don't have to account for them." He stuck out his right hand toward Olson as he walked forward. "I hope you'll accept my apology, Sarge. And maybe I could talk you into joining me and the captain for coffee after this little get-together, OK?"

Olson took the general's hand and shook it. "OK, sir, but I need to leave pretty early. I have a wife waiting for me at home, sir."

NINE

Kung was glad he and Hamilton had thought of using the SAT telephone system to pass important messages to Tokyo. This was one of those calls.

The man in Tokyo was pleased. The delivery was a success. Of course, Kung already knew that. The man wasn't upset the attempt to intercept the plane hadn't succeeded. Like all other Chinese, he was patient. It was unfortunate the MiG was lost, but it was neither his nor Kung's fault if the information they provided to the People's Liberation Army Air Force, the PLAAF, didn't result in success. The delivery was made, which was the important point. So long as deliveries continued to succeed, there was no reason to worry about who made them. They'd still try to replace the crew. That would be expected now. The PLAAF knew they could provide information on the flights. However, once the plane was downed, they'd tell the PLAAF the information wasn't available on further flights. And, because the delivery was so much larger than expected, there was a large bonus waiting.

Kung hung up the telephone. Now they could go get the payment for the next delivery. They wouldn't pay for further attacks on the crew in Japan. There wouldn't be any more of them. The man explained the *Kempetai* had pressured the Koreans, and the gangs weren't willing to take further risks because the *Kempetai* could have them deported. But that wasn't important. They'd tell the man in Tokyo about future deliveries, and he could tell the PLAAF anything he wished. Kung wouldn't share the bonus with Hamilton, since Hamilton hadn't done anything to earn it.

Now it was time to call Hamilton and tell him they needed to fly to Tokyo in two days. Hamilton would get back five thousand of his dollars and Kung would get a reward for doing the job himself so it was done right. He'd still have to pay Hamilton the money every trip, even though he still had to do all the work himself, but maybe that could change one day, too.

It was a good day.

* * *

Lindsay hung up the phone with mixed feelings about the trip to Tokyo. Were they going to have to watch carefully every second they were there, hoping a bunch of crazy Koreans wouldn't come after them again? It could be especially dangerous for the girls, which worried him most.

The crew was gone for lunch. Tiger would be happy to go back to Tokyo. So would Li and Anderson, although both of them would probably be as wary as hunted animals. As for himself, Lindsay was looking forward to seeing Marion, even if he had to fight his way through a whole army of Koreans!

He picked up the telephone and dialed the international operator. Within a few minutes, he was connected to the SAT Tokyo office and talking with Calloway.

"Hey, Joe," Lindsay greeted his friend.

"Hey, Lindsay!" Calloway responded. "What's up?"

"Us," Lindsay answered. "Day after tomorrow."

"Hey, good," Calloway was enthusiastic. "I want to ask you some questions about that unfriendly you met."

"Figured you would," Lindsay responded. "How's the unfriendly situation up there?"

"The *Kempetai* says no more unfriendlies," Calloway replied. "I think they got a couple of visits from their friendly neighborhood law enforcement officials, and they're behaving themselves."

"Well," Lindsay was a little skeptical, "if you think they won't be a problem, I'll feel easier. On the other hand, there's a couple of things bothering me, and I need to talk them over with you."

"OK," Calloway agreed. "Get on up here. We'll go over the whole thing."

"OK," Lindsay said. "Now, how about letting me talk to Marion?"

"Lindsay, I'm sorry," Calloway sounded serious. "Marion's not here right now."

"Oh?" Lindsay was concerned. "What's the matter?"

"Nothing," Calloway tried to calm the situation. "She's running an errand for me, that's all. I had some papers that needed to go to the SAT corporate offices. But you sound like you're worried, buddy."

"Maybe I am," Lindsay responded. "You know how I feel about her."

"Yep," Calloway agreed, "and she feels the same way about you. And that's why she gets so balled up about you and this job, you know."

"Yeah," Lindsay acknowledged, "it's not like I don't understand how she feels, Joe. But I gave my word to do a job and that's what I'll do."

"I understand," Calloway answered. "I think she understands, too. But she can't bring herself to tie herself to you when she's scared of losing you."

"I know, Joe," Lindsay sounded miserable. "Before I got into this, it didn't make any difference what happened to me. Now that's changed and I don't know what to do about it."

"Come on up here," Calloway encouraged him, "and we'll talk about it! Maybe we won't find the answers, but at least we can try, OK?"

"OK," Lindsay agreed. "See you day after tomorrow."

* * *

The trip was uneventful. Standard flight to Tokyo, the cars waiting, Kung and Hamilton leaving in the limo, as usual. The trip downtown was uneventful, too. They were greeted warmly by the girls. Even Kumiko and Paul's date had showed up, with Kumiko grabbing Li's arm fiercely.

The standard part of briefing Calloway went well. Calloway asked lots of questions about the MiG and its radar, and was especially interested in the fact Lindsay was able to listen to the MiG pilot and his controller. He did more listening than commenting, which Lindsay realized was unusual. However, Lindsay kept quiet – Calloway would comment later, he knew. There were questions about their security in T'aipei, which Paul answered, and then the briefing was over. The younger men left the office, ready to go out with the girls, who again had the afternoon off.

Lindsay saw the crew to the door. "I'll be along soon," he told Tiger. "You guys go ahead and have a great afternoon. We'll see you later."

"OK, Colonel," Tiger replied, aware that Lindsay wanted to talk to Calloway alone. "We'll see you at the *ryokan*. Maybe we can have dinner together."

"Maybe," Lindsay said. "Check with Marion," he joked. "She keeps my calendar when I'm in town."

Tiger laughed as he went out the door.

With the door closed, Lindsay turned to Calloway. "Joe, I don't like the fact the MiG found us so easily."

"Who knew where you'd be?" Calloway asked.

"Only the crew knew the route," Lindsay answered, sitting back down. "If we'd been shot down, they'd have gone down, too."

"Is there some way you could have been compromised?" Calloway asked. "Maybe somebody with access to your documents?"

"No, I don't think so," Lindsay thought about it. "We keep the stuff in a safe, and I changed the combination myself."

"You still feed the information on your drops to Hamilton, don't you?" asked Calloway.

"Sure," Lindsay answered. "We don't give him any ingress or egress information, but he gets the drop point and time we've selected."

"And he gives that information to Kung?" Calloway asked.

"Of course," Lindsay answered. "I see where you're leading, Joe, but there's no way anybody could get that information from T'aiwan to the Chicoms."

"Well," Calloway conceded, "it couldn't be Kung – he probably couldn't call his own mother without CAT or the SID knowing about it."

"Maybe he could make calls from Charlie's hotel room, although I'd be surprised if Charlie's involved," Lindsay came up with a possibility.

"I doubt that," Calloway answered. "We could check that out too easily."

"So, if it was him, how would he get calls off-island?" Lindsay asked. "Through CAT?"

"Sure," Calloway answered. "The question is would he be willing to risk having a CAT telephone operator listen in on the calls. He wouldn't be able to speak Chinese to throw anybody off – CAT office workers are all Chinese."

"So what does that leave?" Lindsay wanted to know.

"That's a question I can't answer," Calloway responded. "I can't help feeling we're missing a possibility somewhere, but I'll be damned if I can think of one right now."

"I agree," Lindsay commented, "but this kind of stuff has me on edge, Joe. A couple of months ago I wouldn't have cared about it. Since I met Marion, I've been scared – the kind of scared you get when you think you might not get to spend the rest of your life with the one person you really want to. You know what I mean?"

"Yeah, I do," Calloway nodded. "I was there once, too. Long time ago, long way from here. Like you, I had to keep going, too. But I hung in there, and I survived."

"What happened?" Lindsay asked quietly, not wanting to intrude.

"She was killed in a car wreck three years after we got married," Calloway answered. "But enough of that," he broke the spell and turned toward Lindsay. "What else do we have?"

"Joe," Lindsay looked thoughtfully at his friend, "when I hired on, you said I'd be 'temporary', that you'd hire another pilot to take my place. How's that going?"

"Frankly, Lindsay," Calloway answered, "I've been working on that ever since I sent you and Tiger down to T'aipei. And I'm not having much luck. Like I told Charlie, I can't even find backups for you guys yet."

"Huh? When did Charlie ask about a backup?" Lindsay was surprised.

"Ah," Calloway searched his memory, "your last trip up."

"Funny," Lindsay shook his head, "I didn't think he ever worried about stuff like that."

"Anyway," Calloway changed the subject, "how's Paul doing?"

"A good job," Lindsay responded. "He's contacted all the right people down there. And he seems to get along with them pretty well."

"Good," Calloway smiled to himself. "Paul's a good young man. I think he's got a good future with the company, if he keeps up."

"Yeah," Lindsay agreed. "Well, I guess I'd better get going and let you look through all of your notes, then."

"OK," Calloway replied. "Hey, I may even have to come down and visit you guys on T'aiwan and see what's going on."

"Promises, promises," Lindsay chided. "You keep saying that, and you never show! You just don't want to have to drink our lousy beer!"

"Aw, go give Marion a hug or two," Calloway answered gruffly, a grin starting to show on his face.

* * *

The telephone call was completed. Hamilton had routed the call through the SAT office once again. Kung was sure the counter-intelligence people couldn't trace the calls. It was perfect – Hamilton had the receptionist forward the call, on the pretext of contacting someone about an apartment. Then Kung could talk to the man on the other end without worrying about anyone understanding anything he was saying, even if the Japanese receptionist listened in. It was too bad he hadn't thought of this before.

The man on the other end thanked him, and Kung wondered if they'd be any more successful this trip than the last. It would be better if he didn't have to threaten Chou too many more times. Of course, there were no guarantees a new crew would be more responsive than the current one. On the other hand, maybe he should take a different approach with the new people, offer to cut them in on the profits. Maybe they'd be more successful if they followed that approach.

Of course, it didn't make much difference if the man's contacts eliminated the crew tomorrow night or the next trip or the one after that. Chou would cooperate, and the next delivery was larger than contracted once again, so there'd be another bonus. When the current crew was gone, there'd be a period of training for the new crew, but the larger deliveries would cover that. He'd have to ensure Hamilton accepted only the proper kind of recruits to the program, and the information would have to be kept from Hamilton's other people in Tokyo, especially from Calloway.

Ah, well, enough time to worry about that, later. Tomorrow night was the flight. Perhaps he could get in a little golf tomorrow before he went to talk to Chou in the evening.

* * *

Lindsay glanced at the plane as he left the office. Another trip tonight, he thought. More worry about not being able to get back to Marion.

Somehow, he was going to have to figure out a way to leave this business, but without actually quitting the job he'd promised to do. Maybe he could turn the flying part over to Tiger and Li while he handled the ground end. That might be worth talking over with Calloway on the next trip up to Tokyo.

Lindsay shook his head. Fighter pilots used to have a saying, he remembered – when you started worrying, you were finished. He only wished he was finished with this.

* * *

The *Kempetai* major returned Calloway's call promptly. No, the major explained, the *Kempetai* didn't watch their foreign guests in Japan, even though the old pre-war *Kempetai* had done so. This was a new age, and things were different.

Calloway asked if the major would keep an eye on one of the men in the SAT office, a Mister Hamilton – as a favor to him, of course. Ah, yes, the major agreed, the *Kempetai* could do that. At that point, Calloway told the major he'd probably be notified of the next visit by Mister Hamilton and his client, a Mister Kung.

Ah, yes, the major spoke up, Mister Kung. The *Kempetai* had heard of Mister Kung, through the anti-espionage office of the Nationalist Chinese SID. In fact, they were presently watching for any calls from Mister Kung's department to the telephone where a Communist Chinese was living in Tokyo. One call had been made, and the SID was interested in who might have made the call. No more calls had been made, though, and the *Kempetai* hadn't been able to help the SID any further.

That got Calloway's attention. So somebody in Kung's office called a ChiCom agent in Tokyo? Calloway explained to the major that one call, from an unverified source, wouldn't help in his investigation, but he'd be interested if any further calls were made. The major agreed to notify him. One call, Calloway thought. There must've been others. How else would Kung or one of his people be able to contact somebody to exchange information?

This Communist agent might do business with airlines, the major suggested, since the telephone he used received a lot of calls from them. Wasn't Mister Kung connected to CAT?

Yes, Calloway responded. Mister Kung, in fact, came to Tokyo about twice a month to visit the CAT offices. But, nobody in the SID would be foolish enough to contact a Communist agent through the CAT switchboard because all of the people at the CAT office were Chinese and they might listen in on any conversation. The major agreed, and the conversation came to an end.

Calloway apologized to the major for taking so much of his valuable time, and the major answered he was more than happy to help. And that was that.

Calloway sat back, thinking. Interesting. So somebody in Kung's office could be in touch with a ChiCom agent in Tokyo. The question was why.

Maybe it was a contact point to be tipped off where and when the supplies would be delivered, so the ChiCom Air Force could try to shoot down the plane! But to do that, the agent would have to have last-minute information from T'aiwan on the drop point and time. And that information couldn't be passed in a way so somebody could hear it. And understand it, of course, Calloway reminded himself – hey, anyone could arrange anything he wanted, right in front of Calloway even, if he did it in Chinese!

Oh, hell! Calloway suddenly sat upright. There was part of the answer! Whoever it was didn't have to make a direct call to contact the agent. They could call an office in Tokyo and have them forward the call through their switchboard to wherever the contact was located. When the contact came on the line, the two of them would speak Chinese. The Japanese switchboard operator wouldn't understand what they were saying even if she listened in! But where the hell would someone on T'aiwan call to do that?

OK – he needed to have Anderson find out about calls to anywhere in Japan from Kung's offices. Calloway picked up the phone and Yukiko asked him what number he wanted to call.

TEN

Olson looked forward to getting tonight done. Last mid of the cycle, three days off coming up, and not a peep out of "their guy". If they could get through tonight, he'd win his bet with the shift chief who relieved him in the morning. The bet was he could get through a set of mids without having the plane show up again – he had a coke riding on it. The other shift chiefs joked the plane was working his shift cycle, and it was uncanny how it showed up on his mid shifts. But he only had one more mid to go, and it hadn't shown up yet. His shift was already checked into the watch center, and he was finishing his first cup of coffee for the night and getting ready to make a fresh pot. It wasn't going to happen tonight – he felt confident! He'd win the coke, and that was all there was to it!

Smitty looked up from showing Stu how to operate the light switches on the map. "Hey, Sarge," he called out, "think you'll luck out tonight?" The rest of the shift members knew about the bet, of course.

Olson grinned back. "Sure hope so. I really would like to get out of here in the morning and go home!"

"Fat chance!" Stu piped up. "You can't win, Sarge. You know that! He's been holding off to really screw up your mind, and then he's gonna jump out there tonight!"

"You guys are really on my side, I can tell," Olson laughed. "I think you just want to see me lose!"

"Why Sarge," Smitty laughed, "would we do that?"

"Hey, Sarge," it was Chuck, reading the day's reports, "got one here you might like to see. Looks like Fuchou's got a transport staying overnight."

Olson turned his attention to Chuck. "What's that?" he asked.

"They flew the usual transport into and out of Fuchou today," Chuck noted, "but there was another plane that came in late, probably another transport. It hadn't left by nightfall, according to the report."

"Probably some high muck-e-muck doing a surprise inspection!" Smitty laughed.

"Well," Chuck seemed disappointed, "it's something a little different from the ordinary, anyway."

"You're right, Chuck," Olson came to Chuck's defense, "and, one of these days, noticing little things like that will pay off."

* * *

The plane had lifted off the ground when Hamilton turned to Kung. "Did you get the stuff on board OK?" he wanted to know.

"Sure I did," Kung spoke impatiently. "Did you think I wouldn't?"

"I just never know," Hamilton answered. "I suppose Chou will be a good boy again?"

"He'd better," Kung answered emphatically. "He knows what it'll cost him if he doesn't!"

"How long has he been with you?" Hamilton asked curiously.

"About eight years," Kung answered.

"Hmm," Hamilton spoke up, "long time for a guy to stay on a job he doesn't like."

"He doesn't have a choice," Kung commented. "He doesn't have anywhere else to go. Besides, he owes me."

"Well," Hamilton observed, "he doesn't seem very happy. I'd hate to have to trust him much."

"I said he doesn't have a choice," Kung was irritated with the small talk. "The car's ready. Let's go back to town. We'll have to be back here again in two hours, but there's no reason to stick around until then."

"Sure," Hamilton agreed. "Drop me off at the After Hours Club, as usual, and pick me up there when it's time to come back."

* * *

Here we go again, Lindsay thought. They were almost out of radar range of T'aiwan and that meant it was almost time to drop some altitude.

First things first, of course. Lights off. There wouldn't be anyone else in the air to notice, of course – not at this time of night.

Tiger noticed Lindsay was reaching for the lights. "And here we go again, Colonel!" he observed.

"Yep, gang," Lindsay replied. "It's showtime!"

* * *

"You really don't think he'll show up tonight, do you, Sarge?" Smitty teased.

"Let's put it this way," Olson answered. "If he shows up, I lose a coke. I hope he doesn't, so we can go home in the morning and let somebody else handle the mess on their shift."

"Gee," Chuck chimed in, "that wouldn't be any fun. We wouldn't get to have coffee with the captain or anything!"

"I appreciate that," Olson smiled. "On the other hand, if our guy flies tonight, I owe a coke! Not sure I want to pay up!"

"What?" Stu popped off, "the rich tech sergeant can't afford to buy a coke?"

"Not until the rich tech sergeant gets some of that rich tech sergeant pay!" Olson popped back. "And that doesn't come until the end of the month!" The others laughed.

Suddenly Smitty grabbed the headsets from around his neck. "Oh shit, Sarge!" he spoke up, "I think you just lost your bet!"

The others started laughing, but Smitty turned, his face serious. "No laughing, guys," his voice was serious. "It's for real!"

"Aw, hell!" Chuck grabbed Stu by the arm. "Let's go!" They hurried toward the teletypes.

Smitty reached the back of the map and prepared to mark the first of the plots. "Right in the middle of the province!" he called out, placing the first plot almost centered between the cities of Fuchou and Changchou.

"OK," Olson called out from his usual position. "Stu, catch the coffee. I'm calling the captain!" He reached for the phone.

"On it!" Stu called back.

"Here we go again!" yelled Smitty. "Ya gotta love it!"

* * *

"We've passed Ch'uanchou off the port side," Li announced. "Drop to 35 meters in three seconds, two... one... now!"

"Three five meters, roger," Tiger pushed the nose of the plane downward.

* * *

"He's down on the deck," Smitty announced.

"OK," Olson nodded as he rang the captain's quarters. "Keep an eye on the airfields. No telling what they'll do tonight."

"Back room says Fuchou has activity," Smitty called out. "And another plot on him – he's turned west, getting ready to duck down into the river valley!"

"Captain's on the way!" Olson announced, putting down the phone. "Here we go again. Damn, I hate losing that coke!"

* * *

"Sure hope this one's a milk run," Lindsay muttered to himself, not realizing the microphone was on.

"Ah," Tiger replied. "'Milk run', huh? Let's hope so, sir."

* * *

"Faded out," Smitty announced.

"OK," Olson responded. "Anything more on the fighters out of Fuchou?"

"Nothing here, Sarge," Chuck looked at the teletype units, then turned toward Olson and shrugged his shoulders.

"Sarge," Smitty had a strange look on his face, "back room says the action at Fuchou may be a transport. They say the pilot's using a hand mike. It's not normal fighter equipment."

"Maybe that transport's just taking off," Olson suggested. "Getting ready to head home."

"Could be," Smitty reflected, "but two fifteen in the morning is a weird time to go home! Think I'd stick around until daylight."

"Still nothing out of Fuchou on the teletype," Chuck announced.

"Oh, shit!" Smitty suddenly yelled. "He just used a five-digit callsign!"

"What's that mean?" Stu wanted to know.

"It's a bomber callsign, Stu," Chuck answered. "That's a bomber at Fuchou!"

Smitty cut him off. "Back room says the callsign's from the Il-28 base up at Hangchou."

"Ilyushin," Olson said, "Beagle. Twin-jet light bomber, probably the same category as our guy, except it'll be faster."

"What's faster, Mike?" it was the captain, stepping into the room behind Olson.

"Sir," Olson turned quickly, "Fuchou has a light bomber getting ready to take off in response to our guy. It's an Il-28 Beagle, from Hangchou, according to the back room."

"A bomber to catch a bomber?" the captain asked.

"It could work, sir," Olson noted. "The Beagle's faster than our guy. It's probably got a full crew, and it'll be armed. So it can catch up with our guy and probably fly in about the same speed and mobility ranges."

"Shit!" the captain barked the expletive. "When did this damned bomber come into Fuchou anyway? Anybody know?"

"This afternoon, sir," Olson took his cue from Chuck, who nodded agreement. "A transport aircraft came in and stopped at Fuchou, and it didn't leave."

"Sir," Smitty interjected, "the last three digits of the bomber's callsign were the callsign of that transport."

"And it came in this afternoon?" the captain asked.

"Yes, sir," Chuck responded. "Sergeant Olson and I talked about it when we came in. It was in the evening's report."

"Anyone else think that's strange?" the captain asked.

"What's that, sir?" Smitty questioned.

"You mean strange the Beagle came down today, sir?" Olson was thinking.

"Yeah," the captain responded, "just before our boy made this run tonight. Isn't that a coincidence?"

"Got to be our last mid shift this cycle, sir," Chuck threw in half-jokingly. "That's what it is!"

"No, seriously," the captain continued. "How did the ChiComs know our guy was going to be out tonight? I think it's an information leak. That's the only way it flies in here this afternoon to go out on a mission against our guy now!"

"Damn!" Smitty grabbed the headphones and listened carefully. "The Beagle's lifting off from Fuchou!"

A teletype rattled, and Stu jumped to it. "Got one aircraft lifting off at Fuchou," he called out. "They're calling it a light bomber."

"Not much doubt about that," Olson commented. "What it'll do is the question."

* * *

In the plane, there was enough moonlight so Tiger could see the rise ahead of them.

"Red flag," the radio broke in with a crackle, startling everyone. "There is one red flag... one red flag, at one four zero and two. I repeat, one red flag."

"Red flag?" Tiger glanced at the radio. "What's a red flag?"

Lindsay looked at the radio, a question on his face. "Red flag? That's our callsign, not an identification!"

"Colonel," Li spoke up, "Matsu has no names to identify anything other than fighters. I believe they're trying to tell us this isn't a fighter. And it's at Fuchou."

"What, then?" Tiger wanted to know.

"Hmm," Lindsay nodded, "I think you're right, Li. And I think the reason they call it a red flag is because they know we're a light attack aircraft, and that's what they think it is, also."

"I believe you're right, Colonel," Li nodded back. "They wouldn't call it that if it's a transport. Calling it a red flag means it's like us."

"And that leaves us with either of two types of aircraft," Lindsay spoke up. "The Communists have two light bomber aircraft, the Tupolev Tu-2 Bat and the Ilyushin Il-28 Beagle."

"What's the difference, Colonel?" Li asked.

"The Tu-2's prop-driven," Lindsay answered, "built during the second world war and slower than this plane is. The Il-28 is a jet and faster than we are, but almost as maneuverable. They've probably sent the Ilyushin. And the pilots of that plane are good at night flying – light bombers get lots of it, I understand."

"That doesn't sound good, Colonel," Li observed.

"Actually, it's not bad," Lindsay replied. "The pilots aren't fighter pilots, like we are. So, while they're pretty good at flying their plane, they don't know how to fly their plane like a fighter. On the other hand, Calloway taught Tiger and me to fly this thing exactly like a fighter. No bomber pilot would try the things Calloway taught us to do!"

* * *

"There he is!" Smitty called out as he marked a new plot. "Crossing south of the mountain range, heading into the valley."

"What's the Ilyushin doing?" Olson asked.

"Nothing further since takeoff, Sarge," Chuck responded.

As if to make Chuck a liar, the teletype began chattering. "Oops," Chuck announced, "he's turned to the northwest, heading up the river. Altitude's a thousand meters."

"Doesn't look like he's in any hurry, Captain," Olson looked carefully at the point where Smitty marked the Ilyushin's location.

"He looks like he knows where he's going and when he needs to be there."

* * *

Lindsay could see the way through the valley in the moonlight. "Sure is bright out, with the moon shining."

"It certainly is, sir," Li replied. "I'd feel a lot better if the clouds would give us someplace to hide."

"No cloud anywhere I can see," Lindsay commented. "We didn't expect much, either. The forecast said cold and clear."

"You mean the weatherman was right, for once?" Tiger joked. "What'll happen next?"

Lindsay and Li both laughed, but Lindsay noticed that Li continued to look outside the plane, just in case.

"Chou," Lindsay called out, "please keep your eyes open. We may have another airplane trying to find us tonight."

"OK, Captain," Chou called back.

* * *

"Our guy dropped into the valley behind the mountains," Smitty noted. "He's below radar again. And the Ilyushin's headed up the river." He added another mark to the Il-28's track.

"The Ilyushin's not pushing it, sir," Olson noted. "It's like he knows what he's looking for and where he'll find it."

"Shit!" the captain was not pleased. "I just wish there was some way we could be sure our guy knows the son of a bitch is there!"

* * *

"Roger, five four zero meters," Tiger started the plane climbing, even as it completed the turn. "Gonna go buzz your girlfriend in the village, huh, Li?" he teased.

"She wouldn't know it's us," Li answered. "In fact, she should be asleep now, and she shouldn't even know an airplane went by."

"We could drop her a message," Tiger laughed. "At least let her know you're thinking of her."

"That would be great!" Li laughed back. "The villagers hand Lin a message from me, dropped from an enemy plane!"

"Oops," Tiger agreed. "And we're at five four zero meters."

* * *

"OK," Smitty called out, "he just jumped over the ridge southwest of Shahsien, and he's in the valley between Liench'eng and Nanp'ing. Hmm." He listened to the headsets. "Strip alert fighters are standing by at Liench'eng. But they're not reacting."

"Odd, isn't it?" Olson said to the captain.

"What, Mike?" the captain asked.

"No fighter reaction, sir," Olson answered. "Liench'eng's standing by, and no activity at Fuchou or Changchou. They've all got strip alerts posted, but nobody's flying except the Ilyushin."

"Maybe they don't want anybody in the way," the captain was thoughtful about his answer. "Could get busy if there's a fight and fighters try to jump into it."

"Hmm, guess that's right," Olson agreed. "Still, it's unusual."

"This whole damned business is unusual, Mike!" the captain shook his head.

* * *

"Right to three zero, roger," Tiger echoed, turning the plane. "And, ladies and gentlemen," he announced, "off our left wing we see the village of Shahsien, where the Great Li's lady awaits his return." He grinned, but didn't take his eyes off the flight path ahead. "Sorry, Li, just couldn't contain myself!"

"I'll contain you!" Li laughed at Tiger's joke. "For now, just keep the plane going straight ahead! Let's see if you can fly this thing properly and not wobble all over the valley, OK?" Both of them laughed.

* * *

"The Ilyushin's still ambling along up the valley," Smitty noted as he added another mark to the track. "It's close to Nanp'ing, but it's sure not in any hurry!"

"What's its altitude now, Smitty?" the captain asked.

"It's still at a thousand meters, sir," Smitty answered. "That's been pretty constant."

"And that's pretty low for anyone transiting the area," Olson added.

"Which says he's not transiting, right?" the captain lit another cigarette. "He's looking for our guy, or I miss my guess."

* * *

"Roger, heading one zero," Tiger banked the plane. "Up the valley we go."

"When we finish the drop," Li reminded, "we turn and come back down the valley."

"Right," Tiger acknowledged.

"Opening cargo door," Lindsay called out. "Ready, Chou?"

"Ready, Captain," came Chou's steady response.

* * *

"The Ilyushin's headed west," Smitty called from the map as he put up another plot. "Maybe he's not following the river after all, just heading across the hills there."

"Our guy could be in there now," Olson spoke up.

* * *

"Three seconds to drop point," Li called out.

"See the light!" Tiger called. "There he is!"

"two...," Li counted down, "one... now!"

"It's gone!" called Chou.

"On target!" called Lindsay.

"Good," Tiger spoke up. "Now let's get out of here. Please watch for that other airplane!"

The plane banked hard and turned to reverse its course.

* * *

"The Ilyushin's descending," called Smitty. "Altitude's now 700 meters."

"OK," the captain nodded. "Looks like maybe it's going after our boy?"

"Nothing right now, sir," Smitty answered. "Wait! Back room says it was ordered to descend to 500 meters and start looking for a hostile!"

"Damn!" the captain shook his head. "Knew it was set up. That damn ChiCom had prior knowledge when and where!"

"It hasn't reported seeing anything yet, sir," Olson reminded him. "Our guy could still be somewhere else." The captain gave Olson a skeptical look. "Or," Olson continued, "maybe that's just wishful thinking."

* * *

"Captain!" Chou called out. "There's an airplane high up and behind us! It's silver! It's coming toward us!"

"Damn!" Lindsay was thinking fast. "Tiger, double back and see if he's seen us yet."

"Roger, Colonel!" Tiger threw the plane into the turn.

"It's turning to follow us, Captain!" Chou called.

"Shit!" Lindsay spat out. "He's seen us, then." He began scanning the sky to try to see the other plane.

"It doesn't look like a fighter, Captain," Chou answered. "It seems to have its engines out on the wings, like ours."

"Bomber. 'Red flag'!" Lindsay continued to scan. "Matsu was right." Suddenly he saw the other plane, to their rear. "Ilyushin. It's a jet, faster than we are." He looked at Tiger. "Tiger, us fighter jockeys always think we're ten times better than any bomber jockeys who ever lived. We're going to get to prove it!"

"Colonel," Tiger replied, still looking straight ahead, "the Ilyushin doesn't have missiles or cannon. It has only nose and rear machine guns. That means bullets. It'll take special bullets to kill us!"

"Bullets don't worry about who they kill," Li spoke up. "And we're not armored. Besides," he continued, "these machine guns can be aimed independently of the airplane."

"Yeah," Tiger agreed, "but they've got to get close to fire them! And I don't intend to let them get close!"

"Then you'd better do some magic stuff fast!" Lindsay spoke up. "It's getting ready to come in and feed us a few of those bullets!"

"Ha!" shouted Tiger, "here we go!" The plane turned tightly away from the Ilyushin, just as a spray of tracers announced the machine guns were in business.

* * *

"The Beagle's faded out, but it's attacking!" Smitty called out. "It just reported it sighted the target and is attacking it!"

"Hell," the captain suddenly laughed out loud, "we don't even know if our guy has guns! He might just turn and blast the Ilyushin out of the sky!"

"Don't think so, sir," Olson countered. "We haven't had any

indications of him shooting at the planes that attacked him before this."

"You're right, as usual, Mike," the captain's face fell.

* * *

"It's catching up!" Lindsay called, watching over his shoulder.

"Break left!" Li called out. "Now!"

The plane snapped into a left turn as another stream of tracers flowed through the space they'd just vacated. However, as Lindsay watched, the tracers began to track them, catching up quickly.

"Back to the right!" Lindsay called, and Tiger flipped the plane back toward the right as several rounds hit the plane.

Suddenly, Tiger flipped the plane upward, then rolled it over to come screaming downward, directly into the oncoming Ilyushin. He sent the plane directly over the Ilyushin. The ChiCom pilot, reacting automatically, pushed his plane close to a dive to avoid a collision as the A-26 shot overhead. By the time the Ilyushin could turn, the A-26 was running up the valley the other direction.

* * *

"The Beagle just reported the enemy went right over top of it!" Smitty called out.

"Sounds like some fast and furious flying!" the captain responded. "And they're not far off the ground, either!"

"The Beagle reported it hit the enemy aircraft," Smitty was still relaying from the back room. "But the enemy's outrunning the Ilyushin right now."

"That won't last long," Olson answered.

"Sounds like our guy is quicker than the Ilyushin," the captain observed. "He just doesn't have the flat-out speed."

"Beagle reports it's up to speed and chasing the enemy," Smitty called out. "The enemy is down low and dodging around trees."

"OK," Olson nodded agreement.

"Beagle reports it's catching up," Smitty added.

* * *

"The enemy's closing in on us again," Chou called.

"Damn!" Tiger shouted. "Got to reach that stand of trees!"

"He's shooting!" Chou called out.

The plane fishtailed wildly as Tiger tried to avoid the bullets from the Ilyushin. In a moment, the plane reached the trees and dodged around the side while the Ilyushin climbed to cross over. Tiger immediately turned away from the trees and reversed direction. The Ilyushin continued across the stand of trees. When the A-26 didn't appear on the far side, it took a moment before the pilots realized the A-26 had turned and was flying back down the valley once again.

"The enemy's turning!" Chou called out.

"We've got to reach the rise over there!" Tiger aimed the A-26 down the valley. "It's the only place where I can try to scrub him off!"

* * *

"They're still at it," Smitty spoke up, concentrating on the headsets. "The Beagle's having a hard time nailing our guy down. Our guy doesn't want to stand still!"

"Must be a fighter pilot flying ours," the captain offered. "Bomber pilots don't know how to wiggle like that!"

"Could be, sir," Olson spoke up.

* * *

"Here he comes over the trees!" Lindsay could see the Ilyushin. "Firewall it, Tiger!"

"Kick it, Colonel!" Tiger yelled. "Make it go faster!"

"Going as fast as it can!" Lindsay called back.

"No it's not!" shouted Tiger. "But it will!" With that, he pulled back on the yoke, sending the plane up into the sky. The Ilyushin, behind them, also climbed, but not as quickly.

"He doesn't have our rate of climb!" Lindsay suddenly realized the Ilyushin was underpowered.

"Yes, sir," Tiger responded, "but he's got more time to get up than we do. We have to use our altitude build-up to gain speed better than he can!" With that, he drove the nose of the A-26 into a screaming dive toward the earth below.

* * *

"There he is!" Smitty shouted. "There's one of 'em! Oops! Faded off!"

"Our guy," the captain shook his head. "The Beagle wouldn't climb out like that and then just drop back down."

"Well," Olson said, "he's still alive! But why did he dive back down?"

"He's trading altitude for speed," the captain answered thoughtfully. "The Ilyushin can't climb as fast as he can. But it's faster on the level."

* * *

"We're going to make it!" Tiger shouted above the scream of the plane.

"Yeah!" Lindsay shouted back, "right into that damned ridge! It's dead ahead!"

"The enemy's right behind us!" Chou shouted from the rear. His voice was cut off by the sound of bullets striking the plane, and Lindsay felt a hard sting in his left shoulder!

Just then, Tiger flipped the plane up and to the left, barely in time to clear the ridge. The Ilyushin, still firing, tried desperately to turn, but couldn't. It crashed directly into the ridge, throwing a fireball upward and outward.

"It's gone!" Li called out.

"So are we!" Tiger replied. "That last burst killed our number one engine and number two's losing oil pressure." He fought to control the dying plane. "It won't last another two minutes. Dumbass ChiCom! He killed himself to get us!"

"Keep it flying, Tiger," Lindsay managed to speak through the pain in his shoulder. "Get us out of here."

"I'll get us as far as I can, Colonel," Tiger answered. "After that, I think Li needs to take over!"

"I don't think he heard you, Tiger," Li was bending over Lindsay. "He's been hit!"

"Oh, no!" Tiger's pain was obvious. "He's got to be OK, Li!"

"He's just passed out," Li answered. "Get this thing down safely, as far away from that crash as you can. I'll do the rest."

* * *

"Nothing more," Smitty shrugged. "Back room hasn't heard anything more from the Ilyushin, sir."

"I'd say there's a plane down over there," the captain looked a little uncertain. "Maybe more than one."

ELEVEN

Lindsay came to. The plane was stopped. There was a lot of dust in the air, but no fire.

Lindsay checked himself. Damn! His left shoulder hurt! But nothing else did, and the shoulder told him he was alive. The others! The thought jumped into his mind and he reached to unbuckle the harness. His left arm wouldn't raise to reach the buckle. Just have to do it with his right hand, then, he thought. And then an arm reached across him and Li undid the belt.

"Looks like you were hit in the shoulder, Colonel," Li's voice was steady. "It's probably broken. We'll have to put your arm in a sling."

"How's Tiger?" Lindsay asked.

"He's fine," Li replied. "He was out of his seat about the same time I was. He didn't look like anything was wrong, so I sent him back to check on Chou to get him out of the way."

"That's Tiger for you," Lindsay tried to joke. "Take away his airplane and he goes hyper!"

"Frankly, sir," Li continued, "I really wanted to check your condition without having him right behind me! You were unconscious, and I couldn't tell anything at that point. But it looks like I didn't need to worry."

"Not sure when I passed out," Lindsay gritted as pain shot through the shoulder again. "But I remember the plane being hit."

"Well," Li helped Lindsay up, "the enemy signed his death warrant with the last burst. He could've turned away, but he flew into the side of the ridge."

"Li! I need you back here!" Tiger called from the rear of the plane. "Hurry, please!"

"Coming!" Li replied and turned toward the back, Lindsay behind him. In a moment, both men were at the back of the plane, where Tiger was bent over a bloody Chou.

"Li!" Chou groaned, "Is the captain OK?"

"I'm here, Chou!" Lindsay responded from behind Li. He stepped around into Chou's view.

"Oh, Captain," Chou's face was a mask of self-torment, "I failed you! I brought all of this down on us." He caught his breath in large sobs. "And now we'll die because of it."

"Chou, what're you talking about?" Lindsay asked firmly. "We're alive and we're going to stay alive!"

"Oh, Captain," Chou sobbed, "I'm dying. I feel the cold coming in my arms and legs."

Lindsay looked at Li, and Li shook his head in return. Tiger nodded toward Li in agreement and pointed a finger toward his stomach, indicating Chou had been hit in a vital place.

"Chou," Lindsay held his voice steady, "you're not to blame."

"Oh yes, Captain, I am!" the man insisted. "I dropped the opium. I made the Communists come after us. It's all my fault!" He sobbed again.

"Opium?" Lindsay's mind raced. "What opium are you talking about?"

"The opium in the packages," Chou spoke between sobs. "The packages Mister Kung gave me to drop. The one I opened contained opium! I know it because the women in the whorehouse used it sometimes. I couldn't say anything because Mister Kung threatened to tell the police."

Opium! Lindsay was livid. It wasn't morphine, then. And damn Kung for forcing Chou to do it! But there were other things to worry about now.

"Chou," Lindsay spoke with as much strength as he could muster, "it wasn't your fault. The Communists wouldn't have known where to find us if they hadn't been told where we'd be. Hamilton and Kung were the only ones who knew where we'd be and when we'd be there, and they were the only ones who could give the information to the Communists."

"Captain, I dropped the drugs," Chou continued to sob. "It's my fault."

"Chou, I'm your captain and I'm telling you, you did nothing wrong," Lindsay made the pronouncement. "Kung forced you to drop the drugs, and it's not your fault. It's Kung's fault. Now, you need to rest, because we have to leave the plane. You're part of our crew, and we won't leave you behind. What's happened is the fault of a couple of greedy men, and not your fault. You're our friend, Chou, and we won't leave you."

Chou's face calmed and the sobbing stopped. "I won't go any further with you," he said, "but thanks for being my friends." With that, he closed his eyes, and his breathing became shallower with each breath. In moments, it ceased.

"He's gone, Colonel," Li's hand touched Lindsay's right shoulder.

"I know," Lindsay answered. "I just hope we get to nail the bastard who caused it."

"There must be a lot of money in this, Colonel," Li commented as he lifted Chou's lifeless body, "to cause men to be so willing to kill others."

"Maybe the best term would be 'greed', Li," Lindsay replied. "The amount of money may not be important. But let's make sure Chou has a proper burial," he turned to the tasks at hand. "Then, we've got to get away from here as soon as we can." The speech brought another surge of pain and Li stopped him.

"Colonel, let me bandage that shoulder," Li asked. "We've got time. We're far enough away from anywhere that no one will come looking for us, probably until daylight."

"OK," Lindsay gave in, since the shoulder was hurting more. "But let's make it quick. We need to be a long way from here by morning."

"We will, Colonel," Li assured him. "And in a direction they won't expect." The plan was forming in Li's mind – not only would they escape, but they'd take care of a few loose ends while they were at it.

* * *

In the alert center, Olson stared at the map. There wasn't any more activity.

"Another one?" he looked at the captain. "Two fighters and now a light bomber?"

"I don't know," the captain lit another cigarette. "He may have met his match this time."

"Well," Olson breathed out gently, "the valley's not that big. He should be popping up before long."

"If he survived," the captain added.

"We should know pretty soon, sir," Olson continued. "Less than five minutes."

"I don't think he's coming," the captain turned away from the map with a drop of his shoulders. Suddenly, he stopped and looked up. "Mike, I'm not sure how we're going to brief this one to the general, but I'll bet it'll be hot and heavy in there this morning! We need to be ready!"

"I think we will be, sir," Olson replied evenly.

* * *

The shoulder was hurting badly. Lindsay grimaced as Li finished pouring sulfa into the wound and bound up the bandages. Good thing he couldn't see the wound, Lindsay thought. It could put him into worse shock than he was already in. He didn't need to be any more of a burden on Tiger and Li than necessary.

Tiger was outside the plane, digging quickly with an entrenching tool from the emergency gear. Chou would have a shallow grave, but he was a part of their crew and they wouldn't leave him to be buried by strangers.

Lindsay stood up, his arm now in a sling. The pain was still strong, but it had subsided. He no longer felt the nausea he'd experienced after the adrenaline had worn off. He exited the plane through the gaping wound that had been the upper rear window. Tiger helped him with the last step.

"Colonel," Tiger was calmed, "sit down and rest. Li's getting our things, and we'll finish Chou's grave and be on our way." He pointed toward a faint glow beyond the hills. "You can see where the Ilyushin crashed."

"Which way's the coast?" Lindsay asked.

"I'm not sure," Tiger answered, "but Li's been here, so he knows the way. Besides," he grinned, "we have compasses in our survival gear."

In moments, Li was out of the plane, carrying the bags. He came over to where Tiger and Lindsay sat.

"I brought Chou's bag, too," Li said. "It may be added weight, but it has extra medicine and some currency we can use. Tiger," he asked, "how much more digging do we need to do?"

"Not much," Tiger responded, showing Li the hole he'd made.

"That looks fine," Li spoke up, turning toward Chou's body. "Let's get rid of these flight fatigues, say farewell to our friend, and be on our way!"

* * *

"It's been half an hour, Captain," Olson said. "We need to wrap it up. There'll be transports out looking for the wreckage in the morning, sir, and we'll need to have that ready for the general, too."

"We won't wait until then, Mike," the captain stood up. "Let's get on the phone now and let him and the colonel know what's happened, especially the part about the Il-28 being in the area, and then we may be able to delay the wrap-up so we can have some words on what's happened."

"Sounds good, sir," Olson turned toward the phone. "You want me on the other phone again?"

"You'd better believe I do!" the captain grinned at him. "It's your turn to keep *me* from getting raked over the coals!"

* * *

Li used one of the uprooted tea bushes to obliterate the signs of their digging. As they finished, Lindsay bowed his head for a moment and asked his own God to have mercy on Chou and give him the peace he deserved, then turned to see both Tiger and Li standing with bowed heads, too. Then the three men started out, Li leading the way.

They hadn't gone far when Lindsay realized he could see the stars, and the North Star was behind them, not to their left. They weren't headed eastward, toward the coast, but southward, toward another range of hills!

"Li!" Lindsay called out, "is there a reason why we're not headed for the seacoast?"

"Yes, Colonel," Li replied. "First of all, we're going to confuse the enemy by not going where he expects. Second, we'll find a friend of mine -."

"The girl!" Tiger interjected. "She lives just over those hills, doesn't she?"

"Yes, Tiger," Li answered. "We can use her help getting to the seacoast, and I'll keep my promise to take her to T'aiwan!"

"Is that safe, Li?" Lindsay asked.

"I think so, Colonel," Li responded. "Unless she's changed, she doesn't like the Communists. They mistreated her."

"But will she assist a foreign devil and one of the hated *Kuomintang*?" Lindsay wanted to know. "She may not want to help either of us, regardless of her feelings about you."

"Colonel, I can't say for sure," Li answered truthfully. "But, even if she won't help us, she won't give me away to the Communists – I'm willing to bet my life on that!"

"Then I guess we'll go along with your bet," Lindsay turned to Tiger. "Any objections?"

"None," Tiger answered simply. "I don't think we have any better alternatives. Besides," a grin crept onto his face again, "I want to meet this girl who ran all over the mainland with Li. She's got to be pretty special!"

* * *

The general and the colonel listened quietly to the entire report over the conference call, not breaking in once to ask a question. Finally, when the captain finished, the general spoke up. "Sergeant Olson, is that how you saw it?"

"Yes, sir," Olson answered.

"OK," the general sounded thoughtful for a moment. "Guys, I want you both to stay there until we can get there, OK? And then," he went on, "I need somebody I can trust to stay on top of it until it's over. Will you do that for me, both of you?"

"Yes sir," Olson answered. "This is my last mid shift this cycle. I just need to let my wife know about it."

"No trouble for me, sir," the captain answered.

"OK, guys," the general sounded relieved. "Thanks. The colonel and I will be at my office by seven. I'll call after the staff meeting to see how things are going. OK?"

"Fine by me, sir," Olson responded.

"I guess I'm going to miss the afternoon golf game," the captain grinned as he chided the general. "That may be the only way you guys will beat me, sir!"

"Well, Bill," the general laughed, "We'll take you any way we can! And thanks, guys. I'll talk to you later."

* * *

They had to stop frequently. Lindsay was still losing blood, and the pain wore on his reserve of strength. Li made him drink lots of water. But they'd reached the base of the ridge when Lindsay suddenly stumbled and sat down on the ground, his head hanging down.

"No further," he gasped. "Got to rest before I can go any further."

Li spotted a stand of trees nearby. He half-carried Lindsay there, followed by an anxious Tiger.

"We'll stop here," Li spoke quietly.

Lindsay dropped to the ground and fell fast asleep.

Tiger spoke up. "Will he be OK? Can he make it?"

"He'll be fine," Li responded. "And he'll make it. We've got to be patient and careful, but it won't be hard to get away."

* * *

"Captain," Olson spoke up, "we're coming up on deadline for the ops report, sir. Do you want to release it, or would you rather I do it?"

"Hey, Sarge," Smitty broke in, "the controller quit calling that Il-28. But at least two Il-28s are going through comms checks at Hangchou. They'll probably take off at daylight."

"Let's get the report out then," the captain took it from Olson. "I'll deliver it to the comm center, Mike. You keep an eye on things here."

"OK, sir," Olson agreed. "And I'd better call the wife and let her know I'll be late again."

"Will this cause a problem, Mike?" the captain asked.

"Only if hugging your wife to let her know she's number one in your life is a problem, sir," Olson answered with a grin. "I get to do a lot of that when I work late."

"Then I guess it sure won't," the captain chuckled as he left the room.

* * *

"So you think," Tiger asked, "we should be off the mainland within a week, then?"

"I'd rather make it quicker, maybe only two days," Li said. "But we can't sustain that speed with the colonel. Lin won't slow us. She'll keep up."

"Well, I have to admit," Tiger grinned, "she's made an impression on you, and that speaks for itself!"

"And now," Li waved toward the sleeping colonel, "we've got to wake the colonel and get him to the top of the ridge before sunrise, so we can hide before daylight. This valley will be busy when the sun comes up."

"If you'll take first shift with the colonel," Tiger volunteered, "I'll take the bags." With that, he lifted the bags and swung them over his shoulder.

"Why, Tiger," Li looked at him with feigned surprise. "I believe some of that strength training's actually rubbed off on you!"

"*I'll* rub off on *you* if we don't get going," Tiger growled. "These damned things are heavy!"

* * *

The captain returned from the comm center. "When will those Il-28s start hunting for the wreckage, Mike?" he asked.

"They should be in the area by daylight, sir," Olson answered.

"OK," the captain looked at his watch, "that gives us about two hours before things start up again. Maybe you can lay down on a desk and catch some sleep. Smitty can keep an eye on everything." He turned toward Smitty. "Will that be OK?"

"Sure, sir," Smitty answered.

"Good," the captain smiled. "The general asked us to stick around and brief him, probably around eight-thirty. We'll let sarge get a nap. Today may last awhile."

"OK, sir," Smitty nodded. "We've got it. Good luck to sarge on sleeping on those desks, though! They're not built for sleeping, more for keeping you awake."

* * *

The climb to the crest wasn't easy. Li worked hard to keep Lindsay from falling, while Tiger cursed as he stumbled a time or two himself. Finally, Li took the bags from Tiger and had him help Lindsay, at which point Tiger found a few other things to curse.

They finally reached the crest of the ridge. Standing on the crest, Li could see the village of Shahsien. He smiled. He'd been here before.

They needed a place to stop and rest through the coming day. One of the caves along the ridge would do nicely. Tonight, after sundown, he'd descend to the village. He should be able to find Lin readily. The hard part would be getting her away. If he only had letterhead paper with the provincial seal, it would be easy to forge a letter to have her leave with him. Without the letterhead, he'd have to tell the villagers the papers were on the way from Fuchou because he had to come get her in a hurry, and then hope they'd allow her to leave. Unfortunately, the villagers would eventually have to explain why they let Lin leave without paperwork. Too bad, but it couldn't be helped.

Enough of that, though. He needed to fix the bandage on Lindsay's shoulder, and then rest. The cave he was looking for was only a few yards away.

* * *

"Captain," it was Olson. "Time to wake up, sir. Not long now until the Il-28s should arrive in the area where the planes went down."

"OK, Mike," the captain lifted his head. "Coffee?"

"It's ready, sir," Chuck was behind Olson. "Here's your cup."

"Thanks," the captain smiled back before taking a sip. "What's going on?" he looked toward Smitty as he pulled a cigarette from his pocket and lit it.

"There's four of 'em coming, sir," Smitty answered.

* * *

They were safe in the cave, Li knew. The others had eaten and were sleeping while Li stood the first watch. It was sunrise; the enemy search planes would be here soon. They'd find the wreckage of the Il-28 quickly, since there'd be smoke rising from it. The A-26 would be harder to find, though.

Li knew they wouldn't have to worry about the People's Liberation Army, the PLA, trying to catch them. The deputy governor, Chang, had confined the PLA to their bases while Li was on the mainland earlier. The provincial militia would try, but Li knew they couldn't do the job. So long as the enemy chasing them was only the militia, they wouldn't have tracking experts, and Li was sure they probably wouldn't do anything more than try to cover the coastline.

In the meantime, evening was coming soon, and he'd be able to contact Lin.

* * *

"There's broken clouds at about a thousand meters," Smitty

called out. "Back room says cloud cover's eighty to ninety percent."

"They'll have to stay below the clouds," the captain commented. "Otherwise, they can't see. That's pretty low to cover a lot of area quickly."

"Sir," Smitty called out, "back room says the Il-28s are being directed to break formation. Their controller's giving them a heading and separation distances. They're being deployed in a group pattern."

"May be easier on the controllers," the captain noted wryly, "but not the aircrews. The pilots have to work hard trying to keep distances and headings."

"Communists won't let them take any initiative, sir," Olson responded. "Too much chance they'll take it and run away."

"Yeah," the captain nodded, "I guess that's so."

"They're formed up, sir," Smitty announced, "and starting their first sweep."

* * *

Tiger and Lindsay were asleep at the rear of the cave, and Li was close to the front, watching the mouth. His chance to sleep would come later. For now, it wasn't difficult to stay awake and think of seeing Lin again.

A shadow passed over the mouth of the cave. The sound of jet engines followed. A plane was passing above the ridge. Perhaps later he'd go out to the top of the ridge and look back into the valley they'd left behind.

* * *

Six forty. Olson was startled as the new shift came into the center.

"Hey, Mike," the oncoming shift chief greeted him. "Time for break!"

"Afraid not, Al," Olson answered. "I have to stick around. We had a real night of it, and it's not over yet."

"What happened?" Al asked, and Olson explained it quickly. "Wow, man, I win the coke! You think they got him, though?"

"He didn't come out," Olson answered. "Back room hasn't reported any search results yet, but four Beagles are flying patterns."

"Got a sighting!" As if to contradict Olson, Smitty called out. "One of the Il-28s reports a crash site on a hillside." He hesitated, then added, "Now it's confirmed."

"Any indication what kind of aircraft?" Olson asked.

"Nothing, Sarge," Smitty responded. "There's smoke coming up from it, though. One of them reports seeing a silver wing and engine."

"It crashed and burned," the captain interjected. "No survivors."

"Silver wing?" Olson asked. "Captain, that first MiG pilot said the plane was black! Remember, we briefed that."

"Yeah, he did," the captain remembered. "They've found the Il-28, then."

"Looks like it to me, sir," Olson nodded. He turned to Smitty. "Any idea where they found it?"

"Nothing yet, Sarge," Smitty called back. "Hey, Al," he added, "can I stay on the headsets with Tony? This is too good to miss!"

* * *

Li made his way to the crest of the ridge, where he lay under a bush and looked down into the valley they'd left the night before. He quickly picked out four silver airplanes, flying where smoke was rising into the air. That, he thought, is where the Ilyushin crashed.

Looking down into the valley, he noted patches of fog. It was going to be difficult for the Communists to find their airplane.

Li rolled over and looked the other direction. He could clearly see the village of Shahsien. He was pleased at the thought of seeing Lin tonight.

* * *

Calloway peeled off his jacket. A cup of coffee and he'd be ready to start the day, looking over some more new candidates for the crew. He was supposed to have lunch with a guy from personnel, and then an afternoon of working on a list of parts. Another routine day.

He hadn't gotten to the coffeepot when Yukiko caught up with him.

"Oh, Mister Calloway!" she was crying. "Mister Hamilton just called. They didn't return from the flight last night."

"Where's Hamilton now?" Calloway asked.

"He called from his office," Yukiko replied tearfully, "and said you should call him there."

"Damn!" Calloway's upset was obvious. "What's the number, anyway?"

"I have it, sir," Yukiko answered. "Let me dial it."

"Let me get a cup of coffee, OK?" Calloway shook his head. "And where's Marion?"

"She's in the ladies' room, sir," Yukiko sobbed. "Do you want her?"

"Not just yet," Calloway was thinking as he spoke. "Be ready to get her when I get off the phone, though, OK? Maybe I'll be able to tell you something then."

"Yes, sir," Yukiko turned. "I'll get the telephone number and start the call."

* * *

Olson was glad he'd gotten a chance to nap. The coffee was helping, but a long set of mid shifts was ended, and his body wanted more rest.

"Back room reports military people on the ground near the crash site, sir," Tony reported. "The aircraft crews are trying to guide them to the site."

"Thanks, Tony," the captain replied.

"Sir," Smitty broke in, "the back room thinks the ground people aren't PLA."

"More of that stuff about the PLA being restricted to base?" Olson turned toward the captain. "Sir, a report came out a few months ago that said PLA troops in the province were restricted to base because of clashes with the local militia."

* * *

"Damn, Charlie!" Calloway was upset. "We've got a crew down over there! What kind of communications do they have, anyway?"

"They've got radios," Hamilton responded. "There was a tactical radio in each survival bag!"

"Oh, crap!" Calloway barked. "Those things can't transmit thirty miles! Have you sent anything on their frequency?"

"Well, no -" Hamilton was taken aback. "I don't have any equipment, and I didn't think anyone would be alive!"

"Until we know different, Charlie," Calloway asserted, "we assume all of them survived."

"Look, Joe -," Hamilton started, but Calloway didn't give him a chance to continue.

"Charlie, I'm on my way down," Calloway cut in. "I need to talk to the American military advisory people. I need to talk to somebody in the watch center at T'aipei Air Station, too. I want you to get hold of a guy named Art Ramsey at the embassy and tell him I'm coming."

"Hey, Joe!" Hamilton protested. "Hold on, here! I -."

"Charlie!" Calloway cut him off. "Call Art and tell him I'm on my way down and I'll see him when I get there. OK?"

"Hey, I -." Hamilton started to protest again.

"Just do it, OK?" Calloway insisted. "Look, Buchanan's going to call you in just a bit, and ask you what you've done. Now save yourself the embarrassment of having to tell him you haven't done shit and call the embassy, you hear me?" With that, Calloway slammed the phone down on its receiver and immediately yanked it up again. "Yukiko!" he yelled out the open door.

Yukiko was on the line instantly. "Yes, Mister Calloway!" she answered.

"Get me Mister Buchanan, please," Calloway was in a hurry. Buchanan was the SAT director for Special Ops.

"This is Buchanan," Buchanan's voice sounded directorial.

"Jesus, Dan," Calloway winced, "you sound like a frigging executive!"

"What do you want, Joe?" Buchanan asked. They knew each other well.

"I've got a problem," Calloway answered. "I'm working the A-26 project with Charlie Hamilton, we've got the plane down in a bad place, and he's freezing up. Can you convince him to help out?"

"Sure," Buchanan responded. "You sound like you're in a hurry, so I'll wait for the after-action to find out what it's all about. What do I need to do, lean on him?"

"A little anyway, Dan," Calloway answered. "I want him to make some contacts for me and get some things started. Oh, and

I'm taking the company plane, too. I'll need your signature for that, I guess."

"OK," Buchanan agreed. "Your secretary have the number to call?"

"Nope," Calloway answered, "but the receptionist does. Let me talk to her for a minute and then she'll help you. I'll have her call when she's back on the switchboard."

"OK," Buchanan responded. "If there's anything more you need, let me know. And get the mess fixed, OK?"

"I'll try," Calloway replied, "and you sign the paperwork for the money, OK?" Calloway hung up the phone. "Yukiko!" he called, "please get Marion and the two of you come in here!"

* * *

"Four of them are still orbiting where the Il-28 crashed, General," the captain explained. "Sergeant Olson found a report about regular troops being confined to their bases and everything like this being handled by the militia."

"OK," the general answered. "In the meantime, though, you have no idea what happened to the other plane?"

"No, sir," the captain replied. "The terrain in that area is rough and steep."

"Sir," Olson broke in, "There's no report of other smoke, and they've made a complete sweep of the valley. I'd say the penetrator probably made a crash landing, and we could have survivors on the ground."

"Hmm, Sarge," the general was thinking, "is there any way we could contact survivors?"

"Sir," Olson answered frankly, "I don't think so. If they use the radio, the ChiComs can find them easily. They know that, too!"

"Then we're looking for a needle in a haystack?" the general asked.

"Worse than that, sir," Olson answered. "The needle doesn't want to be found by the wrong people, so it'll hide from us, too."

"OK," the general said, "let me come out there. I want to see a map where all this has happened. Maybe we can come up with some other ideas at the same time. I'll be there in about twenty minutes."

"Yes, sir," the captain answered.

* * *

Both women had been crying. Calloway understood, but there wasn't time for sympathy.

"Look," he spoke, "I'm sorry the guys went down. I understand how you feel, but I'm convinced they survived. And we've got a lot to do to get them back."

Marion looked at Calloway in surprise.

"I've already got permission to go to T'aiwan to get together a rescue effort," he went on.

"Joe," Marion asked, "what makes you think they survived?"

"Because I know how they fly an airplane," Calloway answered. "Now, I have to get to T'aiwan and I need your help to get there so I can find out where they are and how I can get them out."

"What do we need to do?" Marion asked.

"First," Calloway replied, "tell the crew of the company plane to get ready to head for T'aiwan. Next, I need money and travel orders, and I need to have my clearance sent to Art Ramsey at the embassy. And I've got to go pack. So I'll head for my place, and let the two of you do the rest. Don't worry," he stopped any questions, "I've already cleared taking the plane with Mister Buchanan. Just hand him the paperwork, Marion. And Yukiko, please help him call Charlie Hamilton, OK?"

"Sure, Joe," Marion answered. "I'll go ahead and set up the flight." She turned to Yukiko. "Yukiko, after you finish with Mister Buchanan's call, please cut a travel requisition to get Mister Calloway money for the trip. I'll take it to Mister Buchanan when I take the plane authorization to him and he can sign both at the same time." The two women started out the office door, making plans to support Calloway's trip.

Calloway thought to himself, yes, the guys survived. A visit to the watch center at T'aipei Air Station would help confirm it. Ramsey would have things set up by the time he got there.

And now he'd better quit lollygaging! He had a crew down on the mainland with a lot of work ahead to get them out of there!

* * *

The general and his staff crowded into the room.

"Gentlemen!" Olson started. "May I have your attention please? General, would you please step toward the map?"

The crowd quieted as the general joined Olson.

"Morning, Sarge," the general nodded, then turned. "Folks, let's give Sergeant Olson our attention and find out what he has to say."

"Thank you, sir," Olson continued. "As we told you earlier, we had another penetration of mainland airspace last night. As you know, the Communists have responded by sending aircraft in reaction. This time, however, they sent up an Ilyushin Il-28 Beagle, a light bomber."

The crowd gasped with excitement.

"The penetrator entered ChiCom airspace here," Olson pointed toward the map. "He dropped below radar coverage here," he pointed out the location. "At about the same time, we picked up reflection of an aircraft taking off from Fuchou. We thought it was a transport that flew into Fuchou late yesterday and hadn't returned. However, we soon determined it was a light bomber, using a callsign from the Il-28 unit at Hangchou."

The general's face suddenly became quizzical. "Sarge," he started, "you know what that means?"

"Yes, sir," Olson replied. "The ChiComs had prior knowledge of the penetration. After the Il-28 took off from Fuchou, it flew up the valley at an altitude that indicated it wasn't transiting. That's here," Olson pointed out the location. "In the meantime, the penetrator eventually dropped into this valley, where the river runs toward Nanp'ing. Finally, we believe the penetrator entered the valley to the north before the Il-28 suddenly turned and crossed into the same valley. Shortly after that, it was ordered to attack. We know that neither aircraft left the valley, and the Ilyushin's controller called it for some time after that. This morning, we've had information that confirms the Ilyushin crashed, probably with no survivors, but the ChiComs haven't found the penetrator yet."

"What kind of search efforts are the ChiComs putting up?" one of the colonels asked.

"Hold on, Jimmy," the general spoke to the colonel. "You finished, Sergeant Olson?" the general turned back.

"That's all for now, sir," Olson nodded.

"OK, guys," the general looked toward the others, "questions are one at a time. Jimmy, you got yours in first."

"Sir," Olson turned, "four Beagles from Hangchou were in the crash area by sunrise. They found the Ilyushin almost immediately. A second group of four Beagles flew several sweeps of the valley with no sighting of the penetrator. They were in the area for about an hour, and were relieved by a third group of four Beagles, which is now sweeping the area. Four more Beagles are coming in right now. No one's spotted the penetrator. And ground forces haven't reached the crash site yet."

"How do you know the crash site's the Ilyushin and not the penetrator?" a man in civilian clothes asked.

"The first group of Beagles reported seeing a silver engine and part of a wing, sir," Olson replied. "The penetrator was black."

"Why haven't the search aircraft been able to find the penetrator, Sarge?" another officer asked.

"There's low cloud and light fog in the area, sir," Olson responded. "It's hard to see a dark aircraft with the shadows, especially with poor light. The Ilyushins have to stay at low altitudes under the clouds, and they haven't covered all of the ground yet."

"Sarge," one of the officers spoke up, "do we have any idea what happened to the crew?"

"No sir," Olson answered. "At this point, we know as little as the ChiComs do about the location or status of the aircraft or the crew. The aircraft apparently didn't burn, so there's a chance the crew could have gotten out alive."

"Sarge," a senior Army officer was next, "you said no ground effort had reached the crash site. Can you elaborate on that?"

"Yes, sir," Olson replied. "We've had reports the PLA is restricted to its bases, and this operation is under control of the provincial militia. They're not well equipped or trained, and we think they also had to start a long way from the site. We do expect them to reach the site within the next hour."

With that question answered, the group seemed to wait for the general to take the next step. He did.

"Sergeant Olson, thank you for an outstanding briefing," the general spoke up. "If you have no further questions, gentlemen," he addressed the group, "then we can break this up. We'll have a briefing here this afternoon at sixteen-hundred. Please call my secretary by fifteen-thirty to confirm it. That's it, then, and thanks for coming."

Dismissed, the officers began to leave the room. Several turned to look at the situation map once more, and some shook their heads in disbelief.

"We'll all be back here this afternoon," the general spoke to Olson and Captain Armstrong. "Looks like we won't be able to play golf this afternoon, Bill."

"Hell, General," Captain Armstrong shook his head, "it's supposed to rain today, anyway."

* * *

Lindsay awoke with dull, heavy pain in his left shoulder. He turned his head – where were Li and Tiger?

"Good afternoon, Colonel," it was Li's voice, soothing. "How are you feeling, sir?"

"Like I've got a hot poker in this shoulder," Lindsay growled.

"Would you like some tea, sir?" Tiger asked. "It's even hot! We started a fire," he explained. "The clouds settled in around us and nobody can see the smoke."

"Anybody looking for us?" Lindsay asked. "And have they found the plane?"

"The Communist planes found it about noon," Li answered. "The clouds settled in at about two o'clock. At that point, the ground people were a long way down the valley from it, and wouldn't get there soon." A frown crossed his face. "The ground forces aren't regular PLA troops, Colonel," he commented. "I doubt they're anywhere near the wreckage yet."

"Where are we now?" Lindsay asked. "Didn't we cross a ridge before we found this cave?"

"That's right, sir," Li answered. "We're near the top of the ridge south of our plane. Below us is the village of Shahsien. I'm going to contact my friend there tonight. In the meantime, we'll be safe on the ridge, even if the soldiers come this way."

"OK," Lindsay agreed. "The shoulder hurts, but it won't stop me from helping. You obviously have a plan, Li, and that's better than anything I have. So let me know what I can do."

"Glad you're back on your feet, Colonel," Tiger said, "but don't hurry things, OK? Just let your strength build up and be ready to move."

"Right, sir," Li seconded Tiger's words. "We're not in a hurry. We can survive for several weeks before we begin to run low on supplies."

"OK," Lindsay nodded. "Have you tried to establish comms? Radio, specifically?"

"No, sir," Tiger answered. "We're too far inland to make contact. You gave Hamilton a set of frequencies to use for messages if we went down, but I'm not sure he could find a radio strong enough to reach us."

"He could," Lindsay responded. "OK, though, first things first. Let's get an antenna strung and one of our radios turned on to receive. Use the primary frequency we set up with Hamilton, Tiger. Next," he turned toward Li, "my left arm's useless, but that doesn't mean I am, Li. So I can do things to help, and I expect you to let me know what, OK?"

"Yes, sir," Li hadn't expected the colonel to recover from the wound so quickly. "We can use your help, sir, especially at making wise decisions. And we can use your help in organizing our travel."

"Well," Lindsay was amused at Li's discomfort, "that's better than just being a drag on you guys, I guess!" He needed to stay busy. If he didn't, it would be too easy to let down to the pain and feel sorry for himself. And that could only lead to a downward spiral in his physical and spiritual strength. He couldn't allow that if he was going to make it back to Marion.

* * *

Calloway sat back in the soft seat of the company plane. It wasn't often he got to ride in the back.

Marion and Yukiko had put things together quickly, and he was on his way as soon as he arrived at the airport. Hamilton had called just before Calloway left the office and said he'd contacted Ramsey. It was a six-hour flight to T'aiwan, and he'd get there late, but at least he was on his way. Maybe he'd be early enough to have dinner with Art.

Calloway reviewed the known stuff in his mind one more time. The reports from T'aiwan were brief but good. The ChiComs had found the plane in a tea patch. There were no signs of life around the plane, but it wasn't broken up much. The ChiComs also reported their ground forces were a long way from it. Unfortunately, Calloway would have to wait until he got to T'aiwan for further information. It would have been nice, he mused, to catch a ride in a jet from Tachikawa. All he could do, though, was sit in this tub and try to figure out what the guys would do. Had to figure that at least one of them was injured enough to slow the group, though, Calloway thought to himself. That way, he wouldn't get too anxious if things went slowly.

* * *

There wasn't much news, Olson thought. The ChiComs were putting up roadblocks – as though any survivors would travel on roads. The swing shift was already on duty, and the afternoon briefing to the general was done. Olson had called Marie to explain he had to stay at work. She understood, and Olson was glad of it! The captain's wife had sent over lunch, and now she was getting dinner ready. They'd have to stay around until dark. After that, the swing and mid shift supervisors would call the captain on anything further. And there wouldn't be much happening now it was dark. Olson could go home and get some rest.

* * *

Li got ready to move. He needed to catch Lin between the evening study session and bedtime. He briefed the others as much as possible on ways to reach the coast and where they needed to be before they tried to use the radios to contact help.

The radio remained silent. Lindsay was disappointed there wasn't any apparent attempt to contact them. Li finally requested they save the batteries. They certainly should have heard something on the frequency they'd given to Hamilton.

"It's time," he announced after checking the colonel's bandage once again. "I have to start now. I'll see you here tomorrow morning." Li turned and started down the hillside.

* * *

The plane finally landed. Calloway was getting his carry-on bag out of the storage bin long before it was even close to the terminal. He wasn't going to be slowed by any flight attendants in his hurry to get the hell through customs and into contact with Ramsey! And then he spotted Ramsey's big Irish frame at the foot of the steps, a car behind him.

"Welcome to T'aiwan, Joe." Ramsey laughed at Calloway's hurry. "Get in the car and let's get you checked through customs."

"Did you get my clearance and request to visit T'aipei Air Station?" Calloway asked as they climbed into the car.

"Sure did," Ramsey grinned that big redheaded grin of his. "And the ops officer there, guy named Bill Armstrong, is waiting for us."

"Jesus, Art," Calloway had a sour look, "I don't want to talk to officers. I need to talk to the guys who do the work. This isn't some frigging inspection. I need information."

"Hey, Joe," Ramsey laughed at the look, "you'll enjoy Bill – he's an old ex-sergeant with captain's bars. And he's got some damned good people – I've been to a lot of their briefings. And I know what you're here about."

"Yeah," Calloway responded. "Art, I've got to find out about my guys over there. Sorry we can't talk about it now, but I'll tell you and the guys at the watch center the whole story. OK?"

"OK," Ramsey replied.

* * *

Captain Armstrong met them at the entrance into the controlled area. He stuck out his hand and introduced himself as "Bill". That made points fast.

"Mister Calloway," the captain led them down a long hallway, "this is our watch center. I need to warn you that the information you're exposed to here is specially controlled."

"Kind of like burn before reading?" Calloway responded. "And I'm 'Joe,' OK?"

"Worse than that, Joe," the captain was straight-faced. "We can tell you all this stuff, but then we have to shoot you." He opened the door. "This is where it all happens. And there," he waved toward a young sergeant who was busy reading, "is the guy who knows what's happening, Sergeant Olson. Mike!" he called out, and Olson looked up quickly, then got to his feet and started toward them.

Calloway stuck out his hand. "Hi, Sarge," he greeted Olson, "I'm Joe Calloway and this is Art Ramsey, from the embassy."

"Mister Calloway, Mister Ramsey." Olson shook the proffered hands. He looked at Ramsey again. "I've seen you at our briefings, sir."

"That you have, Sarge," Ramsey chuckled. "Now Mister Calloway here, will get to see how you brief."

"My name's Joe, Sarge," Calloway spoke up.

"OK, sir - Joe!" Olson agreed.

"I've got a problem, Sarge," Calloway went on. "I need information on the penetrator that went down this morning, so I can try to set up a rescue. The plane was a modified A-26 Invader, or B-26 owned and operated by Southern Air Transport, contracted to the ChiNats. It was being used strictly as a fast transport over hostile territory. It had a crew of four – pilot, co-pilot, navigator, and cargo kicker. OK," he smiled, "now, I need to know everything that's gone on since this morning. Good enough?"

"OK, Joe," Olson looked toward the captain. "Let's go to the big board. I'll try to give it to you exactly as it came in to us."

"You've been on duty all day?" Calloway asked.

"Since eleven last night," Olson answered.

"The general himself asked Mike to stay on," Captain Armstrong added, "and keep up with it."

"Don't forget, sir," Olson said to the captain, "he stuck you with it, too. Anyway, Joe," he pointed toward the board, "here's the last information we had on the plane. About five minutes ago, the ground troops reached it. The wreckage is located here." He pointed to the map.

"No way to guess whether or not anyone survived?" Calloway asked.

"No, sir," Olson answered. "We're hoping the troops who arrived will report in, so we'll know what they've found."

"Excuse me, Mike!" the on-duty shift supervisor suddenly appeared alongside Olson. "We just got a report the ChiComs found very little at the penetrator crash site. There was blood in the cockpit and the rear of the plane, but no bodies."

"Did they say where in the cockpit?" Calloway asked.

"The pilot's seat, sir," the sergeant answered, "but there wasn't much, and it was all on the left side of the seat. There was a lot in the back of the plane, though."

So Lindsay and the kicker, Chou, were hurt. Damn! "Anything else?" Calloway asked.

"No, sir," the sergeant answered. "They're setting up camp, and they only did a quick once-over before darkness set in. They said they didn't find any tracks."

"That sounds like Li's handiwork," Calloway grinned.

"Li, sir?" Olson asked.

"Commander Li of the ChiNat navy, Sarge," Calloway answered. "He's their navigator and he knows the area over there. And he's a frogman, meaning he's been trained in escape and evasion and a few other things the ChiComs may not like to be up against."

"Ah, I see, sir," Olson knew something about the frogmen.

"Sarge, the reason our plane was there was to drop supplies to ChiNat frogmen and to drop medical supplies for the villages out in the countryside," Calloway spoke quietly.

"That sounds hairy," the captain spoke up. "It's sure one hell of an explanation, though, isn't it, Mike?"

"Yes, sir," Olson answered. "Don't think we would have ever come up with that as a reason."

"Anyway," Calloway continued, "it sounds like we've hit a little bit of paydirt. I suspect the pilot's wounded, and the kicker may be badly wounded or dead, with that much blood lost."

"Joe," the captain broke in, "we need to get a report off on this information and call the general about it. If you'll give us ten or fifteen minutes, we'll answer any more questions you've got – providing, of course, you don't mind us answering questions over dinner. By the way," he looked at both Ramsey and Calloway, "if you haven't eaten, I'll tell my wife to throw a little more water in the stew."

"I've already eaten," Ramsey answered, then turned to Calloway, "but I doubt you've had anything to eat, Joe."

"I really would appreciate it, Bill," Calloway responded. "I had a quick lunch before I left Tokyo, but nothing since then."

"Let me holler at Cris, then," Captain Armstrong grinned. "She likes cooking, even when I bring folks at the last minute."

"Joe," Olson stopped. "There's one more thing. The Ilyushin

flew into Fuchou yesterday afternoon, and then took off just about the time our guy first penetrated the coast."

Calloway's attention was suddenly directed completely at what Olson was saying. "You mean the Ilyushin might have been at Fuchou to react to the A-26?" he asked.

"Yes, sir," Olson answered. "And the way he wandered up to the intercept point, it looked like he knew when and where he'd meet up with the A-26."

"That's damned interesting, Sarge!" Calloway thought quickly. "Damned interesting, indeed!"

* * *

Lindsay sat back against the wall of the cave. The fire was well enough hidden it couldn't be seen. The warmth felt good, and the hot meal felt better.

"You're a good cook, Tiger," Lindsay chided his co-pilot.

"I just warmed up what Li cooked, Colonel," Tiger responded. "He's the one you need for a cook and maybe even a bottle-washer!"

"Actually, I think I'd prefer Marion's cooking," Lindsay commented. "Only one problem – I don't believe I've ever tried anything she's cooked!"

"Oh, Lord!" Tiger's face showed mock horror, "what if I marry Yukiko and she can't cook?"

"Don't make me laugh, Tiger," Lindsay winced. "It really does hurt when I laugh!"

* * *

Li reached the valley floor well after dark. It was late enough so everyone should be in the evening study meeting.

Li smiled at the idea of Lin's surprise at discovering he wasn't the Li she thought she knew. The smile faded when he remembered his family had partly caused her difficult life so far. That would change, of course. But he hoped it didn't make her too upset with him. She really could give them all away to the Communists!

And now it was too late to turn back. Here was the edge of the village, and he'd already been seen by someone down the street, someone who knew who he was from the last time he was here.

* * *

The two ladies who brought the food into the staff room outside the special area received a warm greeting, Calloway noticed, especially since one of them – the young sergeant's wife – was obviously unexpected. Olson was surprised, and the captain's wife was pleased about it.

Calloway decided it was best to delay asking any further questions. The ladies probably weren't cleared to hear about it. Besides, it was difficult to talk while his mouth was full.

* * *

"I'll take first watch," Lindsay said, getting up from the fire.

"You let me know when you're tired," Tiger responded, "and I'll give you a break."

"Tiger, you know I have to push myself, don't you?" Lindsay asked.

"Sure, Colonel," Tiger answered. "If you don't push, you lose your drive. Don't forget," he chuckled, "I went through survival school, too. You just remember we need you rested and ready, OK?"

"OK," Lindsay replied. "You remember I can't quit trying to get home to Marion."

"I understand," Tiger agreed. "Yukiko's waiting for me, too."

"Get your beauty sleep, then," Lindsay moved to the cave entrance. "I'll wake you up when it's time."

* * *

"OK," Calloway was glad to be back in the watch center. "There are survivors, and they wiped out their tracks so the ChiComs can't tell which way they went. That means Li survived. Tiger too, since they didn't report any blood in his part of the cockpit. Blood on the upper left side of the pilot's seat says Lindsay was probably hit high, in the shoulder."

"Couldn't it have been the head, instead?" Olson asked.

"I don't think so," Calloway answered. "Not enough blood for a head wound. It's the left shoulder. Lindsay's right-handed, so it won't stop him. But it'll slow their travel."

"How will they escape?" Olson asked. "Do they have a plan?"

"Nothing formal, Sarge," Calloway answered. "But Li will have a plan and there's no telling what he'll do. In the meantime," he continued, "I have to find a way to contact them. They have small tactical radios, so I need a good, powerful transmitter." He turned to Armstrong. "Do you guys have anything like that, Bill?"

"We don't have anything here," the captain was thoughtful, "but the guys in the Military Assistance and Advisory Group – the 'MAAG' – do. And if they don't have it, the ChiNats do. Let me call one of the MAAG guys I know."

"Sounds good," Calloway nodded.

* * *

The door of the dining building opened and people started coming out. Several of them greeted Li, welcoming him. He watched for Lin, and saw her leave the building. She noticed the knot of people, and then saw him. With a whoop of glee, she ran through the group.

"Li! Li! My dear friend!" she wrapped her arms around him in a hug. "You've come back!"

"I told you I would," Li chided her. "I've come to steal you away from here!"

"Oh!" Lin stopped abruptly. "Then you really meant it when you said you wanted me to go with you? Oh!"

"Before we go," Li spoke gently, "we have to talk. You need to know some things before you decide whether or not you want to go."

"Oh, Li," her excitement eased, "we'll talk. But first, have you eaten?"

"I ate earlier," Li had eaten a cold rice bar while descending from the cave. "But I'd like some tea, if you have it."

One of the villagers scurried off for tea. The villagers finally drifted away, leaving Li and Lin alone. They went into the building and sat down.

"Lin," Li started, "I need to tell you some things that may seem strange. I'll start by apologizing to you for not telling you the truth about me before this."

"There's no need for apologies," Lin's pragmatic side came out. "You're my friend. You proved that."

"I'm glad you believe that," Li spoke sincerely, "and I hope you continue to believe it."

Lin's face sagged. "You can't take me with you?" she started.

"Not that!" Li took a deep breath and continued quietly. "Lin, a long time ago, my family was forced to leave a beloved servant behind. You are that servant's daughter. My family hoped to send for you and your mother after we were established in our new home, but the Communists came too soon. We never heard any more of your mother or you."

Lin's face registered shock. "You're – you're the boy I remember from my childhood! Your family was kind to my mother and me." She began to remember. "But your family went to T'aiwan. My mother said someday we'd go there, too, and be with you again. I'd forgotten that!"

"You'll still go there with me," Li replied. "Lin, I'm sorry I couldn't tell you before this, but I came to learn about the countryside. That's when I first met you in Fuchou. For awhile I was afraid you might recognize me, but then we became good friends and I wasn't concerned. And I knew I'd come back to get you when I could. I'm here."

"But why did you come?" Lin's curiosity grew.

"Lin," Li admitted, "I'm a member of the Nationalist navy. I was sent here to learn the land so I could help an airplane drop supplies to other men who came here to learn about the Communist government's military things."

"Oh, spies, then," Lin's comment held no hint of blame.

"Yes, spies," Li admitted. "But we dropped medical supplies for the villages, too."

"Yes," Lin nodded. "We found some near the village last month. There was a note which said they were provided by friends from T'aiwan." Suddenly, recognition dawned in her eyes. "You were in the plane that flew over!" she exclaimed.

Li nodded. "Yes, we flew over here a couple of times, including last night."

"Oh, my," Lin smiled, "I sleep lightly, and I've heard the plane pass overhead at night!" Her face suddenly straightened. "But how did you get back here tonight? Did you parachute?"

"No," Li admitted, "we were shot down last night, although most of us survived. There are three of us, and we have to get to the coast to return to T'aiwan. And that's why I'm here. I want to take you with me, to T'aiwan, where you'll be part of my family again."

"Oh!" Lin's face registered her surprise. "I don't know!"

"You won't be a servant, Lin," Li vowed. "My family promised me you'd be a family member."

"Even as a girl?" Lin was skeptical. It was still common for female children to be sold into slavery.

"Things are changing on T'aiwan," Li assured her. "It's common for women to be educated. Even poorer families see that young women with an education can find jobs with good pay. Fewer and fewer are being treated badly. I think you've been educated enough to qualify to attend the university. And my family will be sure you can go."

Lin looked at him with wonder in her eyes. "Li, this is like a dream come true," she finally said. "I'll be sad to leave here. But I'll certainly go with you. However," her disappointment showed, "I've got to have permission to leave."

"That's a problem," Li answered. "I've thought about it. I may be able to take you with me without the paperwork."

"How's that?" Lin asked.

Suddenly, a door opened nearby and an elderly woman looked into the hall. "There's tea!" she called out. "If you want to have more, please do so, but please turn off the lights before you leave the building! I'm leaving."

"Thank you!" Li called back. The woman put a hand to her ear and he called again, this time much louder.

"Ah," she nodded, "you're welcome, young man. Don't be too late!" With that, she left the building.

"Whew!" Li turned back to Lin. "I didn't realize there was still somebody in the building."

"She can't hear," Lin reassured him. "She barely heard you the second time you called out! But you didn't answer my question."

"I'll tell the village leader I've come quickly from Fuchou because we have to go to an important job right away," Li explained. "If I say the papers weren't ready when I got to Fuchou, the leader might let you go with me without question."

"Hmm," Lin was thinking. "What sort of papers would it take to have them let me go?"

"A letter from someone in the government, I suppose," Li replied. "I could forge one easily, but I don't have the paper."

"What kind of paper do you need?" Lin asked.

"I need 'letterhead', with an official heading," Li said. "I can only get it at the provincial offices in Fuchou, though, and there's no chance to get to Fuchou quickly to obtain it."

"Li," Lin smiled secretly, "I worked in the provincial offices in Fuchou when you met me."

"Yes," Li shook his head, "but -" He stopped. "Do you have some of the paper?" he asked.

"Yes," she replied, "at the dormitory. I took it so I'd have paper to write letters to you! I also have a brush and ink."

"Ah, Lin," Li chuckled. "We're both rascals, I think."

"You're right, Li," she chuckled in return. "And I'll get the paper and things in a little bit. But first, you have to tell me about flying."

* * *

The captain had called his friend at MAAG headquarters, and Calloway and Ramsey were now on their way to see a sergeant about the radio Calloway wanted. Things were moving forward, and Calloway was happy about that. He still had to contact Hamilton and get information about the radio frequencies Lindsay had set up.

At the headquarters, they were ushered into a secure office by a young military policeman and met by an Army sergeant. "Sergeant Major George at your service, Mister Calloway!" the sergeant announced as he shook the proffered hand. "Captain Armstrong said you needed some help, sir."

"It's 'Joe', Sarge," Calloway replied. "And you can help me by finding me a long-range radio with enough power to reach all the way to China – that's a joke, but not as much of one as you might think!"

"I understand, Joe," Sergeant George nodded his head. "By the way, I'm Alex, OK?"

"OK, Alex," Calloway nodded.

"Let's see about a radio, then," George got back to business. "What frequency range?"

"Probably the three to five megahertz range," Calloway responded.

"Easy enough," George nodded. "The ChiNats have some good radios out on the islands that operate in that range. I think you'll find the antennas are aimed in your direction, too." He grinned.

"Any trouble getting to use the radios?" Calloway asked.

"Shouldn't be," George answered. "We furnished them in the first place, and the ChiNats are glad to let us use anything they have."

"Good," Calloway nodded. It was time to get the information he needed from Hamilton. They might even be able to start sending radio messages tomorrow. He turned back toward George. "Only a couple more questions, Alex."

"Fire away," George offered.

"First of all," Calloway started, "I need somebody who can use the radio and who knows how to work with codes. They'll have to use a book I've got to send coded messages."

"That's easy," George nodded. "My son-in-law's with Army Security Agency here, and he works with radios and codes. I can probably get him loaned to us."

"OK then, where can I find a bed and a cold beer around here?" Calloway asked. "Oh, yeah – it would help if there was a telephone, too. I have to make a couple of calls before I can enjoy the beer."

* * *

Lindsay sat quietly on the crest of the ridge. It was calm and peaceful here, and there wasn't much need to move, so the pain in his shoulder had subsided. The clouds had cleared away during the early evening. He could see stars in the sky, and the moon was on the horizon. He wondered if Marion could see the sky tonight, too. Damn, the stars were bright. They looked almost close enough to reach up and touch.

* * *

The phone rang in Hamilton's room. He reached across the sleeping bargirl and picked it up. "Hello," he muttered.

"Charlie, this is Joe," it was Calloway. "I'm in town and setting up the rescue operation." Hamilton woke up quickly. "I need help from you, right away. Can you meet me somewhere?"

"Now?" Hamilton asked. "Hey, it's -" he looked at the clock alongside the bed, "damn, Joe, it's almost eleven! Can this wait until morning?"

"I need the emergency information you set up with Lindsay, Charlie," Calloway explained. "It looks like the crew survived the crash and they're loose somewhere in there. I've found a radio that can reach them. I need to know the frequencies to use."

"The crew survived?" Hamilton was now wide awake. "Are you sure, Joe?"

"Yep," Calloway replied. "Li and Tiger are OK, but Lindsay's wounded. I need the information you have so I can make contact and start trying to get them home."

Hamilton's mind raced. The crew survived! That meant there wouldn't be any attempts to find another crew until this one was caught. Double-damn! Kung would be upset. They wouldn't be able to make another delivery for months, and the customer would be furious. Hamilton knew he had to meet Calloway. "Joe, where are you? Can I meet you there?"

"Sure," Calloway answered. "I'm in room 415 at the Dragon Palace."

"OK, I know the place. It's about fifteen minutes from here," Hamilton estimated. "Look, I'll get dressed and be on my way there as soon as I can. Room 415 at the Dragon. See you there!"

"What's that?" the bargirl asked sleepily as he reached for his clothes.

"Business, buttercup," Hamilton answered crisply. "Time for you to get dressed and go home, right now. I have to go see a man."

"OK, I go," the girl agreed quickly, jumping out of bed and quickly picking up her scattered clothing. This customer would come back to the bar and spend money again, so long as she did what he wanted.

They both dressed quickly.

Hamilton finally spoke again as he tied his shoes. "I'll give you a ride back to the bar. But I have to make a telephone call first, and you need to be outside."

"Why?" she asked.

"It's business, I said," he sounded irritated, and she quickly started for the door.

"I wait outside, then," she said, hurrying. She didn't want him to become angry!

* * *

Li smiled at the package Lin handed to him. Inside were a brush and a block of dry ink and the glorious letterhead paper that would let him take her away from here.

"I have to go back now," she smiled. "But I hope these help. And thank you for what I learned tonight. I thought of you as my friend, and now I learn that you're almost my brother!" She hugged him. "I have a family!" She turned and walked away with a proud, determined step.

Li smiled. The paper was a miracle. Now he had work to do, and then they would leave in the morning. It wouldn't take long to write the letter. But he did need to be careful to make this look as much like the deputy governor's handwriting as possible!

* * *

"Damn it!" Kung was upset. "Calloway is beginning to irritate me! We may have to do something about this!"

"I can't do anything, Winston," Hamilton pleaded. "I'm going to his hotel now. I just called to pass on what he said about the crew. I'll call you in the morning, because I don't think I'll get away from there for awhile."

"Call me then," Kung was thoughtful. "We have to respond to this. We *can't* afford to delay in getting a new crew and plane in place!"

"I understand," Hamilton agreed, "but I have to go now."

Ah yi, Kung thought as he hung up the phone, I'm surrounded by enemies and idiots, and there's no way to tell which is which! But it's fortunate that Hamilton is still in Calloway's good graces. We may be able to use his information to help our neighbors find their intruders! I imagine anything we can furnish will be welcome, and Hamilton should be able to get that information from Calloway. I'll talk to him in the morning.

* * *

Calloway was waiting in the bright lobby of the Dragon Palace when Hamilton walked in.

"Over here, Charlie," Calloway called out. "I came downstairs for a beer. You want one?"

"I could do with one." Hamilton took a chair.

Calloway waved at a waitress who was standing in the doorway of the bar, and she turned and disappeared into the bar.

"Joe, I don't want to change the subject," Hamilton started, "but I'm sorry I clutched when you called this morning. I was upset about the plane not getting back, and Kung was upset because he didn't know if they were able to make the delivery. And then you caught me off-balance wanting me to do that stuff, and I guess I reacted badly. I owe you an apology."

"Not a problem," Calloway replied. "I understand. Been there a time or two myself." The waitress approached with two beers. When she left, Calloway turned back. "Charlie, this is probably your first time to have a project go down in unfriendly territory, so I hope you won't mind if I take over and try to get things back on track. I've been in a few of these before, and I've learned how to get things done." He tipped his beer up and took a drink.

"You're right," Hamilton agreed, "and I'm not sure how to do any of this. That was probably bugging me this morning, too. I just hope you'll let me stick around and watch, so I can be ready next time."

"Be happy to," Calloway nodded. "Now, about the information I asked you for -"

"Right here in my pocket," Hamilton pulled out a folded piece of paper. "Lindsay handed this to me when they took off."

"I hope nobody else has seen this," Calloway spoke quietly.

"It's been in my shirt pocket since I got it," Hamilton assured him. "I wasn't sure anybody could use it, but I guess you can."

"Well," Calloway took the paper, "I've contacted some folks here who will help. I'm surprised Kung didn't offer any help."

"He was rattled about the plane," Hamilton answered. "You know, his man was the kicker. After you called, he backed away from getting involved – said he didn't want to interfere."

"OK," Calloway dismissed the situation. "Look, I've gotten together with a guy who can help us tomorrow. He'll get us access to a high-powered radio, and I'll use that to contact the guys."

"Joe," Hamilton asked, "how do we know the guys are still alive?"

"I've got sources," Calloway answered. He had no idea whether or not Hamilton was cleared, and he wasn't about to give him information he shouldn't have. "They say the ChiComs didn't find any bodies at the plane, so somebody was alive enough to bury any bodies and get out of there."

"OK," Hamilton nodded. "So can I tag along with you tomorrow? I have a car we can use." Maybe it was a good idea to stick with Calloway to see what kind of success he had. Kung would want to know, and this information would help satisfy him. Maybe Kung could even transmit the information to their contact in Tokyo, to send along to the mainland.

"Sounds good, Charlie," Calloway answered. "I'm supposed to meet Sergeant George here about nine in the morning. He said he'd have a staff car, so I guess you can leave yours here. He's supposed to take us out to the islands to meet the people who will let us use the radio. Be sure to eat breakfast, because it'll be awhile until lunchtime, and I expect the food out there isn't the greatest."

"OK," Hamilton appreciated the advice. "Nine o'clock it is. Guess I'd better head for it. I've got some lost sleep to catch up on." He finished up his beer and stood up. "See you in the morning, then, Joe."

"Get a good night's sleep, Charlie," Calloway advised. "I have no idea when or where we might get any sleep again!"

"Appreciate the warning!" Hamilton called back as he headed for the door.

* * *

Li looked at the letter critically. It would do. These people didn't see letters from Fuchou often, and nobody would recognize the deputy governor's handwriting. Now came the hardest part of the task, forging the "chop", the mark that verified the authenticity of any document. The red ink was available almost anywhere, but each stamp block was uniquely carved.

However, Li had saved papers from Fuchou when he'd been there previously. There was an impression of the deputy governor's "chop" at the bottom of them. He pulled a small piece of wood he'd found earlier from his pocket and, using the sharp penknife he always carried, carefully shaved it to fit the size of the stamp block that had created the "chop".

TWELVE

Morning came early. Li needed to get the papers to the village leader for validation and leave quickly. The Communists might be able to put together a search effort soon and find where the crew had gone.

Li left the dormitory and started toward the dining room. He saw Lin leaving the women's dormitory and coming toward the dining room also. She was smiling – he hoped it was because she was happy about what would happen today.

He caught Lin's eye and nodded, letting her know he'd finished his work and they'd be able to leave this morning. Her smile brightened.

* * *

On the ridge, Tiger saw the lights come on in the village. They weren't the first lights on – some had come on down the road, where there wasn't a village, and a truck had made its way from there to the village.

Tiger thought about going back into the cave, but changed his mind. He'd watch to be sure nobody was coming. Colonel Lindsay needed more sleep, and he could last a lot longer before needing more rest. When Li came, they'd have to be ready to move out.

* * *

Li was surprised to see the soldiers at breakfast. He asked Lin if she knew about them, but she shook her head. Finally, the man across the table said they'd come in for breakfast from the new security checkpoint just down the road. It was there, he said, because some bad people might be in the area, enemies who came from an airplane crash back in the hills.

"Checkpoints!" Li spoke disgustedly. "*Ai yi*, this will delay us! It means I can't get back to Fuchou quickly. I wanted to be there at least by tomorrow, but this may delay us several days!"

"*Ai yi*, comrade!" the man shook his head. "We have to live with it."

"That's true, comrade," Li agreed. "Bend with the wind and survive."

"Yes," the man nodded in agreement. "I hope this doesn't inconvenience you."

"It really won't," Li replied. "It's just a nuisance."

The man smiled knowingly and turned his attention to his food.

Hmm, thought Li, so we have checkpoints to avoid.

* * *

Calloway was awake early, and had time to think about what he'd learned the night before. He was upset because the Ilyushin had prior knowledge of the A-26's flight plans. That meant the MiG-19 also probably had prior knowledge. The question was, if this Chinese guy in Tokyo was the transfer point, how did he get the information from T'aiwan? It wasn't hard to figure the routing after the T'aiwan-to-Tokyo link. But there was no real way to pass information from T'aiwan to Tokyo except by phone.

OK, then, he thought, could Hamilton make calls from his room without charging them on his hotel bill? He'd turn that over to Anderson. There had to be a way the information got from T'aiwan to Tokyo.

He picked up the phone and dialed Anderson's number at the apartment.

* * *

Li handed the paper to the leader. "Here's my authorization, Comrade Yang," he said. "Lin and I need to leave right away."

"Sure, Comrade Li," Yang smiled pleasantly. "Please wait while I check the chop."

"Of course," Li answered.

Yang lifted a book from the center drawer of his desk. He opened it carefully, then held the paper next to an entry in the book.

"Good," the man said. "I'm sorry to lose Lin. She's a credit to our school program. But I suppose she can serve the people better as a surveyor."

"I sure hope so, comrade," Li smiled. "She learned quickly during our work together. She'll be good, I'm sure. And now," he added, "we need to leave for Fuchou right away!"

"How do you plan to travel?" Yang questioned. "There probably won't be any transportation through here today."

"I thought we'd wait at the Army's checkpoint down the road," Li answered. "There will be Army vehicles going through there, and maybe we can catch a ride."

"Ah!" Yang exclaimed, "good thinking, comrade! Have a good trip then! And come back this way some time."

"Thank you, comrade," Li bowed. "I'll come back if I can." With that he left the building. Time to get Lin and be on their way!

* * *

There was daylight now and Tiger had watched the truck depart the village a while ago. Everyone in it was in military uniform. And now he could see two individuals departing the village. He couldn't be sure it was Li and his friend, but it wouldn't hurt to wake Colonel Lindsay and let him look also. Besides, it was time for Li to be coming. Colonel Lindsay wouldn't mind waking early to verify it was Li.

* * *

As they started out, Li checked how much of the road was visible to the village, so he could tell where they'd be able to leave it without being noticed. It wasn't far.

"I just hope," Li spoke quietly, "the soldiers don't send anyone else to breakfast. They may hear about our departure and wonder where we've gone."

"Well," Lin spoke ironically, "even if more soldiers do go to the village, they won't find any breakfast now. Everyone's already gone to work. Anybody who sleeps this late won't get much from these people, including civility. And the soldiers don't pay for their food in *yuan*, but in worthless government chits. You saw how little respect the soldiers got in the dining room."

Li smiled. He understood.

* * *

Lindsay looked through his binoculars at the couple moving down the road. "The guy's Li," he commented to Tiger, "and the other one's probably a female, lots smaller."

"The bag Li's carrying is a giveaway," Tiger replied.

"You're right," Lindsay agreed. "But they can't leave the road yet without somebody from the village seeing."

"They'd better not wait too long," Tiger noted. "See that checkpoint down the road? It's not that far, and it can see a lot of the road, too."

"I don't think there's much problem," Lindsay swept along the road with the glasses. "There's plenty of road where nobody can see them. In fact, they're almost to a place, now!"

"We'd better get ready to go, then, Colonel," Tiger advised. "I'm sure Li wants us to be on our way as soon as possible."

* * *

Anderson's voice sounded tired. Calloway knew he hadn't slept much since last night.

"Paul," Calloway said, "this is Joe. I need some help."

"Count on me, sir," the younger man answered. "I'm ready."

"I need to have you check some stuff," Calloway spoke up. "First of all, please check the Grand Hotel to see if Hamilton's made any calls off-island that aren't on his bill. Then please ask somebody in the SID's internal affairs office if there have been any recent calls out of Kung's SID office to Japan. You might also check with the CAT business office. Tell them you're with Air America, and they'll be glad to help. See if any calls from Kung's office to Japan have gone anyplace besides the CAT office."

"OK, sir," Anderson was wide awake now. "What do I do with the information?"

"I'm going out to one of the off-shore islands this morning," Calloway answered. "I probably won't be back until this afternoon. I'll call the SAT office here when I get back and let them know where I'll be, and we'll use them as our clearing place. Think that'll be OK?"

"Sure, sir," Anderson agreed. "The director here likes Lindsay a lot. He'll be unhappy if we don't keep him involved!"

"Good," Calloway was pleased. "I'm looking forward to hearing what you find out."

"Hope I'll have it all by the time you get back, sir," Anderson was ready to go.

* * *

"And what'll you accomplish by going out there?" Kung wanted to know.

"Look, Winston," Hamilton was irritated, "this won't be settled until that crew's caught. If I can find out where they are, I can let you know so you can tell our friend. And his people can catch them."

"Charles," Kung nodded, "that's an excellent idea. You can call me here, of course. Then, I'll call through SAT's switchboard and let our friend know what to do. And we'll be back in business soon."

"How will you pass the information through my office?" Hamilton asked. "You can't just call through the switchboard."

"You're still talking to the landlord up there about a place to live when you get back, aren't you?" Kung asked.

"Of course," Hamilton answered.

"Then I'm calling for you while you're out on the island trying to help our crew," Kung finished.

"That'll work," Hamilton agreed.

"Good, then," Kung was pleased with himself. "I'm sure Calloway will let you know the details. You get them to me, and I'll send them on."

"OK, I have to go," Hamilton said. "I'll call your office later and let you know what's happening."

"Good," Kung agreed. "And I'll use the telephone in your office for my calls to Tokyo."

* * *

Lindsay returned from checking the other side of the ridge. "Still no activity," he announced. "The soldiers are still in the crash area. They're not having much luck finding our tracks."

"Their luck may get worse," Tiger smiled faintly. "It looks like rain, if the clouds continue to build."

"We'd better get our stuff ready to go," Lindsay suggested.

"Already done, sir," Tiger grinned. "I did that earlier. We'll be ready when they arrive."

"They might be tired," Lindsay said. "It's a long climb. They might want to rest for a few minutes."

"Li won't need much rest, Colonel," Tiger replied. "And the girl isn't slowing him down."

* * *

"Let me finish my breakfast," Calloway said. "You're early, and I still haven't had my second cup of coffee! Care for some?" he offered.

"Sure" Hamilton sat down as Calloway poured a cup. "I just didn't want to be left behind."

"We've still got time," Calloway noted. "Enough for another cup, anyway."

"I guess we won't get much of that out on the island?" Hamilton asked.

"The Chinese prefer tea," Calloway nodded. "We probably won't get much coffee wherever we go. Better enjoy it while we can."

"I didn't ask last night," Hamilton asked, "but would it help if I stay with the radio operation? I'm not much of a radio operator, but maybe I can help a little, and I can get hold of Kung to help out if there's any problems."

"That's not a bad idea, Charlie," Calloway was pleased. "Having one of us out there will help, I'm sure. And I have to get back here to work on a plan to get them out."

"I'll need to come back and get some stuff," Hamilton said. "I can feed details to the radio people. How will we do this, anyway? Is there a code or something?"

"Yeah," Calloway nodded. "I'll fill you and the radio guys in on it when we get there."

"OK," Hamilton responded.

Calloway finished his breakfast. "This won't be a picnic, Charlie, but it's got to be done. We won't know whether or not they're reading our transmissions."

"Is there some way they could do something to let us know they've heard us?" Hamilton asked.

"I can't think of anything," Calloway shook his head. "But maybe something'll come to one of us. In the meantime, it won't hurt to transmit in the blind, so long as there's a chance they can pick it up. They should have a receiver turned on, waiting for us to broadcast."

"Well, I'm anxious to get started," Hamilton reached for more coffee, "and get this done."

"It'll take its own time, Charlie," Calloway spoke seriously. "They won't hurry coming out of there."

Hopefully, Hamilton thought, they won't come out at all!

* * *

"Colonel Lindsay, Tiger," Li said, "this is Lin Yu-feng. Lin," he turned to her, "meet my friends, Colonel Lindsay and Tiger Ch'en."

"Lin," Lindsay bowed, "you're much prettier than Li said." Lin's face flushed at the compliment, delivered in her own language by a foreigner.

"In fact," Tiger followed up, "I believe Li didn't want us to know just how pretty you really are." Lin's face flushed even more.

"You see, Lin," Li turned to her, "didn't I warn you about them?" The girl nodded. "Of course, they're right, too."

"Well," the girl spoke, "I'm pleased to meet you two. And I appreciate your compliments." She bowed pertly to each of them in turn. "But we need to leave right away."

"We need to be at the top of that ridge," Li added, pointing to a ridge about 20 kilometers away, "as soon as possible, before it rains."

"We figured there'd be rain," Tiger noted. "The weather forecaster the other day said there'd be showers today."

"Well," Li pointed out, "I'd rather move at night and rest during the day, but we need to go as soon as we can. It won't take much to figure out we didn't go to the roadblock. And I'd like to be gone before they figure it out, so we won't be stuck up here while they look for us down there."

"Let's go, then," Lindsay agreed. "If that's where we need to be," he looked toward the ridge, "then we'd better get started."

"Colonel, your shoulder -?" Li left the question hanging.

"It'll go where I go," Lindsay answered. "Your bandage is doing fine, Li, and the pain's not bad."

* * *

"- this is my son-in-law, Gary Johnson," Sergeant George introduced Calloway and Hamilton to the young man driving the car. "We've got him for the radio work!"

"Hi, Gary," Calloway greeted the young man. "I'm Joe, and this is Charlie. We're going to work your butt off, son, but I hope you understand why!"

"Yes, sir," the young man nodded. "Sergeant Major told me about it. My overnight gear's in the trunk. I expect to stay for awhile. And I don't mind working!"

Calloway smiled. "Let's go, then. By the way, Gary, Charlie will come back to get his stuff this afternoon, but he'll go back out there as liaison. Will that work?"

"Sounds good, sir," the young soldier answered, then turned toward Hamilton. "We'll be living in rough quarters, Charlie, sir, and I'd suggest you get some fatigues – Sergeant Major can help you with that."

"Well," Hamilton had half a smile on his face, "I just hope we can find a cup of coffee now and then!"

"The coffee supplies and the cups are in my bag!" the young soldier laughed. "I like my coffee, too!"

"We'll do just fine!" Hamilton laughed back.

* * *

At the bottom of the hill, Li stopped them. "I'll go ahead and see if it's clear," he said.

The others nodded, and Li crossed the road, quickly moving into the field of tea bushes beyond it. He looked both directions and waved them across the road.

Lindsay was first, and next was Lin, who dropped to the ground lightly alongside Lindsay. The last was Tiger, and, just as he reached the road, Li saw motion out of the corner of his eye and motioned to Tiger to drop and hide in the bushes beside the road.

The old woman who had been in the kitchen the previous night came slowly down the road. She was carrying an armload of sticks and bending to pick up more as she moved along. Lindsay and Lin held their breath as they realized she'd probably look right where Tiger was hiding. Li suddenly began moving in her direction. Lindsay realized Li was probably moving into position to attack her if she discovered Tiger. Damn, Lindsay thought – there should be another way to stop the old woman! Nobody wanted to see her hurt!

Li was almost in position when the old woman stopped to pick up another stick, then straightened up and turned back toward the village, plodding along until she was out of sight.

Li and Tiger were alongside Lin and Lindsay in seconds.

"I thought she might spot Tiger," Lindsay said. "I'm sure glad she didn't!"

"Colonel," Li smiled, "I thought she might, too, but I was going to stand up and greet her first. She'd probably think Lin and I were fooling around, and I wouldn't have had to harm her. My apologies to Lin, of course."

"If it would save her life," Lin said, "I'd have taken my tunic off and stood there in my underwear to back you up!"

"Thankfully it wasn't needed," Li shook his head. "But we have a long way to go."

"Let's be on our way, then," Lindsay spoke up.

"Yes, sir," Li agreed, "let's go."

* * *

The plane was an old C-47, its engines crackling and popping as they arrived at the airfield.

"OK, Alex," Calloway turned to George. "Where are we going, anyway?"

"We're headed for Matsu," the sergeant replied. "They've got the best radios, and they don't have to spend every other day hiding while the ChiComs shell the place, like they do at Quemoy!"

"The ChiComs shell Quemoy every other day?" Hamilton looked semi-upset. When George nodded, Hamilton continued. "What do they do on the off days?"

"That's when the ChiNats shell the ChiComs," George answered. "Let's load up."

* * *

The rain started when they reached the bridge. They stopped for a quick rest and pulled ponchos from their bags, including one for Lin.

"Those are OK for you men," she wouldn't accept the poncho, "since they're like the ones the soldiers use. But they're not for women." With that, she gathered rice straw from the edge of a nearby paddy and quickly formed a crude raincoat and hat that shed water as well as the ponchos.

When she finished, she smiled. "Now I look like an ordinary woman, trying to help poor soldiers find their way!"

"I doubt you're an ordinary woman, Lin," Lindsay said quietly.

"Thank you, Colonel," she acknowledged. "Now we'd better move before the rain stops."

* * *

The radio room was well equipped and the equipment was well cared for. The young lieutenant, Han, smiled brightly. "As you see, Mister Calloway," he spoke excellent English, "we're proud of our equipment. It's the best we could have, thanks to the MAAG."

"I can tell you're proud of it," Calloway responded. "You take good care of it."

"Thank you, sir," Han answered. "My troops will appreciate your compliment!" He turned toward Johnson and Hamilton. "If you like, I'll be glad to show you the operating procedures while Mister Calloway and Sergeant George visit my commander."

"Maybe you ought to come with us, Charlie," Calloway said, then turned to Han. "Mister Hamilton won't be operating the equipment," he explained. "He'll be my liaison. He'll also report to your government's project officer."

"I see," Han smiled. He turned toward Johnson. "Shall we go to work then?"

The two young men began talking between themselves, and the others turned to leave.

* * *

Platoon Leader Kao of the People's Liberation Army was furious. His cousin, a militiaman, had baited him about not being allowed off the division's base. And now his cousin rubbed it in again, telling Kao the militia would catch the survivors of the enemy plane crash in the valley. But the provincial governor restricting the PLA to their bases made Kao maddest. The old governor was one of the original patriots, but Kao served in the People's Revolutionary Army when the old man sat in his rocking chair in Hunan while the young men drove the *Kuomintang* from the mainland. And now his division commander bowed and scraped in front of the civilians!

Kao looked at his platoon. They were good men, well trained and proud to be the best. With them, it would be easy to catch these survivors. The militia sure couldn't do it!

* * *

They stopped at the bottom of the ridge to rest a moment.

Lin was concerned about the colonel. Lindsay's pain could draw him down quickly, she knew.

"Colonel," she asked, "can I look at your bandage? I may need to change it."

"Sure," Lindsay answered. "But let's not change it until we stop."

"I only want to look, sir," she explained.

A quick look convinced her the bandage would be OK until she could change it properly. Li had done a good job, but she wasn't sure what was under it.

* * *

Calloway was pleased with the results of the discussion with the station commander. The radio used to pass warnings to the crew was now theirs to use as long as they needed it.

The next step was his first message, telling the crew he knew they'd survived. He couldn't confirm it was received, of course. But he needed to verify the message was from him.

Calloway laughed at his idea. The beer on T'aiwan was as bad as Lindsay said it was! The hard part would be finding the word "beer" in the Officer's Guide they used as a codebook!

* * *

Olson looked dolefully at the coffeepot. Another cup and his insides would slosh! Nothing had happened. The ChiComs had gone over the plane thoroughly this morning, but they hadn't found anything. The search party was trying to find any tracks left by the surviving crewmembers, with no success.

Another sheaf of reports arrived at the desk. Olson scanned through them. Suddenly, he called to the shift chief to call the captain and have him come over, right away.

As Captain Armstrong came in, Olson handed him a page. "This is the first one, sir," he said.

"Hmm," the captain looked the paper over carefully. "A surveyor and his assistant are missing in the area south of the crash. The village chief reports the surveyor took the assistant away and they haven't been seen since they left the village this morning." He looked at Olson. "So?"

"This came back from the provincial government office, sir," Olson answered, handing over a second piece of paper.

"The surveyor isn't authorized to be there, and doesn't have permission to take the assistant," the captain read. "What's this all about, Mike?" He looked at Olson, questioning.

"Sir, I'm not totally sure," Olson started out, "but we agreed that the people in that plane had to know the area really well. That surveyor's assistant was there, which means the surveyor's been in the area, sir. And now he magically shows up and both he and the assistant disappear."

"I'm still missing something," the captain was puzzled.

"Sir," Olson said, "the surveyor isn't authorized to be there. He can't get there, the middle of the province, without having to show an authorization at least once or twice. Unless, of course," he continued, "he drops out of the sky! Sir, he's one of the crewmen!"

"Wouldn't the assistant turn him in?" the captain asked.

"Not necessarily, sir," Olson countered. "This assistant's probably a friend."

"OK, then," the captain asked. "Why didn't the village chief ask this guy for an authorization?"

"The village chief probably knows the guy, sir," Olson answered, "from when he was there before. You know, the gate guards let you in here without looking at your identification, because they know you."

"Jesus, Mike!" the captain agreed. "This is our first lead since the crash! Let's get it written up. And I'll call the general and let him know we've got something."

"The only problem, sir," Olson shuffled through the papers again, "is that we seem to be the only ones who realize it. I'm not sure why the ChiComs haven't caught on yet."

"Maybe that's personal recognition again, Mike," the captain's eyes twinkled. "Maybe nobody believes this surveyor's a 'bad guy'. Maybe he made friends with lots more people than just the assistant."

* * *

Calloway was briefing Johnson and Han on sending his first message. "Make sure you repeat it at least every half-hour," he told them. "Especially around dusk."

"OK, sir," Johnson answered. "We've already worked out our schedule. We'll transmit all night."

"You're not going to transmit during the day?" Hamilton asked.

"They'll probably sleep all day, Charlie," Calloway answered. "If it were only Li and Tiger, they'd travel any time, but they can't afford to have Lindsay seen. And if they've got Chou with them, they may have to carry him. That'll attract attention during the daytime." He turned back to the two radio operators. "Best time is just about sundown or sunup. They should have a radio on then, while they're tearing down or setting up camp."

"Sounds good, sir," Han smiled. "We'll make sure they get your messages."

"Thanks, guys," Calloway replied. "Now for the important part. How are you guys fixed for goodies out here? Like beer and sodas?"

"Not very well, sir," Han grimaced.

"Well," Calloway continued, "we'll have to make sure you have a beer or a soda once in awhile out here. I'll send some back with Charlie."

The commander came into the room. "Mister Calloway," he called out, "there's a call for you from T'aipei, sir. You can take it on the phone there." He pointed to a telephone near the radio.

Calloway picked up the phone. "Calloway here," he said.

"Bill Armstrong at T'aipei Air Station, Joe," the captain announced. "We've got something here you ought to see, as soon as you get back."

"We'll be on our way shortly," Calloway looked at Sergeant George questioningly, getting a large nod in return.

"We'll be expecting you," the captain signed off.

* * *

Kao's anger hadn't subsided. His platoon felt it. Only the second squad, under Squad Leader Yang, shrugged it off. Yang would do that, Kao understood – Yang was a PRA veteran, like himself. Yang also understood Kao's anger.

If only this politician of a commanding general would get off his fat ass, Kao knew he could take the second squad and catch the enemy quickly. The stupid militia figured they'd set up roadblocks and have the enemy walk into their arms! He and second squad would show the militia how military men really did things! If only they were allowed to!

* * *

The sky darkened as the afternoon wore on. They'd reached the opposite ridge and found shelter. It would be a short rest – they had to make as much distance as possible. Following the ridge would be slow. But it was far safer than traveling in the valley, where they could be seen.

Lin removed Lindsay's bandage, concerned about his condition. However, she was relieved to see the bleeding was stopped and the wound wasn't infected. Li had used some sort of cleaning agent!

"Is it OK?" Lindsay had a positive attitude.

"It's much better than OK, Colonel," she smiled at him. "There's no infection, and the bleeding's stopped."

"Before you put the new bandage on," Li spoke up, "sprinkle on some more of the sulfa."

"I'm afraid I don't know much about sulfa," Lin admitted. "Here, we use alcohol to control infection."

"Oh, that's fine," Li chuckled, "for internal infections!"

"Li!" she admonished, "I'm serious!"

* * *

Calloway listened to the captain and Olson before he finally spoke up. "Li picked up the girl. That's the one he said he'd go back and get one day."

"Is she a girlfriend?" the captain asked.

"More like a sister," Calloway answered. "She was his assistant while he got acquainted with the area."

"OK, then," Olson nodded, "we've got one person located. We still don't know about the rest of the crew."

"That's right, Sarge," Calloway nodded. "But we know which direction they headed. And we know they had to cross a ridge to get there. So the guy in the back probably didn't survive. He lost too much blood to travel like that. Not sure about the pilot, but there wasn't enough blood to kill him. So the three guys from the front-end crew are probably still alive and moving. Where we go to get them out of there is the question."

"You should probably send them to Quemoy," the captain suggested. "It's only a couple of miles from the mainland, and it has medical help."

"Not sure I'd agree with you, sir," Olson volunteered. "It's logical, but it may be too obvious. I really think they should head for Matsu. That area's not as well developed as Quemoy, and there are lots of places where they can be gotten off the mainland without anybody knowing they're around."

"Think I agree with you, Sarge," Calloway nodded. "But I'll let them pick where they go. We'll suggest they go north, but it's their decision."

"OK, then, Joe," the captain nodded. "Let's go tell Mister Hamilton what's up, so he can pass the messages on."

They walked out of the restricted area and met Hamilton.

"Charlie, we think we've found a reflection of Li, at least," Calloway didn't bother to explain. "We figure they should head up to the seacoast north of Fuchou. How does that sound to you?"

"OK," Hamilton replied. "How do we get them out of there, though?"

"Probably put in a submarine with frogmen," Calloway answered.

* * *

Li stretched out the wire for the antenna, then turned the radio on. It immediately began to crackle and he tuned it. What he heard surprised him.

"Hey!" he called the others. "We're getting a message!"

"How do you know it's for us?" Lin asked.

"It's six-digit groups in English," Li explained. "That's the code Colonel Lindsay set up." He found a pencil and paper and began to copy the message. Soon, he held the paper up triumphantly.

"We've got the first message!" he proclaimed. "Now we have to decode it."

Lindsay handed him the book. When he finished, Li gave the message to Lindsay.

"Joe knows we're alive," Lindsay announced. "He knows we can't respond, so he'll repeat his messages all night. He says if this frequency's jammed we need to try the next frequency on our list. And that's it," he looked up, "except to verify it's him sending the message."

"He didn't say where we should go?" Tiger questioned.

"He probably doesn't know the best pickup point," Lindsay answered. "I'm sure he'd like to ask us about our preferences, but we can't tell him."

"Colonel," Li said, "there's something bothering me. That Ilyushin wouldn't have been where it was if it wasn't told to be there. I'd be willing to bet somebody gave away our location."

"I know," Lindsay responded. "Joe and I talked about it, but we don't know how anyone could pass the information along. Everyone involved in the project has been watched carefully by your government, Li, and they haven't been able to catch anyone."

"Well," Li went on, "I think we need to be careful Mister Calloway's messages to us aren't compromised the same way our flight plans were."

* * *

Darkness allowed Kao to slip off base without anyone knowing. He'd found this route not long after they closed off the base, and he could come and go freely, so long as he didn't wear a uniform. In fact, he could probably drive a truck off the base here and nobody would notice it.

In the village, he listened to the gossip. The enemy was still loose, and some people from Shahsien had disappeared. Some of the villagers thought the enemy might have killed them. And Shahsien was only a few dozen kilometers down the valley. But the militia still sat at its roadblocks, while the enemy freely moved around the countryside!

* * *

Hamilton hurried back to the hotel. He was on the telephone to Kung within minutes.

"I'm back," he reported. "We're successful. I'll go back in the morning. And the crew's supposed to go north."

"Good," Kung was pleased. "I'll tell our friend. When you arrive, call and let me know what else happens."

"OK," Hamilton smiled. Kung was pleased. Now, if everything went OK, the crew would be caught, and they could start a fresh operation. Maybe he should see about some horizontal action with Buttercup tonight, since he might be gone for several days.

* * *

"Look, Tom," Calloway shouted into the phone, "I don't give a rat's ass what the ChiComs say! The damned plane might be American-built, but somebody in Washington needs to remember we sent 'em all over the world. We even sold them as war surplus."

"Easy, Joe!" the voice on the other end of the line tried to calm Calloway. "I'm just telling you the politics here. The Chinese blame us for violating their airspace and shooting down their airplanes because we built this airplane. So far, nobody here's been able to respond. If we tell them it's the Nationalists, all hell will break loose! The United Nations will probably try to give the island to the mainland. You know that won't happen, but it'll put our government in the nasty position of having to use its veto power to override something the UN has already decided."

"Tom -" Calloway tried to interrupt, without success.

"If we even think of admitting it's us," the voice went on, "then *we're* the bad guys. You know *that*'ll never wash here!"

"Tom, dammit!" Calloway finally wedged the words in. "There's no way to connect the plane to anybody, so long as you did what I said and laundered the money we paid for it. Did you?"

"Well, yeah," Tom admitted. "We used SAT money, like you said, and replaced it through another contract."

"So the plane's paper trail leads to SAT," Calloway explained patiently. "SAT's a private company. Nobody will chase SAT away just because the Chinese complain. Around here, they're all using SAT to move troops against their own Chinese–backed rebels! And nobody will tell SAT to give away client information, because they don't want their own information given out! So SAT sits tight and keeps its mouth shut and nobody's the wiser. The only loophole we've got to close is getting the crew out of there!"

"What does the crew know?" Tom asked.

"Not enough to worry about," Calloway responded. "They know SAT owns the plane and they work for SAT Special Ops."

"OK," Tom was quieted. "So SAT sits on any information and stays quiet. Nobody can trace the operation. What about the contract? Do we need to restart the operation?"

"I don't know," Calloway responded. "That's not my concern right now. I just want those guys out of there."

"OK," Tom agreed. "Do you have anything more on the possible compromise of the flight plans?"

"Nothing yet," Calloway answered. "I've got suspicions, but one question stops me from accusing anybody."

"And that is -?" Tom questioned.

"I can't figure out how the information got off the island," Calloway answered. "The people I suspect were monitored, and there's nothing."

"Are we covering the right people?" Tom asked.

"We're covering everything I can think of," Calloway responded.

"Well, I hope you find out," Tom offered. "I'll get back with our people here and tell them how to cover our end. And you get your crew out of there."

"OK, Tom," Calloway agreed. "And remember, SAT bought a plane that was converted for transport use, and that's what it was used for. You might remind SAT's customers we don't get involved in shooting."

"Good," Tom agreed. "I think it's covered then."

* * *

Kao was back in the barracks, making sure his platoon was ready for lights out.

"Sir," it was Yang. "There's a rumor going around about enemy in the area. Why won't they let us off the base?"

"Yang," Kao responded, "there aren't that many of the enemy. They're survivors of an airplane crash. They may have even killed some people. But the militia thinks it can catch them with roadblocks!"

"Pardon my saying so, sir," Yang countered, "but I don't think the militia has a chance. Nobody's going to walk into a roadblock."

"I agree," Kao replied. "If it were up to me, I'd take you and your squad and a truck and we'd catch these people by tomorrow morning!"

"I bet we could, sir," Yang agreed.

* * *

Li decided; they'd go north, then east to the seacoast where a submarine could meet them. Even if the ChiComs tried to block this route, they still had to cover the route to Quemoy, as well.

Covering both should stretch the militia far enough to allow them to slip through. For now, though, they needed to head northeast.

It would be time to start soon. They'd follow the ridgeline tonight. There were lots of overgrown places where they could find cover for the day's rest. Then, when night fell again, they'd cross the river and be into the hills the following morning. From there, the trip to the seacoast should be easy.

* * *

Kung smiled to himself. He had called SAT's Tokyo office and explained he needed to talk to the landlord about Hamilton's rental. The receptionist had patched him through. He'd passed the man the information, and was assured it would be sent on. Kung wasn't concerned how the man sent the information to his contacts on the mainland, only that he did so. And, of course, that the contacts acted on it.

Now the man in Tokyo knew whatever survived of the crew was headed north, to Matsu. Most importantly, Hamilton would tell the crew where to go, and he could tell the man in Tokyo exactly what the crew was being told to do. This was almost too easy.

* * *

"So it's a blind alley?" Calloway was disappointed. He'd hoped Anderson could find a lead. That was their best chance of learning how the information was getting off the island and who was passing it.

"Yes, sir," Anderson was frustrated. "The guy in SID internal security, P'eng, told me there haven't been any further calls from the SID offices to Japan. He also said they've checked on SID folks using their home telephones. The Grand Hotel says Hamilton's calls are all on his bill. Kung calls Tokyo's CAT office almost daily as part of his job. Hamilton calls our office in Tokyo frequently, but nothing out of the ordinary. I even asked the SAT director here if they used any of SAT's phones, but no dice."

"There must be something, somewhere," Calloway couldn't believe there was nothing.

"I sure wish I knew what, sir," Anderson apologized.

"So do I, Paul," Calloway shook his head. "Ah, well," he went on, "I guess all we can do now is get the crew out of there."

"Yes sir," Anderson looked at his dinner plate, without interest.

* * *

"So where to now?" Tiger asked, stretching.

"North," Li answered. "Do you agree, Tiger?" he asked.

"North," Tiger agreed, "unless you want to go another way, Colonel."

"I'm outvoted if I say anything else," Lindsay replied. "But I'll vote for north, too."

"Good!" Li nodded. "Now, we'd better eat while we're packing."

"You're going to make me fat, Li," Tiger said in English.

"You might look good in fat, Tiger," Lin responded, also in English.

All three men stared in amazement. "You speak English!" Li stated the obvious.

"Of course," she answered. "What did you think I taught to the children?"

"Where did you learn English?" Li asked.

"You forget, Li," she smiled, "after your family left Fuchien, we still lived there until the Communists came. I went to the foreign missionary school. They insisted I learn English. I believe I learned it well."

"I'll say you did!" Lindsay volunteered.

Lin smiled at Li. "You know, Li, all things happen for good. Something good will happen because I know English. Some day."

* * *

Kao lay on his bed after lights out, thinking. It would take a truck, Yang's squad, and a day or two of pursuit, and the enemy would be caught. Tomorrow morning, he'd take the platoon to camp where he could get on and off the base. While the other two squads did routine activities, no one else would realize that one squad and its truck were missing until they came back with the enemy. He could even say he'd caught them on the base! Then he could laugh at his cousin and the militia.

* * *

Calloway gave the message to the Chinese lieutenant over the phone.

"OK, Mister Calloway," Han sounded eager to start work on the new message. "We'll get started right away."

"Good, Han," Calloway agreed. "I trust you guys to do a good job on this. You're the only lifeline our folks have over there."

"I understand, sir," Han was serious. "By the way, were you able to get transportation for Mister Hamilton tomorrow?"

"Sure," Calloway replied. "And he's bringing a couple of cases of beer and sodas!"

Calloway hung up the phone. With a smile to Olson, he turned toward the door. "A good day's work, Sarge," he smiled. "Now, can I give you a lift somewhere?"

* * *

Lindsay took out one of the radios. It crackled with the sound of the message as soon as he turned it on. He quickly copied down the numbers. As soon as he finished writing, his good hand scrabbled in the bag for the codebook.

"OK," Lindsay announced. "Calloway suggests we go north. That means we need to be careful, since we're heading that way anyway."

"Does Calloway know which way we're going?" Li asked.

"I don't think so," Lindsay answered. "There's not really a way he could tell." He hesitated a moment. "Unless, of course -."

"Unless what?" Tiger wanted to know.

"Unless the ChiComs know and talk about it," Lindsay guessed. "They might pass information on the radio, and Joe may know what they're saying."

"Oh," Tiger grinned, "that's rich! We're worried about a spy giving away our location, and Joe's spying to find out what the spy tells the ChiComs." He laughed.

"Let's hope the spy hasn't told them we're heading this way," Li wasn't laughing.

THIRTEEN

The guard called to notify Olson that Calloway was outside. The day was starting early, Olson reflected.

Olson signed Calloway in. "Thought you'd be half-asleep at this hour, sir," Olson chuckled, "or maybe still in bed."

"The thought of a decent cup of coffee was just too much to resist," Calloway replied.

"Then you haven't had breakfast yet, sir?" Olson asked.

"Nope," Calloway answered succinctly. "Thought I'd head out later and find a place to eat."

"Chow hall's open until eight," Olson offered. "They serve a pretty good breakfast here."

"We may have to head over there, then," Calloway nodded, "as soon as you let me know what happened after I left last night."

"Then you might as well head over right now, sir," Olson shook his head. "Nights around here are quiet. Last night was no exception."

"I meant you, too," Calloway offered.

"Appreciate it, sir," Olson smiled. "But my wife already fed me."

"Well," Calloway laughed, "I'm afraid I don't have a wife to feed me. Guess I'll head over there and fill up my middle. If you'll just point the way -."

* * *

They could see the river and the mountains from where they'd stopped.

"I'll miss the quiet mornings," Lin spoke.

"You'll live where the mornings are quiet," Lindsay answered. "Li's village is out in the country. It's wooded, with lots of birds."

"Our government says T'aiwan is desolate," Lin said. "They say it's covered with military bases, and the people are afraid to leave their homes."

"It's not like that," Lindsay smiled. "There are military bases, but the streets are full of people on bicycles, with lots of cars and busses."

"Do all of the cars belong to the government?" Lin asked.

"No," Lindsay shook his head. "In fact, most of the cars belong to private citizens."

"Could I learn to drive?" the girl asked.

"You can if you want to," Lindsay suddenly realized that he was enjoying this question-and-answer session. It would be fun to acquaint this young lady with the capitalist world.

* * *

"Here's what we have so far, sir," Olson briefed Calloway. "A platoon-sized patrol departed Nanp'ing shortly after daybreak, headed downriver, and they're spreading the squads out along the road."

"I don't think they've made the link between the couple at the village and the crew, Sarge," Calloway said. "They should've come up with that right away."

"Not necessarily, sir," Olson responded. "If the guy was known, they may think they've run off. I think they're on the back burner for now."

"That's not very smart," Calloway replied. "Li will make them pay for it."

* * *

Lin suddenly put her hand on Lindsay's good arm.

"On the road, near the river," she pointed. "A truck stopped and some men got off."

"Let me have the glasses," Lindsay said. He took the binoculars from her and adjusted them. "Soldiers, with rifles and packs."

"Are they coming this way?" Lin asked.

"It looks like they're staying near the road," Lindsay answered.

* * *

The company leader was pleased Kao was taking his platoon on an unannounced bivouac. "Commendable, Kao," he nodded. "Good training for your men."

"Thank you, sir," Kao smiled. "This will test their ability to set up and protect a camp from an enemy force."

"How will you do it?" the leader asked.

"I'll take a squad from camp, sir," Kao outlined his plan, "and allow the other two squads to get ready. Then we'll attack without warning."

"You'll be gone for a week?" the leader asked.

"If all goes well," Kao answered, "we could be back sooner."

And we'll bring prisoners, Kao thought.

* * *

"You guys enjoy that beer," Calloway told Hamilton.

"OK, Joe," Hamilton nodded. "You'll be back in about a week, right?"

"Yeah," Calloway confirmed. "They should be getting close to pickup by then. I have to go, Charlie. Don't forget to get the next message off right away."

Damn, thought Hamilton as Calloway left, I need to get busy. We need to get that crew caught soon!

Maybe the new message would help. Hamilton read it again. The ChiComs were patrolling north of the river, it said. How Calloway knew, he had no idea, but he could change the message and send the crew right into the arms of the patrols.

* * *

Ramsey had already made the appointment with the ChiNat admiral.

The admiral smiled as he shook their hands. "What can I do for you, gentlemen?"

"Well, sir," Ramsey started, "your government leased an airplane recently from Southern Air Transport."

"Ah, yes," the admiral replied. "One of my frogmen, Commander Li, is temporarily assigned to them."

"Yes, sir," Calloway agreed. "He's a good man. Unfortunately, he's on the ground over there, along with the rest of the crew. We'd like to get them back."

"I see," the admiral nodded, "I know the airplane was down. How can I help?"

"Sir," Calloway said, "we knew we couldn't communicate with survivors if they crashed, so we decided they'd go to one of several predetermined locations. They'd send a radio message with a codeword for the location, which would be our signal to get them. That's where we need your help, sir."

"Ah," the admiral said, "you'd like to have a quick reaction to their call."

"Yes, sir," Calloway replied.

"OK," the admiral was pleased. "I think we can have something ready when the time comes. Let me introduce you to one of my staff to start the planning."

* * *

Yang reported quickly. "Sir, the camp's set up. We're ready to start the 'exercise'."

"Good," Kao answered. "Get your squad into the truck. Are they ready?"

"Yes, sir," Yang replied, then turned to load his men. Each man's pack contained civilian clothing.

Kao spoke quickly to the other two squad leaders, giving them last-minute instructions. When he finished, he climbed into the truck. It was time to go catch the enemy.

* * *

Hamilton handed the message to the soldier. "OK, sir," Johnson acknowledged, "it'll be on its way shortly."

"Good," Hamilton responded, "and the beer Calloway sent is in my refrigerator."

"Thanks, Mister Hamilton," Han smiled. "I won't drink much – beer tends to get to us Chinese pretty quickly."

"OK, there's sodas, too," Hamilton replied as he left the radio room.

Good. The message would send the crew into the hills north of the river, right into the path of the patrols. Now he needed to tell Kung what he'd done. And Kung could pass that information to their contact.

* * *

Li woke them all as the sun went down. While they ate, Li turned on the radio and tuned in the message that came. Tiger copied the numbers, then handed them to Lindsay.

"This isn't right," Lindsay said. "It tells us to go north, across the river. It's not from Calloway."

"If this message isn't from him," Lin was puzzled, "then how do you know the one this morning was?"

"Two things, Lin," Lindsay explained. "First, he won't tell us what to do. Second, I have a special way to tell when he does, an authentication. This order isn't authenticated."

"I understand," Lin responded. "But now what do we do?"

"We need to keep on the way we planned," Lindsay proposed. "Stay along the river until we get past the patrolled area, then turn north."

"I agree, Colonel," Li replied.

"Me, too," Tiger agreed.

"How about you, Lin?" Lindsay asked.

"You don't have to ask me, sir," she replied.

"Yes, we do," Lindsay answered. "You're one of us now. You're as important as any of us. So what do you think?"

"I agree with you, then," the girl stammered. "And thanks for honoring me."

"You're welcome," Lindsay replied. "Now let's get moving."

* * *

The roadblocks weren't a problem. Kao's forged papers identified them as a militia work crew building roadblocks and they passed through the roadblocks readily. Although he wasn't sure where to start, they stopped and got information from the militia at a few roadblocks, under the guise of trading stories.

The village of Shahsien was the best place to start. The missing people had departed from there yesterday morning. Despite the rain, the trail would still be warm and Yang's trackers were well-trained.

* * *

"Good thinking," Kung praised Hamilton's initiative. "You'll send them right to the patrols. I'll contact our friend in the morning to let him know they're coming. Be sure to let me know about anything else."

"I will," Hamilton was pleased. "But I doubt anything will happen tonight."

"Talk to you tomorrow," Kung hung up the telephone. Good! Hamilton would send the crew right into the ChiComs' hands. Kung smiled.

* * *

Olson met Calloway at the gate and escorted him to the watch center.

"Any further word on their militia?" Calloway asked.

"Yes, sir," Olson answered. "Two groups are patrolling along the river, and several more are in the hills north of the river. They haven't found anything yet."

"So the crew's still south of the river," Calloway nodded.

"Well," Olson shrugged, "if it actually was your friend and the girl, I don't think they could make it to the river in time to beat the patrols."

"Which means they've either gone toward Quemoy," Calloway said, "or they're staying parallel to the river until they find a place where they can cross."

"There's no activity to the south," Olson replied. "It's almost like the ChiComs know the crew's going north."

* * *

They moved quickly, but Li knew the weather would slow them down. The clouds had been building since right after sundown. They had to reach the mountains before morning.

The rain started. They came to the stream right after that and began following it.

As they traveled along, the stream began to swell. Within an hour, they weren't able to follow its banks. Li was concerned about reaching the safety of the mountains before morning. This could be dangerous.

They entered the village almost before Li realized where they were. Visibility was so poor that he could only see one or two lights at this end. He motioned for the others to stay back, and then heard a familiar voice.

"Work for the good of the people," it was a villager he had met when he and Lin were here, one who quoted Chairman Mao's red book. "Comrade Li, isn't it?"

"Yes, comrade," Li answered, surprised the man would remember him.

"You shouldn't be out on a night like this, comrade," the man spoke gently. "But stop for a moment's rest at the far edge of the village, where our new hostel's being built."

"Thanks for the suggestion, comrade," Li nodded. "Will we disturb your fellow villagers?"

"You won't," the man smiled. "They should all be asleep in bed. So should the militia, in their camp between the village and the river. That's the only way you can bypass the village. The militia's trying to catch some war-mongering foreigners. I hope you and your friends won't run into any such people, Comrade Li."

"I hope so, too, comrade," Li answered. "And thanks."

"And we thank someone for the medical supplies we've received, Comrade Li," the man smiled. "I think we should show our gratitude by helping others. Especially friends."

"We'll pass along your kindness," Li nodded again. "Thank you, friend, and may your way be smooth and peaceful. *Yi lu p'ing an.*"

"*Yi lu p'ing an* to you also," the man nodded in return. "And please be careful of the roadblock on the other side of the bridge."

"We will," again Li nodded. "Thank you."

The man smiled again.

* * *

The rain was heavy and Kao was frustrated. "Damn this rain!" he growled to Yang as the two huddled inside the truck cab. "It'll wipe out the trail."

"It's not a problem, sir," Yang calmly reasoned. "It's obvious which direction they'll go. Their tracks show there are four of them, and one's the girl. They're headed along the ridge, moving parallel to the river. We're not far behind them. Don't forget, they're on foot and we have the truck."

"The truck won't help much in this rain," Kao responded darkly.

"Sir," Yang tried to calm his leader, "we have good people. We'll catch them."

* * *

Calloway lay in bed, wondering why the ChiComs were concentrating their attention to the north. There had to be a reason, but there weren't any indications they'd spotted the crew or had any knowledge of their movement.

It would be a long night. Tomorrow morning, he'd have to warn the crew of the increased patrol effort along the river and to the north of it. He'd call the guys on Matsu early and try to get the message off right at sunrise. In the meantime, he wasn't having any luck getting to sleep.

* * *

The rain continued to pound as they reached the bridge. On the other side was the roadblock. However, maybe they could cross the paddies and not be seen.

As they crossed the bridge, Li noticed the water was high. If the rain continued, there'd be flooding. The bridge was sturdy and wouldn't fail, but the riverbank could collapse.

They came to the end of the bridge, and Li saw light at the roadblock. He stopped the others. The light would obscure the vision of the soldiers. Li waved to the others to walk along the dikes that separated the paddies and circle around the roadblock. Lin understood immediately and started forward. She hadn't gone far when she suddenly stopped. The paddies ahead of her were so flooded the dikes were under water.

"There's nowhere to go," she whispered. "We'll have to find another way."

"I hope we can," Li was concerned. "We can't delay much longer." He led the group as they retraced their steps. Soon he found another dike that seemed to go parallel to the road, and he started that direction.

They'd walked for a few minutes when Li realized that this dike was turning, heading toward the light at the roadblock. He looked to try to find another way, but there wasn't one. They'd have to go forward or return to the bridge and try to find some other way. Maybe, he thought, they could bypass the roadblock on the other side. With that in mind, he told the others to remain where they were while he scouted the roadblock.

The rain continued to pound down for what seemed an eternity. Suddenly, Li was in front of them, calling them softly to follow him. He led them past the lighted roadblock, but there wasn't a challenge.

As they passed by, Lindsay noticed that part of the road on the far side of the roadblock was washed away. Maybe the sentries were washed away with it. He wasn't going to ask Li about it, though.

* * *

The wakeup call came early, and Calloway woke up grudgingly. He hadn't gotten much sleep. But he had a phone call to make to Matsu, and he'd just have to start firing on all cylinders – he didn't have a choice!

Thankfully, he could call from the hotel, he'd learned the previous night. He needed to get the message put together, then call it to the guys at Matsu so they could put it on the air. There wasn't much time – he'd better start right away. He went to the door to get the coffee and donuts the bellboy had left with the wakeup call.

* * *

"Are we ready to go?" Kao was impatient to be on the way.

"Almost, sir," Yang replied. "The last man's getting on the truck. I'll have to be careful driving until it turns light."

"I know," Kao responded. "But the rain will slow our enemies, also. We still need to hurry or they'll get away."

"We're loaded now, sir," Yang started the truck.

* * *

Hamilton took the message. Calloway wanted to tell the crew there were patrols out along the river and in the hills north of the river, did he? That meant Kung got the word through to his contact in Tokyo. Good! Now Hamilton had to change the message to tell the crew to cross the river and get into those hills for safety. He wrote out a message telling the crew there were patrols active on the south side of the river. That should force the crew to head northward.

* * *

Kao returned from the roadblock and climbed back into the truck.

"What did they say?" Yang asked.

"Two militiamen were washed away at a roadblock," Kao reported. "Part of the road collapsed into the river."

"Did the roadblock wash away?" Yang asked.

"No," Kao replied.

"No militiaman would leave shelter in this rain," Yang sneered. "Does that suggest something?"

"Yes," Kao responded. "That's why we're headed there."

* * *

Lindsay looked at the decoded message.

"This is bullshit!" he told Li. "Joe's not sending these messages. There's no authentication." He wadded up the piece of paper tightly. "I think we're being bushwhacked!"

"What do we do then, Colonel?" Tiger asked.

"We keep on doing what we're doing," Lindsay responded. "We go the way we've planned, but be careful not to do what we're told, until we get Joe's verification."

"OK," Li nodded. "Let's finish setting up camp. The rain's easing, but it's already daylight and we need the rest."

* * *

"Gentlemen," Olson started the briefing, "there's a report this morning that a couple of militiamen are missing from a roadblock south of Nanp'ing. The area flooded in the rains last night, and part of the road alongside the roadblock washed out."

"Any suspicion of foul play?" Calloway was alerted.

"Not that anyone could tell, sir," Olson answered. "Nobody at the nearby village knew anything, and the militia camp next to the village hadn't seen anybody. Right now they're trying to see if they can find the bodies."

"Anything else, Sarge?" Calloway asked.

"Only more about the flooding, sir," Olson answered. "The rain's supposed to get here later this morning."

"Well," Calloway encouraged, "let's hope they've found a place where they can be safe and dry, anyway."

"Can't say I envy 'em, being without coffee," the captain commented, lifting his cup. "Dry or otherwise!"

* * *

Kung hung up the phone. Good, he thought, the incorrect information Hamilton was passing to the crew should get them captured soon. Lindsay was a maverick, but he wouldn't disobey orders from Calloway. Then only the ineptness of the military could cause the plan to fail. Kung would bet that not all of the army could be stupid enough to allow the crew to escape.

Of course, he and Hamilton would continue to provide misdirection to the crew and inform their contact in Tokyo until they knew the crew was captured, and they might not find out about the capture until days after it happened. Kung knew he could get the information more quickly than that through SID, but he didn't want to call attention to his interest. It meant he'd have to call the contact on a daily basis to keep things in motion. He was glad he'd found the way to call through Hamilton's office in Tokyo. It was even more delicious since they were using SAT's communications to help capture the crew!

Kung laughed to himself. Now he had to go call Tokyo.

* * *

It was still raining as Lindsay awakened Li. The rain was so heavy it was impossible to see far.

"We probably won't see much activity by the ChiComs today," Li commented. "We might be able to start early and use the roads, as long as we're careful."

"Good," Lindsay answered. He was feeling stronger and Lin had told him the wound was closing well.

"We should be past Fuchou in two more days," Li continued. "Then we can call Matsu to come get us."

"How far do we have to go after we pass through Fuchou?" Lindsay asked.

"Probably two days on foot," Li answered. "Maybe I can find a truck in Fuchou to speed our trip. The roads aren't good, but a truck travels almost as far in an hour as we can travel in a night!"

Lindsay smiled. It would be nice to ride.

* * *

"I'm sorry," the militiaman was adamant. "You can't leave."

Kao's anger was rising. "We've been ordered to build the roadblock at the bridge to Fuchou!" he barked.

"That's impossible now," the militiaman insisted. "You have to stay here and help us."

"We can't take orders from you," it was Yang. "We have our own."

"I don't care about your damned orders!" the militiaman was getting angry. He waved to the two men behind him, who raised their rifles. "You *will* stay here and help!"

From the rear of the truck came the unmistakable sound of automatic rifles being cocked. Fear filled the militiaman's eyes as he looked into the barrels of the squad's AK-47s. His men lowered their rifles.

"Please understand," Yang smiled gently, "our orders are from higher authority. We're already late, and we've got to go now."

The truck rolled away from the militiamen, as Kao breathed a sigh of relief and a prayer of thanks for Yang.

* * *

It was Calloway's first chance to slow down. He and Anderson sat in the MAAG Compound Officers' Club, looking out at the rain.

"So no news is good news?" Anderson asked.

"Maybe," Calloway answered. "At least, nobody seems to know

where they are right now. But why would the ChiComs concentrate their forces in the north? They can't have any more information than we do."

"It's weird," Anderson spoke thoughtfully. "It's almost like they think we're telling the crew to go there."

"I don't know enough to tell the crew where to go," Calloway replied. "The best I can do is give suggestions."

"Well," Anderson continued, "the ChiComs might know more about what the crew's doing than they're saying."

"Yeah," Calloway acknowledged. "I just wish I was sure we haven't overlooked anything."

"Hey," Anderson was suddenly thoughtful, "how about giving me a copy of your code and the frequencies? Maybe we're transmitting something that's telling the ChiComs where to look."

"OK," Calloway agreed, "if you can hang on until I finish the steak I've got coming!"

* * *

Li awakened the others as the light failed. This would be the hardest part of the journey, since there wasn't much cover left between here and Fuchou.

The group ate their cold meal in silence. The rain continued to obscure the countryside. There wouldn't be much light, and it would be tough making their way through the paddies tonight.

* * *

Yang parked the truck on the side of the road. They'd sleep in it again, the men in the truck bed while Kao and Yang stayed in the cab. The only thing good about this, Kao reflected, was not having to attend evening meetings.

"Sir," Yang was thinking, "they were at the bridge last night, you know."

"Yes," Kao answered. "We're on the right track. But the activity along the road's scaring them away. They're staying to the south, but they want to go north."

"Would they go where we did coastal defense duty last year?" Yang asked.

"It's a perfect place," Kao replied. "The defenses on the beach are thin because it's a stupid place to attack. But we'll catch them before they reach Fuchou."

* * *

"Sir," Olson looked tired, "this afternoon, a patrol reported they found where somebody went off into the rice paddies. The locals think it was somebody tending rice shoots, but that's unusual in this weather."

"Anything else?" Calloway asked.

"Well," Olson continued, "they've put together a convoy from Changchou, heading up the coast road. They're supposedly going up northwest of Fuchou into the hills. There's lots of complaining - nobody wants to spend time up there. Other than that and the situation at the river, the ChiComs seem pretty quiet with the weather, though."

"OK, Sarge," Calloway shook his head. "We still don't know why the ChiComs are moving their people north of the river, do we?"

"Well, sir," Olson replied, "they've mentioned information from Peiching. We can't get that level of information, though. Most of what we see is tactical level stuff."

"OK," Calloway understood. "Keep a watch for the crew. Anything like a bunch of people moving quickly into an area may be a response to the crew. Now, if I can use your phone to call out to Matsu -."

* * *

Hamilton chuckled at the message. He almost wouldn't have to change this one. Calloway mentioned a troop movement coming from the south, which would go along with what Hamilton had already sent out. Kung would laugh at the irony!

As if that wasn't bad enough, Calloway thought the crew was in the mountains west of Fuchou, but wouldn't move because of the heavy rains. Kung would love to hear that, too.

Hamilton wrote out the text, then began encoding it.

* * *

Kung was excited to hear the crew should be in the mountains west of Fuchou. This was the best information yet! He didn't understand why the crew hadn't crossed into the hills yet, as Hamilton had told them to do, but maybe they'd spotted the patrols. They'd probably stay near the river until the patrols ended, then cross.

It was too late tonight to call Tokyo. He'd have to make the call first thing in the morning. He had to re-direct the militia toward the mountains west of Fuchou. It was time to capture this crew. They'd wasted too much time already.

* * *

The flooding wasn't as bad in the plain as it was in the valleys. Li picked the way for them, finally following a stream before stopping to rest.

"We'll be in the open," Lin noted. "There's not much cover between here and Fuchou."

"True," Li agreed, "but the rain will cover us. I wanted to cross the river before this, but we'll probably have to go through Fuchou." His face darkened. "I have a few things to settle there, anyway," he continued.

"Not on my account," Lin looked at him with alarm.

"Only if your account coincides with mine," Li responded. "I think I'll find a frogman named Wang there. He's the one who received the opium and delivered it. I'll probably catch him with the deputy governor or the governor – they're the only people in this province who can afford opium. And the opium's the reason the ChiComs got our flight plans."

"Why do you say that?" Lindsay asked.

"Because of the problem we had with the 'morphine'," Li replied. "We made it hard to deliver the opium. So we have to be eliminated and a new crew found that will deliver."

"Who sent it?" Tiger asked.

"It must be Kung," Li continued. "He might be backed by others, but I don't think so."

"Calloway and I thought it might be him, too," Lindsay agreed. "We couldn't figure out how he got information to the ChiComs, but we never told anyone else about our destination."

"That's not my problem," Li responded. "But I can and will take care of Wang. He's dirtied the reputation of all of us frogmen."

FOURTEEN

They were hidden behind a clump of bamboo, almost at the river's edge. There were villages nearby and a bridge, but the bamboo would keep them from being spotted. They'd crossed the road at the junction and Li had carefully eliminated their tracks. This place was as safe as any.

Li watched the others prepare the campsite. Perhaps tomorrow they'd be in Fuchou. He'd find a truck for the others and then take care of Wang.

He pulled the radio from his pack. It was time for the report from Matsu. The rain would cover any noise from the radio. It crackled lightly as he turned it on and tuned it.

* * *

Calloway padded to the door to get the coffee and donuts. Another early day. Day after tomorrow he'd head to Matsu to prepare to go after the crew. They should be near the coast by then, and he wanted to be there when they called to report their intended location. The ChiNat navy would send a submarine to bring them out. So long as they remembered to take him along, Calloway would be happy.

Time for a shower and shave, and then off to T'aipei Air Station to get the morning's news. Calloway poured a cup of coffee.

* * *

Kao awoke stiff and tired. Another night of sleeping in the truck was over. He wasn't happy, but the rain stopped them from setting up camp. Yang and the men were already preparing the morning meal. He'd better eat. It would be another hard day, but they should catch the enemy today.

"We need gas today," Yang reminded him. "The tank's low. Maybe we can get some from one of the roadblocks."

"Aren't there any militia bases nearby?" Kao frowned.

"Yes, sir," Yang replied, "but they won't let us have gas. And our papers may not stand the close scrutiny."

"We've got to do something," Kao stated. "Even if we have to take it by force."

"I'm not sure that's a good idea, sir," Yang cautioned. "Maybe we can get gas at one of the roadblocks."

"Then let's find one, and soon," Kao said.

"Yes, sir," Yang agreed.

* * *

Li and Lindsay looked at the decoded message sourly. They had a major problem.

"A militia convoy's coming north," Li told the others. "It should arrive in Fuchou this afternoon. The message says we should either go north immediately or remain in the mountains for further instructions." He turned to Lindsay. "This still isn't from Calloway, but we have to get through Fuchou before the convoy gets there."

"I agree," Lindsay nodded. "I think we need to move more quickly than we planned."

"OK, Colonel," Tiger said. "We're ready to get this over with, right, Lin?"

"If we have to move quickly, Colonel," Lin responded, "I won't hold you back."

"She won't, either, Colonel," Li added. "She'll outdo all of us!"

"Well," Lindsay considered their options, "there's not much else we can do. Let's get ready to go." He turned to face east. "Fuchou, like it or not, here we come!"

* * *

Kung hung up the telephone. Another call to Tokyo completed. This time, he'd told the contact the crew seemed to be located at the northeastern end of the coastal mountains. The contact was excited at knowing the whereabouts of the crew, and felt Fuchou would act on the information within an hour. The only problem, the contact said, was that the rain might slow the militia. But they'd surround the area where the crew was hiding and capture them today!

Kung rubbed his hands together. Soon, very soon, the money would start coming in again. He wondered how Hamilton was enjoying the life of a soldier on Matsu.

* * *

Calloway stood in front of the map.

"The convoy won't make it to Fuchou by nightfall," Olson explained. "The rain washed out the road and they're delayed." The telephone rang. "Just a moment, please, sir," Olson excused himself.

In a moment, he handed it to Calloway. "It's a Mister Anderson, sir," he explained.

"Paul," Calloway acknowledged, "what's up?"

"Joe," Anderson asked, "did you tell Matsu to tell the crew to either head north or sit tight in the mountains this morning?"

"No," Calloway replied.

"I didn't think so," Anderson continued. "I bought a short-wave radio last night and copied the message from Matsu this morning. It said the convoy would arrive today and the crew should stay in the mountains or go north."

"That's not the message I gave Hamilton to send," Calloway's anger flashed. "As soon as I hang up here, I'm going to find out what the hell he thinks he's doing out there!"

"OK, sir," Anderson replied. "Let me know if there's anything I can do."

"OK," Calloway anger showed. He became aware another phone was ringing.

"Mister Calloway!" the young airman who answered the phone held it toward him. "It's for you, sir!"

"Calloway!" Calloway barked, expecting to hear Hamilton's voice.

"Joe!" It was Art Ramsey, "Glad I caught you! I've got your secretary on the line! I'm patching her through."

"Joe!" Marion's voice was excited, "I'm glad we found you."

"What's the matter, Marion?" Calloway was impatient to call Matsu.

"Joe, Yukiko's here," Marion continued. "She just overheard something. You need to hear about it!"

"What the hell?" Calloway asked.

"Mister Calloway," Yukiko broke in, "they were talking about Tiger and Mister Lindsay and Li and someone!"

"Who was?" Calloway's attention focused immediately.

"The man who called to help Mister Hamilton, sir," Yukiko continued. "He's Chinese, and he's called Mister Hamilton's new apartment several times lately to help Mister Hamilton get the apartment ready. His name is Mister Kung, and I thought he could use help talking to the Japanese landlord. And so I listened this morning to see if I could help. But they were speaking Chinese, and they were talking about Tiger and Mister Lindsay and Li and someone else with them. And then Mister Kung said he told the crew to go north or to stay in the mountains, and the man could tell the soldiers to catch the crew in the mountains, since they didn't want to cross the river."

"When did you hear this?" Calloway asked sharply.

"Oh, Mister Calloway," there were tears in Yukiko's voice, "it was only ten or fifteen minutes ago. Oh, please help them, Mister Calloway."

"I will, Yukiko," Calloway replied, "don't you worry. We'll get them out of there!"

"Just be careful, Joe Calloway," Marion spoke again. "No foolishness, OK? You get them out of there, and I swear I'll even marry that lovable dummy, just to keep him out of airplanes!"

Calloway thought fast. "Marion!" he replied, "I want you and Yukiko down here, right away." He went on. "Tell Buchanan it's company business and you'd better be here before noon if he wants to keep his director's chair!"

"OK, Joe," Marion answered. "We can catch a flight from here and be there about noon."

"Good!" Calloway responded. "I'll have Ramsey meet you at the airport!" He thought for a moment. "Does Yukiko have a log of the calls Kung's made through our office to that number?"

"Sure, Joe," Marion answered. "She logs all pass-through calls, even the ones Hamilton makes. It'll take a little bit to find them all in the records, but they're there."

"OK," Calloway was excited. "Bring everything you've got on the recent calls by Kung, especially since the crew's been down. I'm sure his bosses here will be interested in them. Now, Ramsey will get you to me, so trust him and do what he says, OK?"

"OK, Joe," Marion agreed. "Get that big, sweet guy home for me, will you?"

"How can I resist a request like that?" Calloway laughed, popping the hook up and down to get Ramsey's attention.

In a second, Ramsey broke in. "You need something, Joe?"

"Yep," Calloway replied and told Ramsey what he needed.

Moments later, Calloway was talking to Sergeant Major George about transportation out to Matsu.

"What's the rush, Joe?" George asked. "Can I help?"

"Yep, Alex," Calloway replied. "My guy's sending bad messages!"

"I'd like to go along, then," George sounded worried. "You know, my son-in-law might try to do something foolish if the situation gets out of hand, and I'd just as soon be there to try to keep things in hand."

"I understand," Calloway agreed.

"See you at the airfield in about half an hour, then," George rang off.

Calloway dialed Anderson's number once again. "Got a job for you, Paul," he told the young man.

"Yes, sir," Anderson replied.

"I need to have you get hold of that guy at the SID internal affairs office," Calloway said.

"P'eng," Anderson responded.

"Yep," Calloway answered. "Tell him we have proof coming from Tokyo that Kung's talked repeatedly to a suspected Commie agent in Tokyo through a telephone connection at SAT the past several days. This morning, one of our people listened in when he told the Commie agent the location of our crew. P'eng might like to hear that."

"I'll bet he would, sir!" Anderson replied. "He might even want to act on it!"

"Thanks, Paul," Calloway said. "And now, I'm headed out to send Mister Charlie Hamilton on a trip to Leavenworth. That son of a bitch has not only been passing bad instructions to the crew, but he's the only one who could have passed the information along that Kung gave to the Commie guy in Tokyo."

"Hard to believe Charlie would do something like that," Anderson was taken aback. "He always seemed like a nice guy."

"Nice guy or not, Paul," Calloway responded, "he's given away a lot of information. I just hope we can undo the problems he's caused us. Putting him in Leavenworth is tame compared to what I'd really like to do to him!"

"OK, Joe," Anderson said, "I'll get to Mister P'eng right away, and let him know what's going on. Good luck with Hamilton."

"Thanks," Calloway answered and hung up the phone.

"Mister Calloway," it was Olson. "We have a problem, sir."

"What now?" Calloway's stinger was out and Olson had just run into it.

"The ChiComs just ordered their roadblock units to converge on the northeast end of the coastal mountain range, sir," Olson wasn't letting Calloway's temper bother him. "They're talking about going after the crew of the crashed plane, sir."

"Oh, shit!" Calloway stared at the map, the stinger forgotten. "I think that's where the crew is! Sarge," he turned to Olson, "how long will it take to get those troops to the mountains?"

"Probably an hour, sir," Olson answered. "They're taking trucks out of Fuchou, picking up people on the way."

"I've got to go, then," Calloway looked at the clock. "Sergeant George will meet me at the airport in about fifteen minutes, so maybe I can get to Matsu in time to warn the crew."

"Sir," Olson broke in, "why don't you just call and have the GI who works the radio send the message for you, if you don't want Mister Hamilton to do it?"

"Good idea," Calloway replied. "Hamilton probably won't be in the radio room at this time of day. I'll use your phone for just a minute longer, then."

He dialed the operator.

* * *

The truck was refueled. Two militiamen lay dead by the gas drums and another at the gate into the dump. They wouldn't give up the gasoline and the truck's gauge showed empty. Kao had even tried to pay for it, but they refused. When Kao insisted they give it up, they'd pointed their weapons at him. Yang's men opened fire to protect their officer. There was no more to be said, Kao told them. The enemy was loose in the country, and their task was paramount. Dead militiamen might be the price they had to pay to catch the enemy.

Yang's men bandaged their two wounded while Kao and Yang pumped the gas. As soon as the truck was filled, Yang climbed behind the wheel and they continued on their way.

* * *

Li watched from the bushes as the troops near the bridge began stirring.

"What's the matter?" Lindsay asked. "Are they going to block our way?"

"I don't know, sir," Li answered. "Something's upsetting them. They're apparently getting ready to go somewhere. See, they're carrying their rifles and packs."

"Are they pulling everybody back to Fuchou?" Tiger asked.

"I can't tell, Tiger," Li answered.

"Li," Lin tapped him on the forearm, "several trucks are coming up the road across the river."

Li looked in the direction Lin pointed. "They sure are, Lin," he agreed. "And they're in a hurry."

"Would you want to bet they're headed where we're supposed to be?" Lindsay suddenly said.

"I think you're right, Colonel," Li agreed with him. "Maybe it's a good thing we decided to move on today. It's a long way, but they'll cover it quickly in the trucks."

The crew watched as the trucks crossed the bridge, then stopped to pick up the soldiers at the roadblock. They were soon on their way and out of sight.

"It looks like the troops are gone," Li looked skeptical, "but they've left a truck behind. It's partly hidden in the bushes." He turned to the others. "I'm going to see if I can get it!"

"Just be careful," Lindsay cautioned him. "We'll wait here."

* * *

Calloway arrived at the airport on time, the staff car screeching to a stop at the ramp where the C-47 was warming up. Calloway didn't waste a second jumping out and yelling a quick thanks to the captain behind the wheel. A quick sprint across the ramp, and Calloway was into the C-47.

"Let's go!" he said to Sergeant George, who pulled the stairs up.

The plane began to taxi out while George and Calloway closed the door, then quickly sat down.

"Here, Joe," George handed Calloway a bag. "It's the best I could do on short notice. It's a Colt .45. I grabbed it from my commander, but I don't think he minds. And I trust that look to the sky was his way of praying for our safety."

"Not bad, Alex!" Calloway pulled the gun, holster, and belt from the bag. "Even extra clips of ammunition. Thanks!"

"You're welcome," George replied. "I figured you might like to have it. You really think we might have trouble with this guy?"

"I have no idea," Calloway answered. "I hope not, but he's

looking at a long time behind bars, and Leavenworth isn't much of a retirement village."

* * *

The truck pulled to the side of the road. Li smiled from behind the wheel.

"I remembered how to start it," he said.

"Let's be on our way," Tiger threw his pack into the back of the truck and climbed in, followed by Lin.

"Not so fast," Lindsay calmed things down. "Let's organize what we're doing."

"Go ahead, Colonel," Li nodded to Lindsay.

"OK," Lindsay continued. "We don't want to attract attention. I think we should have the three of you in the front seat. The truck itself looks pretty much everyday."

"There's not much difference between the civilian and military models," Li replied. "The government owns them all, anyway."

"OK, then," Lindsay continued, "with the three of you in front, and me hidden in the back, we shouldn't be stopped, except at random."

"I should stay in the back, sir," Lin spoke up. "That's the usual way."

"OK," Lindsay agreed. "The two guys in front and you in the back, with me under cover. And everybody keep your guns handy. Anybody have anything better?"

"Sounds good," Li answered, and Tiger nodded. "But let's knock out the rear window, so we can communicate!" He clubbed the rear window with his pistol until it fell out.

"This'll be better than walking!" Lindsay said as he climbed into the truck.

"Don't bet on that, Colonel," Li replied. "Faster, yes, but it rides like a rock!"

"Li," Tiger chimed in, "let me drive. It'll leave you free to handle gunwork if we need any!"

"Good idea," Li replied. "Just don't get any speeding tickets, OK?"

* * *

Anderson was shown into P'eng's office.

"Ah, Mister Anderson," P'eng smiled in greeting. "It's good to see you again. And what can I do for you?"

"Mister P'eng," Anderson replied, "I'm sorry I couldn't speak openly on the phone. We've learned that one of your people has been in direct contact with a Communist agent in Tokyo."

"Ah, yes," P'eng broke in, "we know about that."

"Well," Anderson continued, "we have proof that this person contacted the agent several times in the past few days and passed information about our crew, to try to capture them."

"You have proof of this?" P'eng asked.

"Yes, sir, I do," Anderson answered. "It's coming from Tokyo and should be here soon. It consists of telephone records showing that this person has contacted the Communist agent almost daily the past few days and has probably been in contact with him several times in the past."

"How did they make contact?" P'eng questioned.

"It was simple, sir," Anderson answered. "The SID agent called the SAT project office in Tokyo, and had the call forwarded to the phone where the Communist agent was waiting."

"Ingenious," P'eng almost smiled. "What gave it away, Mister Anderson?"

"Total accident," Anderson replied. "SAT's receptionist in Tokyo speaks both Japanese and Chinese. She thought the caller might need help when he talked to the Japanese man she was supposedly calling for him, and she listened in. Of course, she understood what they were saying. She reported the situation, and my boss, Mister Calloway, told me to come see you about it."

"This is serious, Mister Anderson," P'eng placed his palms carefully together. "If we have a person in one of our offices who's a traitor, it could result in a death sentence."

"I know, Mister P'eng," Anderson spoke gravely. "But you need to know about the situation and the individual involved. I'm sure you know Winston Kung."

"Kung?" P'eng looked surprised. "And to think I told him we suspected someone in his office! I have to arrest him immediately, of course. Would you care to go with me?" He walked to his coat rack, where a shoulder holster with a gun hung with his suit jacket.

"My pleasure, Mister P'eng," Anderson answered. "The members of that crew are good friends of mine."

* * *

"How are you doing back there?" Li asked Lindsay.

"Tell Tiger to quit aiming at the bumps!" Lindsay shouted back.

"You should see the ones he's missing!" Li replied. "We'll be in Fuchou soon. We may need to stop and get out of the truck fast."

"Understand!" Lindsay responded. "Just tell Tiger I liked his flying better than I like his driving!"

Lindsay looked up at Lin, whose face had hardened. "You don't like going back there, do you?" he asked.

"No," she answered. "It isn't my favorite place, and I'll be happy to leave. There are too many people there I don't like."

"Hopefully, we won't stay long," Lindsay tried to be encouraging. "But I think I'd better be sure I'm hidden now."

* * *

The commander met Calloway and George. "Ah, gentlemen," he nodded. "It's a privilege to have you with us again. We didn't expect you back so soon."

"We didn't expect to be here so soon, either, sir," Calloway replied. "But let's get out of the way. This airplane's going back to T'aipei to bring some other people here. We needed to get here as quickly as possible."

"Something's wrong?" the commander asked.

"There's a problem with the man I left to help with the radio, sir," Calloway answered. "He's not following orders, and I suspect he's working with the Communists to stop us from rescuing our people."

"That's not good," the commander replied. "What will you do?"

"I'm going to put him under arrest," Calloway answered. "And I need to send a message immediately to the crew. They could be in danger and they need to know it. Also, can we set up a secure phone line to T'aipei Air Station?"

"Sure," the commander smiled. "Not a problem."

"Good," Calloway answered. "The sooner we can call T'aipei Air Station's watch center, the better! Now," he reached down to pat the pistol at his side, "we have some other business to tend to."

* * *

P'eng stopped the car in front of the CAT office building, in a No Parking zone. A policeman hurried toward them, waving at them to move the car, but P'eng held up his identification, and the policeman retreated. P'eng didn't slow his stride, and Anderson hurried to keep up.

Inside, P'eng stopped at the reception desk. "Is Mister Kung in his office?" he asked.

"Yes, sir," the receptionist replied. "May I tell him who's here?"

"No," P'eng answered, holding up his identification, "and I'd advise you not to tell him anyone's here. This is official business!"

"Yes, sir!" the receptionist stiffened at the sight of the credentials, recognizing them immediately.

P'eng turned toward Anderson. "This way," he started toward a stairway.

They'd reached the bottom of the stairs when P'eng looked up and called out. "There he is! Halt, Kung! You're under arrest!"

Kung jumped back up the stairwell and disappeared behind a corner. P'eng immediately ran up the stairs, followed by Anderson.

"Don't let him get away!" P'eng shouted back, pulling the gun from his shoulder holster. Behind him, Anderson reached for his own gun.

They reached the top of the stairs and P'eng rushed into the hallway. A shot rang out, and P'eng was thrown sideways, landing in a heap on the floor. As several more shots rang out and bullets ricocheted off the floor, he quickly scrambled back to the stairway and fell next to Anderson, holding his bleeding shoulder.

"How bad is it?" Anderson asked.

"Hit me in the shoulder," P'eng gritted his teeth. "Stupid move. Should have known better."

"Where is he?" Anderson asked.

"In a doorway about twenty feet down the hall," P'eng's voice showed the pain. "All of the offices have fire escapes."

"Then we'd better get him now," Anderson responded, and dove into the hallway, rolling over as more shots rang out. Suddenly, he stopped rolling and fired once, twice, a third time. A gun fell on the floor, followed by the sound of a body falling, and Anderson stood up, the gun still leveled down the hallway.

Without turning, Anderson spoke. "Mister P'eng, I don't believe we'll have any further trouble."

"Is he dead?" P'eng struggled to stand.

"I don't know for sure, sir," Anderson replied, helping P'eng to his feet, "but I got a good shot to his head. He's isn't moving at all."

They walked down the hallway to Kung's body as doorways began to open and frightened office workers peered out carefully.

* * *

"They were here, sir," Yang showed the signs to Kao. "They went to the road, there. That must have been after the troops were picked up by the convoy."

"Squad leader!" one of the men called. "Come here, please!"

Yang and Kao walked to where the man was looking at tire tracks.

"What?" Yang asked.

"These tracks don't turn the same direction as the rest," the man pointed. "They're headed down the river."

"And right past where the enemy came to the road," Yang nodded.

Another man called. "There's a body here. A dead militiaman."

"The guard," Kao understood. "Now they have transportation. We've got to catch them before they can use their mobility."

Yang called to the men to get into the truck.

* * *

They were in the city, and there weren't any roadblocks. Lindsay hid in the back of the truck, with Lin sitting slumped over him. Li thought the lack of soldiers was remarkable. However, he directed Tiger to drive to the ugly building that housed the provincial offices. When they arrived, he gave Tiger directions to leave the city.

"I won't go without you," Tiger stated.

"You may have to," Li wasn't smiling. "I'll do my best to be back as quickly as I can. But if there's any sort of trouble, leave immediately. Don't worry about me – I'll be gone before they know who to look for. If we're separated, I'll make my way to the coast and use the radio I have in my pocket. You've got to get Colonel Lindsay and Lin to the coast to be picked up – I'm counting on you!"

"Then I guess I'd better do it," Tiger nodded.

The truck pulled to a stop under a terrible picture of Chairman Mao, smiling a glued-on smile, that hung over the main doorway.

"Wish me luck," Li said as he stepped down onto the sidewalk.

* * *

"Hey Joe, what's up?" Hamilton was surprised to see Calloway.

"I came to get some answers, Charlie," Calloway wasn't smiling and Hamilton was instantly wary.

"What do you mean, Joe?" Hamilton asked.

"I mean we just learned that Kung's feeding information on the crew's location to a Commie agent through our own office, Charlie," Calloway was blunt. "He used your phone at CAT and called a number in Tokyo that you called several times. Only the guy he talked to wasn't a landlord, as you told Yukiko – he was a ChiCom agent, and Kung was tipping him off where our crew was supposed to be."

"I don't know anything about that!" Hamilton objected.

"Oh, don't feed me that crap, Charlie!" Calloway was angry. "Kung was telling the Commie the same stuff I told you earlier. Only he was telling the Commie to use it to catch our crew! You were feeding it to him!"

Hamilton's mind raced. What was he going to do? "Joe, talk to Kung!" he clutched at a straw. "He'll tell you it's not so! I don't know who he was talking to in Tokyo, but I wasn't involved!"

"I don't believe that, Charlie," Calloway answered. "And Kung's probably under arrest by now. I sent Paul Anderson to the SID's internal affairs office while I came out here for you."

"Oh, God, no, Joe!" Hamilton pleaded, "I don't have anything to do with it! You've got to believe me!"

"Charlie, shut up!" Calloway barked. "You go with Sergeant George to get your stuff together while I send a message over there and try to get them out of this mess! Get moving! Now!"

Hamilton almost ran out of the office.

* * *

Inside the building, Li recognized the guard.

"Friend!" Li greeted him. "You remember me? I was here with Lin Yu-feng several months ago." He stepped forward, bowing.

"Ah, yes," the militiaman smiled recognition. "Comrade Li, isn't it?" He bowed in return, and was rudely hit squarely on his chin and knocked out cold. Li caught the body and eased it quietly to the floor.

"I'm sorry," Li spoke softly. "You were Lin's friend, but you're in my way." With that, he hurried to the stairway and quickly climbed the stairs to the deputy governor's office.

At the outer office door, Li pushed the door open quickly. The startled secretary looked up to see Li holding a finger to his lips to quiet her as he stepped to the door to the deputy governor's office and threw it open.

Inside, the deputy governor glanced upward from behind his desk. On the desk lay a package, the opium Chou had dropped with his last delivery.

"Where's the man who delivered that?" Li barked.

"Behind you, turtle's egg," a familiar voice called out, and Li ducked to avoid the blow to the side of his head, a blow that smashed into the door instead. With a roar, Wang swung again, but Li spun and caught Wang's arm, then reached to catch his head, snapping it sideways, breaking his neck. Before he could drop the dead man, a shot rang out, and the body was slammed backward against him.

The deputy governor held a pistol in front of him, pulling the trigger again. With a huge surge, Li thrust the body at the deputy governor, pulling his own pistol from his pocket. The next shot struck the body, and the deputy governor ducked away, only to step into Li's bullet, which struck him in the head. He fell, dead before he hit the floor.

Li grabbed the opium package and ran out, leaving a horrified secretary behind. As he pushed out the door into the hallway, the old governor stepped out of his office, holding a rifle.

Li raised the pistol and pointed it at the old man. "Put the gun down, governor," he said quickly, "before I have to shoot you."

The old man stared at the pistol. With a frightened look on his face, he dropped the rifle. "Are you going to kill me?" he asked, fear shaking his voice.

"You'll die soon enough," Li answered, throwing the opium package to him. He then turned and ran down the stairs.

He'd barely started across the foyer when another door opened down the hall. Instinctively, Li dove forward as a gunbarrel thrust out and sprayed a burst of fire down the hallway. Behind the gunbarrel, Lin's former boss stepped forward, trying to get a better shot.

Suddenly, a different gun fired, from near the main doors. Li looked up as the bullet struck the boss in the forehead, then looked toward the doorway to see Lin holding the militiaman's rifle. With a yell to get out, Li rushed across the foyer and pushed Lin ahead of him through the main doors toward the waiting truck. He lifted her into the back of the truck before jumping into the front seat himself. Before he could close the door, Tiger jammed the vehicle in gear and sped off down the street, pounding on the blaring horn as traffic scattered to get out of the way.

Twisting and bouncing, the truck rushed through the streets of Fuchou, suddenly exiting the city. A mile ahead, the gateway to the airbase loomed. If the ChiComs put a truck across the road, they'd be stopped in their tracks! But the closer they came, the more they realized no effort was being made to stop them. In a moment, they were past the gate of the airbase. The truck sped toward the coast.

Li suddenly realized he was holding his breath. It was OK to breathe again, he thought. He reached for the radio in his pocket.

* * *

Calloway finished the message to the crew and handed it to Han just as Johnson rushed into the radio room.

"Mister Calloway," he was out of breath, "come quick, sir. Hamilton's got a gun and he's holding the sergeant major hostage!"

"Send the message, lieutenant," Calloway gave the order. "I'll be back as soon as I can!"

"Roger, sir!" Han called back. "Good luck!"

"Need more than luck, dammit," Calloway growled as they raced out of the building. "How the hell did he get a gun?"

"I don't know, sir," Johnson replied. "I went to see if I could help, and Hamilton had the gun on him. I got away before Hamilton could stop me, and came right here."

"Let's get the sarge out of there, then," Calloway halted as they rounded a corner and saw the barracks in front of them. "Now, how do we go about this?"

"Look, sir," Johnson offered, "I'll wait for the count of thirty and start raising a ruckus out here in the street. Hamilton will come to the window to see what the racket's all about, and you can break into the room then. How does that sound?"

"Sounds good, son," Calloway patted him on the shoulder. "Start your count now, and I'll give him a second or two to go to the window after you start making the racket."

"OK, sir," the young soldier got into position as Calloway hurried to the building, heading for Hamilton's room.

At the door, Calloway halted. Within a moment, he could hear the noise of metal trashcans being upset outside the building. He reached quietly for the doorknob and turned it, and the door started to open. Hamilton hadn't locked it!

Calloway threw the door open, his gun in his hand. Hamilton was at the window, looking out, and George was at the side of the room, his hands on his head while Hamilton's gun was pointed his direction.

"Drop the gun, Charlie!" Calloway took aim, hoping Hamilton would obey. Instead, Hamilton spun toward him, bringing the gun around, and Calloway fired.

One shot.

The heavy slug struck Hamilton in the chest, slamming him through the window, and he fell outside. Calloway ran to the window to see Hamilton lying on the ground, eyes staring, struggling to breathe.

"Damn you, Charlie," Calloway cursed. "I didn't want to shoot you, you dumb shit!"

"Ah - ah," Hamilton tried to speak, then went limp. Calloway climbed out and checked for a pulse. There was none, and he pulled the eyelids closed, then looked up to see George standing in the broken-out window, Johnson behind him.

"He wouldn't let you take him alive, Joe," George said. "He said he wasn't going to Leavenworth. He had that gun in his stuff."

"Damn!" Calloway was upset. "I wanted to know why he did it!"

"He said something about money in the bank in T'aipei he'd gotten for opium they sent to the mainland," George responded. "Maybe that was it."

"Opium – oh, shit! But what the hell did he hope to accomplish by taking you hostage?" Calloway asked.

"I don't know," George replied. "He couldn't get off the island. I'm not sure he had any idea what he was doing, he just did it."

"Damn," Calloway shook his head. "It's about to cost us a crew, unless the lieutenant sent that message through." He looked up as large raindrops began falling. "All we need now is rain! Let's get back."

* * *

"Which way do we go from here?" Kao asked Yang as they entered Fuchou.

"Sir," Yang replied, "they'll go through the city to the coast highway, and to the coast to be picked up."

"That's where we'll go, too," Kao nodded. "Let's hope they're not too far ahead of us."

* * *

"Are we close enough to use the radio?" Tiger asked.

"Not yet," Li answered. "I'm getting ready. When we reach the large turn in the river, I'll start calling. After that, we'll be heading directly toward the coast. Our only problem now is to pick the place to meet our rescuers. I'd prefer we didn't go a long way up the coast, but it will be some distance, at least, before the coastal defenses thin out."

"Well," Tiger offered, "we have to make a decision soon. It's starting to rain again, and this road will get worse as we go."

* * *

Yang noticed the increase in activity as they approached the capitol building. "Sir," he spoke up, "something's wrong. There are troops at the capitol building."

"Stop and let's find out," Kao answered. "Hello, comrade," he called to a man in front of the building. "What's the matter?"

"Comrade," the man responded, "there's been shooting inside. The lieutenant governor and several others are dead."

"Does anyone know who did it?" Kao asked.

"No," the man answered, "but one of the dead people in the lieutenant governor's office is an enemy. And a truck left here quickly after the shooting."

"When did this happen?" Kao asked.

"Only a short while ago," the man replied. "Fifteen or twenty minutes."

"Thank you, comrade," Kao turned to Yang. "Let's go."

"Yes, sir," Yang answered and the truck started forward once again. "Tell the men to hold on tight, please."

FIFTEEN

"Sir," Han spoke up as Calloway entered, "I've transmitted the message already. I'll wait a few minutes and transmit again."

"Thanks, lieutenant," Calloway responded. "Is there anything we can do to help?"

"Nothing, sir," Han answered. "Just stand by and pray."

"We'll help with that prayer," a woman's voice broke in. Calloway turned to see Marion and Yukiko enter the room, with Ramsey and the Chinese admiral close behind, followed by the comm unit commander. The women saw Calloway and quickly came to hug him.

"Joe, where are they?" Marion asked.

Calloway shrugged his shoulders, "I don't have the least idea, Marion. If they're where I *think* they are, they're surrounded by half the ChiCom army, and we're trying to let them know about it! But what are you doing here? You were supposed to go to the SID internal affairs guy with the evidence against Kung!"

"By the time we got to SID," Ramsey broke in, "Anderson and the internal affairs chief had already taken care of Kung. The internal affairs chief will see the girls later on, after the doctors dig the bullet out of his shoulder."

"And Paul?" Calloway asked.

"Hell, Joe," Ramsey chuckled, "he shot Kung after Kung shot the internal affairs officer. He's waiting outside."

"Admiral," Calloway acknowledged the Chinese officer. "Sorry about the lack of military bearing, sir, but a lot has happened."

"It's OK, Mister Calloway," the admiral smiled. "I understand. It was a pleasure accompanying the ladies here to meet you. I felt it wouldn't be totally inappropriate for me to come along."

"Joe," Marion asked, "Art said Charlie Hamilton was involved in this. Where is he?"

"Marion, I hate to say this," Calloway was uncomfortable. "He's dead. In a gunfight not more than ten minutes ago. He was holding Sergeant George hostage. He tried to shoot me when I went to stop him, and I had no choice."

"I'm sorry, Joe," Marion winced. "I know you two worked together, and it must've been tough."

"You're alright, Mister Calloway?" Yukiko asked.

"I'm fine, Yukiko," Calloway smiled at the young woman. "It's the crew I'm worried about right now."

"Mister Calloway, sir," it was Johnson, "there's a Sergeant Olson on the phone from T'aipei Air Station."

"Calloway here!" Calloway shouted quickly into the phone. "What's up?"

"Sir," Olson replied, "I can't talk on this line, but there's a hell of a mess over there. They've called the real army out. Something big is going on, sir. And things are so confused we can't make out much of what it is."

"OK, Sarge," Calloway thought a second. "Keep us advised, OK? Send any information you get to us through your back room people – they've got a secure link here, OK?"

"OK, sir," Olson sounded relieved. "I know what you're talking about. We'll pass any information we get. And I'll get out of your way, sir."

* * *

The truck leaned in the corner. Lin was ready for the turn and leaned with it, but Lindsay, sitting on the bed of the truck, tumbled over.

"Are you OK, Colonel?" Li had seen Lindsay fall.

"Damn' kid drivers!" Lindsay yelled back. "Tiger, must you drive like a maniac?"

"Sorry, Colonel," Tiger called back. "I'll try to go easier around the next one, sir."

"At least give me some warning!" Lindsay called back.

Li lifted the radio and switched it on. "Black dragon," he spoke into the microphone, "this is red flag, do you read me, over? I say again, black dragon, this is red flag, do you read me, over?" He released the transmit button and waited for a response.

* * *

The receiver in the radio room crackled, and Johnson jumped to tune it to the incoming signal.

" - over? I say again, black dragon, this is red flag, do you read me, over?" It was followed by stunned silence.

"Jesus!" Calloway shouted. "They're in radio range! That's only thirty miles! They're on *this* side of Fuchou! They're not in the mountains at all!"

Han rapidly moved the dial on his transmitter to the same frequency as the receiver. When it got there, he keyed his microphone and replied.

"Red flag, this is black dragon! Stand by for authentication!" He looked toward Calloway.

Calloway turned to Marion. "Take the microphone, Marion, and tell them the beer here is really lousy."

Marion gave him an uncomprehending look, but did as she was told. "The beer here is really lousy," she repeated Calloway's words. There was a short silence.

"It's better than no beer at all," squawked the radio, and Marion almost jumped – it was Lindsay's voice!

"That's the authentication!" Calloway grinned. "It's Lindsay!"

Yukiko's face was pale. "Is Tiger -.?"

Calloway grabbed the microphone. "Red flag, this is daddy," he spoke up. "What's status on people?"

"Two and three are fine, daddy," Lindsay responded. "Two's playing juvenile delinquent behind the wheel. Four's gone. We have five with us."

"Roger, red flag, daddy reads that." Calloway turned toward the room, "You heard it. Lindsay says Tiger's driving, Li's fine, Chou's gone, and they've picked up somebody, probably the girl Li was talking about bringing back."

He turned back. "Red flag, daddy. Tell us your destination and situation, over."

"Daddy, this is red flag," it was Li's voice. "We're rolling, ahead of the hounds. We're going to Plymouth Rock, with estimated arrival in about an hour. Do you read, over?"

"Got you, red flag!" Calloway acknowledged, looking toward the map. "We'll see you at Plymouth Rock, hopefully in an hour. This is black dragon out."

"And red flag out," Li ended the conversation.

"Damnation!" Calloway shouted. "How much do you want to bet they just raised holy hell going through Fuchou?"

* * *

Lin could see Lindsay was happy.

"The woman who spoke," Lin smiled, "is she your woman?"

"I hope she will be," Lindsay smiled back.

"And the man," she asked, "he's the man you work for?"

Lindsay replied, "Yes and no. He's really more of a good friend. But he's in charge of getting us out of here."

"They're coming to meet us, right?" Lin asked.

"Well," Lindsay answered, "I hope they bring help. They may have trouble with the PLA if they don't." He hesitated, then added, "Unless Li knows how to make us invisible to get past them."

"We may not have much trouble becoming invisible," Lin spoke up. "The rain's like a wall in front of us."

* * *

"Admiral," Calloway turned, "I hope you're ready to go a little earlier than we'd expected."

"Well, Mister Calloway," the admiral responded, "I'm not sure. The weather won't allow us to take a helicopter, and a submarine can't make it in time. There's a patrol torpedo boat, but only the captain and mechanic are here. It'll take hours to get the crew here."

"That's too long, sir," Calloway said. "Can we man it ourselves?"

"I don't know why not," the admiral replied. "We have enough people here to handle it." He turned to the commander. "Get the PT boat captain and tell him to get ready now," he ordered in Chinese. "We're going after the airplane crew!"

The commander saluted and hurried away to find the PT boat captain. "Lieutenant," the admiral addressed Han, "go to the weapons room and get at least seven automatic rifles for the boat. And plenty of ammunition." Han saluted, and he and Sergeant George raced off.

"Alright, Mister Calloway," the admiral grinned. "By the way, you're right. Chinese beer isn't very good. We don't drink it much, and we really don't know how to make it. Now let's get to the boat."

* * *

The truck reached the mouth of the river and started up the coast. Tiger drove fast, even through the small villages along the way. It startled those few villagers out in the poor weather, indicating no one knew they were coming. Perhaps, thought Li, the

ChiComs weren't prepared for anyone to act so violently and so quickly.

They'd arrive at their pickup point soon. But how would they get by the coastal defense forces? The place where Li wanted the pickup to take place was too open to be able to hide easily in the daytime. On the other hand, there was nowhere else to go. It was that beach or nowhere, Li thought.

The truck crashed into the wall of rain, and Tiger had to slow down to see through the flood that smashed into the windshield.

* * *

The rain increased as they arrived at the PT boat. The boat captain came running along the dock behind them, and the mechanic was already aboard, with the engines running. The comm unit commander followed the boat captain, who quickly saluted the admiral and then jumped on board. The commander joined the group alongside the boat.

"While we're waiting for the guns," the admiral spoke up, "let's get organized."

"Sounds good, sir," Calloway responded.

"We'll only need five or six to go with the boat," the admiral went on. "That should include you, Mister Calloway, and Mister Anderson, myself, Sergeant George, your young American soldier, and you, Mister Ramsey. Commander, please stay and take care of the ladies. Also," he continued, "the lieutenant should stay here to operate the radio while we're on the boat."

"Understand, sir," the commander replied.

"Here come the guns!" the admiral said, pointing toward the men who came down the dock, struggling under their load. The others quickly ran to help.

When everything was aboard, Marion turned to Calloway. "Good luck, Joe," she smiled. "Bring them all back, and you, too. Bring Harry back for me."

"I will," Calloway smiled back. "See you in a little bit."

"I hope so," she waved as the boat pulled away from the dock. "God, I hope so!"

* * *

"Straight ahead, Tiger," Li called out. The truck sped up, still hampered by the lack of visibility. "We have ten more miles to our turn," Li noted, "and another twelve to the beach where they'll meet us. We're not going to get there quite as quickly as we thought," he added.

"Sorry I can't make it go any faster," Tiger apologized.

"You're doing better than the rest of us could," Li responded. "Just keep going. Let's hope the boat's also slowed by the rain."

"I still don't see anyone chasing us," it was Lin, peering behind them.

"They'll be recovering by now, though," Li answered. "Someone will take charge, and the pursuit will start. They'll block the roadway ahead of us. Hopefully, we'll be off the road before we get to them."

The radio crackled. "They're going to tell us we're trapped," Li ventured a guess.

* * *

The sea was choppy, and the boat was going as fast as the captain dared, but it seemed awfully slow. The boat smashed against the waves, shuddering each time. In the cockpit, most of the makeshift crew frantically loaded the weapons. At the same time, the mechanic briefed Anderson and Ramsey on firing the large machine guns mounted on either side of the boat. All of them were soaked, but nobody seemed to notice.

"I sure hope they're being slowed by the rain, too," Calloway commented. "I'd hate for them to have to hold off the Chinese army while we're puttering along out here." He picked up another empty magazine and began stuffing bullets into it.

"The visibility out here's poor," the admiral replied. "Maybe it's a limiting factor there, too."

"Let's keep our fingers crossed we don't get there too late," Calloway commented.

"- or they don't do the same," Sergeant George added.

The radio alongside the captain crackled. "River dragon, this is black dragon." It was Han at the radio room.

The admiral grabbed the microphone. "Black dragon, go ahead."

"The watch center's reporting, sir," Han reported. "The enemy's sending forces to trap red flag. They've established a roadblock north of point Boston. They also report a truck departed point

Baltimore awhile ago, headed for the coast. I've already informed red flag, and I told them you're coming by PT boat."

"Excellent, black dragon," the admiral replied. "Keep us posted. River dragon's out."

"If anybody's slowed by the rain," Calloway commented, "let's pray it's the Commies!"

* * *

"There's the turn!" Li pointed to where the road turned off into a water-covered track.

"Jesus, Li!" Tiger was appalled. "That's not a road, it's a river!"

"It's sand, Tiger," Li answered. "It's solid under the water."

"We're still twelve miles from the beach?" Tiger asked. He turned the truck onto the narrow, watery track.

"That's right," Li responded.

"Can we drive all the way there?" Lindsay asked. "Or will we have to abandon the truck?"

"In some ways, I wish we could go on foot, Colonel," Li answered. "It would attract less attention. On the other hand, maybe the soldiers will think we're other soldiers in this truck."

"Well," Lindsay looked at his watch, "we need to move, Tiger. We're already late."

"I'm driving as fast as I can, Colonel," Tiger answered. "And that sounds strange, especially coming from me!"

* * *

"There's the point!" the captain shouted. "Once we're around it, we'll run straight to the beach!"

"I hope they don't have any big guns in the area where we're landing, Captain," Calloway said.

"They do, but not near the shore," the admiral replied. "They don't need to be, since they can cover the area behind the beach very well. The ground's too exposed, with radar sitting almost on the point," the admiral continued, pointing to a radar site back in the sand dunes.

Calloway stared at the water beyond the point. "Well, I don't want to take us into the face of an ambush!"

"That may be the only way to rescue the crew," the admiral spoke up. "We have to be ready to face that possibility."

"Let's hope Li has a better plan than getting us bushwhacked," Calloway commented.

* * *

"They've been through here," Yang noted as they sped through the village. "These people are still excited about it."

"And about us, too," Kao noted. "I still haven't seen them. They must be driving fast to stay ahead of us."

"Yes, sir," Yang was driving fast too. "After the shooting at the capitol, I'm sure they're in a hurry."

"Well," Kao said, "the weather will slow them down."

"It's doing the same to us, sir," Yang replied. "And we need to be alert so we don't miss where they turn off the road."

* * *

"What's the plan?" Tiger asked.

"My plan," Li replied, "keys on the fact the ChiComs know the Nationalists aren't strong enough to attack. They actually defend this open stretch of beach from back in the hills. All we have to do is pass the few emplacements here on the beach, and we'll be gone."

"How do we do that?" Lindsay asked.

"The ChiComs are deployed to stop penetrations, not invasions, Colonel," Li explained. "They only have overlapping fields of fire with light machine-guns. We have to break the overlap where the boat lands, so they can't fire at it."

"How?" Tiger asked.

"If we time this right," Li responded, "we'll arrive at the coast as the boat comes in. Nobody will watch behind them. We'll take out three sites in a row and break the overlapping fire. When we do that, the boat can come to the middle, and we can get to the boat while the boat's crew holds off anyone trying to chase us."

"Sounds good," Lindsay commented. "How do we start?"

"Well," Li replied, "the first site is only about a mile ahead of us."

* * *

The boat was now headed toward the shoreline. Another squall line suddenly moved from the shore and obscured the beach where they intended to land.

"The rain might help," Calloway said. "Except for the radar, the troops couldn't see us out here, and they wouldn't know where we're headed."

"The radar can see us," the admiral responded, "but the troops on the beach don't know where we are. There's no communication between them and the site. The Communists don't have enough equipment to provide radios to their small defensive positions. They have to rely on their eyes to see where we're going, and the rain will obscure their vision."

The captain was now guiding the boat toward the shore, and the wind was from the side, so the boat rolled through the troughs but maintained a higher speed. The squall line continued to move toward them and the boat was into it in moments.

* * *

"Stop!" Kao shouted. "That track! The water in the ruts is muddied! That's where they've gone!"

"Doesn't that go to the beach behind the point?" Yang remembered the area.

"Yes!" Kao replied. "Back up and take it! Hurry!"

"Not too fast, sir," Yang pleaded. "This track twists a lot. I could tip the truck over or miss a turn!"

"They're not far ahead!" Kao's excitement increased. "And this is a dead-end. They're trapped!"

* * *

The boat continued, still covered by the squall. Calloway's nerves were stretched taut, all of his attention to the front. There was still a ways to go to the beach and it wouldn't be good to run out of the squall right in front of the enemy's guns. He looked up to where Anderson and Ramsey were also sweeping the area in front of them with their concentrated gaze, their fingers ready on the triggers of the heavy .50-caliber machine guns. Those guns, Calloway knew, could fire a mile with good accuracy, while the guns they expected to face weren't accurate over half a mile. Even so, if they broke out of the squall within half a mile of the beach, the Communist emplacements in the dunes would have the advantage of surprise, being able to see the boat before people on the boat could spot them. There was a ways to go before they'd be within half a mile of the beach, but, if the Communists saw them break out of the squall and were ready for them, it could be hell.

* * *

Li helped Lindsay move the machine gun into position so it could be used to fire down the beach toward the next emplacement. The three soldiers who manned the emplacement only moments before glared at them from where they sat tied and gagged.

"When you see the boat," Li advised, "be ready for the enemy to fire at it. Don't try to suppress their fire, just get away before they realize you're not shooting too and come to investigate. Don't try to be heroes – run to the next emplacement, and Tiger will cover you from there. I'll be at the emplacement beyond that, and we'll try to guide the boat into position at the middle emplacement."

"Be careful, Colonel," Tiger added. "We've come too far together to lose you now."

"Well," Lindsay replied, "you take the same advice, yourselves. Be careful, OK?"

"We will, sir," Li nodded. "We'll see you at the boat."

* * *

Calloway stared ahead into the squall.

"Maybe it won't break until we reach the beach," the admiral said. "Hopefully it won't break until we're gone."

"I'm still not sure how to get them aboard when we get there," Calloway replied. "I sure wish we'd hear something!"

The admiral turned and spoke to the boat captain, who pointed toward the radios in front of him. The admiral began turning the dial of one of the radios, finally stopping when he thought he'd reached the correct frequency. He picked up the microphone and spoke into it.

"Red flag, this is river dragon," he intoned the callsigns. "Do you read, over?"

To the surprise of everyone, the radio crackled to life. "River dragon, this is red flag one and five. Go ahead, over."

The admiral immediately passed the microphone to Calloway. "This is daddy dragon. What're you guys up to? Over," Calloway barked.

"Two and three left us at the first position to your left," Lindsay responded. "They've gone on to the center and right positions. We can't see you in the rain – where are you right now?"

"We're still about five miles out," Calloway took the admiral's five fingers in the air to mean that. "That's maybe ten minutes before we hit the beach. How far are you from where we planned to come ashore?"

"This location's only about three hundred yards from where you'll come in," Lindsay continued. "We have about a six hundred yard buffer on either side of the center. I think two's going to wave a poncho so you can identify the position."

"Good thinking," Calloway felt better. "We'll see you at the beach."

* * *

"OK," Li nodded to Tiger as they hoisted the stick with the poncho tied to it. "I'll go take the last position now. Remember to cover Lindsay and Lin as they come down the beach. Make sure you fire over their heads."

"How about you?" Tiger asked.

"Don't worry about me," Li replied. "I'll be fine. You remember to cover them."

"And if you're not 'fine'," Tiger was skeptical, "then I'm facing down the beach while I've got the whole damned ChiCom army charging up my back?"

"OK, OK," Li rolled his eyes skyward. "So keep an eye *up* the beach, too. Stop anybody coming from that part of the beach – except me, of course! It's only about three hundred yards to the next emplacement. You should be able to hit anything you want at that distance."

"Not the way I shoot!" Tiger shook his head. "You know better than to ask me to shoot at anything that far away!"

"This is no time to tell me that!" Li looked skyward again. "Besides, I know better! You just want to come with me. But I need to have you stay here and cover the center!"

"All right!" Tiger grumped. "You made your point. If the Communists shoot you in the ass, it's not my fault! But you'd damned well better meet me on the boat!"

"I will!" Li barked back, vaulting out of the emplacement to return to the truck. "Just make sure you don't shoot me while I'm getting there!"

* * *

"About four more minutes," the admiral repeated what the boat captain had just said. "Please get ready – we're only two miles from the beach, and we'll have to slow down so we won't run up onto the sand."

"Admiral," Calloway was still worried, "we still don't know whether we're where we're supposed to be or way off course and heading right toward an emplacement where the Commies aren't cleared out."

"Trust the captain," the admiral was confident. "He knows where we're going and how close we are. And remember, the rain that keeps us from seeing the coastline also keeps the coastline from seeing us."

"It doesn't necessarily keep the coastline from hearing us!" Calloway responded, referring to the muffled roar of the boat's engines.

The admiral looked at him balefully.

* * *

Tiger heard the boat. The sound was out there, muffled, but he could hear it. And maybe the Communists could also hear it.

Suddenly, Tiger realized the rain was no longer pounding down. He glanced outside the gun emplacement, and saw visibility had improved. He turned toward the beach – the squall line was moving out over the water. Suddenly, there was the PT boat, coming toward shore, heading just a bit toward his right.

Tiger quickly grabbed the stick with the poncho and began waving it in the air, trying to catch the boat's attention. That was when he heard the truck behind the emplacement, and saw it going the direction Li had gone. Oh, shit, the thought passed through his mind in a flash – Li would need help. Tiger waved the poncho wildly one last time, then grabbed one of the automatic rifles from the stack he'd collected and began running along the dunes toward the next position.

* * *

"There's the truck!" Kao caught sight of it through the easing rain. "It's behind that position! Hurry!"

Yang stopped the truck behind the smaller vehicle and the men piled out quickly. Kao motioned to them to be quiet and break up into two groups, one going to the left of the position and the other following him to the right.

* * *

Li also heard the truck as it came to a stop. There were still two soldiers he hadn't tied up. He quickly hit the first at the base of his neck with the edge of his hand, knocking the man out, and then swung at the other man. That one ducked, and Li caught him alongside the head, a painful blow, but not disabling. In quick reaction, Li continued through with a fist to the side of the man's jaw, knocking him cold also.

It took too long. The men from the truck were almost at the position – Li could see the top of the first one's head. With a strength born of desperation, he threw himself out of the position toward the beach, just as the first of the arriving people began firing at him.

* * *

"There's one!" one of the men to the left cried, firing his weapon. Kao ran forward and jumped into the position, his gun ready. The only people in the position were tied up or lying on the ground. They were all soldiers. Where were the other two enemy?

* * *

"There's the beach!" Calloway shouted. "And there's the poncho! Head there!" He pointed the way out for the admiral, who was still wildly looking for the now-disappeared poncho.

"There's somebody running along the dunes toward the right!" Sergeant George called out, bringing his gun up.

"Don't shoot!" Calloway heard the shots from the next emplacement over. "Watch that emplacement over there!" He pointed to the right.

* * *

Kao stood and looked out of the position toward the beach. My God! There was a PT boat trying to land! He and his men would not only capture the enemy spies, but a PT boat, as well! He jumped out of the position to run across the sand.

* * *

"We'll hit the beach in a moment!" the admiral called out.

Suddenly, an emplacement to their left down the beach began firing, sending tracers into the water short of them.

"Get that site!" Calloway shouted at Anderson, who didn't hesitate to fire in the direction of the emplacement. "Here comes somebody!" Calloway shouted, as two figures jumped from a closer emplacement and began running toward them. "It's Lindsay! Cover them!"

The admiral and Johnson moved quickly to the side where Calloway waved, their weapons ready. Calloway moved to the other side of the boat, where Sergeant George watched the dune area around the emplacement to the right. The figure running in that direction continued to move quickly, nearing a point where Calloway thought it might be dangerous to get any closer to the shooting that had started at that site.

Suddenly, the figure fell forward.

* * *

Kao saw the man running toward the beach in front of him and quickly dropped to one knee to fire. As he tried to line up his sights on the man, several bullets whistled through the air around his head. He ducked and rolled along the ground, then got back onto his knees to see where the bullets had come from.

* * *

Calloway couldn't see what was happening clearly, but the sound of more firing came through amidst the thumping of the heavy gun on the other side of the boat. The figure he'd seen suddenly jumped up and moved quickly, obviously bobbing and ducking, the weapon raised and firing.

"Hold on," Calloway cautioned Ramsey, who was getting edgy with the second big machine-gun. "That's Tiger, and he's probably trying to get Li out of a scrape up there!"

The boat was now moving slowly, only a few dozen yards from the shore and headed directly at the beach. Suddenly it came to an abrupt halt as the nose found the sand. Calloway leaped to his feet and ran to the front of the boat, jumping into the shallow water and starting to splash to shore. "Cover me!" he shouted back to the boat. "I'll be right back!" With that, he started off up the beach toward where Tiger had last disappeared.

* * *

From the corner of his eye, Kao saw the man coming over the sand to his right. He turned quickly to fire, only to have the sand around him start to spurt as another gun fired at him. He swung back to his left and snapped off a shot at the first man, who was now running toward the boat again, his gun still pointed loosely in Kao's direction. Where were his men?

Kao turned to see that at least one man behind him had been wounded, and the others were pulling him back across the sand toward shelter. It looked like Yang.

"Come with me!" he shouted. "They're retreating!"

The sand began to spurt up around him again, and he ducked.

* * *

Lindsay was running, the AK-47 held in his right hand, the pain shooting through his left shoulder. He couldn't let up now! A heavy-sounding gun on the boat fired in the direction of the emplacement he and Lin had just left. They had to hurry! But where were Tiger and Li? He couldn't see them at all. And then he saw Calloway jump from the boat and head toward where Li should be at the third emplacement.

Shit! Lindsay slapped Lin's arm and pointed toward the boat, telling her to go that way, but she wouldn't turn and kept running alongside him. Damn! Lindsay thought. Just like a woman. Wouldn't listen!

* * *

Kao rolled to his knees again as the firing slacked. The two men who'd engaged his people were now running along the beach, escaping. He jumped to his feet, and then saw the other two also running toward the boat. Four people? But one had been killed at the capitol building, hadn't the man said so? Kao hesitated.

No matter! They'd get away if he didn't hurry! He hurried forward to the top of the rise, several of the men following him.

* * *

Calloway was sprinting up the beach when he saw Tiger and Li come over the dunes toward the beach, then turn to run parallel to the dunes along the beach toward the boat. Calloway dropped to a knee as he saw the figures following them arrive at the top of the dune. He fired into the sand in front of them, and they responded by falling and firing back.

Several spurts of sand kicked up around Calloway as he tried to return the fire and then there was a sudden hard pain in his shoulder as he was knocked backward. As he began to fade, he noted that the sand in the area of the figures was being thrown high into the air while the sound of heavy machine-guns pounded in his ears.

* * *

The one from the boat had started firing at them! Kao dropped to the sand and fired back, seeing the figure spin and fall as one of Kao's rounds hit him. He swung his rifle and fired again at the two men who were running toward the boat.

Sure he had hit one of them, Kao started to jump to his feet when the sand in front of him suddenly erupted in huge spurts. He barely heard the sound of the big machine-gun that fired the round which hit him squarely in the chest, driving him backward and downward. He was dead before his body landed in the sand.

* * *

Li felt the bullet hit him from behind, but then he saw Calloway fall and changed the direction he was running, heading toward the body on the sand. At the same time, Lindsay and Lin realized Li and Tiger were running toward the boat, and they also turned that direction. Lindsay saw Calloway was down, and dropped to one knee to fire in the direction of the dunes, but Lin grabbed him by the arm and tugged him toward the boat. Lindsay realized there was nothing more he could do, and he jumped up and continued running toward the boat alongside Lin. When they got to the boat, a Chinese man in a blue uniform jumped down from the boat and quickly hoisted Lin up onto it. She was grabbed by a young American soldier, and the Chinese man helped Lindsay up to be grabbed by another American soldier. In a moment, Lindsay saw Li with Calloway over his shoulder. Tiger was running backward, firing wildly at the area that was already being sprayed by the big machine-guns on the boat.

Li raced up to the boat and tossed Calloway up onto the deck easily. He then turned to grab the backward-running Tiger, who was still firing.

"Damn', Tiger!" Li threw his friend up onto the boat. "Don't you ever give up?" With that, he also grabbed the admiral and boosted him onto the boat, then caught the admiral's and Sergeant George's outstretched hands and pulled himself up, to fall on the boat deck.

The boat captain had already crammed the gears into reverse and he now pushed the throttle to full. The boat jumped clear of the sand, and backed speedily away from the beach. Anderson and Ramsey continued to pound the beach with the heavy machine-guns as the boat spun and picked up speed, pursuing the now-retreating squall line.

"Welcome aboard, Commander Li!" the admiral called.

"How's Calloway?" Li asked from where he lay.

"He's fine, Lin has him," Lindsay responded. "She's working on his shoulder. What the hell happened, anyway?"

There was no answer. Li had shut his eyes tightly, and then shuddered. The bullet had found its way home – it had simply taken this long for it to overcome Li's strength. His body went limp, and Lindsay realized Li was gone.

Tiger scrambled past Lindsay and fell alongside Li, trying desperately to breathe life back into him.

"No!" Lin wailed.

The rain began again.

SIXTEEN

Calloway opened an eye to see Lindsay standing alongside the bed. "Don't you look ugly?" he asked, wryly. "At least sit down, so I don't have to look so damned far up."

"They let me out of bed," Lindsay said, pointing to the sling that held his almost-useless arm as he sat in the chair by the bed.

"Well," Calloway replied, "I'll get out of here soon, too. What did they say about the shoulder?"

"I won't pass any flight physicals for awhile," Lindsay answered. "Looks like I'll have to find a ground job somewhere."

"You can apply with SAT," Calloway suggested.

"I'm not exactly excited about a ground job for a flying company," Lindsay responded. "They usually don't pay anything."

"I think SAT needs a project officer to replace one I shot," Calloway stated. "And the director will listen when I tell him to hire you."

"You mean I'd be working with flying projects?" Lindsay's eyes brightened.

"Don't get anxious," Calloway warned. "They still won't let you fly, just do all of the grunt work. But the pay's pretty good, usually better than most of the pilots get. It'll give you a salary you can afford a wife on, and put you on the ground so she'll marry you in the first place!"

"Hmm," Lindsay glared at the sling. "Maybe this isn't such a bad thing, after all. I can live with this."

"Speaking of living with it," Calloway responded, "they tell me Li's family's going to adopt Lin."

"Yeah," Lindsay replied. "Tiger and his dad went to talk to them about it. They weren't happy about Li's death, but I think they gave up on him ever having a normal life when he went into the navy, and they've taken it pretty well."

"Bunch of shit!" Calloway showed his upset. "He shouldn't die just because of a couple of packages of opium."

"Well," Lindsay replied, "he didn't go by himself. I talked to that young Air Force sergeant, Olson. He called to find out how you were doing. We chatted for a minute or two, and he said something about Li killing a bunch of people, especially the deputy governor and another ChiNat frogman, while we were on our way through Fuchou. His captain also said to tell you to get on your feet soon."

"Maybe I'd better listen!" Calloway chuckled. "Armstrong's a pretty big guy, especially alongside a shrimp like me!"

"Shrimp, hell!" Lindsay shook his head. "I saw you out there, acting like you were ready to take on the whole damned ChiCom army to get us out of there!"

"Yeah," Calloway replied, "and I got my ass shot doing it, didn't I?"

"Well, at least your shoulder," Lindsay answered. "I'm glad you didn't catch a bad one."

"Maybe I should be glad, too," Calloway sat back against the pillow. "I'm just happy we shut down the opium deliveries – at least, I hope we did."

"Well, we put a cramp in the flow," Lindsay answered. "Hell, there's no way to tell what all Kung was involved in – even Hamilton probably didn't know all of his doings. But there are people over there with money, and I imagine they'll find other ways to satisfy their appetites."

"Yeah," Calloway responded. "And there's lots of folks around who're as greedy as Kung and Hamilton."

"Well," Lindsay shook his head, "it sounds to me like we were lucky Yukiko was the right person in the right place at the right time. Not that I'm complaining about it, of course!"

"You'd better not!" Calloway laughed.

"So what happens with the operation, now that the plane's gone and we're out of action?" Lindsay sat back in the chair.

"I doubt the ChiNats will want to resume deliveries," Calloway replied. "They lost two frogmen in this deal, and I don't think they want to risk losing any more, especially since the ChiComs know about the penetrations."

"Yeah," Lindsay nodded agreement.

"In addition to that," Calloway continued, "the SID's probably just a little embarrassed about sponsoring the flights without providing proper oversight."

"By the way," Lindsay spoke up, "that reminds me. Paul Anderson said to tell you P'eng, the SID counter-intelligence guy, is here in the hospital with us. In fact, Paul wandered down to visit with him after he found out you were still asleep. He'll probably be back to see you pretty quick."

There was a knock on the door.

"Speak of the devil," Calloway said to Lindsay, then called to the door, "come on in."

Tiger's head peered around the door. "OK to visit with you, Joe?" he asked.

"If it isn't, then I'm in trouble," Lindsay replied. "Come on in."

"Good!" Tiger stepped back, and Marion and Yukiko came into the room before he closed the door behind them all.

"Good to see you guys," Calloway grinned. "Damn, you girls look prettier than ever!"

"No amount of bull will get you out of trouble with me for getting shot," Marion announced, taking Lindsay's good hand in hers.

"Marion," Lindsay spoke up, "Joe says he's going to get me hired on as a project officer with SAT, since the doctor says I probably won't be able to fly anymore."

Marion's eyes registered her pleasure.

"So," Lindsay continued, "I'll ask you again, will you please marry me?"

"Do it," Calloway insisted, "and put him out of his misery, OK?"

"Of course I will, Harry," Marion smiled, then turned to Calloway. "You mean you didn't tell him what I promised when you left to bring him back?"

"What was that?" Lindsay asked Calloway. "You holding out something on me?"

"Shoot," Calloway drawled, "the girl was under duress and stress. All she did was promise that, if I got you back, she'd marry you." He looked at Marion. "What did you call him, a 'big dummy'?"

"Does this mean a double wedding?" Lindsay looked at Tiger.

"Well," Tiger started. "I got a very nice offer from the SID. They wanted me to go to the states and learn how to fly the U-2. But then China Air Lines showed up with an offer I couldn't refuse, and I decided it's time to settle down and start a family.

Besides, my folks say they'll adopt Yukiko whether I marry her or not," Tiger grinned. "I guess that means I'm hooked!"

"Couldn't happen to a nicer guy," Calloway grinned back. "Now if I could just find a decent beer -."

Marion reached into her purse. "Quit complaining and look what I brought you from Tokyo," she smiled, holding out a bottle of Japanese beer.

EPILOGUE

"Congratulations are in order, Mike." The captain was sitting on the edge of the desk with a cup of coffee and a cigarette as Olson came into the center to relieve.

"Thanks, sir," Olson replied. "For what?"

"Hell," Armstrong grinned, "you got two of your guys promoted! The results from the promotion board were just announced. Thought you'd like to know right away. Smitty and Chuck both put on stripes."

"That's great, sir!" Olson was pleased.

"One more thing," the captain stood up from the desk. "The general wants to know if you'd like to do what I did and go to OCS for a commission. He said he'd be glad to recommend you, and he's sure you'll be accepted. And I think you should think pretty hard about going for it!"

* * *

This might be the story, and then again it might not be. You won't find it in any history books, of course – stuff like this is never mentioned there.

And those of us who were there can never confirm a thing, can we?

The End

Denlinger's Publishers, Ltd., "The InstaBook publisher for tomorrow's great authors... today!", hopes you have enjoyed reading this book.

We will forward your emailed comments to the author upon request. [support@thebookden.com].

Visit our on-line bookstore for additional **InstaBook** paperback and electronic (**eBook**) titles.

Contact:
http://www.thebookden.com

This book was produced by **InstaBook** system technology.

Mission Statement

We will earnestly strive to enrich and entertain our customers through reading by promoting one of our constitutional rights, "freedom of speech." And, with honesty and integrity, strive to recognize and promote authors by publishing their works.

Denlinger's Publishers & Bookstore
P.O. Box 1030 – Edgewater, FL 32132-1030